GULLIVER
TAKES FIVE

GULLIVER
TAKES FIVE

BY JUSTIN LUKE ZIRILLI

Published by AmazonEncore
P.O. Box 400818
Las Vegas, NV 89140

ISBN-13: 9781612184234
ISBN-10: 1612184235

In memory of my father

Have fun laughing obnoxiously and dancing in Heaven

A NOTE FROM THE AUTHOR

Have you ever asked yourself the question, where was HE last night? I know I have, quite often. Whether you've wondered where a friend was during a wicked-crazy party, or where your boyfriend was when he was supposed to be at home sleeping, or where YOU'VE been when you've awakened the morning after, still in your clothing, on the floor of your apartment.

Well, turns out readers ask that question too! In my first novel, *Gulliver Takes Manhattan*, I introduced a gay twenty-something Angeleno named Gulliver who left home to escape an asshole exboyfriend, moving to New York City to live with his best friend, Todd, in the up-and-coming gayborhood of Hell's Kitchen. There, he quickly became friends with Todd's core crew: Rowan, Servando, Shane, and Brayden. Due to a couple of bad decisions (including secretly dating Brayden's ex-boyfriend, Marty, and engaging in some extramarital adventures with a seemingly random guy named Chase on Fire Island), Gulliver found himself homeless, jobless, and caught in a struggle to stay in the city. Desperate and driven, Gulliver ultimately chose to work in porn, and became an adult film celebrity in the process.

In the original novel, there comes a pivotal, dramatic, and surrealistic scene where Gulliver does something he probably would never have imagined he was capable of. I won't ruin it for you if

1

you haven't read it yet. In that scene, all of Gulliver's exes, friends, and confidantes are strangely (mostly) absent. Where are they? How are they not at this major event? Everyone wanted to know. And, luckily, so did I.

This novel will show you that each of those other characters had VERY good reasons for his absence. I penned the collection of five first-person accounts you are holding in order to answer this question: Where were Brayden, Marty, Chase, Todd, Servando, and Rowan on the night when Gulliver took the stage at the "Gay Party of the Century," otherwise known as eWrecksion?

Why did I call it *Gulliver Takes Five*? Two reasons, really. One, we have five tales within these pages. And two, Gulliver gets to take a blessed break from talking your ears off about his drama. (Don't worry, he'll be back in the third book.)

Writing this so soon after my original novel was an exciting adventure. I got to jump into each of my characters' heads and write five tales that all occur on the exact same day, a day that occurred during the timeline of *Gulliver Takes Manhattan*. Just think of this as my written version of the Oscar-winning film *Crash*, except with a lot more sex and bitch slaps. Hopefully you're in the mood for something of that nature.

Okay, you've heard enough from me. I'm going to shut up and let my gay boys do the talking. Have fun.

—Justin Luke

BRAYDEN'S ROUGH REVENGE

Christian isn't up yet. He's breathing deep, sprawled in a position that looks like a marathon runner midstride, about to sprint through the wall and out to the street below. And if the past four Saturdays are any forecast for today, he'll be down for the count for another hour. Loverboy didn't get home from spinning his weekly gig at Splash until 5 this morning. That means I have plenty of time to make this absolutely perfect.

So that's what it's going to be.

There's a "Happy Anniversary!" card hidden under a stack of *Next* magazines in the kitchen. There are four more drafts in the garbage, buried under Chinese take-out containers, just in case Christian decides to dig through the trash for some reason. Those first four didn't get my feelings right—either too sappy or too presumptuous or too formal or too blasé—but the fifth time's the charm. I really hope he likes it.

I also got him that plug he's been drooling over since he first fell in love with it at Sam Ash. I have no idea what it does or how it does it, but he said it'll make his sound even brighter, cleaner, crisper. If you ask me, none of these adjectives should be applied to music, but what do I know about being a DJ? For the one hundred bucks

7

it set me back, it better be one hell of a fucking plug. Please, please let it be right.

The apartment is silent, my guy's slow, rhythmic breathing the only sound. Roommate Shane never came home last night (witness my jaw NOT dropping), which means Christian and I have the apartment to ourselves, to celebrate however we see fit. Will this include naked breakfast making? Stay tuned. It very well might.

Shit. Christian's phone is unplugged. It's sitting on his crumpled pants at the foot of the bed. When he gets up, it'll be dead. That's going to piss him off. Then our morning is already off to the completely wrong start. We'll just consider a fully charged phone his OTHER anniversary present.

I pick up the phone, sort of accidentally waking it up with a clumsy thumb. A notification pops up on the lit screen.

I shouldn't.

I must.

I can't.

I might…

He's dead asleep, right? We've been seeing each other for a month now. A month to the day since our first, oh-so-promising encounter. Someday we might share bank accounts, credit cards—and phone bills. What could he have to hide? Plus, I'm sure he has password protection. Who doesn't these days? So what's one quick peek? I swipe the thing into action, only to find that not only does he not have password protection, he also has a text message waiting for him.

I'm staring at the name *Grant Majors*, the Broadway gay we met through my good friend Todd DiTempto the same night we met each other out on Fire Island (Todd made ALL the introductions that night, per usual). We've hung out with Grant a couple times, since he only lives a few blocks away, once to grab drinks and once to watch a DVD—plus he always has the hookup for free tickets to see his show.

Should I? No. But why not? I'm scrolling down.

It's a photo: Grant's ripped abs—and then some. His rock-hard dick takes up a large portion of the screen. "Good Morning Starshine!" says the caption underneath. I'm instantly pissed, and slightly aroused. I zoom in.

"What are you doing?"

Shit. My guilty hands lose their grip on the phone, sending it clacking and careening to the floor and under my bed.

"What?"

Christian sits up in bed, his hairy torso and chest puffing up and out of my bunched-up sheets. "What were you just DOING?"

"I…I was going to charge your phone. You forgot to plug it in."

"You weren't plugging it in. You were looking through it. I saw you!" He's reaching for his shirt, putting it on. "And now you're LYING about it? Son of a bitch. How crazy are you?"

Shit. The C-word. The dreaded C-bomb. When a guy drops it, I know everything around me is about to explode and collapse, leaving me with only a charred ruin to remember it by.

"How crazy am I? I'm not the one getting morning-wood sexts from our mutual friend!"

"What? Who?" He looks genuinely confused.

"Grant fucking Majors!"

This was not at all on my itinerary for this morning.

"Were you going through ALL the texts on my phone?" He drops to the floor and scrambles under the bed to rescue the lost phone, moments ago so harmless with its almost-drained battery, now a lightning rod electrifying both of us into fits of fury. "I don't care if I'm getting underwear photos from every twink in New York State. You don't go through someone's phone!"

"Why is Grant Majors sending you his cock? Why is his cock on your phone?" I rush to him, pulling him up from the floor, our faces colliding.

"Why are YOU on my phone?" He pushes me away, looks down at the screen. At the incriminating cock shot. "This is the first I've ever seen of it. Digitally or otherwise. I have NO idea why he sent it!"

"Do you even know what day it is? Did you have to pick TODAY?" My voice is getting higher and higher, toward the breaking point. I know what's coming next.

"I didn't pick anything! He sent it to me! What are you talking about?"

I know I'm going to cry.

"I'm talking about..." I begin. Then have to stop. These first words are barely a whisper; that's all I can muster. Because there's a sob in me looking for any excuse to break free.

"Our anniversary."

I had intended it to be a joke. Well, half a joke, at least. Who gets someone an anniversary card after one month of dating? And not even full-on, seriously committed dating, because we've never really discussed where we are or where we're headed. We've been spending more nights together than apart, enough for me to know Christian wouldn't have TIME to be dating anyone else, regardless of whether or not he had the desire. So, naturally, I'd just assumed things would keep going in this direction...And yeah, maybe an anniversary card would get that conversation rolling.

But a quick meet and greet with Grant Majors's dick? THAT Christian might make time for.

Now it's no joke. Before I can stop myself, I'm marching into the kitchen and digging under that pile of *Next* magazines, returning to the bedroom, and flinging the sealed canary-yellow envelope at him. "Happy FUCKING anniversary, asshole!"

"Anniversary?" He reaches down to pick up the card carefully, like there's some delicate, valuable clue inside that will demystify the confusion between us. I'm simultaneously reaching up to the shelves in my closet, behind a stack of folded towels, and unearthing the plug he so dearly desires. Brighter, cleaner, crisper? My ass. I hurl it at him.

"Yes! We've been together for a month!"

He looks down at the card, and the plug, and I'm not sure he understands how either of them fit into what I'm saying yet, but then he looks back up and says, "You mean we MET a month ago…"

"And started dating. God, do you have to downplay everything?"

"Well, yeah, we've been seeing each other, but…anniversary? One month after meeting me? And you think that entitles you to go through my phone like we're MARRIED? Sorry, but that is fucking crazy."

There it is again. C-bomb. *Kapow!* My hands are around his throat, with a more violent effect than I'd like. *Oh, I'll show you crazy*, I want to say, but fortunately have the presence of mind not to.

"People told me about your reputation. Going ape-shit on guys for no reason."

"I have reasons," I growl. "And just who, exactly, are these anonymous sources?"

"Doesn't matter. The point is, I guess neither of us knows each other like we thought. If you can't even trust me..." Christian hesitates, choosing his words carefully. "I don't think we're...um... on the same page. And we should end this, before somebody gets hurt."

My face crumbles. My hands release. "END this? No. I'm sorry..."

But he's putting on his pants, shoving his phone in his pocket. "Too many sorries, Brayden! I can't be with someone who will go through my phone before just ASKING me if I'm sleeping with somebody! I don't care who did what to you in the past, okay? That has nothing to do with me!"

"It has everything to do with you!" I shout at him, chasing him out of my bedroom to the living room, grabbing whatever isn't nailed to the wall to chuck at his head. "How do you think it starts? With someone's cock on your phone! If I'd started checking phones the first ten times it happened, I would have saved myself a lot of fucking trouble!"

"Yeah. I'm so glad you saved US that trouble."

"Before you go, just tell me why his fucking cock is on your phone."

"I don't fucking know! Okay, Brayden? Jesus! Why don't you ask HIM?"

I can barely hear the door slam because I am screeching, tearing my throat apart, throwing books from the living room bookshelf in the direction of the door. I do this for five minutes, until there are no more books to throw. Until I realize that he's actually gone.

I am heaving, crying, when the door opens—it's Shane, still dressed up from last night, a little more wrinkled than when I last saw him. He looks down at the pile of books at his feet, then back up at me.

"Anniversary surprise didn't go as planned, huh?"

I can't help but laugh as Shane stares at me: in Christian's rush to get out of here, the asshole left his fucking phone charger. I am calming down, I am breathing easier, I am letting acceptance wash over me, all those other stages (bargaining and anger and whatever else) be damned. It was only one month, he is only one boy, I can handle this. I can overcome my pain and sadness and fury, because I have done it before. I've survived. I can cope like a mature, rational adult and not spin myself into that Tasmanian devil cyclone of destruction I've perfected like it's an art. I have learned from past mistakes, grown wiser, become a stronger, more stable man. Shane is here, my best friend. I will tell him what happened and he'll suggest we get a cocktail or two and then we'll laugh it off through our tingly midafternoon buzz.

Yes. That's exactly what I need right now.

For some reason, my body disagrees with this plan. Instead, I am still screaming, crying, flinging even more things at the door as Shane backs up cautiously in the direction of his room.

"I'll let you chill out, boo. Don't worry about the books, I'll clean them up."

He slips into his room and gently closes the door.

I grab the charger as Christian's final few words bounce around in my skull: *I don't fucking know! Okay, Brayden? Jesus! Why don't you ask HIM?*

I fling it at the door with one last scream.

***

FUCKING BITCH!

Hit the buzzer.

Wait.

Punch the buzzer.

Wait.

Kick the buzzer.

This FUCKING buzzer!

Buzz. Buzz. BUZZZZZZZZZZZZZZZZZZZZZZZZZZZZZZZZZZZZ ZZZZZ.

Police sirens wail in the distance like a sick baby crying into a megaphone. I want to punch the sirens. Shut them the fuck up. The buzzing and blaring in my head is goddamn noise enough. My life is all the emergency I can handle right now.

The rain has drenched my hair, which I just bleached this fucking morning an hour after Christian split. The color is Ultra Ivory. Like a ghost flying out of my brain.

Well, it WAS flying out of my brain. Now it's dead, stringy, and pasted down on my itchy, wet forehead.

Answer answer answer!

No.

Buzzer buzzer buzzer!

STELLA! STELLA!

In my pockets are four of those little bottles of vodka they sell for five bucks a pop at any liquor store. All empty. On my phone is a text from Shane. *"Hope you're feeling better? I'm worried, boo. Where did you go this morning? Answer my texts! Oh…Looks like maybe you were right about C and GM. Just saw them walking up 9th together toward his place. What a dick!"*

Now I, too, am outside Grant's apartment, with two plans: one to execute if Christian is still in the apartment, and one if he isn't. I would've gotten here quicker, except I was drinking with some of my girlfriends downtown, pounding back shots to cleanse Christian out of my system.

Needless to say, it didn't work. But the travel time back to Hell's Kitchen gave me all the minutes I needed to scheme. It's now almost 11 p.m. and the only thing NOT working in my favor is that Grant is NOT answering his fucking door.

The shit-eating, backstabbing, STD-infected ho bag!

A click, a beep, a voice. Oh, right—I have a purpose here, don't I?

"Chill out!" Grant screams over the static. "I was in the shower! Who is it?"

What a great greeting. The cunt. What took you so long, you theater fag? Fucking my man? Did you have to wipe all his cum off your face before hitting the speaker button, in case I might hear it drip? Is he in the shower too, wiping your jizz out of his hole?

"It's Brayden," I say into the buzzer, straining so my voice is heard over the fucking police sirens now zooming by, smiling hard to make my voice sound friendlier so it's not obvious that I'm about to bust inside and set the fucking apartment on fire.

"Brayden? Oh. Brayden. I'm kinda busy. Have to run in a few. I'll catch you another time, okay?"

No. You'll catch me right the fuck now. "Is Christian there?"

He's silent. For a bit too long. Because I caught him. Would Christian try climbing out the window? No, Grant lives on the fourth floor. I check the fire escape anyway. Nothing but the corpse of a Christmas tree that's eight months dead. The rain is pelting me now. My hair is in my face, itching like crazy. I want to yank it out. Instead, I shake my head, slick it back. It flops back onto my forehead. I am going to start screaming again. My shirt is sticking to my arms, itching too. I HATE getting wet. I must have been a fucking cat in a past life.

"Uh. No. Should he be? Brayden, I really don't have the time to do this right now."

Bullshit. Liar. Let me the fuck inside. I'll check every fucking closet. Under your bed. In the bathroom. Behind every door. I'll sniff him out like a fucking hunting dog.

"No, I guess not! But can I come in?"

"For fuck's sake, girl, take a HINT!" His voice sounds like a million eyes rolling.

"It's pouring out here, Grant!" I yell, dropping my faux-peaceful performance. "Let me in, please!"

"You have five minutes," he says. The door buzzes and opens after I jam my shoulder into it, slamming it against the wall. I sprint up the stairs, three at a time, rocketing myself up the flights.

I am rage. I am fury. I will not be stopped. My fists are missiles and the crosshairs are flying this way and that. There will be blood. There will be crying. There will be sweet, sweet revenge. When I find him hiding in the bathroom or in a closet, I will pound Christian's pretty face into a pile of rare roast beef. His nose into a mashed potato of veins and cartilage.

Floor 2.

Christian Robert Molson. Or "Christian Robert," as he prefers to be called at the clubs. With his swoopy Justin Bieber hair—so fucking out-of-date! Not cute. Bullshit. When I'm done with him, his dental records won't even be conclusive ID.

And I almost didn't know! I almost had no fucking clue! Me! The guy who suspects everyone and doesn't trust a single damn person in this world. ESPECIALLY a guy I'm sleeping with. That bitch snuck in under my radar. Tricked me. Even this morning, when he had the nerve to call ME crazy, I was ready to forgive him. I was thinking it was ME who was out of line. Maybe Grant just sent him the damn photo out of the blue, like he said. Maybe one month wasn't enough time to get so bent out of shape about it.

But THEN. I hear they're spotted together mere hours after his steadfast denial. The nerve. The fucking nerve, right? That's how slutty this kid is. This kid, who claimed to be so pure and relationship oriented, who once told me sex does nothing for him without intimacy.

Floor 3.

Still sprinting. My chest, throat, and stomach all burn because I keep forgetting to breathe.

I knock a woman back into her room as she tries to walk into the hallway, her umbrella flying open and trapping her inside.

So funny. I would probably be sitting at home by myself right now, staring at my phone, wondering when the best time to apologize to Christian would be. Fuck! I'd be jerking off to something over-long and underlit on XTube. Well, XTube would be on, but I'd be thinking about Christian and his fucking pencil dick that—until tonight—I didn't even mind. That I somehow found endearing. Now I won't let that tiny thing anywhere near me.

Shit! I'd be writing his name over and over on the back of a take-out menu, like I'm some fucking fifth grade girl drawing hearts around a photo of Zac Efron. I'd wait until he came back to my place with the copy of keys I made him last month, then I'd jump into his arms, promising to never even look in the general direction of his phone ever, ever again. Really meaning it this time.

But that's all changed. You DON'T use Brayden Jesse Castro.

An admission of sexting would earn him a less harsh sentence: a bitch slap and me screaming at him until he ran from Hell's Kitchen back to his Upper East Side studio, making sure every fucking tourist and neighborhood whore knew to stay the fuck away from him, that he's mine, and anyone who tried to take him from me would have his throat ripped out.

But then, a few days later, I'd take him back—after he came to my apartment with a bouquet of flowers (the expensive kind, not the bodega value shit) and begged me to give him another chance. I'd look at him like he'd broken my heart and shake my head until he was drowning in his own tears.

I might not have even been so pissed if it weren't Grant Fucking Majors, a mutual buddy, who, I'll admit, I was very attracted to at first. Probably even more than I was initially attracted to Christian. But Christian is the one I ended up going home with, and he's the one who's been in my bed almost every night since...

But now knowing that the corpse of our relationship hadn't even gone cold before he swung by Grant's bachelor pad? Oh, fuck no. Dumping him would be charity; I'd be a goddamn saint. No, I'm going to leave him like Nagasaki—burned-out craters everywhere, women and children mutilated and puking blood, running around screaming through chapped lips. He'll wish he didn't fuck up his shot at the one good guy he'll EVER meet in his public bathroom floor of a life—ME. God, why doesn't anyone I date ever recognize a good thing once they've found it?

Floor 4.

I am lightning shooting down the hall to Grant's apartment. I calm my fist like I'm holstering a gun and gently tap on the door—because if I don't, I'll probably pound the fucking wood down into pulp.

The door opens.

Heeeeeeere's Johnny!

I smile, sufficiently squelching the crazy. "Hey, Grant."

"Fuck, you're soaked!" he says, stepping away from me like I'm covered in bees. I take that as an unspoken invitation into his apartment, let myself in, and close the door.

Grant is fully dressed. Cute and all done up to leave for the night in tight designer clothes that show off his many musical muscles. I have to strain to keep from rolling my eyes at how labored it all is.

"Yeah," I say. "It's hell out there."

Grant doesn't wait for my sentence to finish; he goes right back to dressing up.

"Just…Stand on that doormat right there. Don't touch anything, especially the walls."

Grant's hair doesn't look any more messed up than it normally does. No sweat or post-fuck sheen on his skin. When I take a big sniff for a hint of recent-sex stank, I come up with nothing. He must be heading to some Broadway party. A place where the swishy tenors are bragging about their motivation and whining about their expiring equity contracts and gossiping about who's got photos of which chorus boy taped up next to their dressing room mirror, all while appetizers are passed around on doilies by community-theater-lead losers who think they stand a chance at getting a part in a great big Broadway show just by rubbing elbows with the theatrical elite.

Just the sort of party up-and-coming "talent" agent Gulliver Leverenz would have attended, it occurs to me, if he hadn't up and disappeared two months ago. Little Gulliver. The last guy who fucked with me. If you ever find him, be sure to ask him how THAT worked out.

Grant's place is a large studio, decked out like a French whorehouse you might find in *Moulin Rouge!*, complete with a queen-size bed stage center, covered in an array of colored, semi-transparent fabrics. Staring down on the bed from all four walls are headshots of Grant from probably the last ten years of his career. He's leaning his chin on his hands and smiling full toothed here, sitting up against a brick wall in a loose hoodie that shows off his toned chest there. The two closets in the studio are wide open. The bed is too low to the ground to conceal anything beyond shoes. Even the bathroom door is open, everything in it in plain sight.

No. Christian isn't here. Plan B it is, then.

"What are you looking at?" Grant asks, standing in the middle of his apartment and staring at me.

"Nothing. Just soaked to shit. I was heading down to Ritz and the fucking skies ripped open! And, being the closest gay I know, you lucked out with an unannounced visit!"

"Lucky me, indeed. Well, somebody up there must like you." Grant smirks. "I'd be at *Mamma Mia!* right now if I hadn't taken the night off for this Equity Fights AIDS dinner."

"Always busy," I say, returning the wink. "Can I borrow a towel?"

"I guess. Fuck! I need to carry an umbrella now? That's going to be SO annoying. I abhor coat check." He stomps past me, keeping his distance from my soggy shirt, and goes into the bathroom, slamming the door.

Actors. Jesus.

The bathroom faucet begins to roar. It sounds like he's practicing some sort of speech. I guess I won't be getting that towel. No biggie. It's not why I came here. I tiptoe to a large antique dresser on the far side of his bed, which is covered in a pile of dirty clothes. It's now or never. No. It's just now.

"Why'd you ask if Christian was here?" he calls out.

My heart stops. I look over my shoulder. False alarm. Grant hasn't left the bathroom. I finish up quickly and tiptoe back across the room to the kitchen, which is right next to the bathroom.

"Just wondering where he is, that's all," I say, peeling off my wet T-shirt and wringing it out over his kitchen sink. "He sort of disappeared a few hours ago."

"Wish I could help you, hon. Maybe he's spinning tonight? You try texting him?"

Grant comes out of the bathroom, wiping a streak of concealer from under his eyes. If he's at all put off by me now standing shirtless in his kitchen, he's too preoccupied with himself to show it. The asshole didn't even bring me that towel I asked for. "How does my face look? Can you tell I just used spray tan?"

"Your concealer is all fucked," I say, meeting him halfway between the kitchen and the bathroom. I use my pointer and middle finger to rub out an invisible glop, taking a lot longer than anyone would need to. "Just curious...How does someone get tan lines when they use spray tan?"

"Tan lines?"

"Mmhmm." My eyes work their way down his body to his waist. "Morning, Starshine."

"What? It's dark out."

Not the brightest ball of gas in the galaxy, is he? Guess I'll have to spell it out.

"Christian showed me the cock shot you sent him this morning."

His eyes, which were just admiring his own headshots on the wall, dart to meet mine. "He did?"

I've been wondering if Christian and Grant talked about our spoiled anniversary before, during, or after whatever happened here. But frankly, I don't think Grant Majors is a good enough actor to play this dumb if he'd been informed of this morning's drama.

So he didn't know we were broken up when they got it on this afternoon? Cheeky. They're BOTH two-faced—which must be really handy when they're going down on each other. Wonder how they decide which of their four faces gets to do the sucking?

"Quite the hot little photo," I say, shoving Grant up against the wall. His eyes squint shut, his face turns away from me. He must have heard stories about the lethal behavior of a scorned Brayden Castro—each of which, I'm proud to say, is a hundred fucking percent true. I can smell the fear on him. Bruises and cuts won't look good under the spotlights. How will he explain it to his cast mates? His director? His agent and publicist? The crowd at this Equity Whatever dinner tonight? I love it. It's been a while since I've felt this rush. Grant's chin feels stubbly between my thumb and pointer finger as I stroke the sides of it, then open his eyes with my other hand. "Have to say I wasn't so happy about it."

Grant laughs awkwardly. He would easily lose in a fight. Wouldn't stand a chance even if four of his dancer buddies were there to back him up.

"I was just messing around, Brayden. Don't take it so seriously. He didn't ask for it or anything. I mean, I must have sent that to like five guys this morning. As a joke, really."

"Well, then how come you didn't send it to me?" I pout. "Christian's dick is a joke. Yours, not so much. Besides, Christian's not even the one who thinks you're cute. He thinks you're too full of yourself. I'm the one who's had a thing for you since that night we all met." (All of this is at least partially true.)

Grant's face transforms from panic to pleased. Of course the easiest way to an actor's heart is through his ego. Now he's interested. Honestly, I could never date someone like Grant, already so in love with himself that there's barely room in his heart for a third party. He could be cute, if you're into that tiny-muscled theater queen thing—but this isn't about attraction. It's about revenge. On Christian. On Grant. And it starts right now.

"Brayden, are you flirting with me?" he asks.

My answer is a forceful kiss. I jam my tongue in between his lips. He offers no resistance.

"Brayden," he says, breaking away. "I don't know..."

"What? Is there a problem?" I back off, smiling just the slightest bit.

"Um...Christian?"

"Christian," I repeat, and let the name hang there in the air for a moment before continuing, "will only know what I want him to know."

Grant smiles and kisses my neck, the side of my chin, sucks on my ear. "Then no. There's no problem."

Huh. Here I am, shirtless in this queen's kitchen, anticipating my very own private production of *Broadway Bares*. So far, this seduction has been a resounding success, and the funny part is that I never would have been so ballsy if I actually cared about hooking up with him. I'd have been shy, demure—coy, at best. And Grant Majors would never have given me the time of day. Deep down, beneath my spiny exterior, I'm kind of a pansy when it comes to guys, too afraid of getting hurt. Maybe if I sought revenge more often, I'd get a lot more action. And Grant is cute, but he's cocky as fuck. Always has been. To me. To everyone I've seen him interact with.

"Can you be late to your little party?" I say, walking my fingers up his chest.

"I'm going to blow your mind, get you off, and have you dressed again so fast your head will spin, sir."

"Big promises," I say.

"But," he says, suddenly serious, "let's just fold my clothes neatly on the chair. I don't do wrinkles."

Actors. Jesus.

He strips down in an unsexy fashion, taking exquisite care with how he unbuttons his sleeves and unzips his pants. I, on the other hand, tear off my remaining clothing and fling it against the wall. Interestingly, he no longer seems to care about potential water damage to his possessions. His dick looks even larger in real life. But, shit, I'm distracted. That's not good. All the red and anger is blinding me so bad that I space out while this self-professed Broadway god does his best to make me shoot, riding me at hyper speed.

That's a surprise too—I'm somehow the top in this show-stopping duet. Word amongst the theater queens and sluts (including Todd and the crew when they introduced us) is that Grant Majors is a total top. At first, when he was grinding into my dick, I thought maybe he was just teasing. Then when he started working me inside him, I thought maybe he was versatile. Now, watching him go, there's no question: he's a card-carrying power bottom. No wonder Christian went after him the moment we called it quits.

And he loves talking dirty, which has never been a fondness of mine. But until I start cursing and belittling him, he can't get it up, keeps giving me hints and asking me if he's a dirty whore or a little bitch. Ordinarily, I might abstain, maybe even leave before sealing the deal—but come to think of it, there are a few choice phrases I'd like to throw Grant's way right now.

"You little slut. You conniving, lying, cheating skank bitch."

I must be a little too convincing with that one, because Grant stops his riding and asks me again: "You okay, sir?"

First off, *sir*? And what, exactly, is he worried about? That I'm suddenly guilty? That I might go and tell my pseudo-boyfriend and ruin whatever it is they're up to on the side?

I snarl. "Don't ask questions, you fucking whore. Just do what I tell you. If you're lucky, I won't tell everyone on the Great White Way how big of a bottom you are. What would they think of that?"

It still feels weird saying this shit, but you gotta do what you gotta do. The bad-cop talk is all it takes to push Grant over. He shoots everywhere, squealing like a puppy run over by a pedicab (yes, that's the actual image going through my mind). He's gasping and grinding his teeth. I'm trying to pull out. I don't need to get off; I need to get OUT. But Grant's hand secures me inside of him—the first bit of force he's used tonight.

"I'm not done 'til you get off, sir," he says. Again with this "sir" business. I feel like a fucking army drill sergeant, for the first and hopefully last time in my life.

"Do your friends know you like calling the guys you get fucked by 'sir'?" I ask him, my chest heaving as he redoubles his efforts.

"No, sir! They'd never let me hear the end of it!" He's smiling. He's licking his lips. "Everyone thinks I'm a total top, sir!" And Christian thinks I'M crazy? I really don't get the deal with this charade—like it's somehow shocking and scandalous for a Broadway boy to be a big ol' power bottom. Leave it to Grant Majors to feel the need to "stand out" by living a total lie. Clearly, he gets off on the subversiveness. Psycho.

"Maybe I should tell everyone at your show that you're some fucking nelly bottom queen who begged me to seed him bareback? Post it on the Broadway Fanboy message boards?"

Grant pushes his face against mine, kissing me and talking on top of my mouth. "What if I told Christian you fuck around behind his back?"

Cute. From the bitch who just gave it to (or with today's revelation, got it from) my ex.

Don't worry, baby. Christian will know soon enough.

"Then I might have to punish you."

Grant's hard all over again. Amazing the power a few words can have. And all this time I've been working with my fists to get a reaction out of people!

"What if I did, Brayden? What if I told him all about how good you gave it to me?"

"I will ruin your life," I play along. "Do everything in my power to see to it that you never see those big, bright stage lights again."

"Oh God, YES, Brayden! Ruin me! Destroy me!" He's hard and turning red again, and I'm pumping into him harder and faster. His head tilts back, his eyes bulging.

Not far enough back, though, to see my iPhone perfectly positioned on the dresser right past the bed, aimed to capture every second of our fuckfest. There's over twenty minutes of tasty footage on there already and we're still rolling.

"I'm close," I gasp. Because I actually am. He knows what to squeeze and how to swivel. He locks his mouth on mine, pumping harder, bouncing up and down and whining through his clenched teeth. He shoots again. I shoot too. And my iPhone's video camera is still shooting, shooting, shooting.

Grant turns to kiss me, but I'm already up and walking to the bathroom, dropping the condom on the floor and snatching my phone as I go to wash his shit and cum off of me. (For a bottom, he could do a better pipe-cleaning job.)

In the bathroom, I catch sight of my face in the mirror and rearrange my hair, which has finally dried. Am I really about to do this? Did I really just do what I think I did? Yes. And yes. I clearly need more to drink because the last thing I need now is to second-guess my gut. Anyone in my path gets destroyed tonight—myself included, if necessary. Go, team, go—to hell, if required. I finish washing and return to the bed, where Grant's still glistening and heaving.

"How was my performance?" Ever the actor. He sidles up close for a kiss.

"Why don't you tell me?" I ask as I spin my phone around and click the Play button.

Grant's curtain call comes quickly after. I tell him I'm ready to send a copy of this ovation-worthy performance to the e-mail box of a friend. (Shane will be serving as this friend, since no one else in my crew would understand what I'm going through or help me with my latest life-ruining bender. Or want to see me naked.) I add that this unnamed friend will be ready to upload the video to XTube and then spread it across Facebook quicker than one of those "Oh my God, look at this video of you, LOL!" viruses. Shane probably won't do this, but I would. Gladly.

Imagine the damage, I tell him. He'll be un-castable! He might even lose his current role, his character and family-friendly persona permanently assassinated by a high-definition video of him taking it up the chute better than Brent Corrigan heffed up on a gallon of poppers.

Grant, meanwhile, is crying, looking at his many smiling and Photoshopped framed headshots on the wall like it's the last time he'll ever see them. The Great Grant performing a shit show, complete with waterworks. What do I want? He'll give me anything. Blah blah blah. Fuck, I could probably have him cut me a check from his bloated bank account—and for a moment, this is tempting. He swears, as he wipes snot from under his nose, that he never fucked Christian, top OR bottom. Tonight or ever. But anyone who enables a cheat like he just did with me can't be trusted. Just like Christian can't be trusted.

"So you want to continue playing dumb instead of admitting you were with Christian tonight?"

"We just bumped into each other! He came by to get that tie he left here last time we all watched *Mean Girls* together!"

The prick is light on his feet, I'll give him that. Christian WAS wearing a tie at some point that evening. We went straight to Grant's from some nightlife awards ceremony, where he took home the prize for Best DJ, and he wanted to look fancy as fuck to accept the honor. And if I remember correctly, his only other tie is still at my place, bunched up on the top of the bookcase I tore apart this morning. "Bullshit," I say. "Why didn't you mention that when I first asked if he was here?"

"He told me you guys had a fight," Grant mumbles. "I just…didn't want to cause any drama."

I have to smile at that one. At the still-naked sad sack groveling before me. "I still don't believe you. Christian was here; I can SMELL him." I raise my hand in the air rather theatrically, with my finger aimed at the Send button.

"No! Please. I'll do anything. I'll be your personal sex slave for life."

"Don't flatter yourself. This one session was more than enough. Took you a LOT longer than you promised too."

"But I'm telling the truth! Just let me erase that video…" He makes a move toward me, his hand outstretched.

I slap his wrist away. "Ah, ah. Didn't anyone ever tell you you shouldn't touch other people's phones?"

And that sets him off crying again. I fake pout. "Aw, why so blue, Grant? I thought you got off on this whole being-destroyed thing." Then I toss him the clothes he so neatly folded prior to our life-ruining fuck. "Better get dressed for your party."

"It's not a party! It's a benefit! And how can I go there with my face looking all puffy like this? Please, Brayden, delete the video. Please! Fuck! I was supposed to find out if I got cast in the First Equity National Tour of *Wicked* tonight! I was so happy!"

Crap. I feel terrible. Really I do.

The trouble is, I feel a lot sorrier for myself. So I issue his marching orders: one, he promptly tells me where I can find Christian, and two, he doesn't tell Christian that I'm coming. Grant looks hopeful, despite the continued crying, and agrees that he'll do this right away. He sends some text queries about Christian's whereabouts to his pals, then apologizes that it's taking so long for them to get back to him; it is a Saturday night, after all.

Grant sits, still naked, on his bed in silence, staring at his phone, urgency growing more evident on his face. I replay the video, turning up the volume so he can remember our time together. This breaks him down into sobs again. It's like prodding him with a Taser. Five minutes later, he gets a text message with an address. I make him check its legitimacy with another friend. Confirmed—they both saw Christian at this Upper East Side address. *"Some old dude's pad,"* one of them writes.

Now I know my next stop. Where I will let Christian know that I know why he really broke up with me, what he was REALLY doing this evening. Also: where I will proudly show him my homemade porn, still fresh from the fuck oven. Two can play at this game, you deceitful shit.

I wish Grant good luck as I head to the door and tell him I hope he gets the part. Because once I'm done with my ex, Grant will want to be as geographically far away from me as humanly possible.

I also tell him to invest in some fucking enemas next time he sluts around. And that "sir" is a weird and creepy thing to say to someone you're fucking.

In the stairwell back down to the street, I decide ('cause why the fuck not?) to upload a choice segment of the video to XTube and Facebook anyway. And when it asks me to title the piece? Only one phrase pops into mind. "Good Morning Starshine." How's that for dramatic irony?

***

Christian loves riding the subway. We used to search out empty cars late at night and swing from the handlebars or dance around the poles in the center like we were the MTA's personal go-go boy troupe. He'd read the ads aloud and comment on how smart or dumb they were. He always tipped the guys who played mariachi music, gave a dollar to the deep-voiced six-foot-five black man who carried a plastic bag full of fried chicken for anyone who needed something to eat that night. Me? I'm a cab type of guy. The subway smells like shit and barely works. Christian made it tolerable—fun, even. But now he's ruined it. I'll never go beneath this city again.

I feel only marginally bad for shoving aside a guy who tries to climb in a cab he rightfully hailed outside the Port Authority. The ride is far too slow, and glaring at the drivers clogging the streets doesn't help. My hands won't stop shaking, my fingers maniacally wiggling. All this excess energy surging inside me and I'm stuck in Saturday-evening gridlock. Having to cross Times Square to get to the Upper East Side is always a nightmare; add to that this fucking rainstorm and you have the worst-possible driving conditions next to a mandatory evacuation of the entire island of Manhattan.

I'm willing Christian to stay where he is. I want to destroy him—then I want to get home and pass out. I swig two Red Bulls and another baby vodka bottle I picked up at a liquor store outside of Grant's apartment to pass the time and sustain my buzz, trying to drive from my mind any cute memories of Christian. Or should I let them have their way with my head? Each one makes me smile, then fills me with rage as soon as I think of him with Grant.

Stay put, Christian. Don't you fucking move.

When I finally reach the Upper East Side high-rise where Christian's presence was confirmed, it is past midnight. I may need some sort of alibi to get past the doorman and up to whatever shindig I am about to crash. Turns out I'm wrong. A pack of cute, screechy gays, most quite a few years younger than I am, strut in at the same time. The doorman sighs, shakes his head, and points us to the elevator; he's probably seen many more like us this evening and doesn't need to ask where we're headed.

For the entire twenty-floor elevator ride up to the penthouse, the boys giggle and spank each other, swigging out of flasks they're hiding in their pockets and checking their asses in the elevator's reflective walls.

"Do you think Marvin's going to be there? I hope so. He says he's taking me to the Tonys—the dress rehearsal AND the live show!"

Just my luck. More actors.

"Nuh-uh, queen. He told ME I'm his date!" says his jealous friend, arms crossed petulantly.

"Shut up, BOTH you bitches. He's got a whole fucking ROW. We're all his dates!"

"Whatever. Let's just make this quick. That eWrecksion party is going on downtown, and I'm not missing it for a fucking seat at the Tonys. I don't care if it's right between Audra and Cheyenne!"

The boys crack up and toast their evening plans with their flasks. Not a one tries to speak to me—probably a good idea for all.

The elevator door opens directly onto a massive duplex penthouse. The entire back wall of the residence is glass. New York City looks so squat and ugly compared to what's here on our side. A jazz quartet is deep in a set in the far corner, just beyond a bar and buffet. The saxophonist wipes sweat from his forehead and takes his solo. Too bad no one else even notices; he's actually really good.

It doesn't take me more than two bars of the sax man's solo to realize I've found my way to a sugar soiree. Twelve old (and very rich-looking) dudes are flanked by five times as many pretty (and no doubt pretty poor) boys that look more like me than I care to admit. The old men guffaw, regaling their twinky charges with stale stories, the listeners nodding as they try to figure out how to hold a brandy snifter correctly.

Christian is here?

Really?

That conniving tramp! Makes sense, though. I don't care how good you are as a DJ, nightlife gigs don't pay all that much, my friend Todd has told me this much for certain. Yet Christian was always falling over backward to buy me gifts, take me out to dinner, drag me to a show at Roseland or Highline Ballroom featuring some DJ I've never heard of that he idolizes. If I pulled out my wallet, he'd look at me like I offended him before taking out his own card. I work retail, plus the occasional bartending gig, so no—I can't always afford a nice dinner out or a concert on my own. But I never expected Christian to pay my way. Certainly never asked him to. If money was a problem, I'd have been just as happy curled up on my couch, watching whatever he wanted on Netflix. Instead, it seems he's been sticking his dick in passageways older than the Holland Tunnel in some kind of effort to impress me with his mountain of riches! Every gift he ever gave me, every dinner out, is in question. I've been living on dirty, disgusting daddy money!

The thought of him letting one of these skeezes crawl his wrinkled fingers all over him just so he can pick up the check when we go out turns my stomach. Tonight is jam-packed full of revelations about the guy I thought I knew reasonably well. Who IS Christian Robert? A Broadway star–fucker? A daddy hunter? Was I really so blind this past month? Is it that easy to pull the wool over my eyes? I need to find him just so I can stop this tsunami of disturbing discoveries. I can't even imagine what other twisted skeletons he's got blowing each other in his closet.

I enter the penthouse, doing my best to keep my distance from the oldest of the guests, and come upon the centerpiece of the party: a stainless-steel table that is functioning as a social magnet, pulling everyone in its orbit closer and closer. And with good reason: its surface is covered by a mountain of whiter-than-white cocaine. While the food sits uneaten near the jazz band, boys and men approach the table at their leisure, scrape off a generous line or bump, and snort it to Brainsville. Well, why not? I shovel up a few, sending them into the soup of shots and martinis already circulating inside me.

Now we're cooking.

My eyes move more quickly, empowered by my super-snort. I survey every face in the room looking for Christian and, unfortunately, come up empty-handed. The bassist is now taking over the quartet's rendition of "How High the Moon." The moon's got nothing on how high I'M feeling right now.

Christian has to be here. Two of Broadway Bottom's buddies confirmed it! But if he is, he's definitely not in this room.

As the cocaine continues to work its wonders, everyone around me starts to grate on my nerves. Every bad joke immediately followed by insincere laughter, every old hand placed on every youthful thigh. Shady bitches—the young and ancient alike. I order a martini and offer the attentive cocktail server a tip. Judging by the shock on his face as he hands me back my five dollars, I've just committed a grievous faux pas. I swig the martini and promptly return to the coke pile to inhale another couple Andrew Jacksons' worth of the stuff.

Boys and men enter and exit the room. Still no Christian. I leave in search of a bathroom to relieve myself and splash water on my face. Things are rocking back and forth; I decide no more martinis for now. More coke? Sure.

Back in the salon, I spot Christian by the bar. My palms break into a sweat. Finally! Wait. No, it's just another swoopy-haired gay, a sight about as unique as a losing lottery ticket. The Christian twin leans on a wall next to the coke table, laughing with a geezer who could be his fucking grandfather. They look ready to strip each other naked—though I think that sort of activity would be frowned upon out here in front of everyone.

The bedroom.

Fuck. Of course!

There must be one or two (or possibly ten) May-December couplings doing their business in private rooms somewhere. And if Christian isn't in this living room milling or meandering…

"Well, hello there."

A hand is on my shoulder. It belongs to a man who looks almost identical to Anthony Hopkins, except he's dressed to the nines, tens, and elevens. He wears a perfectly pressed, fantastically tailored suit. His hair is slicked back, luminous. Slimy, even. He holds an almost-empty martini glass, an olive on a toothpick doing pirouettes inside. He looks like he's about to introduce an upcoming segment on *Masterpiece Theatre*.

"Hey, pops. How's it hanging?"

I am looking for bedrooms. He is making his move very boldly, stroking my neck like he's about to offer an old-fashioned lather and shave. Just. Smile. Deep breaths. Keep it civil.

"You're a very attractive fellow," the crypt keeper says. "Do many men tell you that?" (He sounds like Anthony Hopkins too, thanks to the Brit accent.) I know I shouldn't let him waste his time on me, especially considering how little of it might remain.

I smile off into the distance. "One too many, actually."

"Oh! He's got wit too! My name is Ronald."

So not only does he get the clue, he's decided to let it pass right on by him. Entitled prick. This is what happens when you get used to waving a checkbook in front of people to get what you want.

"Brayden."

I can't go searching this place with Daddy Warfucks following me around like there are insider trading tips hidden up my ass. But if I bash my martini glass over his head and call him an ugly old fuck, it'll only cause a scene. Then my wonderful surprise for Christian is ruined!

"Not one for eye contact, I gather?"

Where the fuck is Christian?

My eyes oblige and meet Ronald's. They have to. Because a guy my age wouldn't be in this penthouse unless he's into guys who'll be wearing Depends in another couple years. "Don't take it personally. These eyes are all over the place all the time. Always gotta be on the lookout."

"For what?" Ronald's eyes light up with a renewed sense of opportunity.

I shrug. "Depends. I know it when I see it."

"Would you like some fondue, Brayden?"

"No thanks, Ronald—swimsuit season and all."

"Well, I highly doubt you have much to worry about in that department. Me? I love the stuff. I might actually be the only guy here who does. They'd all prefer to leave the space open for additional mingling or fill the table with more stimulating substances. But when you're the host, you call the shots."

Ka-ching. If anyone would know where my endangered ex is, Ronald's the one. "Well then, since you asked, Ronald, I'm looking for someone named Christian. Maybe you can help me?"

"Oh, he's a pretty one. Pretty intoxicated the last time I saw him too." He looks around the room. "What is your business with him?"

"I have something to give him. Something he really needs."

"Well. Doesn't look like he's around, which usually means only one thing."

"He left?"

"He's in my bedroom. That's my guess." He smiles lasciviously for a second before his face turns serious. "Unless he left with the others for that tawdry party downtown—eWrecksion." He says this last word with no small amount of disgust.

"Did the host of this poor-boy buffet really just call another party tawdry?"

"We have fondue and a jazz quartet. They have porn stars and someone pushing shuffle on his iPod."

"Right. This is clearly a far classier affair, especially with the table piled in blow."

Ronald chuckles. "Stole half of my regular crowd tonight. But there are still some who prefer more *intimate* encounters." His eyes are practically fucking me at the word *intimate*. I want to throw up on his shoes.

Instead, I caress his arm lightly, initiating flirt mode despite the coke, booze, and repulsion surging inside me. "Well, assuming Christian didn't go downtown, you think he and his beau might like a couple more guests in that bedroom of yours?"

"It's certainly worth inquiring," he says, taking my hand.

And off we go.

The bedroom is past the kitchen, dining room, movie theater, three walk-in closets, and a library. Along the way Ronald tells me the history of the art hanging and lit upon his walls, exciting tales of auctions where he almost missed out on this gem by Matisse, that pure display of genius from Dali. (Like many elderly, he takes his sweet time getting anywhere.) The bedroom door is closed when we reach it. He taps lightly. "Hello? Are you decent?" Then he winks at me. "I certainly hope not." He opens the door.

From inside, I hear low, muffled voices long before my eyes adjust to the dark. There is an undulating mass on the bed that seems totally unaware of our presence.

Then, as if on cue, one of the pairing speaks:

"Oh, yes, Christian!"

That's all I need.

Ronald is far too slow and feeble to stop me. I fly, screaming, across the room and crash onto the bed, flinging the senior citizen part of the screwing couple to the floor. Hopefully he's got good insurance, because I just shattered his fucking hip.

Then I pound the shadow of my ex's face over and over again. My fists come down like the sheets of rain outside as his hands try (and fail) to fend me off. Christian's naked old lover tries to stop me from assaulting his precious little thing, but I put him back on the floor with a thoughtless punch that I don't even turn to throw. If this were an action movie, the audience would've cheered at that one. (Well, if he were a terrorist instead of a defenseless old man in his birthday suit, anyway.)

Light fills the room. And the audience in my head abruptly stops cheering.

Oh. Shit. This isn't Christian. Doesn't look like him at all, actually. He's black, for one—and not only does he not have Christian's swoopy Bieber hair, he doesn't have any hair at all. His head's buzzed to the skull. I'm staring at the bloody face of one of the guys who came up in the elevator with me earlier.

Now the poor kid is naked and crying, his face black, blue, pink, and soaking red. The metallic scent of blood cuts right through the sweat and sex smell.

He was pretty cute too.

Pity.

"Stop it! What do you want?" Ronald screams a little too late. "Are you okay, Christian?"

I fall back on my knees, disengaging from ass-kick mode to allow the poor kid to scamper out of the room, drops of blood following him like breadcrumbs. His gentleman friend follows, not caring that he's hobbling back into the party naked as the day he was born (however many eons ago that was).

I am silent. Just breathing to stop the burning in my stomach that kicked up when I began my attack. Trying to collect my scattered and panicked thoughts. If Christian's not here, where is he? Getting fucked in one of the walk-in closets? Has he not arrived yet? Grant and his friends are in SO much shit.

"Christian," I finally say, turning around. "Where. Is. Christian."

"THAT was Christian!"

A crowd has gathered behind Ronald, filling the wide hallway from wall to wall, all peering in to try and piece together what just happened. Hilarious. I just cock-blocked dozens of desperate losers at once. What a pleasantly productive evening!

"Christian Molson. Where the fuck is HE?"

"I don't know who you're talking about! Now please leave my home!"

"Christian ROBERT. Ever hear of him?" I'm in Ronald's face now. All that swagger and suave shit he seemed to possess by the kilo thirty seconds ago is gone. "ANYONE ever hear of him?" I scream at the crowd. But even though I *know* at least two of Grant's buddies are here and know who he is, none of them dares speak up.

"The DJ who spun at my brunch last weekend?" Ronald finally manages. His poor old face looks so confused. Early onset Alzheimer's must be SUCH a bitch. "He just came by to pick up his check!"

This is getting ridiculous. Like Christian knows what I know and is leading me on this absurd Easter egg hunt. Making me chase him until I pass out from exhaustion or get myself arrested.

"Where did he go?"

"Leave now or I will call the cops!"

Oh, hell no. The trail does not go cold here. I've already committed to this and will see it through to completion. The people in the hallway seem to blink in unison. Frozen in place like a room full of precious, invaluable statues that darling Ronald won at auction.

"Don't you all have an orgy to start? Take out your boyfriends' teeth and GET GOING!"

"No! YOU get going!" Ronald has reached the end of his withered rope, and now it's his turn to take me by the throat. Laughable pressure is applied, like I've accidentally tried on a turtleneck one size too small. I'd punch his head straight out the window if I weren't concerned about being carted off to jail before I got a hold of Christian.

"Not smart, Ronald. I'm giving you five seconds to let go."

Ronald's hands release in one. He takes off like a shot in two. I'm not quick enough to stop him before he runs out into the hall, through the crowd, shouting that there's a violent disturbance in his house. Someone has surely pulled out a cell phone and dialed 911 by this point.

In other words, I better make my exit. NOW. I blaze the trail left by Ronald and cut a hard right to the door. Boys and men try their damnedest to stop me, but they end up thrown against the wall, into the coke table (all over the floor now!), in a puddle of fondue. Hurricane Brayden. Cleanup, aisle everywhere!

I skip the elevator and make a run for the fire exit, setting off a screeching alarm. I speed down five flights of stairs and reenter on the fifteenth floor to hop in an elevator for the remainder of my descent.

The doorman downstairs screams, "Hey! Stop!" as I sprint by, the phone he just answered (no doubt a call from Ronald) crooked between his head and shoulder. I am already on the street and running harder. As soon as I round the corner, I dive into a cab and tell him to step on it. The driver's too busy talking on his own phone to ask why.

Only now do I have time to process everything that just happened. The numbing throb of my knuckles. The shocked faces of the twinks and grumpy old men. My fleeing from the scene like a bank robber. *I told you we should've gone to eWrecksion like everyone else.* I know someone said that at some point during my escape, but I can't quite remember who or where.

And now I recall everything else I've soaked up through osmosis about eWrecksion tonight: the "Gay Party of the Century." The party that caused elder Ronald to turn up his nose. *Everyone who's anyone will be there.*

Well, then I suppose I should probably be at eWrecksion as well. I have a pretty good idea who I'll find there.

***

My driver opts to take the highway from Ronald's apartment, promising that it'll be a quicker ride than avenues and side streets. Quick is good.

To pass the time, I check Christian's Facebook. No updates since yesterday. He's gone completely off the grid—most likely in hopes that I won't find him. Well, too bad, baby. I'm almost there. Already I've made the executive decision not to trust anyone I've spoken to. Christian fucked Grant, no matter what he told me. They traded cock pics overnight, Christian was newly single by noon, and the two of them were spotted walking to Grant's place by happy hour. You don't need to be a detective to figure that one out. Hell, Christian probably went a round with Ronald while the jazz quartet warmed up too. He's on a bender. Maybe because he knows his life in New York is over as soon as I find him—and this is his last meal. So far, he's had a cream puff and a few flights of aged cheese; my guess is now he's going for something more filling. Prime rib. And where's the beef tonight?

Initially, I incorrectly Googled "Erection NYC," coming up with a lot of porn sites and men's health clinics. I should have given the promoters more credit. The actual event is "eWrecksion"; the website promises a "One-Time-Only, Big Fucking Deal." Yeah, right. I get ten e-mails a week promising the same damn thing from ten different parties. This one's claim to fame? The "dorm dudes" of New York Screwniversity are performing live at 3 a.m.—which is bullshit. Public sex at clubs hasn't been permitted in this city since the early nineties (or so I've heard from people who were actually living here back then). So they'll gyrate around in G-strings like any run-of-the-mill go-go dancers. Big fucking deal. This party sounds as phony as the NYScrewniversity "dorm." I'm not familiar with the site, but I'm willing to bet most of the "dudes" didn't graduate high school, let alone pursue a higher education.

One thing on the eWrecksion website does catch my eye, though: its main promoter is Todd DiTempto. One of my best friends—or so I thought up until this very second. Why the fuck didn't he tell me about this party? If the hyperbole all over the site is even halfway true, this will trump any other party he's thrown. And Todd always brings us out with him!

Us. Hmm. Aside from Shane, the crew has been mysteriously quiet today, and not one of them informed me of their evening plans, let alone invited me to come along. That's highly unusual. Are they at eWrecksion? WITH Christian? It would make so much sense. Christian DJs a few of Todd's parties. The whole crew likes him— whereas things between me and the crew haven't been quite the same since I put the beat down on Gulliver. They may not have said much about it after the fact, but they didn't need to: I've noticed the glances they exchange, awkward silences that never used to be there. Maybe this time they're just not willing to sever ties with yet another of their friends I've had drama with. How many times have they rolled their eyes at the shit I pull? Complained about cleaning up my messes? Told me I'm too quick to fly off the handle at a moment's notice, before I even get my facts straight? Are MY friends the "anonymous sources" who told Christian I was crazy?

Backstabbing SHITS. They're having cocktails and laughing at me right now. For all I know, Christian has fucked ALL of them! A three-way with Rowan and Servando in a dark corner of one of Todd's parties. Sneaking out of my room in the middle of the fucking night to cross the living room and give it to Shane. I bet he's banging my trampy ex Marty too, just like Gulliver did.

Fucking traitors. They're ALL there, and Shane led me on this fucking wild-goose chase just to throw me off the trail! Each of them will suffer tonight. They can sit in the waiting room of the ER at New York fucking Presbyterian and try their best to continue laughing at me through their wired jaws. Assuming they're even conscious.

After driving past the supposed address five times, the cabbie pulls up to a corner in the West Village and finally admits he has no idea where we're going. I tip him anyway and tell him to have a good night. I can't blame him—not a single building owner on this street cares to display an address on the walls of their vacant-looking properties. The cab honks and rockets down the street in search of another fare to make up for how far off the main streets I took him.

I'm so tempted to call out for Christian—*Hey, loverboy! Where are yoooooou?*—just to hear my echoes off the empty street. At this point, it's a game. I could easily forfeit and head home, gather up all his shit and fling it out in the rain. Considering that some of that "shit" is very expensive DJ equipment he stores at my place for convenience, it might even be a harsher blow than any attack I could dole out. After the sex and drugs and drinking, not to mention one misplaced ass kicking, I'd say my night is complete. I'm so tired.

As for the rest of the crew? We partied, we joked, we had some good times. But when things got shitty, where have they been? Peeling me OFF whoever I'm laying the smackdown on. Telling me I'm overreacting. Never once have they just listened to what I had to say or truly understood how I felt. So fuck 'em. I'll go it alone. I don't need snakes for friends.

Maybe I'll just disappear. Vanish from their lives. Christian's, Todd's, Shane's—all of them. They'll never hear another word from me, spend the rest of their lives not knowing if or how I figured it out. Wouldn't that, in a way, be the sweetest revenge I could possibly muster?

A flash of blue runs by me so fast I almost fall into the street. A boy, in nothing but underwear and a hoodie, his cerulean hair leaving a blurry trail in its wake. I'm overcome by the desire to chase him down and punch him out for knocking me off balance, but I'm not the only person on the sidewalk. There's another boy standing twenty feet away from me underneath the only streetlight.

"Hey!" I yell.

The boy looks up, surprised. He's not a happy camper—he's been crying, and actually, might still be. I'm momentarily comforted that someone else is enjoying their night about as much as I am.

"Yeah?"

"I'm looking for eWrecksion?"

The boy sighs, his shoulders sagging. "Follow the blue-haired douche bag with the chinstrap. Tell him Graham said good-bye if you catch up with him."

I don't bother to thank him, just turn and follow the path blazed a minute before by my gay, blue version of Alice's White Rabbit. Unfortunately, I crash into a long line of guys—and they don't look much happier than I am. The blue-haired boy is nowhere to be found. Was he some sort of VIP who got to cut the line? I should have caught up with him. Dammit.

Minutes pass before I learn why everyone is pissed: the line isn't moving. Unfortunately for whoever's at the door, my patience left town hours ago. I break from the crowd and walk up to the muscle-bound black drag queen guarding the way. "Excuse me? Excuse me? What the fuck is going on?"

"Oh, do NOT address me like that tonight, dollface. I'll bitch slap you back to wherever you bought that hideous hair dye."

I laugh. First time tonight. Things are looking up.

"Listen, I need to get in there."

"You and every other queen on this fucking line!" she says through an expelled puff of cigarette smoke. "Tough shit. Doors are closed. About to tell the rest. Mind if I tell 'em it was your idea?"

"What do you mean the doors are closed? Is it that packed?"

The drag queen measures me up and down, probably trying to gauge how drunk I am—which, to be honest, isn't nearly as much as I'd like to be. And the coke wore off ages ago. "Did you not read the promo? Did you not hear about this party all over the city?"

No, queen, I didn't. Todd is my connection to nightlife. And since he decided for whatever reason NOT to tell me about this once-a-millennium event he was throwing, I had no fucking clue.

"I guess not."

"Doors close at two. No one is allowed in. And"—she pauses to check her cell phone—"it's now five after two, so you're shit outta luck. Mmkay?"

No. NOT mmkay. Not even on the same planet as mmkay. Not while Christian is in there. There must be a way.

"Todd DiTempto's in charge of this thing, right? Let him know Brayden is here."

Oh, this queen loves me. She sends a text on her phone to Todd while shouting, "Doors are closed, boys! Let this be a lesson not to show up gay late everywhere, mmkay?"

The wailing wall that sprouts up behind me is awe-inspiring. At least two hundred gays commence to bitching and moaning and swearing. I have no pity and neither does the queen, whose cell phone lights up with Todd's response.

"Sorry, sugar. Todd went home for the night. He said he's not the boss and doors closed means doors closed."

I don't believe her, but then see the words for myself on her phone. What the fuck? Todd doesn't leave his parties early! He's the last guy there, helping mop up the puke and shattered shot glasses! It's a lie. Fucking Christian is inside this club right now and Todd is with him. God. How stupid do they think I am?

I steal a glance at the drag queen's hand clicker. If she's been counting honestly, there are more than seven thousand fags in there. Only one of them is Christian. I couldn't find him if I tried.

It's time to give up and just—

NO. Weak! Brayden Jesse Castro is NOT weak. He does NOT give up or let anyone stand in the way of giving assholes exactly what they deserve.

Including this built, black bitch.

I know it's wrong to hit an actual woman—but fake bitches don't count, right? There's a dick tucked and tied somewhere under that spandex jumpsuit. This is a fair fight. I take a shot at her. A clenched fist right at her fucking nose.

"Are you fucking kidding me?" the drag queen howls, clutching the spot where my nails scraped the side of her face.

"Get out of my way, you cunt! Let me inside!"

I come at her again.

And get a six-inch heel in the side of my face.

Fuck that bitch can kick high! The punt is only the beginning of a tight combination of kicks, punches, and slaps, all ending in a hip toss that launches me off the sidewalk and into the street, right on the small of my back, all to laughter and cheers from the handful of stragglers that have yet to give up hope that they'll get into the club. They may not get the triple-X blowout they came for, but they won't be leaving without a show. I'm screaming, soaking the street with spit. I breathe around the exploding pain fanning out from my torso.

The queen looks down at me, shakes her head, and says, "Well, that was a pretty fierce show, girl. Not as good as the one in there, though." She clip-clops into the front door and SLAM.

The echo bounces around the rapidly emptying street. There's a loud metal clank as she bars the door shut from the inside.

I remain on the street as the rest of the dejected crowd disperses, counting the cracks in the concrete. In five minutes, I am alone, and I've lost count. No drag queens, pissed would-be partygoers, or asshole security guys. If that's not the green light to cry, then nothing is. Yes, crying is weakness defined. A private failing to be kept to yourself.

Well, if anyone's failed, it's me.

At finding Christian tonight. At keeping Christian happy. At picking the right guy once again.

Fuck tonight. Fuck the past month. Fuck Christian and fuck me. Fuck Grant for fucking Christian and fuck me for fucking him to get back at Christian. Fuck Ronald and his sugar kiddies and those other materialistic bitches on the Upper East Side, all fucking each other by now, I'm sure. Fuck my cabbie for not getting here fast enough, and fuck me for tipping him. Fuck that blue-haired kid for almost knocking me into the street, and that weepy loser whatever-his-name-was under the streetlight. But mostly fuck ME. Fuck fuck fuck.

The coke and booze have worn off completely. Every bit of tonight's bullshit stares me in the face. Cops are probably casing the city in search of a bright-white-haired twink who tore up a fancy party on the UES. The drag queen may very well tell Todd his friend Brayden attacked her, and if there's one thing Todd won't tolerate, it's me pulling shit at one of HIS parties. Now that I'm thinking clearly, I doubt Christian is even in there. He's constantly surrounded by swarms of people when he DJs; when he goes out, he tends to prefer somewhere a little more low-key.

I'm a mess. Which means I need to drink with someone who might actually understand what the fuck is wrong with me tonight.

I call Servando, who answers on the first ring—confirming that he isn't in eWrecksion, confirming that at least not ALL of the crew is in on some massive conspiracy to shut me out tonight.

Although, from the sound of things, he's somewhere almost as happening as eWrecksion is.

"Bitch, where are you?" Servando's high-pitched voice pisses me off a little less than it usually does. Maybe it has the power to blow open the bolted doors to this fucking club.

"Did you know that Todd was running a party tonight?" I ask him.

"What! You for real? I thought he was going out of town for something! You mean that fuckface didn't tell us he had an event?"

"I didn't know he had an alibi too. Weird. Brunch topic for tomorrow, I guess."

"You okay?"

No.

"Yeah, peachy. So what's up? Where should I be? I could use a few dozen stiff drinks. Maybe a blow job."

"Funny you should mention that—there's this sex party out in Brooklyn serving up a shit-ton of both!"

I was kidding about the blow job. I couldn't be any less turned on right now. A sex party? Ugh. Is there a single event that doesn't revolve around everyone taking it up the ass tonight?

"Where's Rowan? Doubt he'd be too happy to know your location, whore."

"I'm here too, Bray Bray. And you're on speaker, so don't go maligning my character, b'okay? You gotta get down here, *prontissimo.*"

And I thought tonight was Ripley's Believe It or Not weird already! Servando and Rowan still hook up sometimes, even though they broke it off ages ago, but I don't know many people who'd agree that attending a sex party with your ex is anything close to a good idea.

I want a drink. I want a shower. The last thing I want is to somehow find and hail another cab in this ghost town of a neighborhood. My bed sounds so much more welcoming. At least there I can beat the shit out of my pillow and scream until the stupid neighbors register a noise complaint. Sounds like the perfect end to the perfect night to me.

"Hellooo? You there, Bray?"

"I'm not really feeling the whole sex-with-shady-strangers vibe tonight. Sorry, boys."

"Then just do it with Christian!" This is followed by Servando's trademark seal cackle, a noise that would make a stereotypical wiry-haired cartoon witch blanch with envy.

"Christian is there? My Christian?"

"Um, yeah. We just waved hi to him like two seconds ago. We were gonna go over, but he looked busy."

Busy. I flinch. Like a punch to the gut. "What's the address?"

"Oh, NOW he wants to come out? Not for his old buddies, but for some boy toy he's been seeing for like three weeks? Typical!"

"Actually, it's been a month. To the day." If I hear one more of his laughs, I will find him and skin him like a rabbit. "So. Address?"

"Whoa. Sorry, Bray. Hey, Row? Where the fuck is this place anyway?"

***

Cabbies despise driving to other boroughs—especially this late, when they're planning on driving back to the garage to retire their yellows for the night and head back home for five hours of sleep before it's back to the city in time for the morning rush. For this reason, I make sure I am in the backseat, door closed, seat belt latched (and I NEVER wear my seat belt) before I tell my victim where he's taking me.

"No, no, I no go there," he says.

I repeat the address.

"No. No."

"Drive this motherfucking cab right now or I'll call the fucking cops on your ass!"

I can actually get the authorities involved because, in this city, it is against the law to deny a passenger a ride once they've entered the cab. Smarter cabbies refuse to unlock their doors before hearing where they're expected to drive. Mine is clearly a rookie, so this is a teaching moment.

I catch his eyes in the rearview. He's scared. Probably wondering if I'm carrying a knife or something, like those occasional cabbie-murderers the newspapers graduate to front-page placement every few months when they go on a spree.

"Thanks, buddy," I add.

And so the hunt is back on. How long has Christian been at this fucking sex party? All night? For Christ's sake, he could have been there since I got to Grant's. I yawn so wide that the sides of my mouth hurt. I should have gotten a Red Bull.

I drift off and am only startled awake when the road changes under the cab. We are on the Brooklyn Bridge, I think. The familiar Manhattan skyline disappears behind me, the far shorter and stranger buildings of Brooklyn rising up in front. Somewhere in this place I've only visited once (with Christian, the irony) is my slutty ex.

Oh, Christian. It didn't have to be this way—did it? What went wrong with us? We were so compatible. So happy. Right from that very first night.

Okay, so maybe I checked your e-mail a couple times after you used my laptop and forgot to sign out. Who wouldn't? And yes, I looked at your phone this morning, and that one other time you went to the bathroom and left it on the couch. I only had a moment to scroll through texts and look for incriminating names and phrases before I heard the toilet flush and had to set it right back down where I'd found it. But again, who wouldn't, given the chance? You could've password-locked your phone if you were THAT worried. A guy's got to watch his back, particularly in New York. And you've just proven that I wasn't watching it hard enough, despite my efforts.

The cab stops.

"Here," the driver mumbles. "Twenty-five dollars."

I tip him on my way out. He rips the cash from my hand and speeds away as I close the door, proceeding to run red lights to make up for whatever time he lost carting my ass to Bumfuck, Brooklyn.

I'm alone again, just like I've been all fucking night. Just like I've been for most of my fucking life.

FUCK. Someone get me vodka before I start an emo band. I HAVE to find Christian. Punch him until the anger comes back— 'cause, trust me, fury beats sadness and all the other emotions I've been trying to suppress since this morning. Rage is all consuming, leaving no room to feel anything else.

Fuck you, Christian. I bet you don't feel a single twinge of ANY-THING. Must be nice.

There's only one light shining on this dead-end street. It's coming from a three-floor brownstone with the kind of stoop on which you'd sit and smoke cigars with your immigrant neighbors. The illumination peeks out from a side entrance, so that's where I head.

Beyond the door, I hear the murmur of deep bass and not much else. Flashing light seeps out from underneath and paints the tips of my shoes. I knock because I can't find a doorbell.

A plate window at the top of the door slides open and I'm looking at a set of eyes. Is this a fucking speakeasy? Where's the hooch?

"Yeah?" the eyes ask.

"Sexplosion," I say quietly, more out of embarrassment than secrecy. (This, by the way, is the worst password I've ever heard.)

But the code works and the door opens, giving way to a dark then bright then dark again corridor. The music is unbelievably loud, and the man pulls me inside so he can close the door again. The musty smell that fills my nostrils is not what I expected, and I can't tell if the heavy, dank stink has always been here or if it's a byproduct of the activities that are happening somewhere deeper inside.

"Take off your shirt and pants, please."

If only guys were always this direct! My instinct is to protest—but at this point, what does it matter? I do what the doorman asks and submit myself to a "discretionary door exam." He's being paid to make sure every guy who enters this brownstone is hot enough for the other hot guys already inside—that I am either buff or toned and trim and that my dick isn't undersized. He must not be making much, because he is milking this body-check for everything it's worth, taking the one fringe benefit that came along with the gig.

And I, of course, am letting him.

"Sixty dollars," he says, opening a cash box.

"I don't get a discount for being cute?" I joke.

"That IS the discount. Sixty."

Highgay robbery! At least I'm investing in catching my asshole boyfriend literally with his pants down (or off and checked at the door, rather). "How is it in there?"

He looks up from the cash box and smiles in a way that makes me shiver. "Un-fucking-believable, buddy. You're gonna have a great time. Condoms are on all the tables. Lube too. Water sports in the showers in the back room past the main area. If you get caught going bareback, you'll be ejected immediately."

He scribbles a number on my hand with a black marker, a number that coincides with the shopping bag that now holds all of my clothing, including my underwear. I am then left to stumble through the dark hallway on my own as the next guest knocks on the door behind me.

How will I look naked, beating the shit out of Christian? I doubt the crowd would take kindly to me using my iPhone to record the grand climax of tonight's manhunt. Are Servando and Rowan still here? This won't be the first time they've seen me unleash my inner hounds on a bitch.

The hall opens up on a two-story room, which is probably the living room of whoever owns this place. Couches, chairs, and any items of value have been cleared out in advance, the floor covered in blue tarp. Above me is a wraparound balcony and the second floor that shows what this room probably should look like—portraits and a grand piano, tapestries and coats of armor. Robyn's "Call Your Girlfriend" is blasting, competing as best it can with the many entangled couplings, triplings, quadruplings, and quintuplings getting it on in every corner and on every remaining surface.

Hands and the men attached to them find their way to me quickly. I'm too busy searching the room for Christian to care. Unfortunately, only so many faces are in view, what with so many others being buried in assholes, between legs, pushed into chairs and walls. I'll never find him unless I go from pairing to pairing and pry them apart.

Which I will actually do. Because, hey! Look at that! I'm angry again. I'm pissed at the guy who's started sucking my limp (well, now kinda limp) dick. At the couple sloppily rim-sixty-nining right in front of me, preventing me from going farther into the room. And I'm angry at Christian for dragging me all the way out here to drop trou (and sixty big ones) just to humiliate him. I've already cock-blocked dozens at one skeezy sex party tonight. Do I have to cock-block everyone here too?

I would've come here with Christian. If he'd just sat me down and told me monogamy wasn't his thing. For him, I'd have made an exception; I'd have been willing to separate sex and love, even if it took some getting used to. But clearly, I wasn't worth enough for him to try.

He's dead.

He is so dead.

And he is standing right next to me.

Christian is fully dressed. All the way up to that tie he once left at Grant Majors's apartment. God, it feels like years ago.

"Brayden?"

He's spinning at a turntable. And the whole room is spinning now too as it dawns on me:

He's the motherfucking DJ.

Morning, Starshine!

And now I've forgotten how to speak.

"What are you doing here? Besides getting blown."

I am? Oh, right. Well—not anymore. I don't mean to push the guy off me as hard as I do, but it works. He's only flat on his ass for a few seconds before he's off to find the next cock to gobble.

"Huh. I didn't really figure you for the sex-party type."

"I'm not," I manage. The truth.

Christian steps away from his table to get closer to me. "Oh, so there's some other explanation for why you're standing here naked with some creep's mouth on your dick?"

Fuck right there is—but I don't have time to tell him right now.

"What…What are YOU doing here?" I sputter.

"What does it look like?" He doesn't need to say much else, but he says it anyway: "I'm the DJ. Well, I was. I asked if I could cut out a little early tonight. I wanted to stop by your place and maybe clear up all the bad blood from this morning."

"Shit," I say. But he doesn't hear me.

"Did Servando and Rowan tell you I saw them?"

Fuck me.

"Yeah. They did."

Now it makes so much sense why Servando and Rowan didn't detect the seriousness of the situation when they reported my ex's whereabouts. And now I'm crying again. Christian notices, and his face softens, his anger and confusion disintegrating.

"Are you okay? What's going on? Why are you naked?" He has his arms around me. He's moving in to kiss me. "I'm sorry about this morning. It was early, I had a hangover. I didn't mean to call you crazy. It just freaked me out to see you with my phone, and the card…I always do this when things get serious. I do something stupid that fucks it all up."

I pull away and shake my head. Because I'M the one who fucked it all up. Big time.

"Why didn't you tell me you were DJing at a sex party?" I ask, not even bothering to wipe the tears now drenching my face.

"I didn't know 'til this afternoon. I'm subbing for a guy who missed a flight back from Miami. And what does it matter? I've spun at The Cock, Rawhide, The Eagle…Is there a difference?"

I look around at the men who are having far too much fun to care about what's happening a few feet away from them. Christian's right. There is little difference between the bars he listed and this party. In fact, there are probably fewer people having sex here than there tonight, and here, they're a lot better looking.

"Nothing. I just didn't know. Have you been here all night?"

"Since the doors opened at eleven," he says, checking his watch.

Which is about the time I went banging into Grant's apartment.

This is too much. This is all too much and I can't think straight and I can't handle it.

"Check my phone if you want—Grant and I never hooked up, never talked about hooking up. I don't even like the guy! Totally self-centered prick. I only talk to him because YOU like hanging out with him. I'll delete that Broadway slut's number from my phone, you can watch me!"

I'm shaking my head. While Christian's proposed gesture might have worked this morning, now it's much too late.

"I just…" he starts, then starts again. "I've been thinking about you all day. I wanted to text you and apologize, but my phone's been dead since this morning, and you have my charger. I ran into Grant earlier, which I guess you should know. He had my tie, and he offered to let me check my e-mail at his place so I could try and line up a gig for tonight. I almost e-mailed you then, but I thought that would be impersonal. Then I had to run to pick up this check so that I'd have enough money to—well, I was gonna go get you some flowers and then come by and see if you were home. I know it's corny. But it IS our anniversary. Or, it was, anyway. Before we let that stupid fight ruin it."

He's rambling. It's adorable. My heart is breaking.

I can't tell him. I don't want to tell him. And I won't. He'll hear it all from someone else—EVERYONE else, most likely. Surely someone managed to save that video I uploaded to Facebook, long before they yanked it down (and probably deleted my account for such an obscene violation). Even if he doesn't lay eyes on it himself, by now I'm sure Christian's entire circle of friends knows I fucked Grant Majors. A few of them know I beat up some random naked kid at a penthouse party on the Upper East Side. No doubt even more of them saw my ass getting handed to me by a drag queen in the West Village. The moment he finally fires up that phone of his, he'll be bombarded with texts telling him what a freaky, fucked-up, vengeful loser I am. Then he'll rightfully hate me for the same reasons I wrongfully hated him this entire evening.

Christian called it this morning: I'm crazy. A little crazy when I go after a boy I like. A LOT crazy when I go after a boy I hate.

Well, not just crazy—I'm psycho-fucking-bat-shit INSANE.

The good news is, I have succeeded in my goal to ruin a life tonight. The twist is, it's mine instead of Christian's.

I sniff. "You should probably go."

"Planning on it. Are you...staying?"

Fuck, this is hard. Going from vigilante to villain. Is it possible to beat the living shit out of yourself?

"You should probably stop by my place first and grab your stuff, okay?"

"I'm sorry?"

"No. I'm sorry. Just. Get your stuff from my place, leave the key, and go home. And this time, don't forget your charger."

"Because I spun at a sex party? Because I got an unsolicited dick pic? What?"

I kiss his poor, confused face. I kiss it until my mouth hurts from stubble burn. "You just have to go, baby."

"Are you fucking ON something? Nothing that happened today is a big deal, Brayden! I've been thinking about you nonstop since this morning! That means we have something here. That means we're worth another shot!"

"I just...wish...you would've told me sooner."

"So you came to a sex party. So what? You're single. I don't like it, but I can get over it. And we can talk about what kind of relationship this is…"

I'm silent. He studies me.

"Did you know I was gonna be here?"

I nod slowly.

"So you came here for me?"

I nod again. He reaches out for my hand, hope glistening in his eyes.

"So then what's the problem, baby?"

"There's no problem. I came here to get fucked. You're welcome to stay and watch, if you like. I just figured you'd be tired."

Christian Robert doesn't cry. But tonight it looks like he just might. "Am I allowed to ask why?"

"Because I'm crazy."

Christian's face goes sour. He's angry—but he won't lose his temper. That's MY special power. Plus, he's a professional and this is his party. Instead of dressing me down (no pun intended), he slings his bag over his shoulder and nods. "Maybe we can talk tomorrow? When we're both feeling better?"

I shake my head. I know that's not going to happen.

I won't let myself give in to him. Because then I'M the one who gets hurt—next time or the time after that, whenever Christian decides my crazy is just a little TOO crazy for him. It'll happen—it always does. So better luck next time to the both of us. Somehow I know he'll come out of this fine and I'll be worse for wear. This cookie crumbles the same damn way every time.

"Well, have fun getting fucked. I'm spinning at a brunch tomorrow, so I guess I'll be going home to sleep."

I watch him storm out of the brownstone, the door slamming behind.

It's over.

Happy anniversary.

Now that Christian is gone, I feel alone, even though the sex around me is doing its best to suck me back in. Someone howls as he shoots a load down the throat of a guy he'll never talk to again. Four guys surround me, all jerking off, looking down so the shadows overtake most of their faces.

Disgusting. And this time, I'm talking about me. Because I belong here, and the events of today—tonight—have only served to send me where I was headed all along. Hands take hold of my ass, grab my cock, pluck my nipple ring, caress the scar on my stomach. Instinctively, I want to yank them all off and run for the door to stop Christian. It's not too late to apologize and forget all about this fucked-up hell of a night.

I could do that, right? Just a few small lies and happiness is mine again. I could learn to trust him over time. Actually trust him—no phone checking, no e-mail invading. For fuck's sake, he spun at a sex party fully clothed, then tried to leave early just to win me back!

I could maybe tell him the truth—the whole truth and nothing but. Explain what the hell I was thinking, feeling, while I was laying waste to the city on my way here. Grant. The other Christian. The drag queen. Everything. But how would I explain it? In hindsight, it sounds—well, just as crazy as it actually WAS. Who'd come back to that? Who'd want to be with me now? I can barely stomach what I've done myself, and I've had over two decades to get used to my antics. No one who didn't have to be near me would ever choose to be.

Tonight I've earned these strange hands. These mystery mouths. The wrapped, lube-slimy dick slowly easing its way inside me as I continue staring at the exit like a paralyzed stroke victim.

This is where I belong now. Home at last.

Christian will need half an hour to get to my place. Another thirty minutes to clear his things out and leave the keys. Meanwhile, I'm going to have sex with however many men I can. It's all fading into the back of my mind, every detail of this day just a hazy memory as the immediacy of the here and now finally overtakes me.

Run, Christian. Run as fast as you can. I can't promise I won't chase you, but at least you've got a head start.

MARTY'S BIG BREAK

All I can think of is *A Chorus Line*. The cast of thirteen men and women standing in different frozen poses across the stage, facing the audience.

God, I hope I get it. I hope I get it. How many people does he need? How many people does he need?!

Except, instead of thirteen of us, there's thirteen *hundred*. All guys. All identical to each other. Light-brown hair, around six feet tall, boyish. We're a line of clones plugged into the wall of this hallway in the Equity Building in Midtown Manhattan. I have no idea how anyone ever gets a date at one of these things, though many of my actor friends do. Yes, we're gay and mostly single, but to date someone here is the ultimate feat of egotism. *Hey there, you look just like me! Wanna grab a drink?*

They call these "cattle calls" for a reason. Hundreds of actors crammed into a long hallway not at all unlike a yard full of cows. All of us mooing (or practicing scales—what's the difference?), chewing cud, and swatting flies with our tails. Waiting for the slaughter.

I shouldn't be so negative. It's just that there are only so many of these things that you can take before you begin to wonder, *Am I any good? Are they really considering us?* Every once in a while, Stanford, my recently acquired agent, lands me a private audition. Just me, the casting director, and a piano, plus maybe a few assistants. There aren't hundreds of my long-lost twins just beyond the door, bragging about recent close calls. Nobody mooing but me.

Unfortunately, I've blown most of those private auditions too. So here I sit. And wait. And warm up. Just like the rest of the herd.

"Oh, Jesus Christ, do you hear that? Who the fuck sings 'Lost in the Wilderness'?" one of my twins snorts.

I listen carefully. Shit. The boy in the audition room IS singing "Lost in the Wilderness." The catty trio of doppelgangers breaks down into a loud fit of snorts and giggles, pulling their legs up to their chests as if they're trying to keep themselves from peeing.

"Stephen Schwartz?" says triplet number two. "Really? Someone better tell her Stephen Schwartz hasn't been a smart audition move since Rosie O'Donnell was hosting the Tonys!"

"And still using Tom Cruise as her beard!" closes out the third triplet. "What's next? A one-man rendition of 'Seasons of Love'?"

Now they've had it. This is the funniest thing they've experienced all year! They don't even try to hold back the giggling. All bets are off, and they're rolling around on the floor, kicking their legs up in the air, catching the attention of all my other twins lined up behind me. (I know no one actually laughs like this, but remember, we're dealing with actors here; every action must be performed, otherwise it might go unappreciated.)

"'Lost in the Wilderness'! He's going to be 'Lost in the Slush Pile'!"

More giggling. More uproarious laughter. Meanwhile, my face is burning up.

I shift around on the floor, making sure MY sheet music for Stephen Schwartz's "Lost in the Wilderness" stays out of view. This is the peril of picking a popular and well-known male solo. One, it's been played to death. Two, lots of guys still continue to sing it. Since Hunter Foster first belted it at the Paper Mill Playhouse in New Jersey in the late nineties, every tenor has given "Lost in the Wilderness" a go at least once.

I've stuck with it for five years. Or it's stuck to me. I connected with the song on so many levels: the music somewhat, but mostly the message. I was kicked out of my house when my parents found a copy of *Out* magazine in the back of my desk drawer; I felt just like Cain in this song, exiled from everything he knew and loved. My older sister proved to be my savior, letting me live out the remainder of my high school years with her in her tiny house in New Jersey. She had a piano that she never played—until I moved in with her. Then, every night before bed, she'd settle down at the upright and play "Lost in the Wilderness." Naturally, I provided the vocals.

"Doesn't matter anyway," another twin says. "There's no chance any of us will get this stupid part. I heard Grant Majors already got called in for a private audition last night."

"You serious? I turned down a backup dance gig in a music video shoot this morning for this audition!"

Grant Majors? Jesus. I didn't know he was going for this part! He's a shoo-in for the role—he's already understudying one of the lead male dancers in *Mamma Mia!*, which is something every one of the guys on this line would dream of doing. He's basically my role model, exactly who I want to be in a couple years, and he's the best thing young gay Broadway has going for it at the moment. Grant Majors hosts gay fundraisers, makes appearances at every nightlife event in the city. He's the happy, smiling, family-friendly face of the gay community, and if he's not exactly a gay household name yet, everyone operates under the understanding that he will be soon. This part is as good as his, especially if he got seen before this cattle call. Not only did he get a chance to audition for the role, he's also probably still sleeping, while I had to wake up at 5 in the morning to get a good spot in line at this slaughterhouse.

I should just go home. I have a date in a few hours—a first date, one I need time to prep for. In hindsight, it was probably dumb to schedule two events that involve me being judged and measured up by separate parties in a single twenty-four-hour period. But what can I say? Go big or go home.

"Grant Majors isn't auditioning for anything," another twin scoffs. "He's staying in *Mamma Mia!* until at least next season. Why would anyone go on tour when they can live in Hell's Kitchen and have a five-minute walk to a fat paycheck in the theater capital of the world?"

No one responds, but to me, the answer is obvious: to be on stage, in the spotlight, every single night. Not just waiting in the wings for someone to twist an ankle or suffer food poisoning so you can get your chance. Like Grant Majors, I worked damn hard to get where I am. I graduated two months ago, and I already have a tireless agent who works around the clock on my behalf. A stroke of luck may have brought him to me, but I paved the way for that good fortune with years of vocal lessons. Thousands of dance classes. Staying up late back in high school, committing every cast recording from 1950 to the present day to memory. And I mean *every* single one of the songs, from the company numbers in *Titanic* and *The Sound of Music* to Sutton's eleven o'clock numbers in *Jane Eyre* and *The Drowsy Chaperone*. I worked for this, that's for damn sure. I won't say I was the most talented senior to graduate from the theater program at Millersberg College in Allentown, Pennsylvania, this year. But nobody worked harder. They'd admit it too. When my peers were out getting trashed on fraternity row, I'd be home practicing the same bars from "All I Care About Is Love" over and over again, experimenting with where I could go off the beaten path of written notes to throw in my own flavor. Everyone I graduated with is serving burgers at Times Square chain restaurants or filing receipts at accounting firms, unable to even find time off to attend these cattle calls—if they're fortunate to have found work at all, that is.

But it wasn't all dedication and hard work. I got lucky too. It all happened because of—

NO.

I can't think about him now. Won't think about him. No.

Quick, Marty. Think of something else. Anything else. Songs. *American Idol.* Sutton Foster. Pizza. Your sister. Giraffes. Grant Majors. *Glee.* SHIT. Nothing's working.

I wish for ANYTHING to fill my brain, no matter how sad or maddening or painful. Baby kittens being drowned. Osama bin Laden. Catherine Zeta-Jones winning a Tony for *A Little Night Music*. Because thinking of *him* still hurts too much, and I need to be cool and collected when they—

"Marty Perry?" the exhausted hall monitor calls out from her desk in the far corner.

Dammit.

Cool and collected go out the window. Still here with me? Panic and dread and a sudden onset of perspiration. On the plus side, pangs of heartbreaks past are replaced by the threat of a far more immediate catastrophe.

No, it's not a big shocker that someone else sang "Lost in the Wilderness" in this throng of pretty boys. But right before me? Seriously? I didn't bring a backup, because Stanford insists that I sing this and only this at every audition. It's my musical sucker punch, he swears. Well, it's about to sucker punch ME right back in my own face!

There's no asking the hall monitor to bump me back a few spots. All that will do is dock me points when the producers and casting people meet later to go over the results; hallway etiquette is as important in an audition as anything else.

So here goes everything. I hide my music under my T-shirt as I make my way across the hall to the door.

Ah, the audition room. Always with the squeaky floor, the clanging, banging pipes that snake this way and that inches beneath peeling ceilings. Either sweltering or freezing, so flip a coin and expect the worst. And the walk to the center of the room always takes far too long. This audition has five people sitting at a busted folding table behind a stack of résumés that doesn't yet include mine.

"Come in, Mark," says the balding man in small circular eyeglasses in the center of the panel.

"It's Marty, actually," I say, smiling and apologetic. Because I'd rather it be MY fault he doesn't know my name than have him think I'm copping an attitude. The two women and two men on either side of him nod approvingly. I'm grinning my shit-eatingest grin.

Hand him the résumé. Walk another mile to the piano player to give him my sheet music. Don't look him in the face because I know it'll show annoyance that he JUST finished playing this song. God save me. Turn me into smoke and blow me out the window. (The same window that's refusing to bring a single breath of air into this sweaty hellhole.)

The casting director wipes his face with a handkerchief and exhales dramatically. "We're breaking after this, okay?" More silent nodding from his compatriots. "*Marty*, thank you for coming in today."

"Thank you for seeing me," I say, like they care who shows up at these things. "I'm going to be singing from Stephen Schwartz's 'Lost in the Wilderness.' Perhaps you've heard it before."

No courtesy chuckles. Great. Excellent. Hooray! I can already hear Stanford's consolation: *You'll get one in time, baby. Just keep making that magic happen.* That's Stanford's chosen refrain after auditions. I know he has faith in me—for now. But after each and every disappointing call from a disappointed casting director, I wonder when (not if) he's going to drop me.

"We'll go with eight bars," the director says.

"Eight bars, it is!" I say, probably too eagerly. No matter. I'm about to place my lips on each of their butts and switch my setting to sunshine. At this, by now, I'm a pro.

I snap a few times to give the pianist the tempo and off he goes. Off I go too. I don't know what singing is like for anyone else, but here's what it is for me: an out-of-body experience. It starts in my stomach, a distinct tingling heat that spreads rapidly like liquid from a punctured water balloon. Before I know it, the warmth is flying out of every pore on my body, except I'm not even there anymore. My voice sounds like it's miles away—a speaker in a car thumping four blocks from here. Trancelike. I give myself over to the notes, the words. I am a slave to the syllables and syncopation. It's better than an orgasm. It's better than a full-body massage. If I could sing every minute of every day, I would do it. There is nothing better in this world.

"Stop!" says the casting director.

I am back in my body. Disoriented. Blinking. It's always a system shock to return to my own skin.

"Thank you, Marty," he says.

I nod and whisper, "You're welcome."

I turn to go, determined to hold my head high.

"Wait. Come back. Can you start from the beginning and take us all the way through, please?"

Now my smile is genuine. All of them, including the pianist, are sharing in my emotional high. "Are we okay with postponing lunch for four more minutes?" he asks his tablemates.

"Absolutely," one of the women says.

I snap. The pianist starts. And once again, I exit my body.

***

I can't stop smiling on my train ride back to Astoria. It isn't every day that a group of five exhausted casting directors and producers ALL tell you how beautiful your voice is. (Trust me—I know.) In fact, it's the first time I've heard such accolades since Stanford first heard me sing, the day *he* brought me in to audition for him.

Gulliver.

I guess I CAN stop smiling. Thinking of him is a surefire way to dampen my spirits—and sure enough, now those spirits are sopping. I thought I was done with this—it's been over a month! But no, fifty days is clearly not enough time, because the ache is still as raw as it was on day one, a wound that refuses to scab over.

I stare out the window and, when that doesn't work, try reading the many ads covering the interior of the subway car: Dr. Zizmor will help me clean up my face in time for the beach! My career doesn't have to end here; I can take it to new heights with summer classes at the School of Visual Arts! It's considered good train etiquette to give up my seat for a handicapped person or a senior citizen!

This isn't working, either, so I close my eyes and rewind back to my amazing audition. Close-up on the smiles. Replay the audio of their applause. A reenactment of the light-headedness I felt.

And Gulliver. Gulliver, Gulliver, Gulliver. Suddenly, he's sitting in the panel of casting directors. He's also playing the piano. He's rolling around on the floor laughing with those boys who were unknowingly mocking my song choice. Gulliver is my judge, jury, and executioner. Never mind that it was the best audition I've had yet; no matter that those catty gays ridiculing "Lost in the Wilderness" undoubtedly earned much fainter praise than I. Where there's joy, there's Gulliver, bent on crushing it. The real Gulliver is—well, who knows? Surely he doesn't know I had an audition today, and probably wouldn't care if he did. But the figment-of-my-imagination Gulliver? He's always here, always watching. And he really has it in for me.

Fail. I'm running out of options. Normally, just leaving the chaotic, crass city for my tranquil home base in Astoria is enough.

Its quieter streets, diverse neighborhoods, and actual view of the sky soothe me almost instantly. But not even that works this time.

I plug my headphones into my iPod and hit shuffle. If anything can take me away, it's music. It HAS to be music. My last resort.

The song that comes up is Beyonce's "Halo," which I only have because Gulliver gave it to me on a "Summer Love" playlist. Which I thought I deleted.

There are no more ads to read. The audition happened too long ago. Beyonce can see my halo, halo, halo. The countdown to yet another Gulliver meltdown begins. That boy has taken up residence in my brain, and if history is any proof of the future, he'll stick around for another few hours, at least. It's always when I should be feeling high as a kite that he manages to pull me back down to these trenches.

Now I'm regretting doing so well in today's audition. Because when Gully fever sets in, I am overcome by the idiotic hope that he might come back from the ether. And what if he did? What if I weren't here? What if I were on tour? In my mind, he returns at night in the pouring rain, like it's a classic movie. He's outside my apartment, hitting the buzzer over and over, screaming my name. Then I rush outside, and he takes me in his arms, kisses me long and hard, and begs me to give him one last chance. I say, "But of course, you fool!" (In this fantasy, I sound like Katharine Hepburn.) And while none of this is very realistic, it's a much more definite impossibility if I'm in San Francisco or Charleston or New Orleans with a show rather than at home, waiting for him.

If it weren't for Gulliver, I wouldn't even have had an audition today. I wouldn't have Stanford as the quarterback for Team Marty. On the other hand, I also wouldn't have contracted my first case of chlamydia, wouldn't still feel disgusted with myself and the things I am apparently capable of. And hell, I might actually be HAPPY about blowing away the casting directors at my audition.

God. What am I doing? I didn't land this part, I haven't heard a word from Gulliver. Fuck. Too much Gulliver. Gully OD. Get me home NOW. The train pulls up to my stop and I bolt for the doors before they've even begun to wheeze open.

I sprint the five blocks from the train to my apartment and reach my room just in time to open the floodgates. Thank God my roommates are out, because I'm pretty loud when mess status overtakes me. I slam my door and blast "Halo," making sure it's on repeat so I can't be heard if anyone comes back. Now I will saturate myself with Gulliver to purge him from my system, like he's too much tequila and the consequent spins are keeping me from falling asleep.

I do, sometimes, have trouble sleeping. Because of him.

Remember these walls I built? There's a box hidden in my drawer that holds all that is left of Gulliver. E-mails from when I was still at school, promising a new relationship to wipe away past shitty ones (especially that horrifying bout with bat-shit crazy Brayden Castro). Movie ticket stubs from disappointing summer blockbusters I enjoyed more than Oscar winners because he was there to laugh at them with me like we were silhouettes from

Mystery Science Theater 3000. Playbills from shows we student-rushed because his college ID didn't have an expiration date. He's everywhere—even though nobody knows where he is. I should tell them: he's right here, in this box. In my head.

I should throw the box away. I was close to doing so, until Gulliver pulled his Houdini act. I didn't even know he had vanished until two weeks after the fact, when Brayden clued me in. I still have that text:

"Gulliver is gone btw."

That was it. I sent Brayden fifteen replies that first day alone:

"What do you mean gone?"

"Please tell me! Is Gulliver okay?"

"BRAYDEN ANSWER ME NOW DAMMIT. WHAT THE HELL ARE YOU TALKING ABOUT?!?!?"

But that was Brayden's sweet revenge. He still isn't over the secret relationship I had with Gulliver behind his back, and probably never will be. He gave me just enough rope to hang myself with and not a millimeter more, leaving me to pry the rest of the information (what little there was) from his friend Shane when I ran into them at a party one night. Gulliver just disappeared. Left his apartment in Astoria without a word, without a trace. Back to California? Off to another new city? Or maybe still hanging around the concrete jungle, maybe a mere mile away from me, or even just around the corner? I still look for him, trying to imagine how I'd feel if I saw him. If he looked at me. If he smiled.

We were so close. Almost there. Almost happy. If only we hadn't been sneaking around so much. If only Gulliver had been honest with his friends, or me, or anybody. Gully isn't a bad guy, but he's not good at owning up to the truth if it means someone is going to be mad at him. And when that person has a temper like Brayden, well, I can't say I really blame him. It was bad luck that he was friends with my psycho ex—bad luck and worse timing. I see that now.

And if I never get a chance to see him again and tell him all this, I will never forgive myself. What I did to Gulliver was not something I'd wish on anyone. I ruined his life—without thinking, without knowing what would happen. I just did it. And there's no excuse.

My throat is hoarse from coughing and crying. God, I feel like such a baby. I slap myself across the face. Hard. Again. Over and over in front of the mirror until my cheeks are hot and red. The crying gradually ceases like a case of hiccups.

I need to get my shit together, put Gulliver in the back of my brain where he belongs. Because I have a date in two hours. No—one hour?

Shit. Fifteen minutes.

What? Have I been playing "Halo" that long? Just sitting here, stewing about my fucking ex?

Now I'm going to be at least half an hour late. I should just cancel. I WANT to cancel. In fact, I never wanted this date in the first place.

Oh, his pictures are cute enough—including the slightly slutty MySpace-era one of him shirtless in the bathroom mirror, showing off a tattoo of a pocket watch on a chain that winds around his belly button. Normally this would have been enough for me to avoid spending time with him at all costs, but our consequent e-mail exchanges changed him from a definite no to a potential yes. He's charming, funny, sweet. And he "doesn't mind at all" that I'm an actor, launching him to the front of the line.

But he's also a boy. The first I've agreed to go on a date with since Gulliver. I guess, in a way, that means I'm accepting the possibility that Gulliver may not be coming back, and the more likely possibility that we won't be getting back together even if he does show his face in this town again.

Do I want to accept that? Do I want to meet this random boy who, let's face it, is not my type (except maybe in the looks department)? His name is Chase, and if his OKCupid profile and our conversations are a true representation of who he actually is, he may be the first guy to help me get Gulliver to disappear from my heart as cleanly as he did from Manhattan itself.

But do I want him to?

Yes, I decide, while scrambling to find and put on something cute that doesn't make it look like I've put too much thought into it. I'm not getting any less single crying in my room, pining for

Gulliver. There are thousands of gay boys in this city, and as any casting director knows, you'll never find the right one if you don't hold a big ol' cattle call to weed through 'em.

So bring him in. After this morning's audition, maybe I'm on a winning streak. Let's give today a 2 and 0 record, shall we?

***

Stupid rain! I didn't even think about bringing an umbrella—it was hot as hell when I was rushing back to my apartment post-audition. But now, as I reach Manhattan, the sun has ducked out and left the door open for a blanket of fat, smog-stained clouds. Seems nobody expected this sudden turn, because everyone is scurrying for cover like subway rats just before the 5 train pulls in. Leave it to New York—nothing predictable. Ever.

I duck under a scaffold on Fourteenth Street, which doesn't help at all. I still end up drenched by renegade streams of dirty city runoff. I send Chase a text apologizing for being late, plenty of extra exclamation points dedicated to four-letter words addressing the rain. His text comes back:

"I thought we were meeting an hour ago? Already went home."

Am I a whole hour late? Gulliver strikes again. Bastard.

"I'm so sorry! I'm here now, can you still come out?"

Five soaking minutes pass without a response. During this time, I am treated to a homeless man ranting that the CIA is putting chemicals in our drinking water to turn our children gay. I am just about to head back to the subway when my phone beeps:

"Why not...give me twenty minutes?"

"You got it!!!"

Too many exclamations. The excess enthusiasm isn't going to make up for my flakiness. Dammit dammit dammit. That's strike one, and I'm sure the fact that I look like a twinky swamp monster in my sodden blue-and-yellow-striped button-down and jeans will most likely be my strike two. ARGH. The rest of this date better be the smoothest of sailings, or I'm dead in the water.

I took it upon myself to pick the restaurant—a Thai place on the northwest end of Union Square. I expected us to dine outside on the sidewalk, granting us a scenic view of the comings and goings of the small park and its many occupants to provide handy conversation pieces. Of course, that's shot to shit. The park is now just a small rectangle of grass and concrete filled with murky puddles, its only inhabitants of the homeless and pandering variety. I give change to as many of them as I can, like I'm the weather's personal publicist on damage control. I'm desperately trying to build back my karma.

Despite my proximity to the restaurant, Chase has still somehow beaten me. He looks miserable, ducking beneath an awning that isn't generous enough to keep his entire body dry. The result is a Jekyll-and-Hyde effect: half of him crisp, the other dripping. My God.

"I am so sorry!" I shout as I run across the street. A car brakes and sits on the horn, just missing me. I let loose a scream that belongs in the mouth of a busty blonde in a slasher flick. By the time I reach him, I am both soggy and emasculated.

Oh, boy. I can smell that second date already.

"I am SO sorry, Chase! I lost track of time. I've just been so messed up and stressed out today."

"It's okay," Chase says, squeezing out his shirt and putting little energy into his performance. The result is a less-than-convincing tone letting me know that I'm already skating on thin ice.

"I swear, usually I'M the punctual one waiting on everyone else. That's why I always carry a book with me. Except tonight."

"I said it's okay. Enough with the apologies." He smiles, but it's still forced. Which I guess is better than not making the effort.

When we get inside the restaurant, I discover yet another reason to curse the rain: since the outside seating has been decommissioned, all the tables inside are filled. We have a thirty-minute wait ahead of us. Terrific. Our fellow diners are equally miserable, shifting uncomfortably in wet and heavy skirts and suits. The waiters are perturbed because the drippy customers are tipping less and their bills are wilted from water damage. The entire restaurant smells like a gigantic wet shoe.

I sigh. "Maybe we should…"

"Reschedule?" Chase incorrectly anticipates.

"...try somewhere else?" I eke out just after him.

"Oh." He looks embarrassed. "Yeah. Maybe."

Then I'm blurting: "Look. Clearly this was a terrible idea. It's my fault for screwing up the timing." There are tears sneaking out of my eyes. Not necessarily because of Chase, but man, has today been a trip. "Maybe we should cancel. Our first date hasn't even started and I've already messed it up five different ways. I knew this would happen. I'm a little out of practice..."

"Oh, come on, Marty. It's fine. I didn't have plans anyway. I mean, you're cute enough to take my mind off my wet clothes and the stench of this place. For half an hour, at least."

"It does smell terrible, doesn't it?" I laugh, wiping away my tears. "God, sorry for the waterworks. Like I'm not wet enough already?"

"Nah. I like that you're crying. I mean—it's endearing. Most gays in this city killed off their feelings when they crossed the bridge into town. So. Did you have a bad audition or what?"

I forgot I'd mentioned the audition in an earlier text. "Actually," I sniff again, "they loved me."

"Well, gosh, you poor thing! I'd hate to try and console you after you won the lottery!" Suddenly, I become aware that Chase's smile is gorgeous. Full of bright-white teeth.

"This calls for a celebratory meal in a place that doesn't smell like a ripe scrotum, pardon my French," he says. "I actually know a better place around the corner. And it looks like the rain has stopped. Wanna make a run for it?"

"After you."

Chase sprints a lot faster than me, but he has a firm grip on my hand, dragging me a few blocks to a restaurant that sits below street level. It's designed to look like the backyard of a trailer park and the menu is all deep-fried foods filled and/or covered in Velveeta. The waiters are smiling and friendly, the customers grinning like Buddhas as they try to overcome their food comas. It's like I died and went to deep-fried heaven.

"You're not one of those gays who says they don't eat, are you?" Chase asks once we're seated at a table along the sidewall by the kitchen. I raise my eyebrows and point at the over-buttered slice of Wonder Bread sticking halfway out of my mouth. A waiter arrives with two drinks served in frosty glasses, with little plastic alligators sticking out, tails up, drowning in the booze.

It's a whole new date. Conversation is flowing at hyperspeed. We talk about Armistead Maupin's *Tales of the City* and how we had to spend half of our time on Google to understand all of the now-outdated references. ("Almost as much time as I spent in the companion guide to Joyce's *Ulysses!*") We both hate reality television. Neither of us is on the best of terms with our parents, but we both have kick-ass sisters. Then, even though it's not proper date etiquette, we somehow end up on the topic of guys we've recently gone out with.

"Funnily enough, my most recent date's name was Marty too," Chase says. "We met at a club, went home together, had a great night. Then, nothing."

"That doesn't sound like a date to me," I say. "Going home from a club together?"

"I guess," he shrugs. "Maybe what made it feel like a date is how into him I was. Stupid, I know."

"To fall for someone you just met? Nah. It's pretty common, actually."

"Just not often mutual." Chase smirks. "Anyway, we had...fun. And I don't know, even though it was what it was, I felt a connection. Ever meet someone for the first time and just feel like you've known them before?"

"Sure," I say. "But I have a theory that any relationship that begins in a club is automatically doomed. That's where I met my ex, Brayden. And that was doomed with a capital D."

"Brayden? That's weird. Brayden was MY Marty's LAST name!" Chase laughs, already tipsy from whatever drink he ordered us.

"That IS weird!" I laugh. "Yuck. Marty Brayden. Sounds like a porn name."

"Yeah." Chase is quiet for a moment before assaulting his straw again.

I opt not to go too deep into details about bat-shit Brayden. Just enough to give Chase a flavor of the insanity I put up with. In the end, my conclusion is it was a learning experience. I will never go back to Brayden, and now I have about twenty different signs of crazy to look out for on new dates.

"Notice any in me?" Chase winks.

"Not yet. But we haven't gotten to the Rorschach tests yet."

Now I have a new problem: I'm trying as hard as I can not to dream up our kids' names. How I'll get him out to Jersey to meet my sister. The outfit he'll wear to the opening night of whatever show I get cast in. Maybe he'll travel out of state to see me in the *Wicked* tour if I land it?

This is a problem I can't stand: my proclivity to mentally and emotionally jump ahead forty steps with a guy I've just met. The point where the dumb fresh-love romance is dead and we're picking out what toothpaste we want at Duane Reade or bitching about our double date with that boring couple from Morningside Heights.

Chase slurps his drink down to the bottom. "Oops! Refill time?"

I'm nowhere near done with mine, but I shrug and suck the entire thing down. Brain freeze commences, and I have to grit my teeth, squint my eyes, and breathe roughly out through my nose to fight back the searing explosion in my head. Which Chase finds adorable enough to crack up.

"Gee, thanks. You're really Mr. Sympathy over there. You seem to like me best when I'm in pain or under duress?"

"I can only hope you'll end up in some sort of hostage situation before we say good night. Then I may just fall in love with you, Marty."

Love, hmm? I'm letting that go. Finally, food comes, along with our second round. My God, I've never seen so much macaroni and cheese before—a mountain of it spilling over the trough-sized ceramic bowls plopped down in front of us. Chase digs in and I try to match his vigor.

"Let me say," Chase starts through a cheesy mouthful, "I usually have a no-dating-actors rule."

"You and everybody else in New York," I sigh. "Actors included. We can't STAND each other. Granted, that doesn't stop us from hooking up on tour. I was with *Jersey Boys* as a swing last year. I swear, the Four Seasons was more like the Four-way Seasons."

"What a lonely existence," Chase laughs. "You won't date each other, no one will date you. How do you deal?"

"We're actors. We're good at pretending we're not bitter, jaded, and miserable. So are you anti–ALL theater? Or just the talented boys that bring it to you?"

"I have seen a few shows. Some Broadway. A bunch of my friends go to NYU, so I make a habit of seeing their showcases."

"So do I make a worthy exception to your rule?"

"Hmm. You're not NOT a worthy exception—yet," Chase says, taking another sip. He's drunk. So am I. Apparently, we're both giddy drunks, which is yet another commonality I am enjoying immensely.

"Well, you should stop by a Musical Mondays sometime. It'll help you get more accustomed to actors and theater queens," I say.

"Musical Whatdays?"

"Mondays. It's my favorite party! Every week at Splash. Cheap drinks. Free to get in. And there's a live performance by a touring or Broadway actor at midnight."

"That might be fun. Would you be interested in escorting a virgin?" He grabs my hand as he asks this question. My heart pukes happiness all over the place.

Here we go again. Gulliver? Gulliver who? Already, I'm strategizing about when to ask Chase for a second date, and a third, and a fourth. What to do on each one? I could strategically erase Gulliver by redoing everything he and I did together! I can see Chase fitting in to all those activities. And we'd look so cute together!

"I would love to be your guide," I smile, before taking my hand back to jam more disgustingly amazing mac and cheese in my mouth. "It's actually the only party I really go to. 'Cause other than that, clubs aren't really my thing, you know?"

"You don't like to go out? What, do you hate fun or something?"

"Fun. Ugh. Kids' stuff," I say, doing my best gruff-old-man impression.

Chase smirks and rolls his eyes.

"No, I used to do the bar scene—Deko Fridays and Feathers in Jersey, then some parties here in the city. Especially when I was in college. I was a big party boy on the weekends. But I got over it. It's just so…arbitrary. Everybody's there to have sex with everybody else. ANYbody else. It's like a cesspool! Do you know how many times I've had to pry a guy's tongue out of my mouth, just to watch him stick it right back into the next-available throat? It's disgusting!"

"Well, not ALL parties are that way. Some are just a good time."

"You're right, there's Musical Mondays. Other than that, it's pretty much the same thing everywhere you go. A bunch of people tossing crabs and herpes back and forth. I'll take drinks at a straight bar any night over that sort of scene."

"Right. Because straight people never make out or go home together."

I shrug. "They do, I guess. Gay clubs are just so much more blatant about it. Playing porn and pictures of dicks all over the walls.

And the ones that don't—well, take Splash, for example. Every night of the week they have go-go boys."

"Uh-huh…And what, exactly, is wrong with go-go boys?"

"Um, that's a good question! I'm guessing negligent parenting?" I giggle, a little too tipsy to realize that Chase is far from laughing with me. "They hang their asses out in front of hundreds of strangers, let gross old guys feel them up for less than it takes to buy a scone at Starbucks. For a few dollars more, they probably go home with them. It's just sex in your face, no sense of shame or decency, appealing to the lowest common denominator. It's tacky! And just because I happen to be gay doesn't mean I want to be associated with those skanks when I want to go dancing with my friends and have a cocktail!"

All I can think of is Gulliver, going out every night of the week—every night he wasn't with me, that is. My disapproval of the club scene might have been a problem had there been any possibility we could go out together in the first place. Hell, I might have enjoyed a night out with my boyfriend! But Gulliver was too skittish to take me anywhere there was even a remote possibility one of his friends might see him with me. Bat-shit Brayden, in particular. Instead, Gulliver snuck me around like an illegal immigrant in the back of a van, hiding me out of view just because his nightlife crew believed every word of the poisonous slander Brayden spewed against me. I never even had a chance to explain my side of the story before I was treated like a pariah. If I walked into a Hell's Kitchen bar tonight and found them, I'd be sneered at from across the room until I was driven to leave—if they didn't actually have me thrown out on the street first.

I realize Chase has recoiled like I just slapped him in the face. And why wouldn't he? He has no idea where my opinions are coming from. I'm coming off as a judgmental prick. "Look," I tell him, "I just think gay men have so much more potential than going out, drinking themselves into stupors, waking up with a stranger, and spending the entire rest of the day gaining strength to do it all over again. We have the power to do so much, create so much. I could have spent my college years with my ass hanging out of my underwear for tips too! But instead, I worked that ass off acting and singing. And now it's finally paying off. Sometimes I just feel sorry for the guys who are stuck in that scene, you know? Like slutty robots who don't even realize they're running on autopilot."

I exhale and lean back, suddenly exhausted by my own opinions. Meanwhile, Chase chuckles lightly, looks around the restaurant, then settles on staring at his drink. He doesn't say anything for at least a minute.

What's happened? Up until now, conversation has been flowing so perfectly, a witty tennis match of volleys as delicious as the cheesy carb piles we were shoveling in our mouths. I open my mouth a few times to try and create a new vein of discussion, but I'm too self-conscious. Verbally constipated.

After a minute of us silently chewing and slurping, Chase finally breaks the awkward silence. "Um, Marty?"

"Yeah?"

"I guess I'll come out with this now. I usually hold off until a few dates in. But, up until a few minutes ago, I was liking you…And the last thing I want to do is waste either of our precious time."

"Okay?" I'm immediately defensive, on date-protection duty. Suddenly, everything has taken a turn for the serious.

"Okay. So I'm a dance major at NYU."

"I know! And that's awesome! Clearly you're working hard to get where you want to be too—"

Chase lifts his hand to stop me. I oblige.

"I am working hard. REALLY hard. And this city is expensive. REALLY expensive. You know? College jobs don't cut it. And I sure don't have the time to hold down a full-time day job and still attend all my classes."

That's a plight I can understand. If it weren't for all the money I socked away from touring with *Jersey Boys*, I wouldn't even be able to afford my tiny room in Astoria.

"Right?"

"I help pay down my loans and live in this city by working as a go-go boy."

"YOU'RE a go-go boy? Are you serious?"

"Yeah. I'm serious. I'm sorry if it comes as a shock to you that a go-go boy CAN be serious…"

The snap response catches me off guard. I'm anti-gay clubs, not retarded. Now his quills are up, and I'm stumbling to find the right words to respond. "Well, sorry. I didn't mean to insult your line of work. But I mean, you must be used to it…"

"No, I'm NOT used to it, Marty. Not all of us are as privileged as you. Some of us have to work to support ourselves while we reach for our dreams."

"I wasn't insulting YOU…"

"You just insinuated that I was a stupid, aimless slut. And a prostitute. Not to mention the crabs and herpes. You should share your opinions with my modern dance teacher, she'd be shocked to hear it."

"No! Chase! I'm all for you chasing your dreams and working for it. I understand. But as a GO-GO boy? You couldn't find some other way? You can't deny that at least some of what I'm saying is true. You guys are always rubbing up on each other, making out with each other. And there are strangers all over you all night long…"

"Right, and it's also one of the highest-paying non–sex worker jobs that lets you make your own schedule and work evenings, freeing up the days for class. And it's not like I'm FUCKING them. I'm just dancing, for Christ's sake. In clothing that's no more scandalous than what most of gay New York wears to sunbathe all summer long on the Chelsea Piers. Wow, I didn't realize I was on a date with New York's only virgin. Is your chastity belt on extra tight today or what?"

"I never said I was Mr. Innocent. There's just a fine line."

"You fucking actors. It's all appearances for you. Pretending to be something you're not. It's a job. It's what I need to do. And does it really fucking matter if I make out with a guy in a club versus the privacy of my own room?"

"Yes! At least there's a little privacy! Some dignity!"

"Ever had an STD, Marty?"

"Yeah. I had chlamydia last month. Which I got from my boyfriend who cheated on me with some slut he probably picked up in a gay club."

"Ooh, scandalous. Maybe he was even a go-go boy!"

"It wouldn't surprise me."

Chase sits back. "Well. I don't see any reason why we should see each other again if you can't respect what I'm doing to make ends meet. Clearly you should've met me in a year, once I've graduated and am doing something you find more worthy of your attention."

"What is there to respect? Your lack of tan lines or expertise at spinning around a pole?"

"Nothing at all, Judge Judy. Three nights a week, I strip down to tiny pairs of underwear and dance on the bar at Splash. Sometimes I yank the fabric up my butt to give the clientele more to see. Sometimes I take my G-string all the way off and hold it in front of my junk. At some parties, I dance naked! Maybe someday you'll embrace your sexuality without instantly going soft from shame."

I have no words. But that's unacceptable to Chase.

"Speechless, huh? I must represent everything you hate about the club scene. Or is it everything you hate about the gay community at large? Everything you hate about yourself, perhaps?"

"What?" This is crazy! I haven't said more than ten words since his revelation, and he's acting like I'm a member of the Westboro Baptist Church who just condemned him to hell! "You don't like actors, I don't like go-go boys. I don't see what the big deal is. We can just agree to disagree."

"I didn't launch into a fucking monologue insulting every single actor in the entire universe!"

"No, why would you? We're doing SHAKESPEARE! You're exposing your ass crack to the tune of Britney Spears! I don't think there's much of a comparison!"

Okay, I know I'll never do Shakespeare. But I'm making a valid point here. Questions are sprouting up all over: Does he do drugs too? Does he go home with the heavy tippers? I don't know who he's been sleeping with. The life he leads. And I don't need to spend every waking hour wondering.

There's only one question that HAS been answered:

Chase isn't the boy for me.

"I'm sorry," I tell him. "Seriously, I didn't mean to hurt your feelings. I'm not judging you. But I know myself well enough to admit I'd be way too jealous to let a guy I dated dance naked in a roomful of strangers. In my opinion, in a relationship, that should be for my eyes only. Or else, what's left that's special, just between us?"

"Damn," he says. "Well, I guess in the grand scheme of things, a wasted hour or two is better than dating a jaded, bitter queen."

"Hey!" I say, trying to grab his hands over the table—because I feel bad that I hurt him, not because I want to rescue the date. But too late. He yanks them away and shoves them under the table. We still have a check coming. Can I just get up and leave? Will he make a scene? I can't believe I almost got hit by a car for this guy!

"I still like a LOT about you and where you're going," I say. "And I know I'm spouting every line you've ever read in a bad gay romance novel…But would you want to be friends?"

"You're right, Marty. That does sound pretty fucking predictable. And I'm sorry you can't pick and choose the pieces of me you find acceptable."

I'm back on the defensive: "I'm sorry too." I made a peace offering. Forget him if he won't take it.

"And just so you can be extra sure we both made the right decision here, I'm dancing at this party called eWrecksion tonight. There's a bunch of gay porn stars from New York Screwniversity doing a live sex show on stage! It's right up your alley. Hey, maybe I'LL even get naked up on the go-go box."

"I don't doubt it."

Chase grins. He's not finished with me yet. Something tells me this is the most fun he's had on a date in ages. "Oh, and by the way—Marty Brayden? My bad date? He's the STAR of that gay porn site. We fucked on camera in front of thousands of strangers. That was my most recent 'date.' Maybe we'll reprise it after I see him tonight! Have I thoroughly repulsed you yet?"

"Actually? Yes."

My phone vibrates. It's Stanford. Like a guardian angel here to rescue me.

"It's my agent."

"Oh! Of course! How perfect. Run along, you talented thespian. Clearly you have more important places to be than associating with lowlifes like me. I'll even pick up the check! Hope you don't mind that the dollar bills paying for it were probably scrunched under my taint at some point."

Gross. I already decided I don't like him. Does he really have to hammer it home? Doesn't he realize that, with his admission about that night with Marty Brayden, he just confirmed everything I accused go-go boys of? I want to say so many things now that I'm feeling both righteous AND righteously pissed. But Stanford might have news about *Wicked*. I drop a twenty on the table to cover my food and the tip. "Let me know what you think of Musical Mondays. If you're bored, just head to the bathroom. The stall farthest on the left has a glass wall instead of a regular one. Bet you can still find a dick to suck, even on a Monday."

Aaand scene.

I call Stanford back once I get out of the restaurant and across the street, under another scaffold.

"Golden Goose!"

"Sorry I missed ya. You know actors. I was in the middle of a little drama."

"Naturally. Where are you? In Astoria?"

"Actually, near Union Square. What happened? Did *Wicked* call you back?"

"Even better!" I don't think I've ever heard Stanford this giddy. "We've got two seats at an Equity Fights AIDS dinner at a table alongside the casting director you saw today! And he said he can't wait to talk about you!"

"Oh my God! Are you serious? When?"

"In an hour! How do you look?"

Wrinkly, still slightly damp, and furious at the go-go boy who just went on a bitch bender at me. "Fine, I guess…"

"Fine won't cut it. It's jacket and tie. Do you have those? You won't have enough time to go back to Astoria…"

"Crap! No."

"Okay, okay. That's fine. You're an actor, I used to be one. We can improvise, right? Meet me at the office. I've got a spare getup. It's not the cutest ensemble and you may end up looking like one of those kids in adult's clothing from the old Frosted Mini-Wheats commercials, but it's the best we can do in the time allotted. Defy gravity and get here NOW."

Stanford disconnects and I run to grab a cab, waving frantically. As I hop in the backseat, I catch sight of Chase. He is leaning against a building, his face so angry it looks like someone stuck a screwdriver in his nose and spun it until everything tightened. He taps his cell phone furiously. A cigarette hangs limply from his lips.

I'll happily make that disgusting habit the clincher on the laundry list of reasons why this go-go is a no-go for me.

Onward!

But traffic isn't ready to let me go so victoriously, clogging every street and avenue. Stuck here, now with the knowledge that Chase was nothing like I'd hoped he'd be, I am back on Gulliver. In fact, next to that pole-twirling slut bomb, Gully suddenly looks wholesome.

Trapped in this cab, I start to face the facts: If I get cast in this show, I'll be on the road for who knows how long. What snowball's chance will I have of finding any kind of meaningful relationship bouncing around from city to city? For anyone I meet outside New York, dating me will be like dating a terminal cancer patient, knowing that, in a matter of weeks, I'll be gone for good.

I've been on tour before. I'm done with the shallow sex thing. I don't want to wait a year or two or longer to find someone who's right for me.

Like Gulliver.

I know him. And so I know, even if he did leave New York, he'll be back someday. He has unfinished business here. Unfinished with ME.

Do I really want to miss out on even a sliver of a chance at patching things up with him just to be touring with some silly show?

No. I don't want *Wicked*.

But how can I turn down the role if it's offered? That'd be the last straw with Stanford. He'll never represent me if I refuse to leave Manhattan just because I need to wait like a lapdog for my lover to return. For any lover, but especially for Gulliver. Because if Gully does reappear, Stanford will seriously disapprove of us getting back together. So I'll be hiding Gully from him, just like Gully hid me from Stanford. Making all the same mistakes that led me here in the first place.

So. I DO want *Wicked.*

Ugh. Chase was right. We did waste each other's time tonight. I could have been at home, putting on something that fits and looks right, instead of crossing my fingers that whatever getup awaits me at Stanford's office only makes me look HALF-clueless about how to dress myself. That's something Chase never has to worry about. Is it even possible for a G-string to be ill fitting? I hope he and that gay porn star DO go home together, swapping herpes and crabs. Clearly, they belong together.

The TV in the cab goes through its full cycle of advertisements and movie reviews. I shut it off and turn to my phone. There are no e-mails or Facebook updates to occupy me. And now I'm curious about this porn star that Chase will ostensibly fuck in front of thousands again tonight on the Internet. Because something's not right about all of this—my name, smooshed together with my psycho ex's name? What are the chances? Since I'm stuck here for at least a few more minutes, I figure a quick Googling couldn't hurt.

I type "Marty Brayden" into the search engine and let it take me where it will.

I have a bad feeling about this.

The first site recommended is New York Screwniversity, just like Chase said. I have to promise that I'm over twenty-one to even take a look. The dorm has a thirteen-man lineup, the stars of the site. No, not "stars." They're "dorm mates." This is one of those dumb sites where they act like you're getting a sneak peek at the lives of twenty-somethings who are attending college or in a fraternity or whatever. What kind of pervy idiot falls for this?

The most popular video of the month (go figure) is "Marty Brayden Fucks Midnight Visitor Chase Bliss." I don't have to pay a penny to see twenty full-color, high-resolution photos of my recent date in all matters of compromising positions with this blue-haired punk. Here they are sixty-nining. There's Chase on the floor, legs in the air. And two zoomed-in orgasm shots, their sex parts out of focus and in the foreground, their crystal-clear O-faces in the background. Chase's orgasm face is pretty awkward, if you ask me. And as for this impostor with my name...

My skin breaks into goose bumps.

Gulliver?

No. No way.

I zoom in on my phone, pulling closer and closer to the blue-haired dorm boy who brought Chase into the fold. I have him blown up so large that I'm able to go past the blue hair, the chin-strap, the eyebrow ring. Just his mouth, nose, and eyes.

Vomit. That's what I'm going to do. It's like I just took a huge gulp of milk, only to find out it's five days past the expiration date. I zoom out and click through the other photos, checking, praying that I'm wrong. That it's just a stressful day. That I'm being crazy.

That I'm imagining him now just like I imagined him at the piano, behind the panel of judges earlier.

But no. I'm right.

It's Gulliver. Marty Brayden is Gulliver, bluer and punkier than when we were together. But I'd recognize him anywhere.

Thanks to the sample sixty-second video I play, I can verify my horrible hunch.

Oh, Gully.

You might be able to mask yourself in myriad ways, but your sweet voice is still exactly the same. Marty Brayden? Did you really think I wouldn't have figured it out?

No. You must have wanted me to.

This is his way of getting back at me? Leaving me and disappearing into nothingness…to do gay porn? He expects me to be heartbroken. He assumes this will destroy me. That I'll feel like I pushed him to this and come running to save him.

I guess he never really knew me at all. I've never been so disgusted.

Is it possible to feel filthy in hindsight?

To feel hours and days and weeks of worry and hope suddenly evaporate with futility? All that crying, praying, wishing, exploding like a pipe bomb.

When the dust clears, there's Gulliver, giving away something I cherished in private to thousands and thousands of online viewers. I feel like such a tool.

And I thought Chase wasted my time.

Was Gulliver in porn while we were together? To be honest, I don't want to find out. All that matters is he's doing it now. Which means I dated a porn star. Some would brag about that. Me? I'm mortified. And all of this only thirty minutes after I went on a tirade against go-go boys? At least they keep a shred of clothing on! Well, gee, don't I feel sheepish now?

No—I feel sick.

Gulliver fucked Chase. On camera. In front of thousands. Had I known during our date what I know now, I would have hurled that amazing mac and cheese straight at his stubborn go-go head. Today's events are all too freakily connected for me to ignore. The universe can set things up for a reason. My sister always told me that, and I've always believed it too.

But for what purpose? What good could this disgust, this despair, possibly do?

My revulsion, manifesting itself as an anxious nausea, is actually a strange comfort, because for the first time in what feels like forever, I don't feel like crying. What I feel like doing now is returning to Astoria and setting my Gully box on fire. In my head, I can hear the beginning notes of "Forget About the Boy," Sutton Foster's kick-ass number from *Thoroughly Modern Millie*:

"No canary in a cage for me / This canary's ready to fly free..."

I've found Gulliver, and now he can get lost. Clearly, I saw more in us than he did. I'm just a romantic fool. Gulliver isn't who I thought he was; he was never worth my time. I pull out my iPod and toggle to the actual song that's playing in my head. Sutton starts and I lip-synch along. Stanford awaits. The casting director awaits. My future awaits.

Good-bye, Gulliver. For good.

***

Oh my gosh, is that Sutton Foster? It is. It actually is! Omigod omigod omigoooooodddddd! One table away from me! She's even prettier in real life! That long brown hair. That tiny fairylike face. Wow. Wowwwww!

I need to tell her how amazing she was in *Shrek*...that she's the ONLY reason I saw it...that I'd follow her to any show in any state, or into space, if she's performing there. That she's my inspiration. My inner fanboy is throwing a fit, taking over my body. I'm ready to run up to her table like it's the stage door and I've been waiting outside in the rain just to get her autograph on my crinkled *Playbill*. Such a prize would swiftly find its way to the wall above my bed, the sort of artifact I'd never part with, no matter how much money it's worth on eBay.

Next to Sutton, her brother Hunter (of *Urinetown* and *Little Shop of Horrors* revival fame) laughs between bites of a stuffed mushroom. Across from him, Cheyenne Jackson is checking his phone (probably updating his Twitter). At the bar, Josh Gad from *The Book of Mormon* and Norbert Leo Butz from *Catch Me If You Can* are waiting on their drinks.

My God, I've died and gone to fanboy heaven. It's almost enough to make me forget the roiling nerves in my stomach, creeping around under my skin like a nest of spiders.

Sutton. Fucking. Foster.

I can now happily die.

"You want something from the bar, Goose?" Stanford asks me, breaking me out of my trance.

"Um. Sure. Vodka cranberry?"

"Grey Goose for my golden one, eh? Lovely choice!" Stanford shouts triumphantly. "Two of those, please, my good man," he calls to the cute, stubbly waiter who's putting on a silent show for our table, muscles flexed in hopes that one of us asks for a résumé. That won't happen just yet (only two at our table are agents), so he jots the order down and leaves us for the bar.

Jeez. Everyone here is so beautiful! The guys, the girls, the waiters, the bartenders. The man by the table where all the name tents are sitting (where, might I add, I saw tents for Bernadette AND Patti, who BETTER show up). Even the hosts and hostesses at the door of the restaurant, standing perfectly at the podium in their matching all-black pants and shirts. WOW. This is without a doubt the biggest, most posh event I have ever been to.

Did it have to be tonight?

Even Stanford is more dolled up than usual—his traditional outfit of tight jeans and a V-neck, primary-colored T-shirt replaced by a tailored charcoal suit with a bright-orange tie. He doesn't like dressing up and shows it with his aggressive readjusting, unbuttoning his collar or loosening his tie every other minute while trying to keep up with the conversation at our table of eight.

I, on the other hand, look like a Cirque du Soleil clown doing an impression of a Madison Avenue advertising executive. While Stanford and I are both slender, he's a good six inches taller than me and has the shoulders of a linebacker, which results in his jacket looking absurdly tentlike as it drapes over my shoulders. As soon as it's acceptable, I plan on hanging the jacket on my chair and sticking with my own striped button-down shirt and Stanford's borrowed tie (which, by the way, clashes). I just hope everyone is too busy ogling Broadway stars to notice me.

"Marty here has been doing quite fabulously," Stanford says, shaking my shoulder as he delivers the compliment. "Had three auditions this week alone, right, Marty?"

"Yes, sir!" I say, injecting as much excitement into my voice as I can without tipping over into the obnoxious. "They were all so exciting. Still waiting to hear back!"

I actually blew the first two, unfortunately (I leave that part out). I don't even want to recall the forty-plus before them. Luckily, none of this matters to Stanford. God bless him. He is a good, good man. I mean, I've just about given up on myself, yet here he is, talking me up like I'm Adam Chanler-Berat or Neil Patrick Harris. It's beyond obvious that no one at this table gives half a damn about me, but Stanford knows how this industry works. Everyone must talk about themselves continuously (or, if they're lucky, have their agent talk about them), creating a vicious, self-serving battle won by whoever speaks the loudest and fastest. Unfortunately for me, the *Wicked* casting director hasn't arrived yet, and Stanford will probably have to repeat this whole song and dance all over again. Like any good actor.

Sitting in this room stuffed to the gills with Broadway elite, I am constantly forced to silently admit that I'm anything but one of them. These people are paid to do what they love, singing and dancing six nights a week. Then there's me, the actor who would be starving if it weren't for the free basket of bread in the middle of the table.

There MUST be at least one other out-of-work nobody here, right? Right? Well, if so, they fit in so well with their employed ilk that I can't find them. Meanwhile, I'm right here in my oversized jacket, the sorest of thumbs.

The waiter returns with my vodka cranberry, and I shove the straw in my mouth, hoping Stanford will do the same and let the others at our table have a chance to brag about themselves. Sure enough, the second Stanford's lips touch his straw, another gay man named Stefan speaks up.

"I did the *Wicked* tour a few years ago." He rolls his eyes and ruffles his black hair. "Talk about a robot factory! Step here. Sashay there. And those Ozian costumes are more uncomfortable than an overheated iron maiden."

Stanford looks at me, ready to pad the comment and keep me positive. Little does he know that now I'd go on the tour even if they DID put us in medieval torture devices every night.

"The pay's great, sure. And the production parks in cities for three or more weeks, letting you explore and experience all the sights. But you sell your soul and your artistic integrity for that weekly check," he continues, making a "money" sign with his thumb, pointer, and middle finger. "I'd rather do dinner theater at the Beef and Boards. Seriously."

I want to ask, *Are there any openings at Beef and Boards?* I'll happily have my headshot featured next to a photo of the pepper steak entrée. I hope I never get to a point in my career where I take work for granted. Work is work. Doesn't he remember a time when he didn't have a guaranteed paycheck?

"The thing you're doing wrong, Stanford," says Karen, a red-headed, heavyset agent, "if I may?"

Stanford nods. Smiling. He's always smiling. (I imagine he'll tell me later in the cab what she "may" actually do.)

"I wouldn't be sending my actors to the cattle calls." She pauses to regard a parmesan-bedazzled breadstick like it's a precious stone before dunking it into a ramekin of marinara. "No one takes those things seriously. They're akin to those *American Idol* casting events. Temporary, unfortunate camps of screaming boys and girls who will be good for a thirty-second clip of comic relief and nothing else. If they're lucky."

"Now, Karen, you know they're not that tragic." Stanford still smiles.

Karen's having none of it. "I've never once heard of an actor being cast at a cattle call, Stanford. Let's be realistic! Send him to the private auditions. Save the energy and time. Spare him the humiliation and rejection, for Christ's sake!"

"Marty's still new," Stanford replies after a moment of silence. "All the feedback has been extremely constructive. We just haven't found the right fit yet."

I am not going to be the one to say that I've also blown the few private auditions Stanford got me, which is why he's sent me to moo with the unrepresented talent.

"And how are the rest of your kids?" Karen continues.

"Great, actually." Stanford lights up—because he needn't work so hard to make THEM look good. I'm the only actor Stanford represents who's here tonight (at this dinner OR in New York City). His other four prize stallions and mares are already working and sending paycheck percentages back home to Papa. Leanne is out in California playing Katherine in an avant-garde reboot of *Pippin*. Cristiano is cross-dressing on tour with *La Cage aux Folles*, understudying one of the cagelles. Jonathan and Zachary are soaking up the Miami sun while turning out rave-reviewed performances in *Altar Boyz*.

And then there's me, Marty Perry, forever reprising the lead in his one-man show: *The Kid Who Just Can't Get Cast in Anything, Ever.*

"A tour de force of pity and shame!" cries Ben Brantley of the *New York Times*.

"I laughed (at him)! I cried (for him)!" writes Terry Teachout of the *Wall Street Journal*.

"Someone put this poor kid out of his misery! Aren't there any open temp positions?" moans *Newsday*'s Linda Winer.

And yet Stanford remains confident and unstoppable. I mean, he even splurged on my ticket to this fundraiser tonight! His charity, both to me and others, is unbelievable. He seems to think having me at the same table as the casting director for the National Equity Tour of *Wicked* will get me cast, somehow. I can only hope his hunch is right.

And I do. Of course I do. More, I tell myself, than I hope for anything in the world right now. This is an amazing opportunity, and I'm beyond grateful for it. Yet I can't help it; there are two of me at this table.

There's the Marty who Stanford's bitchy peers can see (if they can even be bothered to look): the starstruck, endlessly aspiring ingenue in a city full of starstruck, endlessly aspiring ingenues.

And then there's the other Marty tucked away inside that one like a seething, wounded Russian nesting doll. The Marty who's just gorged himself on mac and cheese with the date who, it turns out, fucked his ex-boyfriend in front of thousands of masturbating strangers for a gay porn website.

Just when I'm successfully swept up along with the visible Marty in tonight's REAL business—getting this close to the *Wicked* part, not to mention Sutton Fucking Foster—I plummet down without warning into the dark with that other, damaged Marty.

That's where I am when the drop-dead gorgeous brunette girl next to me (a chorus girl in *Phantom of the Opera*) pipes up and yanks me back out. "Oh, look who's here," she says. "Grant Majors!"

What?! Somebody hold that visible Marty down!

Grant Majors is here? My pulse breaks into a drumroll. It takes a minute to find him in the crowd, which only increases the beating in my ears and chest. Yes! It's him. Holy Jesus—even hotter in real life. Until now, I've only seen him on TV or under blazing stage lights at Musical Monday's curtain call from way across the dance floor. He looks taller. Definitely more muscular. He's at the bar, talking to the lucky bartender who's pouring him a drink. Can I please be cast in the role of that drink? They don't even have to pay me.

"Of course he's here," Karen the agent says through another mouthful of breadstick. "He's hosting the event. And performing a number!"

This night may redeem itself, after all. Grant's voice is the only thing that's more gorgeous than he is. I have to somehow pull him aside tonight, assuming he can get away from his adoring fans. I need to let him know that I've been following his Broadway climb, from chorus boy in *The Wedding Singer* and dancer in the unfortunate Elvis jukebox musical *All Shook Up* all the way to *Mamma Mia!*. I imagine him listening to this, nodding and grinning. And leaning in…and kissing me. Then we're starring in a show together; then we're performing at the Tonys. Our kids watching from the front row.

Oh shit, Marty. Cool it!

But after all the weirdness tonight, could a whirlwind romance with my Broadway idol really be any stranger? Couldn't THIS be where this whole bizarre day has been heading all along? My date with Chase helped me get over Gulliver. Now I'm all primed to give my heart away to someone a thousand times better, a million times more deserving.

No—I'm not that stupid. Also, Grant's not alone. And his drinking buddy is someone I immediately recognize. It's the wiry, bespectacled casting director of *Wicked*, the one who was all smiles and sweat stains with me this very morning.

My heartbeat slows to a comatose thump.

The director is laughing and clapping Grant on the back while they wait at the bar for their cocktails. Whatever they ordered is bright green and sloshing in a martini glass.

"Shit," Stanford whispers to me, no doubt fully aware that I'm thinking the same thing. "This isn't good. Shit."

"Hello, everyone!" the casting director says as he approaches the table, seeing the one empty seat. "Oh! Grant, it looks like the table's filled."

"Good evening, everybody," Grant says, flashing his megawatt smile. God, I'm going to suffer radiation burns if he doesn't turn it off soon. "Sorry Leon and I are late. Anybody interested in swapping for my place? It's over at Table 15, next to some of the cast members of *Naked Boys Singing*."

I'm about to volunteer when Stanford grabs my knee and squeezes to the point that it hurts. I take his unspoken cue and say nothing.

"Sounds lovely," says Stefan the *Wicked* basher. "Make sure they keep their clothes on, and come visit after the buffet opens!"

"No," Grant laughs. "Seriously, could one of you please switch with me? I don't want to abandon my date here. That's just rude!"

"It's fine, Grant," the casting director says, breaking the awkward silence. "We can always stay by the bar for a while."

"I'm sure SOMEBODY at this table will be kind enough to give me their seat," Grant says. "I mean, mine's only a few tables away. And it's closer to the buffet."

No one responds, and Grant stays put. People at other tables turn to see what's happening, since Grant's voice has raised an octave with every entreaty. "Somebody?" And I'm now painfully aware that every single person at this table is thinking that "somebody" should be me. (Myself included.)

Yikes.

"Oh, whatever," Stefan says. "Take my seat. I'll go sit with *Naked Boys*." He storms off, his jacket bouncing on his shoulder.

"First time I've ever heard a sister complain about sitting with a table of naked boys!" Grant snickers, taking his seat next to Leon. "Holy shit! That took entirely too much time! I'm going to have to steal the show in a few minutes!"

"Leon, I think someone poisoned your cosmo," Stanford says in an attempt to break the awkward moment we all just shared. "Yours too, Grant."

"Good." Grant smiles. "Maybe I'll feel it quicker."

Everyone laughs, though I wonder how many of us actually found his comment funny. Maybe his comic timing isn't so sharp when it's unscripted.

"I'm kidding, of course," Grant says. "Can't be too soused if I'm supposed to hit the high notes tonight."

"Leon, I believe you remember Marty Perry, my newest rising star," Stanford says.

"Oh, wow, you signed with Stanford?" Grant interrupts. "I remember when he tried to get me. You begged, didn't you, Stanford? I never felt so important! Didn't go with him, though, as I guess you know. So, Marky, how'd you like his office?"

Ouch. Stanford's office used to be a Midtown East dive. I'll admit—even I, up-and-comer that I am, was a little horrified by the place. Stanford blushes and once again, somehow, comes up with a smile. Within three minutes of sitting at the table, Grant has insulted Stanford in front of his industry friends not once but twice. The fact that he mangled my name might be an additional potshot.

"In his defense," I stumble, "his new office is gorgeous."

"Yeah?" Grant doesn't even acknowledge me with a glance. "That's great, Stanny. After seeing that shithole and the kids you were representing, I was afraid you'd be packing up and heading back to Boston. I'm so glad everything worked out in your favor. Maybe I'll stop by before I go off on tour."

Tour? Well, that settles it. Today is now 0 and 2.

"Oh?" Stanford asks, leaning forward at the table. "I suppose congratulations are in order?"

"You must not have gotten my voice mail, Stanford," Leon says. "I suppose you were already here. Yes, after much deliberation, we have decided to go with Grant for the role."

The embarrassment of being looked over for a role is something I typically suffer in private. It's usually delivered via a call or an e-mail, at which point I go home, stare at myself in the mirror, and play some sad song like Audra McDonald's "Come Down From That Tree" or Cheyenne Jackson and Tony Roberts's "Don't Walk Away," from *Xanadu*, wondering how I ever thought I had talent in the first place. But since we're all industry people at this table, I suppose Leon feels comfortable with making this unofficial announcement before *Playbill* and *Broadway World* break the news tomorrow.

Grant is soaking up the awkwardness of it all, silently gloating over the rim of his green cocktail. And since Stanford can't console me publicly, we need to weather this as best as we can.

Double slap: my vision of Grant Majors as anything but a cocky, self-entitled diva is going down like the *Titanic*, and I've failed at yet another audition.

"When do you leave, Grant?" I ask, hoping it's ASAP.

"Well, from here on in, I demand you call me Boq—just kidding! The fitting and rehearsals happen here in New York, then I ship out, what, in a month, Leon?"

"Yes, sir. Thirty days and you're out of our hair for at least a year."

"It'll be good to leave the city for a while. I need a change of scenery!" He laughs. "Are they passing hors d'oeuvres? I'm positively famished."

"Excuse me for a minute, guys," I say, getting up from the table. Stanford is probably too busy wondering if I'm worth representing anymore to ask where I'm going. It's not like I know the answer, anyway. I just need out of here.

"Can you ask a waiter to come back with more breadsticks?" Grant calls after me.

I end up by the bathrooms, which are down in the basement by the kitchen. My only companions are framed black-and-white photos of Italian farmers harvesting crops on hilltops and piped-in old-world music from a hidden speaker in the ceiling. Leaning against the wall, I'm able to let the busboys run past with plastic bins of dirty dishes. Every so often, an actor (including Sherie Rene Scott and Brian Stokes Mitchell—I die) slips by to use the facilities.

I won't cry, since Gulliver already drained every ounce of salt out of me earlier. But I wish I could.

The weight of this failure is so heavy Grant might as well be tap-dancing on my sternum. Just as pervasive as the joy when I sing, this sensation is a brick of lead in my stomach. I can't go back up there. Everyone at that table knows I'm a loser, and Grant Majors is all but belting it at the top of his lungs. Stanford won't even be able to look at me. I just want to go back to Astoria, throw my Gulliver box in the trash, lie in bed crying, and pray for sleep.

People tell me how lucky I am that I landed an agent so soon out of college. They'd kill for someone to represent them, they say, weary from their temp jobs. I can't complain, but sometimes I wish I didn't have an agent, hadn't gotten that gig with *Jersey Boys*. At least then my dreams would be so ethereal I might give up. Instead, I got a taste of what could be, then went straight from feast to famine with no sign of a second helping. When you're this precariously close to what you've strived for, it stings a hundred times more when you fail. Like you're bobbing in the ocean, close to freezing and drowning, and the rescue boat just keeps passing you by.

I don't want to go back to that table, but I don't have a choice. Stanford paid for my ticket, and now I've left him stranded with that asshole Grant Majors.

Fuck! I can't believe I'm stuck here. In this restaurant AND New York City. An hour ago, I'd almost decided I didn't want to go on tour; now I'd give anything to escape this place.

I take a deep breath and walk back upstairs, preparing for whatever else I must face before I can go home.

At the table, it's obvious everyone has been talking about me. "He truly IS a wonderful singer," says Leon. "I've never really been fond of 'Lost in the Wilderness,' but now I'm sold! I went home from the audition and listened to it on repeat for an hour. If the show ever plays near the city, I'll be first in line!"

Small comfort. Too bad I won't be in it.

"We were just talking about you, Marty," Stanford says, pushing out my chair. "Turns out you were REALLY close."

"Which only counts in horseshoes and world wars or something, right?" Grant asks, laughing. Thankfully, this time, no one joins him. "I'm kidding! Hey, did you ask about the breadsticks?"

"As I was saying," Leon continues, "it was a nail-biter between you and Grant."

"You say that now that he's here!" Grant scoffs, making me wish I HAD asked about those breadsticks. So that his mouth would be too busy to keep insulting me.

"You should take that to heart," Leon says. "The fact that there was even a contest between you and someone of Grant's caliber..."

Grant rolls his eyes and stifles a snort. He might as well be on his back, kicking his legs in the air and laughing, just like my twins at this morning's cattle call.

Though I have to wonder what's up with Grant's constant need to belittle me. Why bother, for God's sake? Could it be he finds the fact that I even came close to stealing a role from him threatening? I like that possibility.

"Grant just has the experience and show history that will make the producers happy. You're a very, very talented singer, Marty," Leon concludes.

I have to smile. "Thank you."

"And I promise you and Stanford will be the first people I call when we are looking to cast for any part in either of the tours."

Stanford rubs my shoulder and smiles. "I don't call him Golden Goose for nothing."

Sooner or later, he will revoke that name. What use is a golden goose who's been constipated since he signed his yearlong contract?

"That's cute," says Grant. "Hey, you can always try to come on the tour anyway, as a stagehand or something. Do you mind being behind the scenes? It's a great learning experience, I've been told."

By now, everyone looks put off by Grant's unnecessary cruelty, but no one will say anything. I wish I could blame it on his being drunk. Or maybe he's had a bad night. Still, there's no excuse. Now it's plain as day: the closest thing I ever had to a role model is a complete and total asshole.

I might have been wrong about not being able to cry anymore. I want to get the hell out of here, in case one more bitchy comment from Boq sends me careening over the edge.

"Well?" Grant asks. "Would you? You'd look fetching in all black!"

My phone goes off in my pocket, making a sound loud enough to nab the next table over's attention. Normally, I'd immediately silence it, apologize to whomever I was speaking with, and deal with the voice mail later. But this is exactly what I needed to get out of here. "I'm sorry, I need to take this," I say, and hurriedly excuse myself.

"Wow! You just can't stay seated, can you?" Grant calls after me. "Please remember to ask about the breadsticks this time!"

Outside, the rain is still going strong, battering cars and benches and people. There are no scaffolds out here, so I duck into the doorway of a closed-down theater two buildings down. The marquis is empty, the lobby barren, the overhang generous in its protection. The cold is a blessing, even though the drizzle smears up my phone's touch screen.

The intrusive alert that saved me was in fact a text message. From one of my friends, another actor/temp who I didn't tell about today's audition because I'd feel guilty doing so.

"Hey Marty! Not sure where you are, but there's something on Facebook you might want to check out."

"What's up?" I write back. *"I'm out right now."*

"Well, your crazy ex Brayden seems to have gone viral. Are you still friends with him?"

Yes, I am still friends with Brayden. Why? Because he never bothered to remove me, and because it's good to stop by his wall every now and again to remind myself of how lucky I am to have gotten away from him.

"Maybe…what is it?"

"I don't want to ruin the surprise. Let's just say he's turned a corner. He's a bit of a Facebook celebrity right now. Most popular post and everything. I recommend you check out his viral video before Mark Zuckerberg pulls it down himself."

Wait. What? I fire up Facebook. The post isn't hard to find. It's the most popular post on my newsfeed too. It has over 500 comments, 28 shares, and 1,700 likes. And it was only posted two hours ago. Some of the comments that I can see include:

"HOLY SHIT BRAY! WHO IS THAT?"

"OMG! You trying to get BANNED gurl!?"

"Dude! Give me his number!"

"GROSS! Why hasn't FB removed this?!"

I don't feel like clicking. I don't need to see. Of course, I do anyway. Let's say because it's a great excuse to stay away from the smug smile of Grant Majors and the pity glances of everyone else at the table.

The video is called "Good Morning Starshine." The *Hair* reference is strange—Brayden's not much of a theater person. Far lower quality than the first porn I saw today, this vid looks like it was shot on a single camera—one that wasn't even set up properly. Brayden is now sporting blazing-white hair, which looks worse on him than his usual color selections. (And what's with my exes dying their hair so damn dramatically, anyway?)

Even stranger? Brayden's actions. He's a hell of a lot rougher than I've ever seen him. To his credit, the bottom is a gorgeous blond with muscles everywhere. Strong cheekbones. Perfect thighs.

No. No way.

This cannot be who I think it is. My brain is just manufacturing more weird coincidences. The video is so blurry and choppy no way I could make a definitive identification. But it does look like…

Impossible. He's a total top! Or so the gay theater rumor mill churns. And regardless of what sexual role he's playing, there's not a chance Grant would ever consent to making a sex tape.

Would he?

I turn up the volume on my phone.

"I'm not done 'til you get off, sir!" the bottom howls, grabbing a tight hold of my ex-boyfriend's waist.

Certainly sounds like him.

My ex barks, "Just do what I tell you. Ride my dick, and if you're lucky, I won't tell everyone on the Great White Way how big of a bottom you are. What would they think of that?"

There are more actors in this city than pigeons and rats combined. It could be anyone. Right?

No. This is all wrong. Around now is when I'll wake up in my bed and ask my temp-worker friends to brunch so I can ramble incoherently about the ridiculous dream I had. "And YOU were there! And YOU were there!"

And so was Boq. Or Bottom Boq, as Brayden has just named him.

It only takes a few more thunderous thrusts before the bottom explodes all over, grabbing ahold of a chair next to the bed to brace himself and keep from falling to the floor.

The very same outfit that Grant Majors is wearing tonight rests on the chair, folded perfectly to prevent wrinkling.

I turn around and peer into the restaurant. Grant is there, arm around Leon. He looks like he's singing. Does he know about this? It must have been filmed earlier tonight!

My eyes return to the screen, but the clip has ended.

I text my friend back: *"Oh. Wow. Thank you for sharing this."*

"How could I not? Have a good night babe. Let's grab drinks soon. I have an idea for a web video series we can start if you've got the time!"

"Sounds good!" I say. My mind is so frantic right now that it takes me a minute to properly type those two words.

I take a deep breath and try to make sense of what I've just seen. Grant isn't dating Brayden, that much I know. Last I heard, my ex was with some DJ. (When did that end?) I consider reporting the video on Brayden's wall, get his profile removed from the site. Except my brain is also firing in four thousand other directions. Playing out the next scene of my life in every possible way.

Gulliver is in porn. Chase guest-starred in a porn with Gulliver. Brayden's now in amateur porn. Even gay everyman hero Grant Majors is an unwitting porn star now. If this got out, it could ruin him.

If?

No. It's already out. It WILL ruin him. Assuming it hasn't already.

I return to my newsfeed. My theater-obsessed actor friends haven't mentioned the video. I click to the *Broadway World* message boards. No new threads about this. The video viewers, so far, don't seem to have connected the dots. Despite all the views and shares, this is far from the viral sensation it will become if a single show queen is tipped off as to who this blond bottom is.

So nobody knows. Nobody besides Brayden. And me.

And most likely, nobody ever WILL know. This can still disappear. When Grant finds out, the video will be taken down. Details will go fuzzy in everybody's minds. There will be no way to prove it was him once this gets deleted. And it's unlikely anyone has all the pieces to puzzle it together like I did.

Yet.

Chalk it up to the fact that one too many people who've pissed me off turned up in a porn today. As angry as I am at Brayden, and Chase, and Gulliver, none of them have earned my wrath in quite the way Grant Majors has tonight.

He thought he was so much better than me. So powerful. So invulnerable. It seems that he is actually none of these things.

I click away from the incriminating video to make a call. Inside, Stanford looks down at his phone, excuses himself. He ducks into a corner by the *Naked Boys* table where the Internet's newest amateur porn star was supposed to be seated.

"Goose? You okay?"

"Yeah. I'm fine. Can you come outside for a second?"

Stanford's straining to be heard above the din. "Sure...Should I be worried?"

"Just get out here, okay?"

Stanford is outside and standing next to me within a minute. From there, he only needs to watch the first thirty seconds of the video before he pushes the phone away. "Why are you showing me that?"

"Does the bottom look familiar to you?"

Stanford shakes his head. "I didn't invite you to this event so you could go outside and watch porn, Marty."

"That's Grant in the video!" I shout way louder than I wanted to.

"What are you talking about?"

I press *Play* on the video again and hold it up. "Just look."

Stanford watches for a while longer, steps away to light a cigarette, giving himself seven seconds to mull over what he's just seen. "It just looks like him."

"Look at the clothes on the chair. Listen to his voice! You can't deny it. Boq's getting bonked!"

"No. Listen, I understand you're upset about not getting the part, but you'll land one soon! Second place is pretty fantastic for a show like this."

"Right. I was so upset I spent the past fifteen minutes searching XTube for a video of someone who looks like the guy who beat me out for a role. His headshots are lining the walls of his apartment, Stanford!"

Stanford takes my phone and holds it right up to his eyes, wiping moisture off the screen. The tinny sounds of Grant screeching get louder.

"Oh my," he says, handing me back my phone. He takes two more deep drags. "How did you get this?"

"How? It's spreading around Facebook like crazy!"

"Really?"

"Yes! What should we do?"

Stanford takes another long moment, sucking deep on his cigarette and blowing it out toward the street. He looks at my phone, on which Grant is still howling and bouncing. My agent's eyes meet mine. We don't say a word, but his gaze asks if we're about to do what we're about to do. If we're bad people IF we do. I raise my eyebrows, looking back to the video.

"If this is about to go viral," he says, "there's only one thing we can do. We need to warn Leon before he announces the casting. Or this will get him all sorts of negative press he doesn't need."

"Okay. How?"

"I'll handle it. E-mail me that link. You just go to the buffet and look busy. Head over there now. I'll finish my smoke and then take care of it."

I follow my agent's instructions. Returning to the restaurant, I am welcomed by the wafting odors of the buffet. I walk nonchalantly to the table and begin scooping baked ziti and eggplant parmesan. It's my second dinner of the night and I'm far from hungry, but I pile my plate high, then position myself at the edge of the buffet so I can watch.

Stanford returns to the table and puts his hand on Leon's shoulder. Leon looks up mid-laugh, meets Stanford's eyes, and follows him outside. Stanford's phone is already out before they make it to the street.

"Enough food there, Marty?"

It's Grant, grinning from ear to ear. His lips and tongue are a toxic green from however many *Wicked*-flavored drinks he has downed already.

"I'm a growing boy," I toss back coldly. "We can't all eat young talent for breakfast."

"Whoa, watch the attitude there, scout. Don't want to come off like a diva who can't handle losing out on a part. You'll land something soon, I'm sure!"

"Yes. I will," I say, watching the entrance to the restaurant. Through the glass, I see Leon looking at Stanford's phone. He recoils, head shooting back toward the doors like Stanford just revealed a rotting corpse under a blanket. Then he leans in, probably confirming that the clothing on the chair matches what's on his beloved Boq.

Confirmed, Leon pulls out his phone and storms to the other side of the sidewalk, his free hand waving in the air.

"Anyway," Grant prattles on, "I'm still trying to decide what to sing tonight. I was feeling 'Lost in the Wilderness,' but even Hunter Foster and Stephen Schwartz know that one is played out by now."

I reply with a blink and a smile.

There's a special place in hell for dickheads like Grant Majors, a place where they perform nothing but *Hot Feet*, *Ring of Fire*, and *Carrie: The Musical*.

I laugh at Grant's bad joke, put my lips close to his ear. "Have you ever tried out for *Hair*?"

Grant's laughter stops. "No. Why?"

I set my mountain of food on the table and wrap my arms around him, pulling his head close to mine so I can whisper-sing in his ear: "*Good morning starshine. The earth says hello…*"

He cranks his face toward me, eyes bulging. "What's that supposed to mean?"

"*You twinkle above us. We twinkle below…*"

"What the fuck? Have you lost your mind?"

Maybe a more experienced actor could pretend like he didn't know what I'm referring to. But not this one.

I stop singing. "Oh. Never mind. Just a tune I couldn't get out of my head. Now don't you have to warm up for your number? Or—well, you've already hit a lot of high notes this evening. I'm sure your vocal chords got all the workout they need. Sir."

Grant gives me a frigid half smile. He sets his plate down, scans the room, eyes pausing on every person who's looking down at their cell phones (even Sutton is checking hers). Are they viewing his latest starring role? Probably not. But if not now, they soon will.

Grant lets go of me, says something I can't make out, walks across the restaurant and out to the street. Neither Leon nor Stanford tries to stop him as he passes them on the sidewalk.

A minute later, a text message hits my phone. It's from Stanford: *"You just couldn't resist, could you?"*

"Sorry!" I text back, adding a smiley with its tongue hanging out.

"I'll bb in a few. Talkin with Leon. PS: he wants you back in the office tomorrow for another audition."

"HE DOES?"

"Congrats, Goose. You're headed to Oz."

I abandon my mountain of food for the bar with an Ozian spring to my step. In my head, the bridge in "The Wizard and I" begins to play.

"Unlimited. My future is unlimited. And I just had a vision almost like a prophecy..."

You and me both, Elphy.

Stanford catches me just as two Boq and punches make it out of the shaker.

"What happened to Grey Goose and cran?"

I shrug. "Grey suddenly seemed so drab. A little too Kansas for this boy from Oz."

"Ah. Don't go getting too big a head now, whiz kid." Stanford picks up his green concoction. "I suppose I'll let you do the honors?"

"Is it too crass to say, 'Ding dong! The witch is dead'?"

"No," Stanford says. Our drinks meet. "It is a little cheesy, though." We sip, and savor, in silence.

When we come back up for air, our lips are green. "You know, that video could have probably gone unnoticed, or at least unattached to Grant. The quality was terrible."

I wince. "It's very possible. Or it could have been discovered. There's no telling." I take another sip so I don't have to look at him, then ask, "Do you hate me?"

"Nah. I'd have done the same. Probably be passing it around the party by now. Little bastard shouldn't have talked shit about my office."

I giggle. "So you think he's done for?"

Stanford takes a long, thoughtful drink. "For now, maybe. Depends. I mean, if Leon and his associates keep this amongst themselves, there's still a possibility the world at large will never find out why he lost the role. And that video will surely be pulled down in a few hours. Unless someone found a way to save it, it may end up disappearing forever."

"Good thing no one in the Broadway world likes juicy gossip, then, huh?"

Stanford raises his eyebrows and sighs at me. "Uh-huh. Hey, by the way, I think this should be your last one of these drinks tonight."

"Why? Too early to celebrate?"

"No." Stanford smiles. "But it seems our evening's entertainment has mysteriously deserted us. Leon needs someone to fill in, and it turns out he's got a hankering to hear 'Lost in the Wilderness.'"

"Are you kidding me?"

"You're going on in five, Goose. Better wipe that green off your lip."

I've been given zero prep time, but I've sung enough today to be in a good place. Five minutes pass like they're seconds, and then Leon is onstage introducing me as a brand-new shining star about to take Broadway by storm. The fact that this message is delivered by the casting director of the most successful show on Broadway and on tour around the world cannot be downplayed. Leon also tips off the actors and press that they just might catch me next month in *Wicked* in Boston.

My God.

I could scream. I could dance where I'm standing. I could hug Leon like he's the father I never had. But that's not what I'm here to do.

I'm here to perform.

I approach the microphone to hundreds and hundreds of clapping hands. My heroes, my idols, my crushes, all applauding me, and I haven't even opened my mouth. I want to point them out one by one and tell them each and every song of theirs I have memorized. How every single one of them is the reason I worked day and night to get here. Their successes have fueled me to break through the past two months of failure, the years of challenges and setbacks. I want to scream, *I love you!* to Sutton. Thank her brother for the song I am about to sing. But spoken words would never do my appreciation justice. In my stomach, nerves and anxiety step into the wings, replaced by an ecstatic sensation of confidence. Not just about what I'm preparing to do, but also the certainty that I'm on the verge of something really, really big.

There's so much I want to think, so much I want to feel. Remorse, maybe, for what I said to Chase. Guilt, for my part in obliterating

Grant Majors's career. Grief, for the relationship I now know I will never have with Gulliver, since the Gulliver I loved doesn't exist.

Also, confusion. Complete and total confusion at the surreal way this all lined up tonight.

And joy, of course.

Satisfaction that years of devotion to singing are finally, here and now, paying off. When I awoke today, I was just a cow in the herd. I worshipped Grant Majors and, deep down, secretly hoped Gulliver would come back and prove he was *the one*. Or maybe that Chase would turn out to be that one. Now I'm going on tour and leaving these boys behind me. I know now, that's exactly how it's meant to be.

But these are not thoughts I can think now; they are thoughts I'll think later. Because when I sing, I don't think or feel. All earthly matters melt away. I know they'll return when I'm done. But for now? I escape.

There's only one place to go from here. I snap my fingers to give the pianist the rhythm, throw a quick wink at Stanford, and toss Leon a warm smile. The first notes of my song begin, and I ride each one up, up, up as I exit my body one more time.

CHASE'S NEVER-ENDING NIGHT

Enter black and yellow and red and blue. Accompanied by bursts of stinging light and chilling dark. The bass is so hard it tickles my eardrums, my nipples, the balls of my feet, and my actual balls. Synth horns sound almost royal as they climb sky-high, scales that no actual horn could muster. I am drenched in sweat, throwing my arms here and there, moisture flying in all directions. My biceps are wrapped in fluffy armbands stuffed with dripping dollar bills—wilting flowers of dead green men. My headband has grown too wet to be of use, so I pitch it into the sea of heads beneath me.

I've never heard this remix of Ke$ha's "Cannibal." Leave it to DJ Mikey Makeout to pull something new out of his magic bag of sonic tricks.

Behind me are near-naked bartenders bursting with more muscles than every guy I've slept with in my life combined, pouring vodka-everythings for the gay men gathered at my feet. I shake my ass and tug my pair of 2(x)ist neon briefs up into my crack. I spin around, bend over a bit, showing the newly exposed flesh to the dance floor, straddling perfectly so drink orders can be pushed between my legs.

Now, as happens every once in a while, a drink-chilled hand takes firm hold of my ankle. I shiver from both temperature and possibility. A potential tip? I follow my standard operating procedure:

I peek over my shoulder, one eyebrow cocked playfully, to find Sir Grabs-a-lot grinning or leering or grimacing from nerves—or, this time, sweetly smiling. A tip, for sure, and a good one. I pop my butt out, emphasizing the dimples on either cheek, and pivot to face him. A slow squat brings my bulge right to his face, and I hold steady like this for just a second before bending forward to bring my mouth to his ear.

"Well, hey there!" I shout.

The man currently down south is named Bruce. He's a buyer for Calvin Klein and a total sweetheart. Many of my fellow go-gos wouldn't know this, of course. They call him Palpatine (or Darth Shade-ius) after the wrinkled antagonist of the *Star Wars* movies. And sure, Bruce isn't much of a looker—but so what? He's one of the more respectful guys who come out on Friday. He is always happy to share his wealth without trying to sneak his middle finger up my butt or his wedding-banded hand around my junk; he just smiles, neatly folds large bills into my waistband, and after we chat, quietly retreats to the blazing darkness of the dance floor.

"Your new underwear is so cute!" Bruce says as he adorns it with a handful of five-dollar bills. "How are you?"

"I'm all right!" I shout over the transition into a mix of Katy Perry's "Firework." "Summer classes are ending soon, and I'm trying to graduate early. So I loaded up on hip-hop and modern workshops!"

"And yet you still make it out here? You are an inspiration, Chase. You're chasing your dreams. Hey, how's that for a nickname? Dream Chaser!"

"Very cute," I say, throwing him a wink. "And how are you, Bruce?"

Do I have to be this chatty? Not really. But every go-go knows that the age of bitchy dancers who ignore you while you lavish them with singles is gone. Maybe in a better economy—but no more. Now you need to be cordial to the potential tipper, be they as nice as Bruce or less lovely, like so many other patrons. You must engage in conversation, smile, and laugh to make them comfortable, even if what you WANT to do is demand that they stop massaging your taint through your jockstrap.

Hardly anyone tips go-go boys anymore, anyway. Certainly no one under thirty. There are just too many stigmas attached—it's creepy, it's dirty, it's pitiful. Nowadays, tippers are mostly drunk and giggly girls dragged to the club by their gay besties, generous tourists who don't know a word of English aside from what their guidebooks tell them, and men like Bruce here (not to mention promoters trying to set an example and keep their dancers happy). Sucks for those of us who depend on this cash to cover the costs of our college tuition, rent, utilities, health insurance, and textbooks.

But I'm not just nice for the money. I'm nice because I'm nice. The very day I was hired here a year ago, I earned the nickname "Friendly Spice" (we go-go boys each have our own Spice Girls moniker). I guess it makes sense. While most of the dancers will say hey, give a hug and cheek-kiss to a potential tipper, and then return to dancing, every time I pop a squat, I end up down there for five minutes. It's not just a pleasantry exchange, either—we're talking full-blown discussions on topics ranging from literature to politics to the weather.

Outside, when I take a rare smoke break, I'm often flocked to by party boys for even more conversation. Everyone wants to gather around Friendly Spice. What can I say? They love me.

And I love them. I find people in general endlessly fascinating—what makes them tick, the things they do and say and dream of. Someday, I'll take all the stories I've collected on the bar and go-go box or out on smoke breaks and put it in a novel or something. I definitely have enough material to write a series. The next *Sex and the City*, maybe. Wouldn't that be a trip?

Bruce reaches into his wallet, rooting through the wad of cash.

"Thank you, as always, for helping me pay my tuition," I say.

"You work hard for it, Dream Chaser. You keep working, and I'll keep helping. By the way, I think your watch is broken."

Bruce makes this joke every week. It's funny because it's so corny, and yet every week he repeats it with such enthusiasm. The watch he's referring to is my tattoo: an old pocket watch on a golden chain. The circular timepiece rests just above my crotch, the chain looping up and around my navel. People always ask what it means, but I never tell them. It's far more interesting to ask what THEY think it means.

I've heard a lot of interesting theories. None close to the truth. That's a tale nobody wants to hear when I'm nearly naked, shoving my ass in their face.

The actual watch my tat is drawn from belonged to my grandfather, who died the day before my high school graduation. All through my childhood, he always had it on him; he'd wind it and hold it up to my face to teach me how to tell time the old-fashioned way. When he passed, I wanted to keep it—but that didn't happen. My mom claimed it rightfully belonged to her, even though I was the one who went to the hospital to see Gramps every day and wind it for him. Last thing I heard from my sister was that Mom hawked it to pay for crack.

Yeah. Seriously. Let's just say I come from an interesting family.

Crackhead drug-dealer mom. My dad, probably dead—but no one knows for sure. My stepdad, one abusive motherfucker.

And me, the gay go-go boy with a full ride to NYU, thanks to his dancing talents. My sister and Gramps were the only two who would speak to me after I legally emancipated myself when I turned sixteen. I lost my grandfather soon afterward. Well, not lost. He's still a part of me. I see his watch every day in the mirror. No matter what else changes in this little life of mine—and plenty has, trust me—for the two of us, time stands still.

Bruce pinches my torso and mimes an attempt to wind the watch. "I think you need to take it into the shop, Dream Chaser!"

"I'll be sure to do that." I laugh. "Now I should probably get back to dancing. I don't want to have to depend on YOU to bankroll my entire night's earnings!"

"Wait," Bruce says, holding me in a squat by my shoulders. "Take this. It should help you get the watch fixed. I expect to see the right time next weekend!"

He's handing me a hundred-dollar bill.

"Whoa, now, Bruce. That's a lot. I don't want you refinancing your home just for this broken-down old watch."

"You'd take it from a complete stranger, wouldn't you?" he says, smiling widely beneath his bristly push broom mustache. "Happy Saturday, Chase."

With that, he smiles, doffs an invisible hat, and disappears back into the fey fray of the main dance floor's strobe explosion.

Wow. It usually takes me a full night to earn the cash Bruce just deposited in my skivvies. Another go-go boy might jump down from the bar and spend the rest of his shift smoking and screwing around with the others. Not me. No longer speaking to my family may mean freedom from their tyranny and terror, but it also means I'm a slave to debt and bills, sinking so deep in the red I can't even remember what black looks like. And so I dance. Gotta make that bacon, baby. Gots to pay dem bills, chile!

Unfortunately for me, Bruce is far more an exception than the rule. Over the next hour, every man that approaches my spot at the back bar is there to cop a feel, and do so for free if he can swing it. I understand that I'm an attractive guy gyrating in close to nothing on a bar…But no one seems to understand that this is a JOB. You don't eat the food a waiter serves and then screw him on the tip. You don't accept a couch the delivery guys lug up to your apartment, then bid them adieu with nothing more than an ass slap. Alas, that's the modus operandi of tonight's crowd. I subject myself to a plethora of scrotal squeezes, rectal exams, and one guy who has the audacity to stick his mouth on the crotch area of my underwear, while giving me nothing more than his phone number. If it weren't for the few guys like Bruce, I wouldn't even make enough to pay for breakfast when I finally get out of here. Well, not until I cashed the check the club pays me, at least.

The truth? I'd rather not be here tonight. I've done four nights in a row at other parties in the city. My legs are sore and I had to use a pound of concealer to hide the dark circles around my raccoon eyes. But when you need to pay bills, it doesn't matter how much you hurt. The box calls and you answer with your feet. Besides, Friday is the night I make the most tips, sometimes more than all the other nights combined.

To pass the time, I run through old episodes of *Will & Grace* in my head, reciting Karen's best lines. Or I think about an upcoming performance I've been rehearsing for, sneaking in a ballet move here or there just to make sure I maintain my flexibility and grace. Robotically, without thinking, I march, march, march, bump, bump, bump, thrust, thrust, thrust. Shimmy, shake, pop that booty, shake the head back and forth, pound fists in the air, rub one hand here up my abs, along my chest, slowly past my nipples, the other hand firmly on the back of my head, elbow up. Lift the face, emphasize the jawline, clench the ass cheeks, let the dimples out to play. Join another go-go boy and do it together. Grind up on him. Kiss (if the tips are encouraging enough).

Visions of my lumpy twin bed fill my head, as tantalizing to me as what I'm currently doing is to the guys below. But no, I've got miles to go before sunrise. Don't wanna be too tired to do the shower show at 3 a.m. All fifteen dancers will be expected on the main stage, where the guys in the DJ booth will throw a switch and water will come pouring out of the ceiling.

The water, by the way, is frigid, and after fourteen minutes of freezing frolicking, the resulting full-body chill doesn't fade for many, many hours. Yet through it all, we're smiling and dancing as sweat and ice-cold water rolls down our chests and stomachs, faces and legs. We dance and dance and dance. Because when you walk in the club, we're the first thing you see across that vague, blurry fog of gay humanity that's dancing and drinking and kissing. We're above everyone else, fully in view. We are the face of the party. And if the owner of that face isn't having the time of his life, what chance do YOU have of enjoying your evening?

I'm checking my hair and abs in a mirror ten feet from the bar, watching my moves and trying my best not to ask someone for the time. (On nights like this, the minute hand moves about as quickly as it does on my tattoo.)

An anonymous hand grabs my attention AND my balls, shooting an immediate, fierce pain straight to both of my heads. OW! Some of the other go-gos would kick the tugger in the face without bothering to look down, but I check just in case. And I'm glad I did.

Hello, lover...

Todd DiTempto, the promoter and host of FreakOut Fridays, stands beneath me, smiling and squeezing. Pain? What pain? It's impossible to conceal a hard-on in the tiny excuse for underwear I'm wearing, and judging from the salacious smile on Todd's face, he realizes that I'm sporting a semi as well.

In my own defense, no one would blame me for my junk's blood-filled reaction. If Todd's power and celebrity in gay New York City nightlife doesn't get you hot and bothered, his muscles, perfect complexion, and killer smile will. Every go-go boy has taken a shot at going home with him, and though tons say they succeeded, anyone who's been here as long as I have knows they're bullshitting. It's an impossibility, because Todd doesn't shit where he eats. This fact doesn't stop the gay grapevine that has reported Todd in the locker room bathroom, or around the corner in an alley, or back at his apartment in Hell's Kitchen, with this dancer or that bartender. Anyway, what was I saying? Oh yeah, I'm now hard as a fucking rock.

I'm also not entirely sure that Todd knows my name.

"Hey, Todd, what's up?" I ask, gently removing my balls from his palm and squatting down to his ear.

"Looks like you're doing pretty okay for yourself," he says, fanning his hands through the money in my armbands.

"There are some very generous benefactors on the floor tonight!"

"Uh-huh. You could probably teach some of the other go-gos a thing or two. They're all bitching about how cheap those guys are. I bet they'd make more money if they took a few minutes away from those nightlong cigarette breaks to actually do what I'm paying them for."

"Nah, they're working too!" I say, even though I'm definitely lying for some of them. Specifically Nick (LI Spice), who hasn't been on the box once since he got here, leaving an empty surface that's been taken over by drunken customers who are a liability for the club if they fall off and crack their skulls.

"Look at you trying to save their asses. You're a good team player, bro. You interested in becoming dance captain?"

"What about Rafael?" I shout back. Rafael has been the dancing troupe's fearless leader since he was hired, just a few weeks before I came aboard. And like me, he's rarely, if ever, away from his assigned station.

"Well, he's going on vacation for a few weeks and needs a fill-in. And hey, if you do a better job, maybe it can be yours full-time."

This is beyond flattering, but not something I would ever do. Bros before bills. "I'll fill in, but I don't want to cause any drama in the ranks. A go-go's only as good as his reputation, right? I'll step down when he gets back, is that cool?"

Todd pulls back so he can show me the grin on his face. "No wonder they call you Friendly Spice."

Okay, so even if he doesn't know my actual name, the fact that he knows my nickname is an enticing development.

"Guess I should get back to doing what you pay me for?" I ask, winking.

"Wait!" he says. "I didn't just come over here to grab your balls. Well. Maybe I did. But that's not it. You working tonight?"

"I'm here 'til you close!"

"No, no. I mean tonight, like, Saturday night! A spot just opened up on the go-go squad for this one-time party I'm hosting. Pay's great. Four hundred up front plus however many tips your arm-bands can carry."

Those two words are music to my ears: "Pay's" and "great." *Ding ding ding!*

I had planned on getting to sleep early, since I'm dancing again on Sunday and already feel like I'm about to drop dead from exhaustion—but there's no way in hell I'd turn an offer like this down. Not when loans are past due and interest keeps growing.

"That sounds amazing!"

"They'll provide the underwear, since there's a sponsor, so you can keep that too. Drinks are free. It'll be a blast. I'll get you the address. Just show up at ten; you go up at eleven. Cool?"

"Totally cool!" I say, unable to mask my excitement. "Thanks, Todd!"

Todd plants a kiss right on my lips, holding it a split second longer than your average, everyday friendly kiss might last. But this is Todd DiTempto. He kisses who he wants to, how he wants to, and for however long he wants to. And it means nothing. Still. Wow. It was nice. "See you tonight, cutie."

And then he's gone, heading back into the crowd of heads and shirtless torsos.

Fuck. I'm going to be exhausted by the time this is through. But there's still more money to be made tonight. I spin around, grab a bartender, and ask for a Red Bull. There's two more hours of dancing ahead of me, and I'm going to need all the liquid energy I can absorb.

***

Raffy has discovered a fiver in my ass crack. Don't ask me what his hand was doing back there. I didn't even notice until he began to pull at the bill.

"Gurl, what you been eatin'?" he asks, yanking the bill out of the back of my tiny orange shorts. He waves it around in the air, gives it a good sniff, and crinkles his nose. "Yuck! You should probably leave THIS as the tip."

Our waiter watches this exchange silently and then whispers, "You like more coffee, sir?" Our booth of ten explodes in laughter as he refills our cups and rushes back to the kitchen.

I take the bill out of Raffy's hand and add it to the stack in my wallet. This means that I made $409 tonight, which might be the most I've ever made in a single evening. Celebration was called for, which is why I've actually ordered food this week instead of sitting pretty and mooching off the other guys.

Raffy (Boss Spice), David (Easy Spice), Jake (Fruity Spice), Luis (Spicy Spice), Franky (Cocky Spice), Nick (LI Spice), AJ (Joisey Spice), Conrad (Stud Spice), Matt (Flyin' Spice), and I are the second coming of the Breakfast Club, except we're all gorgeous, gay, exhausted, and have FAR better hair. And while we're often in trouble, that's not why we're here tonight. Every Saturday at around 3:30 in the morning, we put our clothes back on and leave the FreakOut Friday party at Splash, giggling, flirting, and skipping around the corner to the Hollywood Diner—our weekly haunt. The club stays open for another hour or so, with the last party people still dancing themselves into puddles of sweat. But we have our paychecks and wads of tips in hand, and we're starving.

There's nothing particularly glamorous about our tried-and-true breakfast stop, despite its name. Its title actually comes from a painting that stretches around the walls of the diner—a not-necessarily-beautiful depiction of those famous rolling Hollywood hills. But it's open all night long, it's right next to the club, and the waiters couldn't care less about how loud we get and how obnoxiously we behave. The staff doesn't even bat an eye when Jake lies on the table and shoves AJ's face between his legs, or when Raffy mimes rimming his toasted whole-wheat bagel with butter, or when other late-night Splash party people run into the diner screaming one of our names, glitter and sweat flying everywhere. It's home. We hold court in a large booth in the back corner, often surrounded by others from the party, talking about nothing but this party, past parties, and future parties. Added bonus: the blindingly bright overhead lights do no one's complexion any favors, which is just what you need to make sure the guy you met in the blinking darkness of the club is worth taking back home. And the diner is open 24/7, which means we can stay here as long as we want.

"Did you guys get a visit from Palpatine tonight?" Nick asks, eyes rolling as he sucks up his vanilla milkshake.

"Hell yeah, girl. He tipped me a twenty," Luis says, dipping a french fry in gravy. "He also asked me to marry him. But only after he defeats the rebel Jedis."

The peanut gallery howls with laughter, minus this particular peanut. It would be so disingenuous to join in, considering that there's that hundred still tucked away in my wallet. "He's harmless," I say. "And he's basically bankrolled this breakfast, queens."

"Better than harmless, didn't you hear he gave me a twenty?" Luis says. "But man does he have a set of skeezy eyes! If he wasn't tipping, I'd have Todd call security."

Maybe you should try speaking to him, I think. But I'll leave this potentially toxic topic alone. Many a morning-night has turned into an awkward affair because I went to bat defending the older gentlemen who are the sole reason we leave the club with more than our paychecks. These arguments usually end in laughter and a group conclusion that I'm a daddy-fucker, getting extra cash from the gentry on the side. Whatever. We all need this money, otherwise we wouldn't be here. Go-go boys fall somewhere between janitors and post office workers on the respect spectrum. Surely each of my fellow Spice Boys has gotten plenty of shit about what he does to pay the bills. I'm not about to turn around and disrespect somebody else who is equally undeserving of such scorn. Unlike my scantily clad brethren, I'm actually related by blood to plenty of people who HAVE earned the kinds of low blows my boys are so liberally lobbing at Bruce. I will store up all my shit-talking venom for those who actually deserve it, thank you kindly.

At 6, the sun makes its grand return to Manhattan outside the window, spilling warm, early pink-orange light onto Sixth Avenue. The drunken clusters of boys in torn tank tops and tight jeans have transformed into duos of old women walking their dogs, paper cups of coffee clutched in their free hands and the Saturday-morning paper under their arms. I'm just about ready to go down for the count.

My plans for the day are as follows: Go home. Shower. Jack off to the memory of Todd kissing me. Sleep. From there, we'll see. If I have to work again tonight, I should probably preserve what little strength I'm able. It won't be pleasant, but I can pull it off. The change of scenery will be nice—new faces to stare at, new lights and projections, new music and drag queens. If I'm lucky, all of this change will give me the energy it takes to dance without falling asleep on my feet like a horse and plummeting into the crowd below.

"Chase. Snap out of it, sister!"

It's Rafael, slapping me in the face with a fry.

"Yeah?" I blink a few times and stare down at my uneaten BLT. I take a bite, but I'm not really hungry. Plus, AJ's burger melt looks a hundred times better. I'll have to order it next time.

"Girl, wake up. Eat up. Pay up. We're going to the beach."

"I hope you all have a lovely time." I yawn, taking another bite. "I'll be sure to dream of sandy ass cracks in your honor."

"Riiiiiight," Nick says. "You're coming, Chase. And you don't have a say in the matter!"

"Aw, wifey's putting her foot down," Franky pouts, earning an angry glare from Nick.

Okay. So Nick and I slept together a few times. Or maybe a few more than a few times. Usually when we're both drunk, which allows us to pretend it didn't happen. Well, it allows ME to pretend it didn't happen. This, of course, leaves Nick as the braggart who obviously clued in all the other boys. I don't really dignify their jibes with an answer either way. He's not that good, to be honest. He's one of those pretty boys—short, with a butt that's way too big for his body (in a good way). His Long Island accent, complete with "dawgs" and "cawfee," can be cute sometimes. But he knows he's gorgeous and likes to lie back and let you do all the work. The time he puts in at the gym and the willpower it takes to eat nothing but fresh fruit and salads sans dressing counts as his invested effort. He enjoys your mouth, hands, and dick, and you enjoy the fact that it's your mouth, hands, and dick that he's enjoying. That's it. Much like how he hardly works during his shift, he barely musters any effort between the sheets. I only keep doing it because he relentlessly hounds me into letting him crash at my place and I sympathize with his reluctance to get back on a train bound for Long Island at 5 in the morning. What Princess wants, Princess gets.

Including, I guess, my presence at the beach.

"What beach?" I sigh, knowing this war is already lost.

"My parents have a special pass to this private beach by our house on Long Island!" Nick says. "We won't have to deal with the crowds of GTL meatheads. Just us. The sun. You're coming!"

"I don't know. I'm running on empty, bitches."

"Come on, Friendly," Nick says, rubbing my exposed thigh. "I owe you for all those nights you let me crash at your place."

"Yeah, and crash on his cock," AJ adds.

"Shut up!" Nick howls, flinging a sugar packet at AJ, who bats it back at him.

"But I gotta work tonight!" I say.

"You do?" asks Matt, aka Flyin' Spice, our own tight-package twinky aerialist-in-training. "Since when do you work on Saturdays?"

"Just tonight." I tear open the battle-worn sugar packet, pouring it into my already-cold coffee. "I'm doing that eWrecksion party."

"No way!" Conrad says. "DiTempto put you on that?"

"Yup!" I try not to sound like I'm bragging, though I'm sure I am, slightly. "I think tonight's the night he's going to ask me to marry him."

"Right," Nick says, clearly jealous. "And he won't be at all distracted by the live sex show when he's down on one knee, ring in hand. How romantic!"

"I'll bet Friendly will be down on BOTH knees, not Todd!" Raffy roars.

"Shut up," I say. "What's this about a live sex show? If I'm going to be doing all that, I think I'll have to raise my fee!"

"Not you, Friendly. You know, actual professionals, unlike your amateur ass?" says Conrad. "They're from New York Fuck College, or something like that."

Uh-oh. The plot thickens. That can only mean one thing.

"You mean New York Screwniversity?" I ask, feigning as much innocence as a go-go boy possibly can.

"Oh, ho! So someone's a paying member!" Nick says.

I shrug. "I just go there to read the articles. So…Some of those boys will be there?"

"Todd said all of them," Conrad corrects me. "He's VERY excited about the crowd they'll bring out."

Wow. The fact that the boys from New York Screwniversity will be at the party makes tonight infinitely more interesting. I'm not really a fan of gay pornography, preferring the detailed and intimate scenes my own brain can conjure over the forced, usually chemistry-free stuff you find online. But I know of the infamous Screwniversity via personal experience. I've been inside it—and it, in a way, has been inside of me.

Full disclosure: I met the thirteen "dorm mates" and even had drinks in their living room. And on one drunken, hazy, strangely magical night last month, I got fucked by one of them. His name was Marty Brayden. And while he may not be the star of the site, he is certainly the most noticeable: a tight, toned twink with an eyebrow ring, chinstrap, and spiky, bright-blue hair.

If Marty was telling the truth, we fucked in front of thousands that night. Despite some slight stage fright, I performed spectacularly. I guess when you dance in front of thousands of gay men in person, it's not the biggest deal when those thousands are invisible and stuffed inside a video camera silently monitoring your exploits.

It was amazing. Some of the best sex I've ever had—which makes sense, since Marty's no doubt had a lot of practice. I've found myself thinking back to that night during my last few hookups with Nick, but that only makes Nick's shortcomings in the sack stand out all the more.

Most one-night stands I've had end up being just that—a hot time and that's it. Most of the guys I never think about again. But for some reason, I can't forget my time with Marty. And I'm severely jonesing for a repeat.

Is that primarily because I can't have it?

Maybe.

I left Marty my number and got nothing in return. Not a call. Not a text. Not a Facebook friend request. It stung even more when I checked NYScrewniversity.com, only to find that our scene was the top viewed on the entire website. Marty didn't even think to shoot me a text to clue me in on our collective victory? Ouch.

While I didn't watch gay porn before that night, I do find myself watching it now. A lot. I blew a full (slow) night's worth of tips to get a monthly membership. Now I spend my few free nights watching Marty get fucked by his dorm mates in every which way, including some epic three-way they advertised the hell out of. And when I jack off, I'm picturing myself as whoever he's getting it on with. I spend hours clicking through the archives, getting to know the mystery boy I never really got to draw a bead on when we shot our scene. And with each clip, I find myself becoming more and more preoccupied with him. My favorite videos are his interviews (weekly testimonials with the dorm mates go up every Tuesday at 2). The more time I spend listening to him, the more I feel like I'm dating him in reverse. Getting to know him little by little, piece by piece.

But does he even remember me? I guess there's no reason to seek sex with someone like me when you have twelve potential partners every night just waiting to give it to you.

I tried sending a few e-mails to the website, but the webmaster clearly had no interest in relaying my requests. And why would he? It's not like I have extra cash to blow on a pricey private video chat. Especially considering that if Marty wanted to see me again, he could easily have texted me. Why waste any more time or money, only to get blown off again?

Tonight, I'll waste neither. When I see Marty Brayden, I'll go right up to him. I'll be direct. I'll tell him I want to come home with him again and repeat our last performance. Outdo it. He'll say yes because, well, our video is still hovering near the top of the most-viewed list. Refusing to do another scene featuring Chase Bliss? That's just bad for business.

Now I've had a month to get buffer, thanks to my membership at the NYU gym. I've had plenty of days out on Chelsea Piers with the other go-go boys, baking my skin to a deep brown that makes me look almost Hispanic. There's no chance I'm not going home with Marty again tonight—and this time I'll make sure I get HIS number.

"So, you coming to the beach, bitch?" Raf asks as he and the other boys gather their gym bags and split the bill. "We're leaving!"

"Yes, he's coming!" Nick says, grabbing my hand and pulling me up from the table. "Right?"

What the hell. My dorm doesn't have AC. I'd probably spend the next few hours baking to death. I'm sure there will be opportunities to sneak a wink in here or there on the train ride out or on the beach.

And I could stand to go a shade or two darker. Might help my chances at landing Marty tonight.

"Okay. Let's go."

***

Penn Station is dead. All the storefronts are closed, except for one magazine stand staffed by a man who can't even keep his eyes open. The janitors are mopping the corridors in preparation for the rush of weekenders who will soon flood the building with suitcases and crying kids en route to Fire Island or the Hamptons or Montauk. It's so empty that the other boys and I are able to race each other from corridor to corridor. Luis said he's the fastest, but I leave him in my dust just as our train pulls into the station.

Our train is just as empty as Penn, so we stretch out across an entire car, our feet illegally propped on the seats opposite us. The sleepy conductor doesn't bother us about this fineable offense; instead, she sits down to bitch about her fiancé and how she thinks he might be gay and cheating on her with his college buddy. Go-go boy therapy. Luis, still pissed from losing the race, is no doubt bitching about it to David, who is busy texting some guy who gave him his number tonight. AJ and Conrad, who may or may not have something going on between them, have fallen asleep on each other's shoulders. Matt is wondering if he can draw a mustache on one of their faces without waking them up. Franky and Jake are likewise asleep. Nick is holding my hand, and I'm letting him.

I don't regret my choice to train it out to Long Island instead of back to my dorm, but I think my body does. I'm weathering that weird zombielike sensation where your brain feels like it's been sucked out of your head, shoved in a blender, and poured back in through your ear. I let my eyes close for a few minutes.

If I were to write a memoir, I'd name it *Breakfast With Go-Go Boys*. Because that's where I'd start it—during one of the many mornings I've spent with my buds after the club.

It would be a memoir of excitement and possibility and camara-
derie, not a fucking sob story. I'll gladly skip the crackhead mom.
The deadbeat dad. The deader-beat stepdad. The actually dead
grandfather. The legal emancipation trial, complete with my mom
not actually showing up to the courthouse, which only helped my
case. My legal name is Winterman, but it used to be Summers. I
think the stark opposite is all the symbolism required to explain
just how far behind me I want to leave my past.

Where would I have ended up if I hadn't split from my family,
borrowed money from my sister, and fled Connecticut for New
York City? I don't know and don't want to. Back in Connecticut, I
was stuck in stasis, like a kid raised by wolves. My life didn't even
begin until I got out here.

Now my dream has already come true: I got away. Everything
from here on is gravy.

And I don't pretend that my sob story entitles me to skate through
the rest of my life with ease or gives me a license to be a bitch to
people. I know people like that, and they aren't fun to be around.
Seriously—after such an unpleasant past, why would I waste any
more time on nastiness? Being Friendly Spice is so much easier.

The way I see it, we all have stories. Marty Brayden, Palpatine,
Todd DiTempto. We never really know who's suffered what. Most
of us have moved on from something or other. And in this city,
you'll rarely hear about it. Here, people don't talk much about their
childhoods or families or friends back home. No one comes to
New York to dwell on the past; we come to live in the now and get
on with the future. We're our own men. Our own boys. Whatever.

Where we came from pales in comparison to where we are now. You can't look back when you're living in Manhattan; you'll get hit by a cab or mugged or raped or robbed or killed if you stop for a second and let your guard down.

Like right now.

"Chase!" Nick yells. "Wake up! We're gonna miss our stop!"

Wow! Was I out for that long? I jump up from my seat, grab my gym bag, and let Nick drag me out onto the station platform. My eyes register nothing but fuzzy blur as the train doors *whoosh* shut behind me.

The sun stings my face. I block it with my hand as we stumble down the stairs to the parking lot.

The town we're in is called Merrick, or so a giant navy-blue billboard with gold lettering says. Fancy. Nick herds us all to two SUVs idling alongside the curb. "Be nice, they're my parents!" he warns us before we get to the open doors.

I didn't know we'd be picked up; I just assumed we'd cram into Nick's car. It's apparent by the looks on the other boys' faces that I was not alone in this assumption. Our first beach trip will also mark our first time meeting a set of someone else's parents.

I end up in the Jeep with Nick, Raffy, Jake, Franky, and Nick's dad. Nick takes the front seat, while we pile into the back. We're all silent once the doors slam, not quite sure what we should (or can) say in front of him. Does he know who we are? How we know Nick?

"Hello, boys," Nick's dad says. "Welcome to Long Island. Hopefully you won't have to stay too long."

Nick's dad is an attractive man, with a full head of gray hair that he keeps cropped short. He has the windows open to let the warm, fresh air into the SUV and the AC on to fight it off and keep things cool.

The silence is so loud. We elbow each other in the backseat, hoping one of us will say something.

Thankfully, Nick's dad speaks up again. "So do all of you guys dance at the same club as Nick?"

"Yeah, Dad, you've got the full go-go boy squad from FreakOut Fridays coming to the house. How does that make you feel?"

"Like a chauffeur to the stars," he says, turning on the radio. "I'll keep the music down—I'm sure your ears have had enough techno for the day."

So Nick's dad knows his son dances on a bar in his underwear for cash? That's something I never would have expected. Franky and Jake look equally shocked and commence to whispering back and forth. I mean, we're not porn stars (well, THEY aren't), but I'll bet very few of us are up front with our parents about what we do.

My mom sure has no idea, but that's because she's in jail, where she can rot, for all I care. I've thought about visiting her unannounced, dangling a G-string in front of that glass partition between the jailed and the free. But the price of the train fare wouldn't be worth the look on her face. Wouldn't she be proud? At least I'm not selling drugs across state lines like she was.

"By the way, Nick, your mom was so excited your dancer friends were coming by that she ran to the Bagel Boss and bought a spread to welcome you home."

"Jeez, Dad!" Nick says. "We just ate at a diner!"

"Who cares?" Raffy says. "Mister...um...Nick's dad...We're happy to eat more."

"Maybe you are," says Franky. "I have a photo shoot this evening."

"Well, we'll get you boys in and out as quickly as we can. And you can chew on some ice if you can't eat anything. Then you can borrow the cars to get out to Point Lookout. Which of you are sober enough to drive?"

"Chase, you have a license, right?" Nick asks, snaking his hand back from the front seat and rubbing it on my knee.

"Yeah, but I don't think your parents want me driving one of their cars."

"Nonsense." Nick's dad laughs. "You sober?"

"Yeah, I am."

"Then that's all that matters, Chase. Just be careful."

My phone buzzes. A calendar reminder.

Shit! I completely forgot I have a date tonight!

This is exactly why I set all my calendar events with a nine-hour advance warning.

This day is getting so complicated. I'm currently on Long Island with a boy who can't stop staring at me through the rearview mirror of his dad's car. Later, I'm dancing at a party with a promoter I've been lusting after for ages and a gay porn star I'd like a second chance with. AND, in between, I'm supposed to grab Thai with this kid I've been chatting up on OKCupid? I should cancel. Get some sleep. He's an actor, which is usually reason enough to opt out. I have enough drama in my own life without adding a theater major to the mix.

But he's also smart, cute, and a pro at back-and-forth online flirting (always a promising omen of real-world chemistry). I guess I'll keep it.

After ten minutes of driving down tiny side streets, we arrive at our destination. My breath catches in my throat. Nick's house is gigantic, a mansion in a neighborhood filled with equally jaw-dropping domiciles. A U-shaped driveway, three (or maybe four) floors rising above us as we pull in behind his mother's car. I guess the luxury SUVs should have given this away.

So Nick's a moneybags? How did he never tell me during all those nights together? I just assumed he was how I imagine the rest of us are—broke as a joke and doing what we can to make ends meet. No wonder he doesn't dance when he's supposed to be on the block. If he lost his job, he'd be fine! Funny, the things you still don't know after dancing nearly naked with someone for nine months...

Nick's mom, a short and tan blonde dressed in pastels from a place like Talbots or Chico's, lets us into the house and ushers us toward the dining room. The foyer, living room, and hallway are all immaculately white, filled with shiny black statues and oddly shaped pots holding exotic and expensive-looking flowers with long petals and crazy-colored leaves. FUCK, this kid is rich. Why does he bother working at all? I doubt his parents force him to dance in his underwear as a lesson in responsibility and independence. Wouldn't his job be better suited for a college kid who needs the money and actually looks like he wants to be there? I've seen all the wannabe go-go boys that Todd sends home because all the slots are currently filled. Those kids need the money, not Nick.

Once we've gotten our food and sat down in the living room, Nick's mom wants to know all about Splash—how we got there, if we like it or hate it. She shoves her son playfully and says she wants to see the place soon, and if Nick continues to discourage her from coming, she'll just sneak in one of these nights.

Nick rolls his eyes. "Right, Ma. Aaron the doorman won't even let you in to get your ID checked."

"I'll take the fact that you think he'd even check my ID as a compliment, you little brat," she says, taking a swipe at him.

"Oh gawd," David laments as he digs into his second bagel, "I can feel my ass getting bigger with each bite."

"You could stand to gain a few pounds," Nick's mom says. "As for those of you not driving, I can whip up a few screwdrivers. But only after you sign a verbal contract promising me you won't vomit all over my floors. I just had them waxed yesterday."

"Chase is going to drive," Nick says. "The rest can get shit-faced."

"Well then, straight-up OJ for you," she says, pouring me a tall glass.

I can't eat. I'm too angry. Wouldn't you be? Since he started staying over with me, Nick's had me pay for everything—breakfast, extra booze, condoms and lube, whatever. I've even chipped in for his cab to Penn Station a few times. And why? To be chivalrous? I assumed he needed it! Now I know he doesn't, and feel like I've been duped. Not to mention the fact that Nick gets along so well with his parents! They take time between bites to brag about how great he is, and he accepts it all with a wide smile and fake modesty. He basks in their gushing, occasionally winking at me as if to say, *Do you have it this good?*

And he knows I don't.

After the others are filled with carbs and cream cheese, Nick takes us on a tour of his place, which feels more like he's rubbing it in our faces than anything. Every room (and there are so, so many) is spacious, high ceilinged, central air-conditioned, filled with the thousands of blinking red-and-green lights of expensive technology. There's a photo of his dad with Barack Obama—signed, of course. His mom met Martha Stewart and apparently baked a cake with her. We walk through his two sisters' rooms, his brother's basement apartment, the pool out back, which has one of those infinity lines that makes it look like it goes straight out to the canal behind the house. His room has its own bathroom, complete with a damn Jacuzzi, quite a contrast to my crummy dorm. And yet he stays with ME on Friday nights.

Why does he feel the need to show off all of a sudden? I thought we were going to the beach. I would pull him aside and ask why he's doing this, but I can't find the right chance.

As far as I'm concerned, he can come back here from now on. I'm done being so charitable to someone who obviously doesn't need my help and is happy to take advantage of someone so clearly beneath him.

Thankfully, it is now time to actually go to the beach. We load our gear into two cars, pull out of the driveway, and honk good-bye to Nick's parents, who stand arm in arm on their giant porch, waving ecstatically.

My nerves about driving quickly dissipate once we hit the road and muscle memory takes over. I put Raffy in charge of figuring out which button controls the AC and which one will open the moonroof. He solves both dilemmas, and we are flying along some highway in minutes. The rushing air helps me step down from my anger.

"Fuck, did anyone know Nick had it made?" Franky asks, his head hanging out the window.

Anger's back.

"I heard he had cash," Jake says. But Jake always acts in the know, and rarely is he telling the truth. I may have to start referring to him as Pathological Spice.

"Bullshit!" Raffy calls him out. "Why? Because he wears Armani and always has new underwear? We all do. But fuck, he's, like, a billionaire! We should make him start picking up the check at the diner."

"Weird that he never really bragged about it until today, though," I say, doing my best to stay as close to Nick's car without rear-ending him.

"Yeah," Raffy says. "Franky is always bragging about that shit, and his house could fit in Nick's garage."

"Fuck you!" Franky says. "My house is huge!"

"It's not the size of the house, Franky. It's the size of your dick that matters," I say, as I turn the volume up on the radio. "And, regarding either, we'll need photos or it didn't happen."

"My dick's huge too!" he yells above Lady Gaga.

The parking lot for the beach is as empty as Penn Station was a few hours ago, just as I was hoping. We pull into two spots adjacent to the boardwalk and unload the gear lent to us by Nick's Hollywood-movie parents. The beach itself, while slightly pebbly where the sand meets the surf, is beautiful. It stretches for miles in either direction without another soul to be seen. We spread out on blankets and collapse into the sand. As soon as we're situated,

Nick pulls a bowl and weed out of his bag, lights up, and takes a strong pull.

"Do your parents know you're a pothead?" I ask as Luis accepts the bowl from him.

"It's my dad's stuff," Nick coughs out. "That's how you know it's the BEST."

So even Nick's marijuana habit is covered by his glamorous family? No wonder he's so bad in bed. He's never expended a single ounce of effort to get anything in his whole life.

Nick cuddles up next to me and lays his head on my shoulder, draping his arm over my chest. And now I feel shitty for being angry. Because being rich is not something Nick did to personally spite me. But seriously, what the hell is he doing with the likes of us? We latchkey kids, poor students, shitty-family runaways?

"Here, baby," Nick says, handing me the bowl, "take a big hit."

"I'm supposed to drive us back," I say.

"Weed doesn't fuck up your driving!" Raffy shouts. "Suck on that shit or I'm taking it!"

"Come on, Chase," Nick says. "That's like two hours from now. One pull for your lil' Nicky?"

I take a pull off the bowl and it goes down smoother than velvet. It takes three hits to get me blazing. This shit IS the best. When the weed is spent, so are we. Within five minutes, everyone is asleep. Everyone except me and Nick.

"You know," Nick whispers to me, "you don't have to go back to the city when everyone else does."

"Yes, I do."

"Oh, come on, we can make up some excuse. Assuming they give a shit."

"What? That you'll fly me back in your private helicopter?"

Nick rolls his eyes. "No! I just like having you here. Like, in my world, you know? Why do you think I suggested this whole trip in the first place?"

"Well. Won't your parents wonder why I'm sticking around?"

Nick kisses my ear and pulls me in tighter. "They already know I have a killer crush on you. They said you could eat dinner and stay the night, if you want."

"I have to dance at eWrecksion," I tell him.

"Oh, right," he sighs, looking out at the ocean. "Well, you can have one of the other boys do it. I'm sure Todd wouldn't care either way."

He's right. Todd probably wouldn't care that Friendly Spice, his future go-go boy captain, is changing his mind, so long as I provide a sub. But I need that money. Most definitely more than anyone else on this beach.

"I'll think about it," I say. Mainly to shut him up. Because telling him why I need to get out of here is a sign of weakness I'm not ready to admit to anyone. I'm Friendly Spice, not Class Warfare Spice. No one likes a whiner. And where's the valor in bellyaching?

Shit was always complicated between me and Nick, but now it's unbearable. I don't know if I'll be able to eat and look at him at the same time. Pre-Nick, there was an ex whose name needn't be mentioned. Let's just call him Patient Zero. He gave me chlamydia, then broke up with me. Not having health insurance really made that a bitch. Then there was Nick and our drunken nights that just kept on happening. Some would call it a rebound. Really, I was just too lazy to say no and deal with his moping. No, you can't stay with me tonight. No, we can't have sex again. Has anyone ever told Nick no? Hell, I'm halfway considering actually blowing off Todd's party just to please him—and that's insanity! Must. Stand. Firm.

"I sorta wish it was just you and me out here," Nick says, his sandy-blond hair itching my nose as he kisses me gently on the mouth. "Hope that doesn't freak you out."

"No, it's cool," I say, because I have no idea what else I can say. And then I'm asleep.

After napping, we tackle the ocean. Literally. We're karate kicking our way through oncoming waves. AJ complains that the pebbles are killing his feet, and if this beach is for rich people, why wouldn't they demand one on the sandier side of Long Island? We're wrestling and lifting each other up in the air, dunking each other's heads under the freezing water. Luis's underwear comes down and Raffy's screeching about shrinkage. The hours pass as quickly as the constant waves gathering strength in the distance and flying toward land to knock us off balance. Then it's time to go.

I wait until everyone is busy shoving his stuff into the cars to pull Nick aside. "Hey, listen. Thanks for the invite to stay."

"You can't, can you?" he asks, his face pulled into a tight smile.

"No. I really need the money," I say. "Rain check?"

"Whatever."

"Whatever? Whatever what?"

"You made like a thousand bucks tonight! You can't take one night off and stay with me?"

It is taking all I have not to dress down Nick right here. So many responses are queued up like cannon balls, ready to be fired.

"No. I can't. Like I said, I need the money."

"Money," he huffs. "Okay, fine, if that's your choice. Todd DiTempto and his porn brigade instead of me. Thanks for letting me know where I stand." He stomps back to the car, leaving me by myself with a beach blanket in hand.

Someone once told me that every gay man is caught in a never-ending love spiral with every other gay man. We're big fish chasing after smaller fish chasing after minuscule fish. I know Nick has a thing for me, but when I'm with him, I'm fantasizing about being with Todd—or, more recently, Marty. Todd's busy with whomever he dates who isn't any of us. Marty's busy fucking whomever. We're all just going in circles, this ridiculous line dance where our bodies never meet and we're forever switching and turning in opposite directions. I don't know a single happy gay couple, just hundreds of guys chasing after guys who are chasing hundreds of other guys. When does that stop? Who's at the front of this race, and will he ever hit a wall or plummet off a cliff?

Luckily, Nick and I will be in separate cars for the ride back.

Nick's parents drive the rest of us to the train station in the early afternoon. None of us want to leave, but the skyscrapers beckon. The boys have appointments, dates, photo shoots, parties, and barhops to attend to. Nick doesn't even look at me as I board the train.

We leave the sleepy suburbs with their highways and cars, their strip malls and bars that close at 2 a.m. I watch Merrick disappear and fight back jealous tears. Nick will get back in the car with his amazing, accepting, welcoming, weed-smoking parents and head back to his castle of a house, where he'll probably lay out by the pool, or play foosball in the game room on the third floor, or get in his Jaguar and head out to the mall to spend his parents' money on things he doesn't need. Even if he's hurt by my snub, he certainly has enough creature comforts to console him. Meanwhile, I have to head back to my tiny NYU summer dorm that I wouldn't be able to afford if not for the full-ride scholarship. Back to that dirty city, where you can't even see the sky unless you venture to the center of Central Park. To my date with The Actor.

Thanks to Nick, I'm in a shitty mood. I feel completely worthless, both personally and financially. I want to crawl in my bed and sleep through the next twenty-four hours, not spruce myself up for a Thai dinner during which I'll have to nod and smile and match my date's no-doubt-theatrical level of energy when all I really want to do is lie on the floor and take a nap. I'm already resenting this kid for taking up my would-be slumber time and I haven't even met him yet.

He better be worth it.

***

Date status: epic fail. I slam back into the dorm, a bottle of hair dye in a soaking Ricky's plastic bag choked in my right fist. The fucking asshole! That fucking piece-of-shit judgmental cunt! I will NEVER give another actor a chance. I should have quit while I was ahead. I have never felt so insulted, so pigeonholed. Backed into a corner by a stereotype that couldn't be further from the truth—especially in regard to me. That wasn't a date; that was a fucking gay arraignment. And he wasn't even that fucking cute.

My room is disgustingly hot. My one window opens crookedly; I have to go from this side to that to even get it all the way up. Ah, my scenic view of the next building's brick wall, a pair of sneakers knotted and hanging from a fire escape. My tiny twin bed with the broken leg and lumpy mattress. My college-issue furniture.

It's all so suffocating. I can hardly breathe.

Everything is spinning and blurring because I made the mistake of getting sloshed from too-sweet frozen drinks. I let my guard down, which sucks because my comebacks weren't half as cutting as they would have been if I were sober. I should have just stayed home and napped, but hindsight is twenty-twenty. Now I'm drunk, SO exhausted, and goddamn, it's fucking hot in here! Turning on the fan does nothing more than spin and blow the gross hot air around like I'm stirring a vat of soup. And, last time I checked, brick walls don't bring cold air in through a window, so I'm fucked there too.

Oh, because I'm a go-go boy, that means I'm some drugged-up, loose-assed slut, right, Mr. Thespian? God forbid at least ONE of us transcend the piss-poor view you have of the whole lot. Have you ever even MET a go-go boy besides me? Irony of ironies is that YOU are like every other fucking actor I've ever met. So self-important. So sure of his stupid opinions.

Wasted time. I could have spent the afternoon out on Long Island with Nick, who's looking much better after a couple hours opposite that drama queen. I would have gotten laid. (Since that's what sluts do, right?) Could've gone shopping to kick up my credit card debt by another few hundred dollars. Instead, all I have to show for my afternoon is this bottle of bright-green hair dye and my grand plan to rock out tonight at eWrecksion.

Oh, I'm not making some radical change to my appearance because I'm pissed about a bad date—don't give The Actor that much credit. It's one-wash hair dye, and I was planning on doing this anyway. It'll be back out by tomorrow (at least, I hope so).

Let's just say that my date's condemnation pushed me over the edge. Tonight, I'm going to make a scene. And why shouldn't I? I'm a slutty go-go boy with no future and nothing but shame to my name; all I have to look forward to is drug overdoses, STDs, and old age (which will invariably render me useless to greater society—no one wants to see an octogenarian rocking a G-string).

So let's put on a show. Something The Actor himself might appreciate—because, little does he know, I give the performance of a lifetime every time I'm up on that box. Why, yes, Skeezy Old Man With Foul Breath, I DO enjoy having my nipple pinched so hard I have to check to see if it's still there after! And thanks for the dollar! If you ask me, there should be a whole separate category at the Tonys for go-go dancers. Tonight, however, I will be reprising my role as Marty Brayden's mysterious, late-night love interest at the Screwniversity.

He'll spot me across a crowded room, with my neon lizard locks. And it'll be love at second sight. Or whatever. Yes, my emerald tresses are an homage to Marty's own shock of blue. If we fuck on camera again tonight, all our fans will see is blue and green and flesh tones flying across the screen like it's an orgy in a Crayola factory.

But not so fast—because Todd DiTempto will be there too. And if Marty Brayden wants another shot with me, he'll have to prove he's worth it. All I know is, I will not leave eWrecksion tonight without either one or both of them leading me by the hand; I will not surrender to the absurd exhaustion burning my bones and mushing my eyes to putty unless it's in one of their beds, after some of the hottest sex this city's ever seen.

You want slutty, Mr. Actor? Well, there you have it.

When the dying deed is done, I have to admit I look cute. Like the lead singer of a ska band. I scoop up a generous dollop of gel and spike my hair into a pure Mohawk, eliminating the sides with a buzzer to make it as punky as possible. I may be getting paid four hundred dollars tonight, but this hair is gonna earn me at LEAST double that in tips.

I still have an hour and a half until I'm expected to make my grand entrance at the club, and the subway ride should take less than twenty minutes. I set about my nightly go-go prep. First there's two hundred push-ups with my feet suspended on my bed. (I have to move my chair and desk into the corner to fit my body on the floor.) Then four hundred sit-ups, mixing up twists, crunches, and hanging crunches with my legs on the bed again. Then to the twenty-pound dumbbells, which are each lifted one hundred times. I do all of this while staring in the mirror. My body screams for a break, but that's not on the menu tonight. To nap at this point would only end with me snoozing my alarm and sleeping through the gig. Nope. We're in it for the long haul, motherfucker, so quit your bitching and man up.

Then I shower—it's a quick one, since I'm too pissed to jack off or anything. I'm still a little drunk, and still PLENTY angry. After so little sleep, even Friendly Spice has his limits. Fuck you, actor boy. I've had about enough of everybody thinking they're better than me. Tonight the spotlight is MINE.

***

Todd wasn't kidding when he said this would be the party of the century. Whoever he's working with rented out an abandoned warehouse and converted it into a four-floor party wonderland. I'm riding high on the temporary boost you get when you cut in front of a line of hundreds wrapped around the block—and get a kiss from Miss Chocolate Bunny, one of New York's fiercest black drag queens, who's in charge of the door tonight. Good luck to her. Those boys looked mutinous and the party hasn't even started yet.

There are no half-price drink specials, no free anything—no need to bait the boys. There's no way they'd be anywhere else tonight. The music is deafening, the lights blinding, the beautiful guys equally blinding. I wander the many rooms, each themed and decorated differently: the Aliens Room (complete with H. R. Giger statues and masks hanging from the walls), the Rancho Relaxo (wooden fences lining the walls, lassos and cowboy hats hanging from the ceiling, even a boot rental), the White Noise Room (everything white, from the bar to the couches to the glasses), Alice in Wonderland, Charlie and the Chocolate Factory, a room made up to look like a French boudoir, two adjoining rooms in red called the Mouths of Hell. Each impeccably decorated space has a different DJ already in the heat of his set as people enter, admire, and leave again to see what else this chaotic complex holds in store. Too bad Mr. Bad Date Actor is a self-loathing loser; he probably would have liked the theatricality of it all.

Whatever—his problem now. For me, it's time to party.

Seriously, how can you not love gay nightlife? Yes, there's sex and drugs, but BFD. There's also so much more. These parties are a chance to escape the dirty streets of the city, the burning sun and judgmental glances. Your stress and your studies and your baggage all just disappear in the dark for a while, your eardrums thumping from music so loud you can't possibly think about anything else. Cold drinks loosen you up, remove painful memories. We're all here for one reason and one reason only: to have some fucking fun. There are a million ways to escape: with a blow job (the shot or the activity, your choice), shaking your ass atop a box for some spending cash, covering yourself with face paint and glitter (trying to outdo last week's almost-as-fierce look), or simply dancing yourself stupid. We are all here to get away, to bring some fun back into our lives before it's time to go home, go to bed, get up, and deal with all the shit that comes with real, regular, retarded life. To miss this is to seriously miss out.

I haven't spied Todd DiTempto, but he must be here somewhere. He's always the first in and last out at these things, running around making sure the bartenders know the special drinks, the DJs are ready for their contests and giveaways. The boys from New York Screwniversity have yet to arrive, I'm sure. First it's the security, bathroom attendants, coat check, and cleanup crew, then the bartenders, barbacks, and waitstaff. Next enter the go-go and shot boys, then come the entry-paying party boys. Then, finally, the entertainment.

I return to the main floor and find the go-go changing station, off the main dance floor in a back room by the stage. A special green bracelet that identifies me as a member of the go-go-dancing troupe allows me entry. There are already fifteen guys here in various stages of dress and undress. According to the roll call list on the wall, there will be over fifty dancers here, most of whom I've never met.

Wow. This party gets more and more impressive. Sure beats a night on Long Island—not to mention a shitty date.

The first shift of go-go boys are pulling off underwear, pulling on other underwear, checking tan lines, wrapping tape around their wrists, applying eye makeup, lipstick, paint, and stage makeup to their abs and pecs. They're doing shots to loosen up, deep in squat stretches, counting off as they go through sets of push-ups and crunches. They're figuring out their stations and the intervals at which they are expected to rotate from one room or block to the next. The management has set aside costumes for us to don as we go from room to room. Cowboy hats for Rancho, ray guns for Aliens, white gloves for White Noise. There's themed underwear too, adorned with peppermint stripes for Charlie and the Chocolate Factory or pitchforks and flames for the Mouths of Hell. There are even two full-time go-go wranglers running around like the harried stage managers at my dance shows, telling boys where to go and what to wear, making last-minute adjustments to the schedule and positions.

Since I'm already prepped as far as workouts are concerned, I only have to slip into a pair of nut-huggers provided courtesy of the underwear sponsor. My first outfit of the night is a tiny pair of briefs covered in vertical stripes of blue, green, and purple (the green being pretty damn close to my do's new hue).

I have twenty minutes until I'm expected to be shaking my moneymaker up on the block in the center of the main dance floor. Ahead of the game, I decide to go back out to find Todd.

"Chase?"

I freeze. Nick is standing in the doorway, in a pair of underwear identical to mine.

"Chase! What the fuck did you do to your hair?"

"Nick? What the fuck are you doing here?"

"Surprise!" he says, summoning a pitiful smile. "I asked Todd if there were any last-minute spaces available."

I catch myself before mentioning that, yes, there is probably still plenty of room out on the smoker's patio, where Nick spends all his time when he's working.

"There weren't, but he said I could come anyway. There's always room for one more, right?"

"Yeah. Hey, that's great!" I say, even though this situation is anything BUT great.

"AND he has us dancing side by side all night!" Nick cheers. "Cool, right?"

No. NOT cool. All my plans tonight were contingent on me flying solo, NOT attached to a guy who thinks he has some kind of dibs on me just because I let him sleep over after work sometimes.

"Guess it's a good thing I didn't stay in Merrick tonight. I'd be dining with your parents on my own."

"Oh, whatever," Nick rolls his eyes. "I felt bad that you had to work tonight. I figured this was at least a good way for us to spend more time together."

MORE time? I already saw him all night last night AND all day at the beach.

"Now you don't have to choose between me and this party."

I don't remind Nick that I already DID choose. I chose to come here and make money. I chose Todd and Marty Brayden. And I am not backing down from those choices.

"Congrats, babe," I say, giving him a cheap, quick hug and kiss. "I gotta run for a few. I'll see you up on the box in twenty."

"Um, I was going to ask if you could hold down my feet while I did crunches."

"Just stick them under a bench. It works just as well."

I leave without bothering to confirm the look of disappointment I know is hanging off his face. Oh well. He's lucky I'm not bruised from him rubbing my face in his fabulous Long Island lifestyle all morning. Then I might actually tell him how I feel about his need to spy on me at parties he shouldn't even be working. Apparently the house and car and perfect family aren't enough. He can't handle the fact that it was ME who was asked to work at the hottest party in recent memory. He can't risk there being ONE THING I might outdo him in.

Back to the throng of gay men, which has metastasized like a tumor since I left. There's no room to maneuver; I have to push through the dancing guys and hags toward the bars and staircases in the back. I run to the second floor, to the third—no Todd. Would he pull a no-show at his own party? That's not like him. I can't make out a single face through all of the fog, lights, shadows, and heads. It's hopeless. I'll never find him here. All I can do is hope he'll find me.

I dash back down to my box, get there just in time. It's smack in the middle of the people-river on the main dance floor. Nick is already up there, dancing and pumping his arms, smiling with all teeth showing. Since I left him, he's applied a Ke$ha-like streak of makeup to his face. He looks like a slutty tiger. On any other night, I might have found it cute. Tonight, I find myself fantasizing about Nick being mauled by a tiger of the much-less-slutty, much-more-hungry variety. Headless Spice—now there's a go-go boy Splash hasn't yet seen.

"I already made a hundred bucks!" Nick says, hugging me when I've finally made it onto the box. "And I've only been up here for five minutes!"

"That's great!" I say, and spin around, putting our backs to one another. If I'm going to be latched to Nick all night, at least I'll make a ton of money in this high-traffic spot.

We dance back-to-back. From Britney to Girls Aloud to Jason Derulo to Flo Rida to Pitbull. I begin slowly, as I always do. My feet are shoulder-width apart and I rock back and forth, popping my ass to each side, my lips pursed and my eyes scanning the crowd. When it gets later, I'll break out the bigger moves. Until then, I preserve my energy. Marathon, not a race. Marathon, not a race.

But there's a problem: Nobody is tipping. More accurately, nobody is tipping ME.

When a hand rises up out of the thousands around us, the extended dollar isn't intended for me. Each donation ends up in Nick's waistline and is then moved to the armbands he never wore before tonight. That little shit! He stole my armband idea, and he's stealing MY money, dollar by dollar.

Nick tries a few times to press his body to mine. He's done this before. He wants me to spin him around, wrap my arms around him so we can dance together. But I can't do that, because then I might bite his face off. I saw the schedule inside the go-go room. I was supposed to be on this box ALONE. Todd DiTempto, with his trademark kindness, just threw Nick up here at the last minute. He probably thought Nick needed the money, just like we all incorrectly assumed. But Nick doesn't need it. I do. And I'm not getting it.

I pull my underwear lower and lower until I'm cupping my dick in my hands. I'm squatting farther and farther down. And still, Nick is making more money. I pull out my more dramatic late-night moves way too early, as if this will get the attention of the guys beneath us and divert their dollar bills toward me. Head-stands and splits. Still nothing. Every hand bypasses me and goes straight to Nick, who smiles like a child at a birthday party and thanks every man for his generosity. I want to slap him. I want to fling him off our box and into the crowd. I want to scream at him to get the fuck out of here. I want to fire him next week when I become the dance captain at Splash. Or perhaps literally set him on fire.

Down in the crowd, I see Bruce. Or Palpatine, as Nick and the others prefer to call him. He's dressed in a suit, sweat visible on his forehead.

And he's tipping Nick too.

A crisp hundred-dollar bill goes under the band, and Nick pops a squat and plants a kiss on Bruce's sweaty head. Bruce disappears into the crowd, not even looking in my direction as he goes.

Fuck this dye job! That's the problem, isn't it? How ironic. Coloring my hair green has led to a dire lack of said color in my underwear and armbands.

I need a drink. NOW.

I hop off the box, ignoring Nick's pleas to tell him where I'm going.

The crowd is now impenetrable. I catch elbows in my chest, drinks spilled on my stomach. My feet get stepped on. I'm going to flip my shit if I don't find a space where I can move my arms more than two inches. I find an additional few millimeters of personal space up against a bar by the staircase to the second floor. The bartender gives me a free drink, then a second one. I can still see Nick from this corner, floating above all the other bodies. Every few seconds, another hand rises up from the masses and slips a dollar here, there. The money armbands grow and grow. His biceps look like millionaire planets. That's MY money, you son of a bitch! Go back home to your family and your Jag and your private beach and your dad's weed and leave those crumpled singles to those of us who actually need it!

"Well, hey there."

Turns out I didn't need to seek Todd out; he's found me. He also seems to have found one too many drinks. He sways back and forth on his feet, his eyes shifting left and right like he's watching a tennis game behind me.

"Hey, Todd!"

Todd covers his mouth to stifle a belch as his eyes bug out. "Oh, hey there, Green Hair."

Wow. So he's not drunk, as I originally thought. He's completely and utterly trashed.

"Had a bit too much to drink, Boss?" I ask.

"Not enough, actually," he says, wrapping his arm around me and looking out over the dance floor. "Party looks awesome, though."

I'm tingly. I can't help it. Having Todd touch me fills me with a warm, sparkling feeling that seems to travel from the points of contact between our bodies. I'm turned on. I'm excited. I think, maybe, this is something? Or am I making something out of nothing? There's only one way to find out.

"Well, what did you expect? Who wouldn't go to a party thrown by Todd DiTempto?" I say, playing one of my fingers down his chest.

Each time I touch him, I am both worried and hopeful. I'd walk my fingers in circles around his body for minutes if I could. Just testing the waters. This is dangerous territory—an employee of Todd's making a move everyone knows is forbidden and hopeless. But he isn't reacting. Either because he is okay with it or he's so tipsy that he can't feel my fingers on him.

I should stop now while I'm ahead. If I become too bold and he pulls back, he might disappear again. I might lose my job.

Todd shakes his head as he looks at me again. "Shouldn't you be dancing?"

"Well, you put Nick up on my box with me, and he seems to be handling it fine in my absence. Shouldn't YOU be running around networking and fending off drunk guys' advances?" My hand is wandering down his giant chest, his rippled abs.

"It's been a rough night, bro. An old friend came out of the woodwork. The little bastard's been so fucking stupid I don't think I can..." He stops his sentence and pulls out his phone, taps it hysterically. "Rough, rough night."

"An ex?" I ask. Because of course this would be the night that Todd rekindles things with an old flame.

"Nah. I wish it were that simple. Anyway. You wanna see the VIP lounge, cutie?"

Cutie? That's a nickname I'm more than happy to accept.

"I'll see whatever you want to show me," I say.

To avoid the crowds, Todd takes me through a de-alarmed fire exit. As soon as the door slams, he shoves me against the wall and engulfs my mouth in his. His breath tastes like a bar. So many conflicting flavors. Vodka? Tequila? Triple sec? Bourbon? All of the above. This bar is fully stocked.

I'm rock hard and so is he. He's thrusting up against me, pushing his bulge into mine, shoving his tongue down my throat like he's digging for buried treasure. And it feels amazing. The first thing today that's gone right. His highness, Todd DiTempto, the reigning Prince of Gay Nightlife, licking the back side of my Adam's apple. I'm giddy. I'm horny. I'm drunker than I thought, helped along by Todd's Long Island Iced Tea–flavored tongue. He grunts as he kisses me harder and faster. The cold of the cinder block wall feels amazing against my back and arms. I'm on my knees, grabbing for his dick.

"No," Todd says, stuffing his hand in my face, shoving me back into the railing. "I don't do this. Not at my parties. Not with my employees."

Fuck. Why can't I do anything right? I'm on my knees, looking up at Mount DiTempto, his cock just out of reach under stretched jeans. He looks down at me with a mix of confusion, pity, and concern. He's saying, "No, no, no," over and over again.

Yeah. I blew it. Or, well, I TRIED to blow it and have now revealed myself to be a too-eager, too-easy, pathetic hussy, one of many who have unsuccessfully tried to hook up with Todd while he was on the job.

Dammit! What was I thinking? I know better than this! Hope you enjoyed this little rendezvous, Friendly Spice, because here's where the pleasure stops. You thought this was going to be your lucky break? Bad-date actor was right: you'll never be happy. Go back outside and scrounge up a few more singles while Nick rolls in riches he doesn't need. Then go back to your AC-less dorm and your OKCupid account and your sometimes-generous donations from Palpatine, assuming he hasn't found a new favorite by now. Back to your mom in prison and your dad wherever he disappeared to and your dead grandfather. GO.

"It's okay," I say, getting back up. "Sorry. I'm drunk. I should go…"

I make a move for the exit—and can't, because Todd is kissing me again. Grabbing me by my shoulders and pushing me back into the wall. Feeling me up over my tiny underwear. "Go? But you're SO fucking hot, you punky little bitch."

What the fuck? I'm grinning as he licks the sweat off my neck, his hands grabbing and groping and grasping. It feels so good, but my confusion cuts into the ecstasy. Maybe I was too harsh in my assumptions? Maybe I wasn't too fast? Maybe he wants to lead? Maybe HE wants to suck ME off. Maybe I need to let go and embrace Todd's strange intoxication. Maybe I should stop with the "maybes" and just start trying to keep up with his lips.

"Bro, that feels big. How big are you?" Todd DiTempto's hands are down my underwear. I could shoot right this second. The combination of his strokes and the fact that HE'S doing the stroking is more than enough to get the job done.

But no. Not yet. Maybe he wants me to play hard to get. I can get into that.

"Big enough," I smirk, pulling his hand back out and readjusting myself. "But I don't want you to get sober and regret doing this. We should probably stop." I lick along his lips to let him know not to take anything I just said too seriously.

"Yeah," he says, pulling away from me again. "Yeah. Guess you're right."

What! Fuck! Maybe not. I push back up against him and suck on his lip, lick the underside of it. "Well, we don't HAVE to stop if you don't want to, Mr. DiTempto."

He's kissing me back. "Fuck. I guess you'll just have to come home with me later tonight. Cool?"

"Cool," I say. "So tell me about this VIP room."

Todd doesn't tell me about the VIP room—he whisks me there. And I thought the other rooms were impressive! This is the first time I've been amongst the elite who are too important to party with the actual party. Man, do they know how to let loose. Expensive couches and chairs are scattered throughout the room. Lights are dim and a DJ spins in the corner for the two hundred VIPs. Bartenders happily take drink orders and refuse payment. There are even gift bags filled with swag from the many lube, underwear, condom, and clothing sponsors who have banners hanging all around the club.

Todd and I squeeze our way to a far corner and end up drinking caffeinated liquor concoctions brought to us on trays by model waiters. He introduces me to this promoter and that host as "Friendly Spice." They think it's cute, and they think I'm cute. I smile and play president's wife as best I can while accepting a second cocktail.

Todd catches up with the promoters and personalities, his arm forever around me, stroking my back. Standing here like this, smiling and laughing and engaging in conversations about nightlife comings and goings, it's hard not to imagine us dating. Todd could waltz around his events with me on his arm, introducing me to everyone, leaving me with them to entertain while he goes about important business. I could be the president's wife, couldn't I?

A commotion breaks up the conversation and my daydreaming.

The head of the party, some guy named Mikey Drama (so Todd tells me), comes bursting into the room, howling for all present to make way, make way, because the boys of New York Screwniversity have arrived.

And sure enough, there they are, just as I remember them. Drake and Zak and Joey leading the pack. And, in the back, as blue haired and cute as ever, is the one and only Marty Brayden. Despite the fact that I've been watching him for weeks, he has somehow gotten even more beautiful. He's ripped, tanned, impeccably hairless. His bright-blue hair is bluer than ever.

Todd seems to have gone pale staring at them. Like he's in a trance. "Fuck," he says.

"What?" I ask.

His attention snaps back to me. The always-on promoter personality relights in his eyes. "Just too much to drink—and yet, not nearly enough. Refill?"

Todd gets us a drink and squeezes us even farther into the corner, turning his back to the crowd. He's trying to talk to me, but it's obvious he's distracted, his eyes glued on the cluster of porn stars reflected in the mirror behind me. Funny—I never figured Todd would be so starstruck by a bunch of adult-film quasi-celebrities. I guess even he has to jack off to SOMEthing (while the rest of us just jack off to him).

"You okay, Todd?" I ask. "You don't look so good."

"Gee, thanks, bro," Todd grins. "You really know how to boost a dude's ego." And before I can correct myself...

"Todd Fucking DiTempto!"

Mikey Drama has spotted his partner from across the room and is now headed in our direction, one arm outstretched. "Todd Fucking DiTempto! Get your ass OVER HERE!"

"What I wouldn't give to have the power of invisibility sometimes," Todd whispers to me.

"Why?" I ask.

"Nothing. Gotta take care of some shit. Be right back."

Todd lets his business partner drag him away from me, to the cluster of Screwniverity representatives. I'm way too drunk to understand what's going on, but his weirdness is starting to bring me down. Do I really want to go home with Todd when he's like this? In all fairness, there's a lot that isn't right with me either tonight. But I've never seen Todd even half this trashed.

Todd shakes Marty Brayden's hand for what seems a strangely long time, holds onto it once the shaking has stopped. It's like how he kissed me a little longer than normal last night. Does that mean he's changed his mind about bringing me home and decided to flee the scene with Marty instead? Hell, who WOULDN'T choose Marty? Everyone in here is staring at him, trying to get his attention, approaching him with the unholiest of intentions. And I'm no different. What the fuck is wrong with me? Did I really think that dying my hair some crazy color would get Marty to notice me? Take me home? Fall for me? Jesus!

No, Marty will not be mine tonight. Not when it's me against everyone else—my competition including but not limited to a dozen drop-dead gorgeous porn stars, anyone who's anyone in gay New York City nightlife, and Todd DiTempto. I can already see how this will unfold: Todd will go home with Marty, because that's MY luck. Nothing changes. The rich get richer; the poor stay poor. Nick prospers; I falter. Grandpa's still dead; Mom remains a bitch behind bars. I can dance my ass off at school and at the clubs trying to change it, eyeing guys I know deep down are too good for me. Yeah, maybe I'm hot enough for one live sex session at the Screwniversity dorm or one roll in the hay with Todd DiTempto (when his inhibitions are way down in the gutter, that is). But I'm not the boy who gets a call or a smiley *"Last night was fun!"* text in the morning. I'm the boy whose number gets inexplicably "lost," whom Todd will grimace with regret at tomorrow: "Oh, that was YOU?"

So why kid myself? Why am I here? I'm not VIP. Todd is VIP. Marty's VIP. And VIPs fuck VIPs, don't they? I should be back down with the not-so-important people, making not very much money. At least there I'll be dancing with someone who, for whatever reason, DOES want me. Well—he wants a place to crash. He wants a mouth on his dick as he lies back motionless like he's watching *Real Housewives of New York* on TV. He wants someone he is so obviously better than in every way. And even that will only last until he finds a guy more like him. Some other snooty Long Island boy with his own Jaguar and private beach.

I should have just ended this night after the diner and slept through to Sunday.

After a final round of hugs, flexes, and flirtatious grabs, Todd returns to me, even more zoinked than he looked only a few minutes earlier. "Fuck, bro. I gotta get outta here."

"Oh, really?" I ask, unable to mask my utter lack of surprise. I hand him another drink, which he chugs in one breath. "Well, it was nice running into you."

Todd grabs me and kisses me again. "With you, fool. We're getting out of here."

Oh. OH! Well, that wasn't what I was expecting...

"Can you do that?" I ask as soon as he releases my lips from his grasp.

"Fuck yeah. I got people here, didn't I? But—shit, I have to introduce the porn guys in twenty minutes. After that, I can leave. Need to leave."

"You're not suddenly wanted by the FBI or something, are you?" I ask. "You're acting very fugitive-esque tonight."

"No." Todd laughs.

"Because if we're going to be interrupted mid-fuck by a blazing searchlight from a helicopter outside your apartment, I just want to make sure I'm looking my best. For my mug shots, you know. Since those always end up on the Internet."

"I'm not wanted by the FBI. Unless YOU'RE the FBI," Todd smirks. "The Fucking...Beautiful...Shit, I can't think of what could start with *I*."

"Me either," I laugh. "If only I were Iraqi. Or an Indian."

"Right. So yeah. I'm going to run down and do that. Meet me by the front door after the first show?"

"You got it," I say, kissing him on the cheek. Kissing him good-bye, maybe? Perhaps this is just an easy way for him to pull an Irish exit and abandon me in the VIP while he sneaks off with Marty Brayden.

He spins my face and kisses me deeply again. "I'm gonna fuck your brains out tonight, bro. Hope you're ready."

Okay, so if this is an Irish exit strategy, he's executing it very bizarrely. "I was born ready," I say before he leaves me, crosses the room, and vanishes through the door.

Well, now I'm excited. Excited and nervous. Is this really about to happen? After all these months of wishing, wanting, and wet dreaming? The outcome of all of those morning conversations at the diner with the other go-gos that would PAY Todd for a single ride? It's still hard to swallow.

Then I notice Marty has vanished from the room, even though his costars remain. Where did he go? Is he with Todd?

Fuck! Of course he is.

Why would Todd kiss me like that and then run off with Marty? Is he planning a doubleheader?

So what if he is? I'd still take him. Is that totally pathetic to admit? Maybe I'm crashing. Maybe I'm not thinking clearly. Remember the last time I slept? Yeah, I don't, either.

A smarter guy would cut his losses and leave now. Leave Nick to make his money, which he'll lug home in a big bag with a dollar sign on it, only to set it all on fire. Leave Marty to get cheered on as his slutty celebrity climbs a few rungs higher on the ladder of porn infamy. Leave Todd to fuck Marty or any other guy he wants, who he can easily get. To be honest, a little shut-eye may actually feel better than an orgasm at this point.

But then they win.

Nick wins. Todd wins. Marty wins. The Actor wins. Everybody but Chase wins in that scenario.

I'm not letting that happen again tonight.

They say nice guys finish last, and that's fine, because what's so great about being first, anyway? Most winners I know are total douche bags. Take Nick, for example. But I'm also not just gonna give up to make things easier on everyone else. I am still IN this race, boys. I may or may not end up with Todd or Marty or anyone else tonight, but if not, it won't be because I threw in the towel.

I hope I don't just pass out when I hit Todd's bed. Marty's bed. Whoever's.

I catch a boy staring at me from across the bar. Well, I catch him, and then he does that thing where his eyes rush to stare at anything else, which is more an admission of staring than it is a successful cover-up. He's cute. And he's back to staring at me. Because when it rains, it whores, right? Well, if Todd can double-dip tonight, maybe I can too.

"Nice hair," he says before I even reach him.

Fuck, he's a looker. Square jaw with short brown hair. He fits nicely in a simple, logo-less solid-brown T-shirt and a pair of neither tight nor short shorts.

"Your hair's pretty nice, yourself," I say, brazenly rubbing my hand through it. "Man, I feel like we're in a shampoo commercial or something."

He doesn't stop me. "Thanks. I had it straightened this morning. Seriously, though, bold color choice."

"It's one-wash," I assure him. "I'll be back to dirty blond after my next shower, whenever that happens."

"Figures that the two cutest guys in this room have ridiculously colored hair, even if one of them has it for tonight only."

"Yeah. Great minds, you know? I see you're without a drink. Want this one?" I hand him a drink off the bar, my eyes locked on his.

"How much is that?"

"Free," I laugh. "First time in VIP?"

"Yeah, I guess," he says, drinking and wincing at the strength of the brew. "Glad I met someone with a little more experience where very important people are concerned."

"It's my first time too," I say, leaning closer to him. "I'm just a quick learner. You new to New York?"

"Sorta," he says, sipping. "Actually just here for the next twelve hours. Then back home I fly."

"Go on."

"I'm from Los Angeles, just in town to…surprise a friend."

"Oh my, a real-live Cali boy in town for one night only? How lucky am I?"

The boy smiles at me and looks down. "Please don't make me blush. I'm red enough from the sunburn. No one warned me that New York was sunnier than LA."

"It's cute." I smile, getting closer. "You wanna duck out and…do something?" I'm not usually this brave, but I'm also not usually this drunk. Plus, he's a limited edition.

"No, not really," he chuckles, backing up. "Man, you New Yorkers don't waste much time, do you?"

The fact that he's smiling doesn't lessen the blow. Am I in store for another judgment and shaming session? Already had one of those today. Check, please?

"Oh. Sorry. I guess I should probably leave you to your West Coast pace." And with typical East Coast lightning speed, I about-face and walk away.

"Hey! Wait, wait!" The guy grabs my shirt, pulling me back to him. "I didn't mean to offend you. Tonight's just a rough night."

"Yeah, that seems to be going around," I say, finishing my drink.

"Don't take this the wrong way—but I wasn't looking at you because I was interested in you. At least, not like that. It *was* actually your hair. Um. Can I ask you a totally random question?"

"After my proposition, I'm curious to see what you consider random. Go for it."

"That kid with the blue hair—do you know him?"

"Ah, yes, I sure do. That was Marty Brayden."

"Friend of yours?"

"Not exactly. Well, I guess you could say he's everybody's friend— friend with benefits. He's sort of a pretty huge porn star."

"Really," the boy says with a sigh. "How big?"

I laugh and have to cover my mouth to stop vodka from coming out. "I'm pretty sure you have to get a membership to his site to find that out."

"I meant popularity-wise," he smirks. "Is he well-known?"

"I think so. The hair certainly doesn't hurt."

"Or that douche-bag chinstrap," he says. "I'm going to introduce myself when he gets back."

"Ah, hoping for a night with the star of New York Screwniversity, are you?"

"Not exactly. Been there, done that."

I imagine he's lying. But whether he's telling the truth or not, I'm not about to tell him anything about MY past with the sapphire-haired superstar. Don't need a bad rep reaching all the way out to the other coast.

"So you do know him?" I ask, looking over my shoulder for signs of Marty's return. "Don't tell me that's why you're up here."

"Isn't it why you're here?" he asks. "The green hair. I thought maybe you were a fan. Or trying to get his attention."

"Attention? Maybe. His? Not necessarily. It works on other people too. Got yours, didn't it?"

"Guess so," he replies.

"I'm Chase Winterman, by the way. Feel free to Facebook me when you get home. I've been thinking about checking out California."

"It's nothing like this place, I'll tell you that. And I'm Graham."

"Well, Graham, I should get going. And I promise not because you shot down my advances."

"I'm glad. Maybe if you ever get out to Cali, we can hang out."

"Maybe so. Good luck with your porn star."

"I'll need it," Graham says. "Have a good night, however it unfolds."

"Wouldn't have it any other way."

I take a back staircase out of the VIP, leaving Graham to get another drink and await the return of the famous Marty Brayden. I sneak back into the go-go dressing room, slip into my street clothes. I also grab my money, guiltlessly, from the wrangler, who pays me the promised four hundred dollars for the set despite the fact that I danced for maybe twenty-five minutes. This must be what Nick feels like when he cashes his trivial checks at the end of FreakOut Fridays.

As I cross the main dance floor, I can see Nick having the time of his life. By now I imagine he's acquired so much green in those biceps that he looks like the Hulk. Good for him.

And now I wait, hoping Todd actually shows. I order and nurse a Marty Brayden, some blueberry-flavored thing that's actually a bit too sweet for me. I'm also double-fisting it with Red Bull because now, more than ever, I need my energy. I wish I could do another couple hundred push-ups and sit-ups just to make sure I'm in my absolute prime when Todd rips off my clothing, assuming that's going to happen.

From here, I watch the first of two live performances by the boys of the Screwniversity. This one is, predictably, tamer—why buy the cow now when you know it's getting milked even harder later?

Marty stands just to the right of the head of the dorm, Joey Gambit. He gives the crowd a peek of his cock and they go nuts. Or maybe the crowd is going nuts because two other guys are giving each other head. Or maybe they're going nuts because they know what's coming later. The show ends, the crowd has a collective vocal orgasm, and the party returns to dancing and drinking. The boys—Marty included—sprint for the VIP area.

Todd makes it just as I finish my third drink. He breaks through the crowd, grabs me by the waist, and kisses me deeply. "Oh, boo, you got dressed."

"Just for now. Lead the way?"

"Absolutely. I'm done here. And if we don't get out before they lock the doors, we'll be stuck until the second show is over. Don't need that, bro."

"Aren't you curious to see what all the fuss is for?" I ask, poking him. "Thirteen hot guys all going at it in public?"

"You're the one I want naked. And in private, preferably. Let's go."

We haven't moved five feet when I hear Nick screaming. "Chase! Where are you going?"

Yeah. I knew this was too easy. Nick is breaking through the crowd, only a few feet away from me. Todd is already by the exit. I'm stuck in between.

I turn back to Nick. So much money in those bracelets. So much love in his eyes.

"Bro," Todd calls, "you coming?"

"Yes!" I yell to him. I then give Nick a big hug and a kiss on the cheek. "Looks like you made out pretty well tonight. Have a safe trip home."

Despite going home a rich(er) boy, the expression on Nick's face as he realizes what's about to happen looks like he's just lost everything.

Should I feel bad? I don't, really. In the morning, Nick will return home to a loving family on Long Island, bagel spreads with cream cheese. His parents will ooh and aah as he counts out dollar after dollar, twenty after fifty after hundred, because he's just that talented a dancer. Then they'll probably roll one of those bills into a joint and all get high together.

Tonight, for at least one night, I'm going home without him. I'm sleeping with Todd DiTempto, New York's hottest gay promoter, in every sense of the word. Is that a victory? Maybe. If nothing else, it makes me feel a tiny bit better about the lack of cash and bagels that will greet me tomorrow morning. There are at least two things in this world Nick's family money can't buy, and they are happiness and a night with Todd DiTempto.

Well, maybe that's just one thing, after all. Because right now, I'm having a hard time remembering the last time I felt this pleased with myself.

To my dismay, Todd spends the entire cab ride fixated on his phone, which is precariously close to dying. No kissing. No heavy petting. Nothing. It's like I'm not here, bumping up Eighth Avenue alongside him. I wonder if he'd even realize if I opened the door and stepped out at the next red light? Occasionally, his phone rings and he sends it straight to voice mail. He's on Grindr, on Facebook, on Twitter. I take out my phone and click through some Facebook e-mail notifications to make myself look equally busy.

"Sorry," he finally says about ten minutes into the ride. "My head's somewhere else."

"Yeah. I noticed."

"Sorry."

"Do you want to do this?" I ask. "We can pull over here, it's fine. No hard feelings."

Todd puts down his phone and stares at me. "Yes, Chase. I'm sure. You're in the cab with me, going back to my place, aren't you?"

"Oh, wow, you do actually know my name," I say, laughing uncomfortably.

"You think I do this often? Bring my employees home with me?"

"Actually, it's pretty common knowledge that the great Todd DiTempto doesn't sleep with his colleagues."

"Don't call me 'great.' Please." Todd shakes his head and rolls his eyes. "Or I WILL ask you to leave. This idolization shit is a bit much for me tonight, bro."

I have to laugh. "Wait, so you don't like the fact that you're a nightlife superstar?"

"Sometimes I do. Not tonight. Sometimes I want to be just another dude at the club, there for a drink or to get some ass. Nowadays, every boy up on my junk is there because I've got a pocketful of drink tickets or I'm their shot at getting a gig as a go-go boy, bartender, or DJ."

"Right. Or maybe they're after you because you're ridiculously gorgeous."

"All the wrong reasons, bro."

"Then what's the right reason? You looking for a boyfriend? 'Cause something tells me that wouldn't be so hard to come by, either."

"A boyfriend who doesn't know who I am at night," he says, looking out the window. "Someone who wants the real me, Todd DiAngelo, not my nightlife persona, Todd DiTempto. But that's impossible."

"Well, I AM somebody else too, Mr. DiAngelo, okay? I'm not just a go-go boy. I don't wear a G-string 24/7. I have a life outside my nightlife too!" My outrage has at last claimed his full attention. "You've only ever known me as Friendly Spice, but that's a persona just like Todd DiTempto is. I don't always like the guys who've got their hands all over me! But it's a performance! You get on stage, you do what's called for, you get paid, and you go home.

"I know a lot of people ask a lot of you, but I've never asked for anything, have I? So maybe you should give us a little more credit. Nightlife is nightlife; every single guy in there has a day life too. The promoters, the go-go boys, and every drunk gay average Joe. Even the Screwniversity boys—they have friends, and parents, and different names too."

"I know they do," Todd grumbles, his face very dark for a second. Then he regards me with cautious eyes. "A little pent up there, Chase?"

"Sorry. A lot of that stuff has been running through my head all night. I had a bad date."

"Sounds that way."

"It's been a very long, very dramatic day," I sigh.

He shrugs it off. "Whatever. This is getting way too serious. Tonight, I'm just looking to forget shit, bro. Let's talk about something else, okay?"

"Okay. Suggestion of topic?"

"How about we talk about Nick?"

I laugh again. "So you know his name too?"

"I know all your names, bro. Who do you think gets your checks printed at the end of the night?"

"Am I also allowed to request a change of subject?"

"Not as long as you're on my payroll." Todd laughs, rubbing my leg. "What's your deal? He didn't look too happy about you leaving with me."

"It's whatever," I say, looking out the window at the passing diners and apartment buildings. "He has feelings for me. I don't think they're mutual."

"They're never mutual," Todd muses. "That's why we go out to bars and get sloshed and try to find the next best thing to take our mind off it. Fucking depressing, right?"

"Yeah, it sorta is, for me," I say. "Not sure why it is for you, since it keeps you in business. If you hate nightlife so much, why are you a promoter?"

"I hate it, yeah," Todd says. "But I love it too. I know that doesn't make sense."

"Actually, I think it makes perfect sense." I laugh. "Sometimes I'd rather be absolutely anywhere else than up on that bar. Please don't use that as grounds to fire me."

Todd shakes his head, gestures for me to keep going. His phone lies facedown on his leg.

"Hearing those same songs and seeing those same people—every week—sometimes I think, 'Hey! I'll just quit and get a normal day job! I'm over this scene. Time to grow up.' But then after three days away, I'm practically jumping out of my skin to get back up again."

"It's a drug, bro," Todd says, tucking his phone in his pocket. "You think you can beat it, get it out of your bloodstream. But then after a few quiet nights home alone, you're ready to go insane. Fuck it, man. Ridiculous." He turns his attention to the driver. "Right up here, man. On the left, please."

Todd swipes his credit card and leads me out to the street. It's drizzling, which is a lot better than the Armageddon rainstorm that hit during my date earlier in the evening.

My heart sinks as I realize he's leading me into a luxury apartment building. Is anyone in my life NOT filthy rich? Well, at least I'll make gay nightlife history somewhere scenic. We take the elevator up in complete silence, both of our eyes focused on a television screen in the wall that forecasts a full weekend of unhappy rain clouds. New York City is going to drown us all.

Something doesn't feel right here. Todd seems almost burdened by the fact that I'm trailing behind him. And I keep thinking, *I gave you no less than half a dozen opportunities to leave without me—so what are you doing, BRO?* But I can't ask this question, because it's awkward enough as it is. And obviously it doesn't bother me too much, because here I am, crossing the threshold of his apartment. Someone is quietly snoring in the darkness.

"Don't mind him," Todd says. "That's my slutty, fat-ass dog." He turns on a light and points to a Scottish terrier splayed out on its back on a doggy bed by the window, legs kicking as it dreams.

"He's so cute," I whisper. "What's his name?"

"Señor," he says. "Don't whisper for him. That whore would sleep through an earthquake. Can I get you a drink?"

"I've had enough hooch for tonight. Can I get some water?"

"Sounds good to me, bro. Think I'll do the same." He disappears into the kitchen.

The apartment is gorgeous. A huge-screen TV, stereo speakers mounted all over the walls, an iPad charging by the black leather couch and sectional. A glass coffee table covered in large hardcover books. The place looks like it belongs to a thirty-something, not at all what you'd expect from a guy whose job is herding go-go boys and throwing dance parties.

Todd returns with two bottles of water, unscrewing the cap of one before he hands it to me.

"Nice place," I say. "You make this much money in nightlife?"

"Fuck no! I wish," he says. "Nightlife pays for my cable and utilities, if it's a good month. I work in finance during the day. And during the night. All the time, really. Boring shit, but it pays the bills. Whatever. You can't take it with you, right?"

"And I thought *I* needed more sleep."

"It's all I know how to do," he says. "If I'm left with five seconds of spare time, I feel useless. Plus, I like buying shit."

"Buying shit? I'm a fan of that too," I say. "So, now that I've seen it, do you want me to go?"

"Are we still going on about this? If I didn't want company, I wouldn't have brought you here." He kisses me on the mouth, rubbing his big hand on my chest. "I mean, I was close to leaving you behind when I saw your hair, but I figured I could put a baseball cap on you or something."

I laugh. "It'll be gone by tomorrow morning, I promise."

"Good," he says, putting an arm around my shoulder, kneading it with his hand. Our faces draw closer. Our lips connect. He kisses slowly, my bottom lip and then my top lip. Then faster. I guide his hand down to my pants, then inside. I'm already fully hard, waiting for him. Dripping. He likewise guides me down to his. And we're off.

I'm shocked when I pull Todd's dick out. It's textbook average. Maybe six or so inches. Which isn't a problem—but certainly not what I expected from someone who's so above average everywhere else. It makes me feel better about my own shortcomings—not my size, but the fact that there is some semblance of justice in this world, if even this deity of gay nightlife is a mere mortal in some areas.

It doesn't turn me off any. Clearly. I'm kissing him. I'm jerking him off. I'm moaning as he jerks me off.

"Fuck, you're huge," he says, falling to his knees in front of me to take me in his mouth. I'm glad the size doesn't bother him. Glad I have something that excites him.

Fuck, his mouth feels awesome. It's so weird, looking down at Todd as he sucks me off. This guy, for whom just about anyone would drop to their knees—HE'S dropping down for ME. Is it too much to say that I feel a bit like a god now myself? I'm so close to shooting, taking deep breaths to keep myself together, trying not to blow my load too quickly. Even if I do, it'll be just the first of several rounds tonight.

As my mind wanders to keep me from losing it, I find myself thinking of Marty Brayden. The show must be over by now. It's been over an hour since we left the club. On that stage in front of thousands, the blue-haired star of the Screwniversity has no doubt been fucked by each of his dorm mates. And now what? Back to his dorm? Some lucky one-night costar in tow?

Have a good night, Marty. I know I will.

Todd and I switch, and now I'm between his legs. I open my mouth wide to take him in, but he shifts himself away from me.

"Not a big fan of head, bro," he says as not-awkwardly as he can. "Just jack me off."

Someone who doesn't like getting head? That's a new one. Then again, in New York City, I've found that every gay guy has at least one strange tic in bed. They keep their socks on. Or they keep the lights on. Or they kiss with their eyes open. Or maybe they refuse to look at you. Or they don't like giving head. Or they want to get rimmed, but they won't let you fuck them. I once hooked up with a guy who put a condom on before fingering me. Whatever, I can make do.

He's moaning: "Oh fuck, bro. Oh fuck, I'm gonna shoot."

I open my mouth again and lock down on him to catch every last drop, but he yanks my head forcefully off him. I try to get back on it again, but there's his big hand, holding me off like a bully in a cartoon keeping some wimp at bay as he swings at the empty air. Todd jerks himself off and explodes all over himself. A sizable blast that reaches all the way up to his neck. Yet another above-average quality to tip the scales.

"Wow," Todd exhales. "Wow."

He looks done. Too bad we're anything but done. That was just the appetizer. Here comes the main course.

"I want you to fuck me," I tell him as I work my way back up to his face. We're kissing as I jerk myself off and finally release all over him, adding my mess to the mix. "I want you to fuck me right now."

"I do too," he whispers, his eyes still heavy from his orgasm. "I really, really want to."

"Then come on," I say, wiggling out of my jeans and standing up. "Show me your bedroom."

"Not tonight."

If I got this far, I'm not about to give up that easily.

"Tomorrow morning, then?" I ask, throwing myself back on top of him. I grab his dick and push it toward my hole. "Well. You're still hard. Might as well get it over with, if we both know what we want." I feel it pressing, right up against me...

"Get the fuck off me!" Todd screams, flinging me off the couch. "What's the fucking matter with you?"

I'm forced into silence, on my ass, on the floor, looking back at the heaving mass of Todd on the couch.

"What did I do?"

"You were about to put my dick in your ass."

"I was just teasing. Jesus Christ. Freak out much?"

Todd buries his face in his hands, his dick now deflated and stuck to the mess on his belly. "Sorry, bro. Sorry."

I don't know what to say. He's right. I got caught up in the moment. I can't say for sure what would have happened if Todd hadn't stopped me. But I want him bad enough that I might've let my guard down tonight. He must think I'm such a slut! Barebacking my way all around town. When I've actually never done anything like that ever.

"Fine. So you don't want to fuck me. I get it. Loud and clear."

"No, Chase. I do. I really do."

"Then what is it?" I ask. "Saving your second load for Marty Brayden? Is he on his way when eWrecksion ends? 'Cause that would make sense. The go-go boy's just a warm-up. Who would fuck a nobody dancer when the porn star everybody wants is all over you?"

Todd sits, blinking. He wipes his hand across his lips, licks them. He sighs loudly, looking at the ceiling. "Marty Brayden? Yeah right. If there's one person in this world I couldn't possibly get it up for..." He trails off. "You don't know what the fuck you're talking about. You should go home."

And then, silence. Was that a serious request? Does he actually want me to go home? Well, I've come this far (no pun intended). I'm not stopping yet. Not until he actually tells me to go home.

"I don't want to go home," I say, crossing my arms over my chest. "I'm getting fucked tonight. And I'm not leaving until that happens."

Todd laughs, easing up my anxiety. "Fuck, you're so cute."

"Tight as hell too," I say, getting on my knees, facing away from him to show off my ass, leaning it just right on the heels of my feet. "You telling me you don't want this?"

"Fuck." He's getting hard again. Playing with himself. "You should go home, dude."

I stand back up and pad over to him, climbing up on the couch, sticking my ass just inches in front of his face. "The sexiest nightlife promoter in the city won't give it to a tight-assed twink who was just literally on his knees, BEGGING to get fucked? Really?"

"No. He won't," Todd says, holding me away, squirming away from me and across the couch. "Well, I mean, maybe?"

I spin around, and land next to him on the couch. I wrap my legs around him, grab his dick and mine in my hand, and jerk them off together. "Make. Up. Your. Mind."

Todd sighs again, his eyes rolling up. He's sighed at least forty times in the past five minutes. "Bro, you really want this?"

I nod.

"Why? So you can tell all the other go-gos you got fucked by Todd DiTempto?"

"I'm sure Nick is already taking care of that." I grin. "As for me, I'm actually a lot more interested in sleeping with Todd DiAngelo. Whoever he is."

"It's been a long night," Todd says. "I'm tired."

"I highly doubt it's been as long as mine," I reply. "Since I saw you last night at Splash, all I've wanted is to go home and sleep. And now that I'm here with you, going home and crawling into my bed alone sounds like the worst fucking idea ever."

"If you want this, you have to earn it."

"Oh, I'm prepared to."

"Okay." Todd stops my stroking and kisses me slowly. "Before we do this, I want you to tell me something. The most personal, most painful thing you can think of."

"That's a weird aphrodisiac." I laugh, utterly confused. "Kinda S and M–like. My pain for your pleasure?" I feel my fingertips gently caressing the tattoo on my belly before I even know my hand has moved. Obviously, I know what I'm going to tell him. Todd DiTempto and Chase Winterman have been working together for about a year; it's about time Chase Summers and Todd DiAngelo met too.

"I'll return the favor, I promise," Todd says. "But you go first. That's the rule. You don't like it, you're free to go."

Do I really want to do this? Wouldn't it be easier to remain the go-go boy and the superstar promoter? No strings attached?

It's so simple the way things are now. We meet in the dark. We hug and cheek-kiss hello. We see each other shirtless or in our underwear, maybe even less. Physically, we're almost completely exposed. Emotionally, we're hidden under layers and layers of thick armor. We wear masks—whatever guise we take with us into the club and then discard like a used condom the next morning. We do it because it's easy, and it's fun, and when the night ends, none of us really owes anybody anything. How much do we really want to know about each other? Aren't we better off being "types" than full-fledged people, battle scars and all?

Maybe it's because I'm just so fucking tired, but I don't have the energy to keep my defenses up now. It's about time someone knew a bit more about me.

"You're sexy." I smile. "And I'm not going anywhere." Why would I? I'm right where I always wanted to be, sitting naked next to Todd DiTempto—everything bared but my soul. And even that is about to change any minute now.

"Okay," Todd says, returning my smile. And then there is an even bigger sigh. "Here we go."

SERVANDO AND ROWAN'S RANDOM REUNION

Okay, so a rat showed up today. I have NO fucking idea where it came from, but once he got inside my and Servy's apartment, he started running around like he owned the place. We called Todd because he's good at solving everything, and just like we expected, he took care of him.

Well, almost took care of him. Though I guess imprisoning the rat was two-thirds of the battle. Still, Todd was as spooked as we were when it started screaming. He shrieked and booked it double-time. Which left ME to drag the stick with its captive, screeching prisoner along the floor, all the way out of the building, to the street, right?

You were freaking too, Servy. Stop pretending you're so butch.

You were freaking your shit too, Rowan!

I was pretending to freak out so you wouldn't feel so bad about actually freaking out.

Right. That's why we had to call Todd to come over with his lacrosse stick like some on-demand jock escort.

I totally would have killed it myself. I have a bat. I would have creamed it.

And yet you didn't. You were too busy, if I remember correctly, cowering on the bed.

Cowering's a strong word for it. And you were right there with me. Don't pretend YOU'RE the knight in shining armor during all this.

Todd's such a good friend. I'd get him a card if there were a "Thanks for Taking Care of That Giant Fucking Rat" section in Duane Reade.

They SHOULD have a section like that! Call it "Manhattan Greetings." It could be all sorts of cards for situations that only happen in NYC.

Yeah, like, "Thanks for Figuring Out How to Turn Off That Car Alarm Down the Street Last Night."

"Our Sympathies That Two Obnoxiously Loud Broadway-Belting Twinks Moved in One Floor Above You."

"Congratulations On Finding an Apartment That Doesn't Have a Shower in the Kitchen!"

"You're Like That Sock Salesman at Every Street Fair: One in a Million!" Uh…Where were we?

We were talking about how you are currently quivering with fear?

It's cold out! It's called shivering.

It's like a hundred degrees, Rowan!

Fine! So it freaked me out! So what? It freaked you out too!

I never said it didn't. I am happy to admit that it freaked the fuck out of me. It was UGLY.

No, girl, it was HIDEOUS.

All those teeth!

Fangs. And those zombie eyes!

Ugh, I don't want to think about it. Hey, do you know where Todd went?

Who EVER knows where Todd goes? Probably back to his apartment. You know how busy he is.

Truth. Well, now what are we going to do?

I don't know about you, but I need to blaze. Right the fuck now. These shakes are going to drive me insane.

All right. Except our weed is scattered all over the floor. Because of the rat. And smooshed because of all the running and screaming we did due to said rat...

Maybe I can try gathering up the little pieces...

Those are beyond "little" pieces. That is now weed dust mixed into carpet dirt. Just give it up, baby. It's a goner.

NO! Fuck me! This shit was like the holy grail of weed! I spent a Benjamin on it! Government Green isn't cheap!

Are you serious? Is it really from the government?

Nononononononoooooooo! Now is NOT the time for us to be dry. Shit! Shit! Shit!

Baby, come on. Chill. It's not crack, okay? Stop acting like a crack-HEAD. Let's just get something to eat. Pizza? Thai? There's a new Italian place that opened up down the street...

No.

Rowan...?

This was already bad. Now it's worse! It's like when you just smoked the last cigarette in the pack and you realize you won't be able to get another one for HOURS. I need it!

Okay. Gosh. So, fine, just call your dealer!

Yeah, good one. Hold on a sec.

Oh. My. God. Is he seriously number one on your speed dial?

Yeah. So?

Your DEALER is number one on your speed dial? What number am I?

Shh.

What number am I, Rowan?

You're number two! All right?

I'm number two? Ugh. That makes me feel like shit!

Will you shut your mouth for five fucking seconds so I can hear Jack Smack on the speaker? It's ringing.

Jack Smack. That's the dumbest fucking name in the world. Is that the best he could do? He sounds like a WWF wrestler, not a drug dealer.

Servando...

They should be held up to the same scrutiny as drag queens! That's all I'm saying. Does he actually sell smack, by the way?

Dude, I don't know. We only go for his green.

YOU only go for his green. I wouldn't know the first thing about weed buying or the integrity of our local dealers.

Whatever. It's always prime, and he gives me a discount because I introduced him to Todd and now he drinks for free whenever he comes out.

Yes, it's always nice when that straight creep shows up at the bar.

Be nice. He's about to save our day.

YOUR day, love. Mine's peachy as is.

Smack comes on the line, at last: "Rowan? That was fast. You out of green already?" His voice is rough and sleepy.

"Oh shit, did I wake you up?" I ask.

"You could say that. At least, I think I was asleep. Listen, I'm super crazed today. I didn't expect you to ring me up for another week, at least."

"Well, yeah, man. It's been a ridiculous morning. We had to deal with a rat. The weed was part of the collateral damage. And if there's ANY situation that calls for some mellow time, it's this."

"I really can't make it out there, Rowan."

"Come on, Smack. We need it!"

Sigh.

"If you were buying something heavier, I'd understand the urgent need for a delivery. But marijuana is nonaddictive. Go meditate or something. Take a yoga class. Go for a run with your boyfriend."

See, he's on the right track! Spend time with ME. When's the last time you went for a run, anyway?

"Smack. Please. I'm begging you! This is fucking serious."

Why don't you just ask him if we can meet him?

That's brilliant!

I'd call it common sense, but I'll take whatever praise I can get.

"Hey, Smack? What if me and Servy meet you somewhere? I don't care where! Where you going today? We'll meet you in Union Square, the Village, the Upper West Side…anywhere!"

"I guess I could make that happen."

"Really? Thank you! Where?"

"I'm gonna be up near the Bronx Zoo in about an hour or so. Meet me there."

"You got it. We'll be there as soon as we can."

"Don't forget the cash."

"Right! See you soon!"

There. That was easy.

Easy? Your sister's easy. Going to the BRONX? Oh, helllll no. I'm not going all the way up there!

Come on! It's just a hop, skip, and a jump!

A hop, skip, jump, and hour-plus train ride! During which you get stabbed no fewer than six times! Are you insane?

Enough with the drama! Was the rat not enough for one day? You sound like I just told you we have to cover you in honey and roll you around the floor at Penn Station to get the herb.

First of all, I do NOT sound like that. Second of all, that's really fucking far away!

So what? It'll be like an adventure! We can grab a bag, go smoke it somewhere, and then go check out all the animals. Weren't you JUST complaining that all we ever do is sit on the couch?

Yeah…

And have you ever been to the Bronx Zoo?

No. I've been to the Central Park one.

That's nothing compared to the Bronx! How did I never take you there before?

Maybe because I never said, "Hey, Rowan? You know what I'd love to do? Get in a subway for two hours to go stare at a bunch of bored-as-fuck monkeys picking shit out of each other's fur?"

It's not that bad and it doesn't take that long. It'll be cute, kinda romantic!

Rowan, we're way past the romantic stage of our relationship. And, come to think of it, we're past the "relationship" part too.

Well, if we're getting blazed, we gotta go uptown. And while we're there, we might as well go check out that new *Dora the Explorer* 3D ride they just opened.

What? I wasn't told that Dora would be a part of this.

I was saving it as a surprise.

I love Dora!

I hope so, otherwise it makes zero sense that you designed that Dora man-bag.

It's explorer couture!

Indeed it is. Go grab it and let's bounce.

Fine. But you owe me. And not just some of this magical government hooker stuff.

Government Green.

Whatever.

***

Most people are mystified by me and Row-Dawg. I can understand that—we definitely don't follow any standard, textbook-defined relationship rules. But it can get annoying.

Yes, okay, we used to date. Then we broke up. And we still live together. Still fuck together. (Guests always welcome! Interested?) And still do basically everything together. Weird, right? Now get over it and let's get a drink or something.

I mean, people do all sorts of weird shit in this world! There are furries who dress like foxes and wolves and Pokémon and get off on that. Other dudes who dress in a diaper and get off on being "changed." Certain dudes grease up their knuckles with Crisco and shove their fists up into other guys. Girls who strap on dildos and plow their boyfriends. Straight men star in gay porn; gay men star in straight porn. In this light, is my setup with Rowan really THAT bizarre? Aren't we all strange in our little, insignificant ways? And what does it matter, anyway, if we aren't bothering you?

Now, don't give me that shit about how it's "people like us" who are setting the gay rights movement back. Monogamy is a cute concept, but it doesn't work for everyone. The gays, the straights—we're all just super horny! And I'm okay with that. I have no interest in some bullshit standard that heterosexuals can't live up to, either. Politicians are cheating on their wives; wives are cheating on their politicians. Don't believe me? Check Gawker. In my humble opinion, nobody's doing a particularly good job of upholding the sanctity of marriage, so just leave me alone about it, okay? Thanks. Moving on.

And listen, I'm allergic to labels, okay? Honestly. I break out in hives. It all gets so much murkier and muddier when there's a label.

If we're boyfriends, we're expected to sleep with each other and nobody else. Snore. Do away with the label and the rule book is yours to write! If I meet a cute guy, I can go out with him (as long as I warn Rowan in advance). And vice versa. It doesn't bother us at all when this happens.

Also, no longer being boyfriends allows us to duck the whole "So when are you two getting married?" thing. Ugh. Don't get me started! It's like, ever since gays won the right to get married, it became an expectation that every single one of us needs to get hitched. Act now! Supplies won't last! Like it's some time-sensitive thing that will disappear if we don't all use it. Enough!

Rowan and I live together, sleep together, eat together, and go out together. What, exactly, would marriage achieve? Our friends would hate us because they would get that "Save the Date" card two years in advance of the magical day. Like we know anyone who can plan two years in advance? Ask any single gay man in this city which bar he'll be at tonight and see if you can get a definite answer. Oh—and then they have to buy us something stupid for our kitchen or our living room? We don't cook, and we live in a studio. Nice try. In fact, I'll bet that's the reason New Yorkers don't tie the knot (around their throats) nearly as early as our suburban brethren— we simply don't have anywhere to put all that shit.

And another thing—our parents don't even know we were ever dating. I doubt they even know we're gay. This is the benefit of Rowan's 'rents being somewhere in Wisconsin and mine retired in Mount Dora, Florida. I'm not saying they would take this news badly. I mean, they might, but it doesn't matter. If Rowan and I aren't dating, then we definitely aren't getting married. And if we don't marry, the in-laws never have to meet, and then we avoid the awkward situations that make perfect fodder for Ben Stiller comedies.

Plus, let's not forget the stress of getting that church or temple or sandy beach or whatever. Don't forget the caterers, the transportation, the flowers, and the cake. Endless stress to have one magical day that will inevitably go awry somehow.

And then what? We say, "I do." We kiss innocently with the same mouths that were just locked around each other's dicks that morning. Everyone claps and throws rice (or more bird-friendly fare). Then we get in the limo with the rattling cans bouncing behind us as we disappear off into the sunset to…our apartment in Hell's Kitchen? All that trouble and pomp and crap and there we are, right where we were that morning.

No. No, thank you. The notion of marriage hasn't even crossed my mind, honestly.

Right now, Rowan and I are doing all the same good stuff we did while we were together. Why mess with that? The word boyfriend *is a label, like one of those "Hi My Name Is…" stickers you put on at a networking event. And I don't fucking wear those, either! Nothing changes if we dive back into Boyfriendville.*

Well, nothing changes for the two of US. Everyone ELSE gets to breathe easy because we're following "the rules" again. Sometimes I think people would rather we were lying and sleeping around behind each other's backs than just being up front about it. At least that they'd "get."

I'm sorry. I hope I didn't just pop your wedding wonderland balloon. If you're excited about hunkering down for the long haul with the beau of your dreams, please go right on ahead. Just spare us all the questions and inquisitive glances. You do what works for you, and Rowan and I will do what works for us.

(P.S. Please don't send that "Save the Date" card too early, 'cause then we'll totally forget by the time said wedding actually happens.)

So, in conclusion, labels bring no pros and a Louis Vuitton wheelie full of cons to what is otherwise a simple, drama-free arrangement. I'll leave labels for other guys to stick to their lapels. And while THOSE guys are sweating and nervous about what, exactly, their kinda-sorta-maybe-whatevers are, Rowan and I will be watching Netflix and getting blazed.

***

The screech is about as loud as the rat we got rid of this morning. The train grinds to a halt, almost flinging me out of my seat. And then, nothing. Everyone looks up from their Kindles and iPhones.

Oh, great.

Relax, babe. It's nothing. This shit happens all the time. This IS the MTA we're talking about.

How comforting. I forgot a great New York City greeting card: "Congratulations on Riding a Train That Actually Reached Its Destination."

I'll be sure to get Hallmark on the horn. Anyway, it gives me an excuse to read these ads on the walls. They're usually pretty funny.

I've already read them, and they suck.

"We're sorry, we are stopped because of train traffic ahead of us," the Moviefone-esque voice of the subway says over a hidden speaker.

Of course there's train traffic ahead of us! That's how train tracks work! There are multiple trains on every track! And if they are all running like they're supposed to, there's no reason for any of them to slow down!

Chill, Servy. Count down from thirty and we'll be back on our merry way to Marijuana Lane, okay? Why don't you tell me what Dora did this week with that monkey friend of hers?

Don't treat me like a child, Rowan. I will slap you right here in front of these drunken jocks.

Whoa. No need to get violent, sugar beet.

Also, why the FUCK are they drunk already? It's not even dark yet!

Like we aren't brunch-drunk by this time on Sundays?

Fine, but are we THAT loud and obnoxious?

We're worse. How many restaurants have banned us at this point?

Point taken. Three, two, one…Okay, I've counted down from thirty. Choo-choo still isn't move-moving…

Then count another thirty seconds and stop acting like a baby.

Ouch. Sorry. Didn't realize you woke up on the bitch side of the bed this morning and then fell into a pile of other bitching bitches.

That doesn't even make sense!

I didn't even want to go uptown! Fuck you, Rowan!

"We're sorry, we are delayed because of a sick passenger at the next station," says the emotionless robot that holds our fate in his hands.

Well, which is it? Train traffic or a sick passenger? I bet you've got hundreds of passengers here who are sick to death of your bullshit!

You know, I heard "sick passenger" is their way of saying someone got hit by a train at another station.

Ew! Who told you that? That's terrible!

It might not be true, calm down. Just trying to make conversation that isn't wholly comprised of you complaining.

Oh my God, is someone dead? Oh my God!

Why did it just get quiet? Fuck. Subways aren't supposed to be silent. The air-conditioning just died! The rumbling underneath the car stopped. THAT isn't good.

Should I count down from thirty again?

"Hiya, folks," an actual human voice says over the speaker system. "I'm sorry about this, but this train is going to need servicing before it can run again. Thank you for understanding while we try to get this all sorted out. Shouldn't be too long."

But it DOES end up being too long, doesn't it, Rowan?

Shut up. I don't want to talk about it.

Fine, then I will. It takes thirty-plus fucking minutes! We're sitting underground between stations. And it's HOT. Ew! Those asshole jocks across the way think they're sooo funny, endlessly repeating the same three quotes from a movie so dumb it's probably what made them stupid in the first place. Two girls are huddled in a far corner, whispering to each other. Everyone else is totally quiet, like we're in a fucking library. Isn't that always the way in New York City? We can coexist smashing into each other everywhere, as loud as can be, so long as we're in motion. But now that we're stuck here, we're in elevator mode: not looking at each other, staring at our shoes and bags and the advertisements and the poles in front of our faces. Anything to avoid actual interaction.

Okay, Queen Servando. It's not THAT bad. Yes, it's warm, and yes, those douche bags are annoying, but so what? We can't be stuck here forever. What, do you want to talk to everyone on the train? Sing "Kumbaya" or some shit? Go ahead! At least then I won't have to deal with you until this fucking train starts moving again.

Wow. Why are you SUCH a fucking asshole today?

I'm not an asshole. You're being a complete bitch!

Really?

Yeah. Really.

What the fuck! Is it that goddamned rat? Big deal! It's gone! And thanks but no thanks, I don't feel like dealing with your attitude. In case YOU forgot, I was the one who didn't need to get blazed in the first place! I would have been fine staying home and getting lunch. But no, you need to have your smokeout to settle your fucking fragile nerves. And now, because of you, we're trapped here just like rats with no idea of when we'll be back aboveground again. It's been an HOUR! Nothing about the fucking MTA ever works! Every train is simultaneously broken down and being serviced! Stations close without warning and trains change tracks and go places they shouldn't every damn day! And all the while, we're getting charged more and more for a monthly pass! While they cut service, put trains out to pasture permanently, close help booths! Why can't anything in this city just fucking work?!

Jesus CHRIST! You've been a sarcastic, whiny, unhinged lunatic all morning! You don't like the subway? Get a bike! You don't want to come to the zoo? Don't come next time. *I'm* frail and need to chill? Look in the fucking mirror! Fuck this! I don't even want to be near you right now. Just shut up.

Oh, I'll shut up.

Do.

I will!

The guy comes back on the speaker: "Okay, everyone, we're going to try this again. Hopefully we've figured out the problem and we'll be back on our merry way. Again, so sorry for the trouble. Thanks for understanding."

Thank GOD.

Air-conditioning comes spewing out of the vents over our heads. The belly of the train starts rumbling, shaking my ass numb. The lights on the wall of the subway tunnel quickly become passing blurs.

"There we go! And we're back online, folks. Thank you for riding with the MTA."

Like we have a choice?

Whoa, Servy. Why are you standing up? This isn't our stop.

...

Why are you looking at me like that?

...

Because I told you to shut up?

...

Ugh. Fine. UN–shut up. And sit down. We're not even close yet.

I'm getting off.

What?

You heard me. I'm getting off. Have fun at the fucking zoo.

Servy, stop fucking around. I'm really not in the mood.

No. Fuck. You. I'M not in the mood. I never WAS in the mood! I'm going home. You go get stoned, since that's your number one prior-ity. You've made it perfectly clear that I am number two.

Can we just talk about this later?

Nope. And don't bother texting or calling me, either. I'll see you when I see you.

What! Are you serious?

The doors swish open, the subway speakers chime, and suddenly, I'm alone.

I don't follow. I can't. Because I've never seen him this pissed before, so I have no idea what he would do—or what I would do—if I went after him. And I'm too fucking proud or stubborn or whatever to scream an apology. Because he WAS being a whiny bitch!

Whatever. It doesn't matter. He's already left the station and I'm speeding away, farther north, to the zoo. Now I REALLY need to get stoned.

***

I've been standing next to this giant wooden cutout of a caterpillar for at least forty-five minutes.

I've read through the Bronx Zoo's list of special events five times, thanks to the paper program I picked up by the ticket booths. Turns out the Dora ride is closed for repairs, so I dodged a bullet there, at least. A special insects exhibit opened up next to the butterfly house (hence the giant caterpillar). The food court is proud to announce that their chicken nuggets are now shaped like elephants and monkeys.

I am in a wide, cobblestoned plaza that stands between a dead-end street and the entrance to the zoo. Families pass every few minutes, taking pictures with the caterpillar before approaching the ticket booth to buy day passes. The parents have cameras dangling around their necks and fanny packs full of snacks and money around their waists. The kids are sometimes wearing animal masks, sometimes shoving candy in their mouths, sometimes begging for the All-Day Pass Plus that lets you ride the Sky Tram in addition to eight hours of gawking at all of the caged animals. Seeing the little ones run wild and scream like hyenas, I can only think, *What a zoo.*

Jack Smack is nowhere to be found, of course. I know this because I've tried calling five fucking times, and each one ended with his damn voice mail: "Yo. It's Smack. Not here. Be smart about what you leave as a message. Peace."

I hang up for the sixth time and return to the bench that's quickly become my second home. This is the worst thing EVER. I can't see the animals, as they're all hidden behind tall walls. That hasn't stopped the pungent aroma of animal shit from reaching me, though. It's getting cloudy and cold, and I'm regretting not bringing a hoodie. But how could I have possibly known? It's fucking August! How did it go from sweaty-balls hot to ball-shrinking cold this quickly?

Normally, when I'm this bored, I'd text back and forth with Servy. Or check Grindr, then see if Servy's interested in inviting someone back to our place for some sexytime.

Not today, obviously, since Servy has declared that I'm a piece of shit who is not to contact him until he deems me worthy of forgiveness.

No Servy for Rowan.

Funny how that one sentence has left me with nothing.

Fuck, man—I blew it back there, didn't I?

Well…blew what?

When people ask why me and Servy do what we do, I shrug. His answer is much longer-winded and more logical. He's got a whole speech prepared. (Have you heard it yet?)

I, on the other hand, am amongst the majority who doesn't really "get" us. (Don't tell Servando.) I don't know why we're not boy-friends. Is "Because" a good enough answer? How about "Because Servy said so"? People think I'm badass when I shrug, like I've got it all figured out and just can't be bothered to explain it. That couldn't be further from the truth. I'm afraid if I tried to put it into words, I would only realize that I actually don't have a reason and have to come to terms with the fact that we are actually boy-friends. Open boyfriends, sure, but boyfriends nonetheless. Just two label-phobe guys. What a zoo, indeed.

Explaining the hows and whys is Servy's job. He's our PR per-son, and he's damn good at it. No one ever asks us more than once—unless they want to watch Servy foam at the mouth just for kicks.

But why the fuck does everyone care? So many of our friends are lonely or jaded, and yet somehow we're the low-hanging fruit (no pun intended)—easy targets for their comments and questions. Bug off, bitches!

Funny shit is, I'm just as upset right now as I would be if we WERE boyfriends. My head is a ping-pong game between *Dude Where's My Weed* and *The War of the Roses*. Trying to think of anything else fails. I guess it's silly that we aren't official, but popping the question now would be awfully moronic.

I get up from the bench and plod back to the caterpillar. It's about six feet tall, which would be pretty fucking scary if it were alive. It's green, with big, buggy eyes and round, fat circles making up its body. A huge clown smile. I'm pretty sure that's not scientifically correct. Judging by its faded color, no one's ever thought to bring him in when it started raining.

Speaking of, the sky stopped being sunny twenty minutes ago. A hopeful umbrella vendor has already dragged a squeaky-wheeled cart to the plaza entrance, where he now leans against the gate, smoking a cigarette and looking hopefully skyward.

It's at least a ten-minute walk back to the aboveground subway station. If it starts raining, I'll be drenched by the time I get there, cheap crappy umbrella or not.

Fuck!

I pull a Clif Bar out of my pocket. Carrot cake flavored, my favorite. I was going to save it for after I smoked; as delicious as it is on its own, it tastes a billion times better when I'm flying high. But that's shot to shit. I'm starving and every growl of my stomach only pisses me off more.

Three bites and it's gone. I abandon my new best friend Mr. Caterpillar for a garbage can across the entry plaza so I can chuck the wrapper. Hopefully that snack will stop the tummy grumbling.

I've been staring at my phone by the garbage can for five minutes when a hand grabs my shoulder.

"Yo, Row."

"Oh my fuck, you actually came." I laugh, turning around and putting Smack in a bear hug. He smells like BO and his clothing

257

probably hasn't been washed in days, but I could kiss him regardless.

"Yeah, sorry. My last guy didn't have enough money for the goods, and I had to wait around while he ran to the damn bank."

Jack is a heavy straight guy who dresses at all times in black Gap jeans, solid-black T-shirts, and a black leather jacket. His hair is just as black as the rest of his outfit, greasy and slicked back. He looks more like some goth kid you'd find sitting by himself at the high school cafeteria than one of the best dealers in New York City. It's even more ridiculous when he stops by one of Todd's parties to take advantage of the bar tab Todd gave him as a favor to me.

"It's fine, Smack. It is SO totally fine. You should probably ignore the crazy-person voice mails I left you. I just thought you flaked on me." I stop babbling to reach into my wallet. "One fifty?"

Jack usually takes orders, but he knows mine by heart. I take an ounce of what he calls Government Green. Apparently it's grown legally in California and then airmailed directly to him. Whether that's true or just a salesman story to boost profits is not important. It brings a great high with minimal paranoia, exactly what I need in life. It costs a few bucks more than his Schwag Weed, but it's a premium I'm willing to pay.

"Two hundred, actually," Jack says, stepping back. "Rush fee plus delivery."

My hand stops as it goes through the wallet. "What?"

"Yeah. Two hundred. Just this one time. When we're back on the schedule, we'll go back to your normal price."

I laugh, almost dropping my wallet on the ground. "You're hilarious, Smack! Take the money so we can get high and move on with our lives."

"I'm not kidding, bud," Jack says, his face not moving an inch more than it has to to get the words out. "Two hundred."

"Wait, what? Why didn't you tell me while we were on the phone?"

Smack looks at me. Or I think he is. It's hard to tell through his gigantic sunglasses. "I didn't say that on the phone?"

"No, I don't think you did, brother. Otherwise, I would have brought that much! When's the last time I've shown up for a deal short? Come on, where is it? Do I have to search your pockets? You know I will!"

"I'm pretty sure I told you, Rowan," Smack says. "I only give you free delivery downtown."

"Smack, I don't HAVE two hundred. And you TOLD me to come up here and meet you. I would have met you at your place if you asked me to."

"Like hell I'd let you near my place. There isn't an ATM in the zoo?" he asks, gesturing past me and in the direction of the caterpillar.

"It'll cost me thirty bucks just to go inside and get to it."

"Yeah," Jack says, rubbing a hand through his greasy hair. "Yeah, I dig it."

"Are we done here yet? Can I get my stuff?" I say, handing him my money.

"No. No. Sorry," Jack says, stepping backward again. "Two hundred, or I'm going home."

"Smack!" I whisper, looking around to make sure this shit show isn't getting any attention. In hindsight, doing a deal in a space as open as this was probably pretty dumb. Then again, I can't think until I get high. "Dude, you know I'm good for it. If you don't take one fifty, then you just leave with nothing. Does that make any sense?"

"It's the principle of the thing, my friend. I can go sell this to someone else without the friendly discount I always give you and make more on the transaction."

Fuck me. He isn't kidding.

The end of my shakes and a blissful blaze is being held hostage by this pudgy, greasy breeder. Is it pitiful to admit that I'm about to cry? I have to take a deep breath to keep from sobbing. I'm at the end of my fucking rope for today, and Smack is standing there, smiling like a dick and patting the pocket where he's probably holding the stuff. MY stuff. I would do ANYTHING for this right now.

"Smack, please. I'm, like, your biggest customer."

He laughs and lifts his glasses, revealing cracked and red eyes. Of course HE'S stoned. I'm so jealous I could scream. "Rowan, you aren't anywhere near my biggest customer. I've got a guy downtown who buys five times as much every other day. And even he's not my biggest customer."

Okay, now I'm crying. Fuck, talk about feeling like an addict! I tell Smack about the rat, the fight with Servando. I beg him to understand. I call him shady for throwing this extra fee on top of the normal amount. I beg him to look deep within his heart to understand and to give it to me for one fifty.

Smack considers this, picking his nose and inspecting what comes out before he says, "Yeah. No. I got some other stuff on me if you want to try something new to take the edge off your day. Otherwise—"

I shake my head. "I just want my shit. My usual shit."

"Then get the rest of the cash and I can hook you up next week. Usual shit, usual day, usual price. Usual everything. But add another fifty to pay me back for coming all the way out here. Who shows up to a deal with the exact amount? That's amateur shit, bud."

I nod and say, "See you next week."

"Two hundred," he says as he turns around. "Don't forget."

I want to jump Smack and take the weed by force. Not only because I desperately need to get high, but also because he's being such a douche about it. He did NOT tell me two hundred. He did NOT. And now he's acting like I inconvenienced HIM. What the fuck? He probably brought me to the Bronx just to punish me for not sticking to my regular delivery. Or who knows what the fuck a drug dealer is thinking? With the element of surprise on my side, I could get him to the ground, grab the weed, and be well on my way at the speed of light before he knew what hit him.

But I'm too smart for that. He's probably carrying, for one—and if he didn't shoot me in the face here in the plaza, he'd at least never sell to me again, then see to it that all his dealer friends knew I was not to be trusted. I'd never be high in this city again. And while I'm ready to lose my mind right here, I'd lose it a lot more if I couldn't buy weed anymore.

I watch Smack waddle back to the dead-end street. He jams himself into a beaten-up Peugeot, keys the stuttering ignition, and putters away.

I stand in the plaza as a family walks by, kids skipping and laughing. We all just came here to have a good fucking time. So why am I the only one going home empty-handed?

Then I feel something. Cold. Wet.

I feel it again.

Raindrops. And the umbrella guy's gone!

Fuck.

I run. Exactly one block later, the sky wreaks havoc. By the time I get to the subway, my shirt and pants have become an additional layer of drippy, cold skin. My sneakers squish and squeak as I run up the stairs to the aboveground station. My hair wilts into my face, releasing warm, itchy drops into my eyes.

I have never needed to smoke more than right now. And that won't be happening until at least Wednesday night. If I can even survive until then.

I take out my phone to text Servando. Because of the rain on the screen, the text message starts typing itself: *"JHShbvasiah-sIUASHHS!?"* Which is a surprisingly accurate transcription of what I'm feeling. I delete the text and stare at the screen.

Fuck. It's, like, an automatic thing, isn't it? Stress calls, text Servando. I know he doesn't want to talk, yet I pulled up our bazillion-message-long conversation without thinking. And since he doesn't want me adding to it at the moment, I decide to go back to the past, see if I can wring some comfort out of prior correspondence. I scroll up, tapping and dragging for minutes until I get to the top. There, I find a seemingly vague exchange: me telling Servando that I miss him and I'm hungry, and he responds that he'll only be stuck "here" for another few minutes. Then he'll pick up pizza on his way home.

I remember now. He attended a coworker's party on a Friday night a few months ago. I decided to be cute and wait for him to come home before I ate. (Well, I totally snarfed a Hot Pocket, but could you blame me? I hadn't eaten since lunchtime.) Servy came back just like he said he would, toting four slices of pizza so hot and wet that they left grease stains on the crinkled paper underneath.

Man, I'm hungry again. I want to be home. I want to be with Servy. Fuck the weed. I need to be in his arms, pigging out, getting sauce all over my face. We could see what's on the DVR and then threaten to call Time Warner's customer service center when the playback skips all over the place. There's a good Manhattan Greetings card in that scenario somewhere…but I can't find it without Servando.

Instead, here I stand, shivering my face off while sheets of rain fall, somehow sneaking between the cracks of the overhang above to keep me sufficiently soaked.

Soggy shoes. No weed. Even the cash in my wallet is a sodden clump of useless tender.

I want to text Servy so bad. Tell him I'm on my way home so he's waiting for me with food and open arms when I splash into our apartment and fall on my knees in a puddle apologizing to him.

But something tells me that's not going to happen.

Something's different this time.

***

And THAT is another reason why I won't date Rowan ever again.

When Rowan wants something, suddenly that's ALL that's important. And, usually, that's WEED. We need to be stoned before, during, and after EVERYTHING. Seeing a movie? Let's get high! Going out to the country for the weekend? Better buy a double order! Lunchtime? Not 'til we get blazed!

Jesus!

Yes, I smoke a lot too. But I'm not some Harold and Kumar weed fanatic who absolutely needs to light up every five and a half minutes. I do it when he does it, and not even EVERY time he does it.

But Rowan? I can't think of more than five occasions on which he's been sober. I haven't seen him without red eyes since we started dating. The apartment always reeks when I get home from work, our studio filled with the nauseating smoke that only becomes bearable if you're high from it as well.

I'd probably never touch the stuff if it weren't for him. No—I know I wouldn't. It never did much for me. Before Rowan and I met, I smoked up at parties every now and then, and only because everyone else was doing it. It certainly wasn't with the habitual regularity and dedication of Rowan, who still denies it's a problem. Because it isn't harmful like other drugs? Bullshit! If it makes you lazy and stupid and the only active thing you manage to do is eat everything in the house, then what's the difference? I'd rather date an alcoholic. At least they want to go out! The only reason I join in on his favorite pastime anymore is because I can't stand being clear-headed when Rowan's on the green. Everything is so funny to him. I hate being left out of a joke.

Now I might as well be stoned because I don't know where I am. I was so pissed when I flew off the train that I didn't bother checking the signs that tell you where the hell you are. The station smelled like homeless pee, so I didn't stick around. Just breathed through my mouth and got back aboveground.

I look around me. I know I'm still in Manhattan—at least I think I am? I just wanted to walk and be pissed, and in so doing have completely lost my bearing. No idea which direction the subway is.

Around me, the crowds on the sidewalks are a far cry from those in my neighborhood. More diverse and ethnic compared to the tight-shirted and tighter-jeaned white boys of Hell's Kitchen. A short old Hispanic woman with her hair in a wrap pushes a squeaky, empty shopping cart. Two women with dark-black hair tied back in tight, gelled ponytails are laughing and joking in Spanish. A fire hydrant across the street has been dismantled, shooting water into the gutter. R & B and salsa music pour out of open windows up and down the block.

Rowan's probably already at the zoo, meeting up with his number one favorite person in the whole wide world. I'll bet he's not even upset. I'll bet he's forgotten ALL about me, since his actual boyfriend, weed, is there and in no short supply. Hey, hey! More for Rowan. Om nom nom. He's surely sitting in the zoo food court with Jack Smack, chowing down on animal crackers, their minds blown by something they saw an elephant do.

And here I am, lost and clueless. Somewhere.

It's getting cloudy. Where the fuck is the nearest Starbucks? I'm pissed, and when I'm in a bad mood, a Mocha Frappuccino is called for.

I don't recognize any of the businesses on these streets. Fried chicken, tons of hair salons filled with people just sitting around listening to music, iglesias *with barbed wire and locked metal gates. A single chain store would put my mind at ease, proof that corporate America is brave enough to tread these streets. But there are none here. The signs above the bodegas are either in Spanish or terrible English.*

I've lived in this city for four years and I've never been up here. An uncomfortable sensation in the pit of my stomach worsens as I wander. No subways. No buses. Just gypsy cabs and the corpses of dismantled bicycles lashed to rusty bike racks or street signs on the corners.

Get me the fuck out of here.

I need to be back downtown, where the faces are friendly and familiar. FUCK YOU, Rowan! Now I'm lost uptown with no idea how to get home. I don't have a dollar to my name, and these gypsy cabs won't take credit cards!

My phone, despite having a signal, stutters and fails at locating me on a digital map. Meanwhile, the sky grows darker.

People I pass on the street regard me as I would if I saw them wandering by themselves down in Hell's Kitchen: with what looks like a mixture of curiosity and defensiveness. I take a deep breath, shove my hands in my pockets, and start whistling a tune I make up as I go.

What if I got mugged? No. I don't need to start scaring myself. I just have to hang on to my anger at Rowan, find a subway, and get back downtown.

On any given day, I usually crash into someone I know on the street, but not here. That would be perfect. "Servy! What are you doing up here? Yeah, can you believe it? We got an apartment— tough neighborhood, but the amenities are worth it! Wanna come by? We're ordering arepas." Yes, I would love for that to happen. But it won't. The only people I encounter are clusters of thuggish-looking guys who are eyeing me like I need to be taught a lesson.

I'm a fish out of water. A stranger has come to town, and the towns- folk aren't about to welcome him.

A loud banging makes me jump and scream, immediately attract- ing the attention of everyone on the sidewalk. Great. It was just a truck driving quickly over a loose metal plate in the center of the street.

Fuck, I'm scared.

Fuck, I want to get out of here.

FUCK.

I have friends who've had their asses beaten by roving gangs in far more gentrified areas of the city than this. I'm just asking for trouble here.

I stop my messy whistling, grab my phone, and pretend to have a conversation with nobody. "Hey, Rowan! How's it going?"

I continue searching for a subway, babbling mindlessly to my dead phone. But is a subway the smart decision? If I go underground, I'm trapped like a rat.

A RAT? Oh shit! This is karma. Payback for this morning. The rodents appealed to a higher power and asked the fates to put me in this shitty mess. What if a gang of guys is waiting down there? Eyeing my iPhone and wondering how much cash I have on my person?

Fuck me.

No—fuck Rowan.

"Hey, buddy. You lost?"

I look up to find a group of five Hispanic men in front of me on the sidewalk. They wear baggy, torn jeans and jerseys that hang off their shoulders, exposing their chests, nipples, and long, detailed tattoos on the sides of their bodies. The one who spoke to me is as big as a house, with a bright-green do-rag wrapped around his head.

Of course the side street I randomly wandered down is empty. No gypsy cabs. No women pushing shopping carts. No kids chasing each other in circles. Just me and this gang of guys, arms crossed and muscles flexed, like they've been waiting for someone like me to happen by.

I shake my head and mutter that I'm not lost, returning to my fake conversation as I walk by.

"ANYWAY, Rowan. Yeah, I couldn't believe they said that, either. What, no, I'm nearby! Oh, you wanna meet up?"

Now I'm even more on edge.

They were just asking if I knew where I was, right? Street thugs can be polite citizens too! Right? So that's the end of that. I can go back to finding my way home.

Fuck! They're following me.

I can feel it: a prickly heat on my back, like I just put on a shirt fresh out of the dryer, covered in static energy. Their footsteps are getting louder. They're intentionally stomping, quicker and quicker, as they catch up to me.

I slip my phone into my pocket and walk a little faster, using the full length of my long legs to cover more ground. My God, I'm wishing I hadn't abandoned Rowan on the train. Would the thugs harass us if we were BOTH passing by? Probably not. Rowan doesn't look half as gay as me, and he isn't afraid to throw down. I've seen him punch. I've seen him scratch and kick and go after people's eyes—always in self-defense. Rowan wouldn't pick a fight if you paid him, but when it's called for, he's like a caged animal that's been jostled and poked and then finally released. Stand back or die.

I really need him right now.

"Hey, pato," *someone else from the group pipes up. "You ignoring us?"*

I know what "pato" means. It's about as close to "faggot" as you can get in Spanish. The last time I heard that was in the stockroom of a clothing store I worked at during college, and I got the dickhead who muttered it fired. Back then, it was merely offensive. Now it's scary as hell. No managers to mediate, no friends to cock an eyebrow and squeal, "Gurl! Did he just say what I think he said? Oh NO he didn't!"

I have no fucking idea what to do. I walk faster. Running would be dumb—that's just throwing meat in a tiger cage. Fuck.

A few blocks away, a siren starts blaring. PLEASE be headed this direction. Those red-and-blue lights would be like taking two Xanax.

Please.

The siren fades instead of getting louder. I have nowhere to go. Every business is locked and boarded up. When the siren goes quiet, my heart has taken its place, doing a breakdance in my chest.

I curse my outfit. Shirts don't get any more skintight than the one on my back. My pants are perfectly cuffed. My hair coiffed and swoopy. And this Dora man-bag! You won't find a more conspicuous "pato" than me. Benefits at a dance club, all of these fashion choices are now a rainbow-colored bull's-eye, indications that I am far, far, FAR from where I belong.

"Look at him, swooshing back an' forth!" *another voice says, followed by four mocking, deep-throated laughs. Someone snorts and spits. It hits the back of my head, drips down my neck.*

I should turn around.

No. I should keep walking. I should wipe the spit off my head. Or should I leave it there? Should I scream? Would that do anything?

Probably not. Not here.

"You scared, pato? You wanna show us how good you are at sucking dick?"

Their footfalls speed up. I imagine them descending on me, all fists and feet and laughter. The bruises and blood. Would they let me out alive if I just surrendered anything of value on my person?

Fuck, I was so stupid to get off here! Where am I? How do I get home?

"Hey! Pato! You gonna suck our dicks or what?"

There's a hand on my shoulder now, grabbing me, pinching the skin hard, turning me around. The owner of the hand, the biggest of them, the leader, says, "Show us how good you use that pretty pussy mouth of yours!"

I'm surrounded. Scarred, pockmarked faces challenge me silently. Their tattoos are brighter, fiercer. I'm trapped and they're enjoying every minute.

My mouth moves without permission. "I'm just trying to get back downtown, thanks."

"Oh, you're not going downtown, pato. You're staying right here." *The leader, with muscles bigger than my waistline, pushes me backward and laughs.*

I flail and crash into the sizable chest of one of the other guys. "Don't touch ME, pato!" *he yells, shoving me back to the guy who pushed me in the first place.*

"Leave me alone!" *I scream.*

The leader of the group has a full beard and mustache. He's holding me by the shoulders, grinning at me. "Hey, boys, should we let pato alone? Let him go back downtown?"

Snickers and giggles.

"No, I don't think we're gonna do that, buddy."

I'm going to cry. I'm going to scream. I don't know what to do.

Wait.

Yes, I do.

I throw a punch. A short uppercut to the guy holding me. Then another. And one more for good measure.

I've never punched someone before in my life; I guess I was waiting for a good excuse.

All my time at the gym seems to have paid off. The three guys I take swings at fall back in shock, clutching their faces. I kick the fourth in the balls, taking a shot to my chest in the process. I lose my breath, but don't need it. To that last guy, I drop all semblance of masculinity and scratch him across his face, poking him in the eye, then swing at him with my Dora bag. The stainless-steel snaps rake across his face, bringing blood after them.

Then I run.

"Fucking faggot!" one of them screams. But he is far behind me. They all are.

I sprint. They pursue, but they don't stand a chance. It's not their fault; they have no idea that Servando Reyes was a track star back in college. That, as recently as four years ago, he took his sprint team all the way to nationals.

Well, maybe they know now.

My brain has shut down. I am all feet. Lift and drop, push forward the moment the sole hits the ground. I'm not wearing running shoes, but I make do. And I'm NOT turning around to check up on their progress. I refuse to do a damned thing that'll slow me down.

I hear the voices getting farther and farther behind, their screams of rage becoming tinier by the second.

I am back on an avenue, sprinting too fast to read its name. It doesn't matter. I can see, in the distant skyline, the Empire State Building. That's all I need to know: south. I will sprint until I know exactly where I am.

And when I get there, I'm going to Barrage and ordering one of those fucking frozen cosmopolitans! I will get the most amazing brain freeze as I suck it down and tell everyone in the place what just happened. Because, right now, I feel like some crazy action movie hero. Jackie Chan or Vin Diesel or The Rock. Except I can also run—and when it's one on five, there's no shame in fleeing.

"Fuck you! Go suck each other's dicks!" I scream over my shoulder, even though the guys must have given up blocks ago. I scream it again and pick my feet up even higher as I speed back to sanctuary in Hell's Kitchen.

Thunder. Lightning. It's pouring. A blessing—the shock of cold gives me an extra kick to hurtle forward even faster. This is the final scene of a fucking movie and I'm the star, baby.

But in the midst of this victory lap, or whatever you want to call it, there's Rowan.

Not on the street, just in my head.

He's the only guy I really want to tell my amazing story to, because I know how proud he'd be. He gets like that whenever I succeed at any little thing: haggling over the price of a new outfit, getting a raise at work, doesn't matter. And that smile he gets when he's proud of me, it's the only time he uses it. Like he reserves it just for me. The story of what I just went through would have him on the ground, laughing his ass off. He'd make me tell it over and over, asking for every little detail, and I would happily recount it—maybe embellish a bit. ("No, it wasn't five guys…It was more like ten!")

But there's no way it'll go down like that now. Not when you consider how pissed off he was.

And yeah, he was a jerk, but I guess I was too. I could have just gone along with the trip to the Bronx, made an outing of it. Maybe I didn't have to be SUCH a bitch.

Nothing like almost getting your ass killed to put things in perspective, huh?

I'd text this revelation to Rowan, but I can't right now. Not until I get home. Not until I am 100 percent positive that the thugs are a distant memory. Then I'll apologize, and hopefully Rowan will too. We'll smoke the weed he bought from Jack Smack, then have some of the roughest, hottest apology sex of all time.

No—I push that thought away as soon as I have it, 'cause it'll be a lot harder to sprint home with an erection (no pun intended).

The crowds get thicker on the sidewalk, forcing me to weave back and forth between elbows and strollers and shopping bags. I take a quick peek up at a street sign. I am in the mid-hundreds. A few miles from home. I cut into the street, sprinting even faster. Man, even my screaming lungs feel good. I need to get back in the habit of running. Maybe try and qualify for the marathon next year.

And who knows? Maybe Rowan is home already. Won't he be surprised to see that his baby came home looking for loving?

Right now, that's all I need.

***

When I get home, Servy is nowhere to be found. Judging from the way things look, he hasn't been here since we left together this morning.

Dammit. It doesn't help that I'm still freaked out, casing the joint like the rat is the killer in a horror movie, hiding in a shadowy corner, always returning for one final scare. I switch on the light and scream, "HA!" to scare it into showing itself. Todd's lacrosse stick is still leaning against the wall by the door, and considering the mood I'm in, I am completely capable of beating the little thing to death.

But there's no rat. We dragged him out to the street hours ago. I'm just some idiot screaming at an empty apartment.

Make that a dripping-wet idiot. Great. I strip out of my wet clothing, hang it in the shower. To address the excess adrenaline running through me, I clean the mess Servando and I created during our early-morning rat race. I pick up scattered magazines and pile them on a bookcase. I switch on the vacuum and suck up the stray green of Smack's delivery from last week. I giggle at the thought of lifting the vacuum to my mouth and lighting the bag. And then that's not funny anymore, and I go back to putting shit away.

As I wash dishes, my ears perk up every few seconds. I find myself hoping that every sound they detect is the creak of our front door opening. But no. It's the PlayStation's fan, or a creak from the heater, or the air conditioner turning itself back on. Never my boyf—

I mean, my whatever.

Ha. Okay, we've agreed not to use that label, and that's fine. But "boyfriend" is how I think of him, in private, in my own head.

My little secret.

It's been thirty minutes. I can't just sit and do nothing. What do I normally do when I'm here alone? Well, I guess I'd be smoking. Stupid addiction. Now, without weed or Servy, I've got nothing. Make that two stupid addictions, I guess.

To keep myself occupied, I drag the vacuum into the studio area and get under the futon, under our bed, under the dressers, and into the closet. When that's done, I make a cup of ramen, filling the room with the aroma of MSG and imitation, freeze-dried shrimp. It burns my lips and tongue when I sip too fast.

Forty-five minutes. Still no Servando. I look down at my phone for the fifteenth time in three minutes and see the same thing: No e-mails. No texts. No updates or notifications whatsoever. No nothing. I almost text him, but no. I can't. He wants to be left alone, and I'm going to show him I don't need to be in touch 24/7, even though that's exactly the fucking case.

Dammit, Servando! Do you know how important you are to me? Clearly, you're my everything, since I'm shit out of things to do when you're not here.

I have other friends, though—right? I'll call them. Todd's phone rings five times and then goes right to voice mail, which is as dead-end as you can get with him. Todd hasn't checked his voice mail since it was invented. Instead, I text him: *"Hey, what's up tonight? Anything good?"*

Five minutes pass with no response.

This is not how it usually works. On weekend nights, Todd sends group texts to all of us—Servy, me, Brayden, Shane. In no more than the maximum amount of allowed characters for a single message, Todd informs us what time we'll meet at his place to pregame. If there's a dress code, that's also included.

But tonight, Todd hasn't texted. Our hot-party alert system is down. By now we should already know how our night will unfold, whether it's a traditional Hell's Kitchen bar crawl or one of his events.

What the hell?

Ten minutes later, I have texted Todd four times and still not received a response. I've called Shane and Brayden, only to spend some quality time with their voice mails as well.

I sit on the bed, staring at the empty kitchen and the door. Then at my legs. Then at the television, which isn't even on. Then at the time display on the cable box. It's been ONE HOUR since I got home? Have hours always gone this slowly? I need to get out of here.

Why hasn't he called? Is he really that angry? Yes, I said some mean things, but Servando did too. This is quickly setting a record for the longest period of time we've not interacted after an argument. And it really wasn't that big a conflict to begin with! Is this the guy I'm kinda dating? Really? Someone who KNOWS I'll be waiting for his text or call, who takes sick pleasure in withholding? Someone who would intentionally leave me here worried and alone?

We fight all the time, no biggie. When you've been together—or kinda together—for as long as we have, arguments arise out of everything. If I left a plate out in the sink, or he didn't text me before he went out to a party.

I guess we have been fighting more than ever lately, but so what? They're never anywhere near serious. We're having tiffs. Bickering. Like cute couples do.

Except…We're not one.

Maybe this is it. The last straw. Fuck.

My stomach flips when I think about Servando coming home to tell me that this is over. Why not? We're not together. Is it easier to end a relationship when it isn't, technically, a relationship to begin with?

I look around the apartment, take stock of everything, separating what's mine from what's his. If Servando broke up with me, how long would we be stuck living together? I wouldn't be able to stay. I'd ask Todd to crash in Gulliver's old bedroom. And when it comes to custody, Servando better not think that Brayden, Shane, and Todd are his. I knew them first. They're MINE.

My goddamned eyes are tearing. Really? Could a stupid fight on the subway be all it takes to turn off Servando permanently? To stomp out whatever was left of us? Or is this the result of a cumulative pile of crap that just got too heavy for what was holding it up?

Fuck, I need to smoke.

I'm DONE with this. How long do I plan on waiting around, just in case Servando changes his mind and decides to call us official again? How many potential ACTUAL boyfriends in this city passed me by as I headed home with my whatever-he-is every day, thinking, *Gee, maybe THIS is the night he'll cave and tell me he's ready to try again. Try the label again. Try US again.*

I never wanted this fucking nameless bullshit. That was all Servando.

I said it was okay that boyfriends are attracted to other guys. He said no. He wanted to play around, and he couldn't do it with this label. He ALWAYS calls the shots when it comes to this shit, and I go right along with it. I let him hold the reins and yank me along. I act like this is enough for me. Enough for ANYONE.

But it's not. Not by a long shot.

And if Todd isn't going to write back and Servando is going to be a dickhead and Shane and Brayden won't answer their phones, either, then I guess I'm all alone.

And if I'm alone, then I'm going out.

I fire up Grindr. I immediately feel better as the *pop!* of incoming messages sounds. Now, that's more like it. Looks like there are at least twenty complete strangers who appreciate me more than my friends and pseudo-boyfriend.

A pop-up message appears on the screen:

"PARTY IN YOUR AREA: DISCREET HOOKUP EVENT! BROOKLYN! ONLY HOT GUYS ALLOWED INSIDE! CONDOMS, LUBE, BOOZE PROVIDED. EIGHTY-DOLLAR COVER. DISCOUNT FOR CUTIES. SPEND YOUR SATURDAY NITE WITH HOT AND HORNY GUYS AGED 20-30!"

That's weird. I've never gotten a sex party invite on Grindr before.

Servando and I actually met at a sex party, back before Grindr existed (GOD, I'm old). We never tell anyone that our first kiss happened AFTER Servy's dick was in my mouth, since it carries an even larger stigma than saying you met online. But despite what you might think, it was actually sorta cute. He looked down, pulled my face off his cock, and said, "Shit, you're pretty." Then he kissed me full on the mouth. That night, we separated from the rest of the homo hubbub to a corner where we got it on with each other, slapping away hands, mouths, and other such appendages that tried to violate our coupling. They could watch, but that was all. We traded numbers after, he called me the next day, and it just sorta picked up from there.

A sex party? Would I really do something like that? On my own? The most recent one I went to was a little over a year ago, with Servy—and it didn't end well.

I'm not even looking for sex. I fired up Grindr out of habit, because it's fun to flirt with strangers and then go silent when the pic trading takes a turn for the more physical and immediate.

But who's to say Servando isn't out fucking someone else now? I could see him doing that, especially if he's about to break up with me. He's ultra-competitive. He'd want to fire the first shot, to say he beat me to the finish line.

I read the invite again. A random hookup with a Grindr guy is a crapshoot. But if the door is as...discerning as the invite says, I'm guaranteed far prettier people at the party. And if I change my mind when I get there, I don't have to do anything. I can stand in a corner and watch. (Voyeurism is a kink that sex parties are more than happy to accommodate.)

But then again, it's in Brooklyn. I can't remember the last time I got on a train and left Manhattan. Oh, wait, yes I can. It was TODAY. When I went to the Bronx Zoo to NOT get weed. And if I went all the way out there for something I didn't end up getting, what's one more long-distance trek? The weed was a bitter disappointment. Hot, willing naked guys seem a fitting substitution.

Fine. I'm doing this.

I jump into the shower and clean myself appropriately, return to the studio, and select a cute jockstrap that will allow fantastic access to any part of me. I grab a tight T-shirt and a pair of short shorts and head out.

I wish I'd come face-to-face with Servy as he walked into the building. With that apologetic smile and his arms open wide, ready to have that makeup sex we do so well.

But there is no Servy. Not in the hallway nor on the sidewalk nor in the subway station.

He's not on the train and he's not at the stop where I get off to transfer to a Brooklyn-bound train. Before going into the bowels of the second station on my trip, I stop by a nondescript ATM, standing alone and dirty in a corner by a shuttered barbershop. I look around again, one last time, even though I am well aware that the odds of Servy being here are slim to none.

Turns out the odds are none.

Fine, Servy. Fine.

I'm going through with this. No turning back now. And this time, I make sure to withdraw MORE than I'll need to get what I want.

***

By the time I'm back in Hell's Kitchen, I'm not in the mood for a frozen cosmo.

For one, I'm soaked. For two, I'm so dehydrated I'd probably die of alcohol poisoning. And for three, all I really want is Rowan. With all this excess energy and testosterone bouncing around inside of me, I'm ready to fuck his brains out.

Except, Rowan isn't home. I buzz three times with no response and finally give up, fishing my keys out of my pocket. When I get inside, I can see that he was here. And busy. Our place hasn't been this spic and span in FOREVER. Why the fuck was he cleaning? The apartment smells like weed, but it always smells that way, so who knows if he was smoking up recently.

"Rowan?"

I can see every corner of our apartment from the entrance, including the open bathroom. If I can't see him, he isn't here.

I'm still heaving, covered in sweat and rain. I haven't run that far in a very long time. Ripping off my clothing, I head to the bathroom, where I find Rowan's outfit from today hanging, dripping into the tub.

Where the hell did he go? Why didn't he text me?

Deep breath in, deep breath out. I peek out the window by our bed, into the unkempt garden space behind our apartment, just in case he snuck out for a smoke. No such luck.

So...He got stoned, cleaned the apartment, then left? I feel like a gay Sherlock Holmes, rearranging clues to figure out where he could possibly be. No answers come to me.

He probably just went to find something to eat. I myself haven't eaten since breakfast, which was interrupted by the damned rat that set this day's many unpleasant, potentially life-threatening events into motion. So I make some ramen.

Oh, wait. NO, I DON'T.

Because Rowan ate my last ramen! I KNOW I had one last cup. It was the spicy-shrimp flavor, and sure enough, the empty container is hanging out of the fucking garbage can, a few stray noodles on the floor. (And Rowan wonders why the fuck we have a rat!)

New clue: he ate my last fucking ramen. And he KNOWS I hate that. We've fought over this at LEAST forty times.

I'm trying not to get angry, but the feeling creeps up as I imagine Rowan getting high, cleaning, eating my food, and then fleeing the coop without a word to me. And to think I was ready to forgive him! I was primed for makeup sex! In the short period of time he was home without me, Rowan's done a bang-up job of doing every single little thing that pisses me off.

Didn't he wonder why I wasn't back yet? For all he knew, I hopped right back on a downtown train after I left him. If that were the case, I would have been home waiting for him. It really never occurred to him to wonder, Oh, gee, where's my boyfriend? Maybe I should call him just to make sure he's not about to get his ass kicked by five thugs in Washington Heights.

But no, why would Rowan take a fucking second to care about anyone except himself?

This, of course, is nothing new. THIS is why I won't be his fucking boyfriend. Rowan gives too many shits about himself and not half a shit about anyone else. Why would I want a boyfriend who's so distracted and stoned and careless all the time? That makes me look like a fool. I deserve better.

I start to text him, but stop myself.

Maybe I'm overreacting. Maybe he thinks I'm still walking off my anger. That makes sense, right? Even though I don't think that a stoned Rowan is capable of such reasoning, I give him the benefit of the doubt. It was I who instituted the halting of communication, wasn't it? Maybe he thought I'd want to be alone when I got back— which would have been an accurate assumption, if I hadn't had my run-in with the violent homophobes earlier.

I take a deep breath, dig through the refrigerator, and come back out with a bottle of Gatorade. I take three huge gulps, the chill of the sugar water cutting right through the back of my head. As I recover from the assault of brain freeze, I send a quick text to Rowan: "Hey, I'm home. Where are you?"

Twenty minutes later, no response. I've finished the Gatorade, and I'm seething. I send another text: "Where the fuck are you?"

That'll get his attention. Whenever I get pissed like that, he writes back pretty fucking quickly.

Twenty minutes later, still nothing. And now I'm worried. What if he and his dealer got caught by the cops or something? No—he would have gotten that one permitted telephone call. He would have called me. And I don't have any missed calls (believe me, I know, because I keep checking my phone every thirty seconds just to make sure I didn't somehow miss him trying to contact me).

Besides, that wouldn't account for the miraculously clean apartment.

I text Todd, asking if he's seen or heard from Rowan. No response. I crash down onto our futon to distract myself with something stupid on TV. Soon Rowan will come back blazed and fed, and who knows? Maybe with more ramen. He does endearing little things like that every once in a while.

Wait.

Rowan's underwear drawer is open. Not all the way, but open enough. I can't believe I didn't notice that until this second! One of his jockstraps is hanging out. I open it farther.

Ha. The fucking asshole.

Conspicuously missing from the tangle of underwear is a certain jockstrap, a blue-and-yellow one we bought together at a boutique in Chelsea. And I know for a fact he hasn't worn it in weeks.

No, this means Rowan is wearing the jock right now. And Rowan doesn't wear jocks unless he plans on fucking around. (Who does?)

That piece of shit. That son of a bitch isn't answering my fucking texts because he's busy getting a dick shoved up his ass by one of his dom top buddies, who's probably got the jockstrap knotted up in one hand, pulling him back deeper and harder.

That's his way to deal with our disagreement?

Yes, we're in an open relationship, but there's such a thing as the wrong fucking time. And our rules have ALWAYS been that we let the other know BEFORE it happens. NOT okay.

There are so many ways I could retaliate. Lock him out. Text the hell out of his phone until it explodes. Break up with him for real. For good.

But no. I have a better idea.

I'll go out and get some myself. Because if Rowan's not going to be back anytime soon, I'm sure as hell not going to hang around waiting for him.

I send out booty texts to my three favorite bottoms. Brendan, the skinny actor/model from Boston with a mop of brown hair. Jay, a sprite of a thing with nipple rings and a penchant for posting underwear pics of himself on Facebook. Travis, a dangerously tall blond who only bottoms for me.

I wait.

Then, finally, my phone beeps. It's Brendan, tonight's big winner. Two can play at this game, Row-Dog. If you're getting some, then I will too.

"Sup Servazoid?" *he asks.*

"Wanna play?"

"Of course I do," *he texts back.* "But I'm not home."

"When will you be back?"

"Not for a while :("

Or maybe not. "Oh. Maybe another time."

"No! Wait! You can come too. Going to a party."

On any other night, I could be convinced to party. But not tonight. In all honesty, I don't even want sex. I want Rowan. But since that's out of the realm of possibility, I can't let him win this undeclared war. He is already en route to victory, and I just can't. Not after this afternoon. No way.

"No thanks, babe," *I text back.* "I don't feel like doing the social public thing tonight. Just lookin for some fun."

Brendan texts back: "Not THAT kind of party. This is more of a… get-together. Of the sexy variety."

"Go on."

"It's in Brooklyn. I can get you in without having to pay the stupid crazy cover. Jockstrap recommended. Everything else will be there. You can be the first of many I take tonight ;) "

Now we're talking.

I've been to three sex parties in my life. At the first, I just watched gorgeous men all around me go crazy; I had enough material to beat off to for the next six months. The second was where I met Rowan, which is probably the most romantic thing to ever come out of an organized orgy. The third was actually where Rowan and I "broke up" and ditched our label. We'd reached that point where we both wanted to fuck other people in public, so who were we kidding calling each other boyfriends? From there came Servando and Rowan 2.0—the open-love revision of what we once had. And that was it for the sex parties.

So perhaps number four will be equally monumental? Maybe I'll meet someone new. It worked that second time around, so I won't rule out the possibility.

"Well? You coming? About to hop on the train," *Brendan texts.*

I'd much rather spend the night with a hot mug of tea and Thai food delivery. All that running tired me the fuck out. I could even go to bed early, wake up, and start a new morning-running regimen.

But who am I kidding? That'd be a great way to spend the evening if, say, Rowan was at work. But right now, he's getting his hole pounded. The very thought of Rowan squealing as he takes that dick—making that half-pain, half-pleasure face he does when you get all the way in—dashes any hopes of staying in tonight. I wouldn't be able to sit sipping tea if I wanted to. I'd more likely crouch in the corner and chomp straight through my mugs, gnashing the ceramic down to dust. Thinking about the positions he's in. How many times they did it. If the other guy was better than me. What Rowan said. What the guy tasted like...

This will drive me insane. If Rowan's doing this, then I am too.

If we're over, then we're really, truly over this time. No more gray area.

It's finished.

"I'll be there," *I text back.* "Meet at West 4th and we can take the train together."

"Hot ;) see you soon, sexy."

I drop my phone on the futon and my shorts on the floor. And I think, What the fuck? I'll help myself to one of Rowan's jock-straps. *The one I grab is brand-new—pure white, traditional sports type. That'll work wonders.*

Have your fun, Rowan. Because I'M gonna have a blast.

***

This night already sucks. Nothing beats a one-hour train ride when it comes to sucking the fury out of you. Now I'm standing outside this sex party and seriously considering turning around and going home. The rain is back to its old tricks, and I'm soaked for the second time today. I'm dying to get out of these sodden threads; then again, I guess a sex party would facilitate that nicely.

The location is a brownstone in Brooklyn, pretty standard for sex parties in this city. I read Larry Kramer's *Faggots* and had to laugh as I took in the tale of pre-AIDS-crisis sluttery that existed in this city back in the seventies. Apparently, a guy could get head or get fucked basically anywhere: the docks, the streets, any bar or club. Not so any longer, friends. If you wanna get down and dirty with a handful of similarly bodied individuals, you're headed to some sort of private property. The Board of Health is more than happy to shut down any actual business that places exposed pubes so precariously close to open containers of booze.

I have been standing under a tree on the corner for ten minutes. I had planned on going inside, but now I'm not. Why? Didn't I want this? Yes, I DID—but now I don't, for some reason. Guilt? Laziness? In all honesty, I wish I'd stayed home instead. Servy would have come back sooner or later. We could have fought or fucked—or both at the same time. (We've done it before.)

But I'm here. I traveled longer than I should have, WAY too far to just turn around and head home. I made my bed, and now I'm going to get fucked in it.

Yes. I'm doing this.

The door has a sliding grate at the same level as my eyes. I knock and the grate slides open with a squeak.

"Password?" asks a tough, deep, throaty voice on the other side.

"There's a password? Uh…It didn't say so on Grindr."

For fuck's sake. Tell me that he's not going to let me in without this magical password. Tell me I'll have made TWO ridiculously long, fruitless journeys in the span of twenty-four hours.

"Oh, fuck it, you're cute," says the voice. "Hold on a sec."

The grate squeaks and slams shut as the door swings open.

***

Brendan has been rubbing his leg against mine for the entirety of this train ride, occasionally leaning over to lick my ear. I'm not saying this is a bad thing, but it's not half as exciting as it should be. I've gotten harder sitting across from Brendan at the table in his family's kitchen, engaging in coffee talk while we wait for his parents to go elsewhere so we can strip down and get crazy.

Could it be that I'm feeling guilty? I shouldn't. I know Rowan is out getting some, and he never bothered to let me know he was off to get laid. But I AM going to a sex party without texting him, which is in direct violation of not-quite-boyfriend rules. These rules aren't that complicated. Anyone who's been in a relationship—or whatever— for as long as we have develops their own body of laws by which they agree to comply. For us, it's like this: we can play together, or we can play separately. If we play apart, we must let the other know in advance, and it has to be somebody we both know well enough.

We haven't really put this into action in months, except with Gulliver. He was new in town; he had that sheen about him. Rowan and I couldn't wait to give him a proper welcome to the city, and in many ways, he was the perfect third, because there was never any danger that he was secretly into one of us more than the other or that either Rowan or I would fall for him. That's always the risk. Theoretically, an open relationship is supposed to free you up so that lusting after a third party doesn't tear you apart. But that possibility never really goes away. Sometimes I've watched Rowan going at it with one of our guest stars and wondered if he was enjoying it more than he enjoyed being with just me. He must, or else, why are we doing it?

Brendan's hand finds its way between my legs, a bold move considering how packed this train is. At least it hasn't broken down. We're making great time, already in Brooklyn and five stops from our final destination. He kneads his hand in deep and finally my dick springs to attention, waylaying my fears that it is permanently down for the night.

He really is cute, with his boyish face, the giant dimples that make him look seventeen.

"Have you been to this party before?" I ask.

"Oh, for sure," he says, ramping up his sexy voice, closing his eyes halfway, rubbing harder between my legs. "You're going to love it."

"Yeah?" I ask, trying as best as I can to tease back, even though it feels weird. "Tell me about it."

"Sixty to a hundred guys. All gorgeous. They check you at the door, and if you aren't cute enough, cut enough, or hung enough, they send you packing. Condoms and lube and toys and slings as far as the eye can see. Live DJ, which is SO much better than the iPod most sex parties in the city have."

"Most sex parties? I didn't know you were a regular," I say, letting my eyes drift down to his hand.

"Definitely. I love them."

It occurs to me that I met Brendan at the last sex party I went to, the one I went to with Rowan. The last time we were ever officially boyfriends.

"How many have you been to?"

"This month?" Brendan asks, smiling.

He keeps talking, and I watch the tunnel through the windows opposite where we are sitting. Three more stops. Two more. One.

We have arrived.

"Come on!" Brendan hops out of the seat and makes a run for the door. I follow and let him guide me through the station, back aboveground. Shit, it's pouring again. We run, heads down, across the street.

"This way!" he screams. "Almost there!"

I am drenched, my legs sore as hell. The rain is freezing cold, and my clothing is sticking to me.

"This better be good, bitch!" I scream, laughing.

"It's worth it, trust me!" he screams back, grabbing my hand and pulling me along.

Four blocks later, we get to the building. Brendan pounds on the door, yelling. It's a good thing he does—the music inside is blaring so loud, the rain outside so heavy, that the doorman wouldn't hear anything that registered below the decibel level of a low-flying jet. A slate in the door opens, Brendan shouts a password, and we're in.

I am bathed in shifting colored lights. This is already unlike any sex party I've ever been to. Staring down a long hallway, I can see the entrance to the main play area, but with the mixture of blasting music and flashing lights, any normal person might assume it was the portal to a regular dance party.

The sex parties I've been to are really nothing more than some rich dude's loft with a lot of guys fucking. This is a full-on production. I guess all of Brendan's experience has paid off after all.

The doorman has us strip down so he can inspect us prior to entry. I quickly comply just so I can get out of my sopping-wet clothing. He gets in a couple more grabs than he actually needs, but it's no problem, considering what I'm about to dive into. Brendan whips off his underwear to reveal his massive dick—a nearly useless tool, since he's a total bottom. Like giving a fish a bicycle. We place our personal effects in large Hefty bags and allow the doorman to scribble numbers on our arms so we can reclaim our stuff later.

"Have fun in there," he says, unashamedly checking us out from head to toe (but mostly focusing just where you'd expect). "If you get caught going bare, your ass is out on the street. Cool?"

"Yup!" Brendan says, walking quickly toward the door. "Come on, Servy!"

Maybe it's the lights. Maybe it's the music. Or maybe it's the freezing-cold rain that's still dripping off my hair down to my now-unclothed body. Whatever it is, I am now excited, both internally and externally.

Let Rowan have his fun, see if I care. I'll worry about him later. Or better yet—maybe I won't.

For now, my quasi-pseudo-ex-boyfriend needs to be the LAST thing on my mind. His stupid face eating all my food and getting high and whatever. UGH. I'm practically over him already. Good riddance!

***

The sex party was something you'd see on one of those Sausage Party porn sites they advertise all over XTube. About a hundred guys. All beautiful, most hung, and buff, with chiseled muscles and rock-hard abs and asses...

Plus DJ Christian Robert!

Uh, yeah…can't forget him. Anyway, I spent my first hour and a half there all alone, against the wall, sort of watching what was going on. I didn't participate. I kept on wanting to leave. At least until…speak of the devil—

Hey! Be nice!

It's an expression!

Well, I don't like it. I'm not the devil; I'm a saint.

Okay, speak of the saint. So guess who walks into the party rock hard, in a jockstrap, with his little VIP bottom boy in tow…?

Hey, be nice. You've fucked him too.

True. Sorry, Brendan. Anyway. I couldn't get hard. Couldn't get into it. I was having a pretty shitty time, especially considering I spent like half a week's worth of weed to get in. So when I spotted my possibly-ex-pseudo-boyfriend across the room plowing Brendan…

What can I say? I love a good gathering of gorgeous gays. And hello, it's a sex party! It sure as hell wasn't MY fault you couldn't get into it!

It actually kinda was, indirectly. But yeah. Servando was plowing Brendan while Brendan was sucking off two other guys…

And?

And THAT got me...excited.

It sure did! AND?

And...I joined in. I walked across the room, got in front of Brendan, and started face-fucking him.

You weren't mad that I went there without permission?

For a sec. But I went without approval from you, either. For exactly the same reason. And you know what? Actually...I was just happy to see you.

Aw! Me too. About you! 'Cause, believe it or not, I didn't even recognize you for a few minutes, because I was...um...busy. Then I looked up, and there you were, giving me that sexy grin. The one where you lift one of your eyebrows, and your eyes squint, and the right corner of your mouth curls up. And after the day I had, and the fight, and thinking we might never be together after tonight... Well, I just kinda fell for you all over again.

And?

And nothing! I just asked what the fuck you were doing there.

And I replied?

"Just fuck this bitch and we'll talk about it later." Which might be one of the hottest things I've ever heard you say.

I can get kinky. You just need to let me know you want it that way.

Noted for next time. As for the time being... Well, I was so excited to see Rowan I completely forgot about Brendan. I don't even know what happened to him...

I think we can guess.

Right.

We just sorta smiled at each other, nodded, reclaimed our clothing, and went back outside. The rain had stopped. And we walked to the subway.

Holding hands.

Yeah. Still not really saying anything. Just...looking back and forth at each other.

The subway didn't come for fifteen minutes. FUCK THE MTA!

We sat in the station, holding hands, mostly without talking.

Until...?

Okay. Yes. Until I started crying.

It was adorable.

Shut up. Yes. I cried. And apologized. For losing my shit earlier. For forcing him to go to the zoo. For not chasing him after he left the subway. For not calling or texting an apology.

And I apologized too.

Turns out one single text earlier in the day from either of us could have saved us a world of hurt and a trip to Brooklyn. Stupid, right?

It's fine. After the Sorry Show, I told him about how I went all Buffy the Thug Slayer on those guys up in the Heights!

Oh. Yeah, that was so hot. I loved hearing about how tough you were. My ass-kicking boyfriend.

That's what Rowan said, right there on the platform. "My ass-kicking boyfriend." After the B-word slipped out, awkward silence overtook us. That fucking B-word. Taunting us. Challenging us. Dancing around.

A giant bouncing question mark. And?

And then...I said, "Ass-kicking boyfriend. That's a label I could get into."

And that was it.

That WAS it.

After a year of bullshit. A year of playing around. A year of pretending we wouldn't end up back together like this.

And you know what? It felt new. Not like going back, but...

...going forward. It felt right.

Now, we're still not talking about marriage...

Oh, God no. Not now, babe. Why would you even SAY that?

Exactly. And, you know, we still might play around.

Maybe. But if so, only together now. An amendment to our rules.

Boyfriends that play together, stay together. Who said that?

One of your fuck buddies who broke up with his boyfriend shortly thereafter because shit got way complicated.

Right. It doesn't work for everybody. We'll see if it still works for us. But I think, for the foreseeable future, we may just see what it's like to star in a two-man show.

Agreed. Because sometimes it's good to have a partner. In a world with untrustworthy weed dealers and gay-bashing assholes wandering the streets, it's good to know somebody's got your back. Whether to help you throw punches or kick in an extra fifty for your weed—or just to listen to your story and hold you when it gets cold in your apartment because the fucking heat is still broken.

Hey, there's another NYC greeting card! "Sorry Your Landlord Doesn't Turn On Your Heat Until Mid-December."

Oh, and I would be remiss to not mention one final bit of irony: the train we rode back to Manhattan from the sex party broke down.

Are we surprised? Clearly the MTA has something against the both of us.

I dunno. It all worked out for the best, didn't it? If that train hadn't broken down that afternoon, we'd probably still be in quasi-pseudo-whatever-land...

You're giving the MTA credit for that? Hell. I'd rather give props to the rat.

And that's a real Manhattan Greetings card we could sell. "Yeah, Everything Sucked Today and Chances Are NYC Will Try to Make Tomorrow Even Worse, but You Still Wouldn't Dream of Living Anywhere Else, Would You?"

I sure wouldn't. Not without my Row-Dog.

Me neither. Not without my boyfriend. I love you, Servando.

I love you too. Muah—oh my God, there's a rat on the counter!

Aaaaaaagh!

Kidding.

You ASSHOLE! That is NOT fucking funny!

But you still love me.

I do.

I do too.

TODD'S MAJOR MELTDOWN

"Todd? It's Kenton. I...Wow. I...I just need to talk to you as soon as you get this. It's important. Please call me. I've been texting you, but...I don't know why you're not responding. But this is really fucking important. Okay? Just...call me. I know you don't want to, but we need to talk. Please. I promise it won't take long."

Beep.

***

"Shit! Todd! Todd! Wake the fuck up, bitch! Oh fuck, man! There's a rat! Oh FUCK! It's as big as my dildo!"

"It's bigger than your dildo, Rowan! And uglier! Ahhh! It looked at me! Its fucking beady devil eyes saw me! Kill it! Kill it dead!"

"I can't! What if it bites me? Those bitches have rabies and shit! I'm too young to die! NO! He's in the DVD rack!"

"Where's your bat, Rowan? Hit it! Ahhhh! Todd! Help us!"

Beep.

And so my Saturday morning begins.

Well…

Maybe it doesn't have to.

I flip over in my bed, so trashed that the fitted sheet came off in the middle of the night. I was too drunk and exhausted to care when I face-planted at 6 this morning, so I've been sleeping on a bare mattress like a squatter. Someone once told me mattresses end up 50 percent heavier after five years of use—fuck, that's gross.

I roll over to the small, scrunched-up island of sheets, jam my eyes shut, and try to remember how to get back to sleep.

I've been so fucking tired lately. Run-down, like I have a cold I just can't shake. I need to disconnect my landline. Who has one of those anymore, anyway? Fucking discounted cable packages and their slick telephone salesmen. "Oh, Mr. DiAngelo, you'll save X many dollars if you combine the Internet and the TV with a land-line service plan. Can I put you down for the Super De-Duper Triple Play Package? If you don't like it, you can always cancel at any time!"

So now I have a phone people have somehow figured out how to call. If they can't get me on my cell, they hit this thing next, and there's no caller ID, no Ignore button. I won't turn it off or unplug it, not since my mother convinced me that I never know when there will be an emergency I'll need it for. The last thing I want is another "told ya so" from her.

I feel for Servando and Rowan, but they can handle a rodent on their own. Right? They're tough guys. I've seen Rowan tackle dudes a thousand times bigger than the biggest rat. It's not like that time he got himself caught in a subway turnstile and needed my help to get him out. (I made sure to snap some pictures beforehand, of course.)

The landline rings again, and the answering machine picks up.

"Sup, bro, it's Todd. Can't get your call now, probably drunk and/ or hungover. Holler at me."

Beep.

"DiTempto! It's Drama. Get back to me. Wanna talk some last-minute things about eWrecksion. Two of the bartenders called out. Fuckers! They'll never work in this fucking town again! And the pop bitch performer's pulling a diva act too. She wants a limo to sound check! Who does she think she is? Rihanna? Give me a fucking break. I told them I'll send a cab, or they can rent a fucking bicycle built for two and we'll pay them back for it. She'll never work in this town again! Like any of the gay boys care about some nobody with a single they've never heard when we've got the Screwniversity there. Oh, that reminds me, we have an issue with the screen projections. There may have been a small typo, they said. They spelled my name Dromo…DROMO! What the fuck am I, a floor-vacuuming robot? A *Star Wars* droid? That's not a small typo. That's the difference between a cyborg and a human being. Fuck me! Oh, Jesus Christ, just got another text. We lost a go-go boy from…food poisoning? Since when do those big-dicked toothpicks EAT something besides ass? Should teach him a fucking lesson. You better believe it, he'll never work in this town aga—"

Beep.

Oh, merciful beep.

None of that was urgent—right? Crap. All of it was. This party's a big fucking deal, which means anything involving it is equally gargantuan.

Then again, if Mikey Drama had his way, no one would ever work in this town ever again. It'd be him barking orders at a bunch of tumbleweeds, which by the end of the first day would also probably never tumble in this town again. The man's the biggest drama queen—but he can also pack any venue he deems worthy of holding one of his events. He's a legend—and like so many legends, the stardust falling from his shoulders is bound to give you a migraine.

Still so beat. So ridiculously drained. The kind of tired where you're nauseous and your eyes are dry and your throat burns. I could splash cold water on my face and try to crawl slowly into the morning light, but it's only 10! Fuck. Four hours of sleep? Even I can't make that work.

My eyes close.

The landline's jangling rips them right back open again.

Beep.

"Todd! Brayden's lost his mind. I get home from the worst booty call I've ever had, and there he is in the living room, flinging books at the door and screeching at the top of his lungs like he just escaped from *Jurassic Park.*"

Paging drama queen number two.

"Now he's bawling his eyes out. Something about looking through Christian Robert's phone, and a dick pic, and how someone named Grant is not long for this world. Or—I don't know! He's blubbering too much. Call me back, boo. He may jump out the window, or push someone else out, if you don't talk him down."

Beep.

Okay, it's time to get up. Fuck me with a Timberland.

I wish I could say this isn't a typical morning, but that would be total BS. This is exactly typical. Some guys wake up to breakfast and a newspaper and a doting husband or wife; I wake up to enough fires to take down Yellowstone. And nobody ever thinks to dial 911—it's up to ME to put them out.

I sit up and rub my eyes, which are dry, sore, and fighting not to stay open. My head bangs like it's getting punched by two punks on either side of me. Oh, and I'm hard. Total morning wood. But I don't think I have time to pull a load out, even if I started now.

Well, maybe...

The phone rings.

Beep.

"DiAngelo, it's Irwin. You gotta call me, brother, we've got a problem with your latest futures forecast. Bill rang me up an hour ago, blew up my BlackBerry, screaming his head off. Somethin' 'bout your percentages being out of whack. Call me *pronto*."

Beep.

My dick deflates like a balloon untied. I can almost hear it sputtering: *thhhhhbbbbtttt*. At least that's one less thing demanding my attention.

I kick my legs to the side of the bed and hoist myself up. Boom, I'm light-headed. From last night, or...? I lean against the wall until everything straightens itself out. Across the room, I catch sight of my reflection in a standing, full-body mirror. I can see my ribs. My face is rough and dark, like someone tied it to the back of a bike and dragged it around the Central Park reservoir. What the fuck? I know I've been skipping the gym lately—but as my two jobs demand more and more of me, I don't have the fucking time OR energy more than once or twice a week.

But really? It's only been a few weeks since I eased up on my regimen, and it's like all the work I did for years came undone in days. That's bullshit! Fuck anatomy.

And fuck this sleepiness. My normal gym routine will kick off again in earnest next week, even if all I want to do is pass out on the elliptical. If my body is a temple, it's turning into a crumbling, crappy one way too fast—like Machu Picchu. No can do, Picchu. People expect more of me.

In the living room, Señor, my slutty Scottish terrier, is on his back with his legs in the air, snoring like a three-hundred-pound dude. The phone is right next to his head and hasn't stirred him. What I would give for that deep a sleep.

On my way to the kitchen, I stop and look into the empty second bedroom across from mine. Like maybe it was magically reoccupied in the middle of the night.

No such luck. Inside is a bare mattress, an empty desk, two framed photos: one of me and my best buddy Gulliver on the day of my graduation from UCLA, the other depicting the two of us one year later, the day of his. No Gulliver, though.

I still get a killer pain in my gut when I see this room and think of what's missing. Yet I can't bring myself to just shut the door.

Where did you go, Gullzo? In gay New York, it is impossible to disappear. The seediest dive bar, the smallest off-Broadway theater. Doesn't fucking matter. The second you do something embarrassing, you can be sure ten people will be calling and texting their friends to update them on your latest social snafu. Yet Gullzo is inexplicably gonezo. And I'm pretty sure it's my fault. That's why I haven't called his parents.

Three days after his disappearance, I got a vague postcard in my stack of magazines and bills. Not very informative, other than serving as proof that he's somewhere, and alive. Wherever that is, he doesn't want me there. He doesn't want me to know. Nor does he want his parents to know. Gulliver is going it alone.

I've thought of turning his room into an office, but it feels wrong. Like I'm giving up on him. The truth is, I'd do anything to have him back—best friends separated by just one thin wall.

Instead, we're separated by—Jesus. So much. Where to start?

A lot of bad shit has gone down in the past few months. Gully going missing, my day job getting shittier and shittier, and... more. A lot more. But I don't have time to throw myself a pity party. Not when there are actual moneymaking parties demanding my time and attention.

I sigh at the empty air and close Gully's door.

***

"The fucking asshole!" I scream, slamming back into the room to find Gulliver right where I left him. "Fuck him!"

Gulliver looks up at me, eyes wide with shock. He's right to be surprised; I'm not supposed to be here. I just left our room, headed to my boyfriend Josh's place, thirty minutes ago. Presents and champagne in hand, my plan was to celebrate our ten-month anniversary.

That, of course, is now all shot to shit and back.

Gulliver is sitting Indian style on his bed in a pair of bright-orange underwear and a sleeveless Abercrombie T, under a pennant of our house's Greek letters, his notebooks spread out in front of him.

"What happened?" he asks, climbing off the bed and walking across the room slowly, carefully, like I might lash out and deck him in the face.

I cry. I never cry. But here I am, letting it out like some sort of pussy.

Gulliver gets closer to me, wraps his arms around me as best he can. Now I'm heaving and sobbing. FUCK, Todd! Get your shit together! Gulliver holds me, says nothing. Squeezing me and patting my back.

"I walked in on him and his fucking roommate," I choke out. "Fucking each other."

"Oh my God," Gulliver whispers.

What else could he say? What else do I want to hear? I caught my boyfriend in the act—with his roommate! I DID deck him in the face. Threw his roommate out of the bed and kicked him in the stomach too. And then I left. Because if I hadn't, I'd probably have beaten the living shit out of both of them, and then Gulliver and I would be having this conversation separated by a glass partition in a prison somewhere.

"FUCK him!" The bottom is falling out from beneath me and Gulliver is trying to catch the dropping pieces. He continues holding on to me. He's so much smaller than me that he actually has to stand on his toes to keep his arms around my neck.

Five minutes later, I'm done crying. For now, at least.

"Well. I think this calls for a celebration," Gulliver says, letting me go and dropping to his knees, crawling under his bed.

I look down at his bubble butt, blinking and confused. "What, bro? Check your ears. Maybe you didn't fucking hear me right."

"Did YOU hear ME? A celebration!" he shouts from under the bed. "Aha! Here we go." He pokes his head back out with a bottle of Patrón and a bottle of Cuervo in hand. "I knew I still had these."

Gully takes the bottles to his college-issue desk, pulls two plastic cups out of a sleeve of fifty, and pours us both the equivalent of three shots. "We still have some salt packets from the dining hall?"

"Somewhere," I say, going to my desk to find them. "But you've got a final tomorrow. I've got a final tomorrow."

"So we'll only get slightly shit-faced." He smiles, shoving the cup into my hands when I get back to him with the salt packets. "Here's to freedom, Todd. You're graduating. You're moving to New York City. And I didn't want to say anything, but Josh always looked like an exhibit from Ripley's Believe It or Not, anyway. Have you looked in the mirror lately? You can do WAY better. So, by my count, that's a triple score for you! Hence, congratulations." He raises his cup.

"You said Josh was super hot!" I laugh.

"Yeah, white lie. Whoops! The truth shall SET YOU FREE!"

"You're a bitch," I say, wiping my eyes. Ten months down the shitter and I'm grinning from ear to ear. "Hey, isn't Graham coming over?"

I ask, sniffing the cup and flinching. "You being drunk ain't gonna help him in any way."

"I'll tell him to take the night off," Gully says, grabbing his cell. "There. Done. He's hanging out with Kevin, anyway."

"Bro, you don't have to do that."

"Shut up. We've got a double date with Patrón and Cuervo. Ai, ai!"

"Dude, you're ridiculous," I say, swirling the tequila in the cup.

"Yup. Down the hatch!"

The magic words. "Down the hatch." I can't remember who started using the chant first, Gully or me, but the rest of the frat picked it up, and now it's set in stone. Now that Gulliver has invoked it, I have no choice but to comply. That's just the way it works.

"NATCH!" I shout back.

Up with the cups, down with the tequila. We suck in and our eyes tear up. We Hoover up the salt.

"Why can't I get my own fucking Graham?" I grumble.

"You will," he says, ripping open a second salt packet and dusting it on our closed fists. "In New York. Right now you need to get a fucking buzz."

"How do you know I'll find someone?"

"Oh, puh-lease," he says. "Name a guy who DOESN'T want to be with you."

"Josh's roommate"—I shrug—"after I kicked him in the stomach, at least."

"Atta boy," Gulliver says, smiling as he refills our cups again with a second toxic load of Cuervo. "It's like I always say. A little violence never hurt anyone."

"Bro, that makes no fucking sense—"

"Down the hatch!" he interrupts.

"NATCH!"

Up with the cups. Down with the tequila. Like I said—no choice. That's just how it works.

***

In the kitchen, I turn on the coffee brewer and try to enjoy the smell of whatever flavor I threw in the basket last night. Hazelnut? Hazelnut mint? It's from a Christmas gift basket my parents sent last year. Eight months later, I still haven't emptied it. The little sausages packed into the giant wicker basket would have gone rotten and drawn flies by now if not for the fact that they don't expire, which is hella disturbing. What the fuck kind of animal are you grinding up? A unicorn? What freaky fucking chemicals are food scientists shooting into this mystery beast if it has no spoil date? I should throw this shit out.

But not now. I'm on the phone with Irwin from The Day Job. My first call, since that's today's (and every day's) highest priority. If I ever lost this job, I'd be fucked harder than the muscle bottom in a prison gangbang porno. It pays the bills, it fills my savings, it helps me live. Ironically, it's also the most life-draining, fuck-boring part of my existence, forcing me to get up at 8 every morning (or sometimes 7 or 6—let's not talk about it). I work for an endangered species—a hedge fund, which these days is like saying you're a lion tamer. Every day, more of my coworkers go missing, back home to their families with pitiful severances and an insincere apology from the managers, who are too busy dreading the fate of their own paychecks to truly offer any consolation.

I run through my numbers with Irwin. Fuck, it *was* my fault.

I rarely slip up when it comes to The Day Job. Can't afford to. One wrong decimal, one incorrectly placed comma, one faulty percentage, and I could send hundreds of investors to the shit house.

That's exactly what I almost did here. Goddammit! That isn't like me. Then again, I've been pretty fucking distracted over the past few weeks—but that's a whole other hole I'm not ready to dive into.

By the time the coffee is finished brewing (turns out it's Christmas Spice, which has me excited as hell, since it's August and all), Irwin has the updated numbers and he can go back to Bastard Bill and calm him the fuck down. Another money meltdown avoided. The end of the fiscal world as we know it pushed farther back in time. I'm sure I'll hear all about my fuckup in a day and a half when I get into the office.

Unless Bill fires me. Which, as always, is entirely possible. Fuck, that's a scary thought. Big savings or not, I'd be in a hell of a lot of trouble.

I mentally tick through my savings, my 401(k), my investments. There's money there, but how much? How long could I survive in New York without The Day Job paycheck? Scary shit, man. And that's what really sucks. I complain about work, and yet, without it, I couldn't afford even half of this life. I'm like a battered spouse, wincing through the bruises of boredom, stress, and constant work just because it takes care of me at the same time.

In another city, the money I make from my parties might have a chance in hell of supporting me. Here? Fat fucking chance.

When I got into nightlife two years ago, I had dreams that by now The Day Job would be long gone. A distant, hazy, only vaguely painful memory, like breaking my wrist in second grade. I'd wake up at 10:30 every morning, go to the gym, grab a bite at that place that sells grilled healthy crap down the block, then work on the parties. I'd figure out the themes, scout for talent, turn down hosting offers that weren't lucrative enough, work with flyer designers and DJs and subpromoters...

Okay, so yes. I'm doing all that now anyway. But the money I make isn't nearly enough to justify liberating myself from the hedge. If I lost my job, I'd be back on that Long Island Rail Road, headed for my parents' place in Huntington by next summer. There are NO other financial jobs to be had. I should know, since all my former colleagues are still trying to feed their families and pay the bills on four hundred dollars a week from the government.

My cell rings. It's Mikey Drama.

"You're up early," I say, pouring coffee and trying to sip it black. Christmas flavored, my ass! Unless it's so named because it tastes like a fucking mugful of ground coal and reindeer deuce.

"DiTempto!" Michael screams. "I haven't been asleep yet! Not in fucking days! This shit is falling apart!"

"Nice day, isn't it?" I ask, emptying the coffeemaker's basket out. "Weather should be perfect for tonight."

"DiTempto! Are you listening to me?"

I have to laugh. "Yeah, bro. I hear you. Thanks for respecting my fucking hangover. You do realize that you are not currently shouting over a booming bassline at a club, right?"

I drop another filter into the brewer, add a few scoops of eggnog-flavored coffee, wish for the best, and set it to brew.

"Shit. Sorry. You do okay at FreakOut Fridays?"

"Amazing, actually. Didn't get to bed 'til four hours ago. So thanks for the wake-up call."

"You want to sleep through the fucking apocalypse, DiTempto, you go right ahead. They're trying to RUIN ME!"

This is how Michael always is: LOUD. Whether he's bellowing from joy, horror, stress, fury, sadness, or boredom, he never spares the exclamation points. If he wrote a book, it'd be entirely in boldface and capital letters.

I'm pretty sure he brought me into this party because I'm his polar opposite: chill, no matter how extreme the problems that arise throughout the night. Or because I've got the twentysomething New York City gay crowd in a ball-lock. Either way, here we are, and here he is, screaming my face off.

"It's going to be FINE, Drama. Didn't you do a dry run of this thing last month?"

"Yeah?"

"And wasn't that shit on the verge of falling to crap too?"

"Yes..."

"And?"

Michael sighs audibly through the speaker, which is a welcome change from his previous decibel level. "And it was fine?"

"It was fine?"

"It was awesome!"

"Exact—"

"It was the best fucking party anyone's seen in this city for fucking decades! Those crazy crack-snorting party monster fuckups from the eighties never even HALLUCINATED a fucking party like that!"

"Exactly," I finish. "AND you didn't even have my help on that one. It's going to be fine. I'll find some replacement bartenders. I mean, hey, I already found a backup for your food-poisoned go-go."

"You did?"

"Trust, bro. Chase. He's one of my Friday boys."

"Is he hot?"

"Dude, he works for me," I say, conjuring up an image of Chase up on the block last night. One of the hottest guys on my squad, that's for sure. A toned and tight dancer boy with spiked hair and a face that belongs in a Dolce ad. I'd fuck him—if he didn't work my parties. If I weren't—

"Right, right. Okay. I trust you, DiTempto. Thank fucking God in the heavens I found you and GuyTime. Best fucking discovery of my life."

"Aw, gee. I'd blush if my face had any color left in it," I say. "So is that it for now? Shall we say good-bye so you can call me wigging out again in twenty minutes?"

"Fuck me! The projections! They fucked up my name, and I'm NOWHERE near my computer!"

"Yeah. Chill, C-3PO. You got the Photoshop file in your e-mail? Just forward it to me. I'll fix it, okay?"

"Yes, yes, thank you! I will have your children, DiTempto!"

"Those would be some fuck-ugly kids. Now get the fuck off my phone, okay?"

Click.

I can't believe I'm putting this event on tonight. I'd rather spend the night on the couch, watching Food Network like I know how to cook. Order some pizza. Grab some beers. Hang out with…

Oh, right.

I hang up for a second of silence. It's a blessing after eight straight hours of throbbing club music followed by ten minutes of Drama screaming my eardrums raw. Then I see the coffeepot, which has been brewing a full pot of coffee on top of the pot I forgot to dump out. It's all over the counter. The floor. And my foot—Fuck! Ow!

I grab my burning hoof and reach for a roll of paper towels on the counter, dropping to one knee like I'm about to propose to my fucking microwave. Ripping off single sheets doesn't do it, so I start sopping all the coal-flavored, eggnog-infused ass juice with the full roll. Meanwhile, my foot is going numb.

My phone rings.

Beep.

"Todd, you fucking shit! Get down here! It's not going away! Either there's two of them or this one figured out how to open doors! Help! Kill it! What kind of a friend ARE you?"

At the same time, I get a text from Shane on my cell. I have to hop over to see:

"On the list of Bray's Most Fucked Up Episodes, this already ranks as #3. NEED YOU. PLEASE!!!!!"

And then there's a smell. Like hamburger meat left out for too long mixed together with taco seasoning and fertilizer.

"Señor!"

The slut pooch hangs his head and farts again. I swear to God he warms the entire room. If only it weren't August—might save some money on the ConEd bill in the winter. Content with the damage, he skips out of the room and back to his doggie bed in the living room.

My cell rings again. Rowan. The landline rings. Servando. Shane sends another text. Somewhere in the middle, there's another e-mail from Mikey Drama, the subject line just an endless row of exclamation points.

Just another Saturday in the life of Todd DiTempto.

Or, as Mikey Drama might put it, !!!

***

"Todd! What the fuck are you doing here?" Gulliver cries, jumping into my arms and almost knocking me down the stairs of his West Hollywood apartment building.

"Whoa, chill, bro. If I'm going to die, it's going to be in an explosion of glitter in the middle of New York City, not around the corner from Hamburger Mary's."

Poor Gully. He looks terrible. Well, he looked terrible—but at least now he's smiling.

"Why do you always show up without warning? What if I was out trying to get revenge sex or something?"

"Cock blockkkk!" I yell, shoving him into his apartment. "Where's your boring roommate?"

"I don't know. Whatever. I'm glad he's not here. I've been busy."

Yes, he has. On the floor are photos of Gulliver and Graham. Or, more accurately, what is left of said photos. The remaining scraps are all over the place, a guilty pair of scissors lying open nearby.

"Ah, yes, destruction. Always a smart way to kick off the grieving process. But I have a better idea."

"I wish I'd known you were coming, I could have planned stuff for us to do..."

"No way, bro. We're staying in tonight. I met a hot couple at LAX, didn't take much persuading to get them to come back with me."

Gulliver looks up from the torn remnants of his relationship. "What? At the AIRPORT? Fuck, I look like SHIT! And since when do you and I have group sex together?"

I reach into my bag and pull out huge bottles of Cuervo and Patrón. "You still go for Latinos, right?"

Cue tears. Gulliver falls into my arms crying. "You piece of shit. For a second, I thought I was going to get fucked tonight."

"Oh, you will. Fucked UP! Where's your salt?"

Gulliver runs to his shabby kitchen and rips open drawers and cabinets, coming back with a plastic saltshaker. "I stole it from In-N-Out," he explains. "Gotta be thrifty 'til I get an income. And speaking of, don't you have a job you should be at tomorrow?"

"Took a personal day. I'm here all weekend, G," I say, wrapping my arm around him. "Chill out and stop worrying. All we gotta think about now is what Disney movie we're gonna watch while we get wasted."

"I love you, Todd," he says, tears welling up in his eyes as I pour us each three shots' worth of tequila and salt our hands.

"No crying, bro. You can do that when I'm gone. Or when you're puking in a few hours. 'Til then...Down the hatch!"

Gully wipes his eyes with the salt-free hand and shakes his head, laughing. "I can't believe you fucking flew across the country, you asshole. Who DOES that?"

"I do? And I said, DOWN THE HATCH!" I slam my glass on a nearby table, scattering the photo bits in all directions.

"NATCH!" he yells, raising his glass high.

***

Servando and Rowan live in a studio apartment on Tenth Avenue in the thirties. They adamantly argue that this is still Hell's Kitchen, even though no one agrees with them. Technically, it's "Clinton"—or, as Brayden has said, the taint of Penn Station. As far as most gays are concerned, Hell's Kitchen exists between Forty-Second and Fifty-Third Streets, between Eighth and Tenth Avenues. Not coincidentally, this area includes all of the neighborhood's gay bars. Priorities, I guess.

On any normal day, I'd walk to the boys' place to get some fresh air on my way, but they've been blowing up my phone every five seconds, so I'm in a cab. Ninth Avenue is filled with early-Saturday-morning traffic, which is basically a few scattered groups of disheveled gay boys in oversized sunglasses, hunched over from hangovers, and enduring walks of shame, getting breakfast, or dropping off laundry. Most of them I recognize, and would enjoy chatting with if it weren't for the fact that I have to go save two of my friends from a bloodthirsty mammoth rodent. All in a day's work.

My lacrosse stick is on the seat next to me. I haven't used it since junior varsity in high school. (And don't ask me why I've carted it with me all these years—I like how it looks on my wall, okay?) I hope I still have the skills to snatch Mickey up—before he disappears again and comes back with reinforcements.

As long as I'm in the cab for a few minutes, I have Shane on the phone so I can simultaneously deal with THAT bit of drama. Efficiency is key when you're expected to help everybody. At least Batman has Alfred to answer his calls and Robin to send out on lesser emergencies. Like this one. It's like I'm in that old Root Beer Tapper video game, running from bar to bar and making sure that every customer has a tall cold one. They drink and get pissed if you don't toss them a new one the second they kill off the last. And if you throw a new one too soon, it ends up on the floor, and they get pissed about that too. The customers in this morning's version of the game are Irwin, Shane, Rowan, Servando, and Mikey Drama, and they're guzzling root beer like it's going out of style. And here I am, running from one to the next, pulling the draft handle and flinging the mug...

Shane's filling me in: This morning, Brayden was caught looking at his boyfriend's phone, and the guy dumped him and peaced out. Called him crazy too—certainly an apt adjective, but invoking it only makes Brayden even crazier. I don't pay much mind to the trials and travesties of Brayden's dating life, since they come along about as often as commercials during prime time. But Shane rarely sounds the drama alarm like this. This is a big deal, he claims. This tantrum beats out all the others Brayden's ever thrown, including the one that left my best buddy lying on the floor in a pool of his own blood on Fire Island. A full-on psychotic/potentially murderous meltdown.

Even worse, Brayden's most recent ex happens to be one of my favorite pop/house DJs; thanks for that added level of complexity, Bray.

"Do you really think he's in danger? Because if this is just Brayden being Brayden, I have a lot on my plate today, and after what happened on Fire Island, he's not that high up the list," I say, looking out the window. The sky is getting cloudy—not too many clouds, but New York City rarely jokes around with weather. If it went through the trouble of bringing out the gloomy gray, it's probably planning on using it. This isn't a good sign.

"No, boo, I'm totally serious," Shane says. "He trashed our living room, and I walked in on him screaming at nobody."

Okay, that IS crazy. Even for Brayden.

"Jesus, is he still there?"

"No! That's the problem. Bitch ran out of here before I was done putting all the books back on the shelf."

"Is he responding to texts?" I ask as my cab approaches the intersection of Servando and Rowan's place. "Have you tried calling or e-mailing?"

"All of it, boo. No response."

"Fuck a duck. Okay, I have to help Rowan and Servando kill a rat. Or a twenty-foot-tall beady-eyed, fanged monster, judging from the way they're freaking out."

"Didn't realize you had 'exterminator' on your résumé too."

"Yep. Happy Saturday. Keep me posted. If you don't hear anything after I've killed Remy, I'll send out a search team."

"Yeah. Wait—who's Remy?"

"*Ratatouille*? Brush up on your Pixar while I'm gone," I explain. "Also, try calling some of his girlfriends if you have their numbers. Okay?"

"Okay, boo, thanks."

The cabbie pulls up to the curb. I swipe my credit card and leave him a 30 percent tip. He thanks me profusely for my generosity, considering how little he had to drive to reach my destination. I nod and smile.

I overtip everybody. Probably because, before I found myself in this place of financial security and gay fame, I was a waiter at a shitty chain steakhouse on Long Island during college summers. I had my fair share of stiffings by cheapskates and verbal abuse from insensitive assholes. Now I'm always super-nice to those who provide services and tip them generously to make up for the fuckwads they have inevitably dealt with all day (or night) long. Go-go boys, bartenders, pizza delivery guys, baristas, doesn't matter. It's my own bit of social charity. A couple extra bucks to cheer everybody up.

Servando and Rowan's apartment is at the back of the ground floor of a four-story apartment building made of faded bricks, next door to a shuttered pizza joint. I hold the buzzer for their apartment and wait. There is a click as the intercom comes to life.

"Todd! Help! Please! HELP!"

There's another buzz. I enter through the double-glass-doored vestibule quickly so I don't get stuck between locked entrances, pass the staircase and wall full of mailboxes, and jog down the narrow hallway of cracked and peeling cream-colored wallpaper, headed for the last apartment on the far right. The hall smells like someone's dinner from last night—just the highlights that were able to cling to the walls before giving up the ghost.

Even if I didn't know where the duo lived, it would be easy to find them with the assistance of the screeching that echoes all the way to the entrance. Have they been screaming like this all morning? That's one brave (or deaf) rat.

The boys' door is wide open and the apartment looks like a tornado ripped straight through. Abandoned breakfast plates with scraps of egg whites on a small side table, glasses overturned next to them. Copies of *NEXT* and *GET OUT* and *ODYSSEY* magazines open and facedown all over the floor like a flock of dead gay birds. A baggie of weed is torn wide open, the green clumps smashed to useless bits. A dildo lies inexplicably in the middle of the apartment. Servando is dancing from one foot to the other on top of a folding chair, his longish black hair ragged and sticking out in all directions. Rowan is backed into the corner on top of the bed they still share even though they've been broken up for over a year. Both are in their underwear, like two go-go boys magically transported to someone's home, rendered confused by the sudden change of location.

"Good morning, boys. How's everything?" I ask, bouncing my lacrosse stick in my right palm with my left hand.

"Get it, Todd!" Servando screams, pointing in a variety of directions, like the rat is teleporting back and forth across the room.

"Where is he?" I ask, clearing the door and slamming it behind me with my ass, cutting off the critter's possible escape routes. Okay, this might be a fun way to start my day, after all. I've got some aggression I wouldn't mind taking out on Servando and Rowan's new furry friend.

"You think I know, bitch?" Rowan yells, like I'm the one who released this creature into their home. "Probably plotting his next attack! Ugh, I hate New York! We never had rats in Wisconsin! I'm gonna move back home!"

"Funny, because you'd think they'd be all about the cheese," I say over my shoulder, casing the joint and monitoring closely for any sort of movement. "Now, shut up, both of you queens. Maybe we can hear him."

Servando and Rowan clam up, their hands on their mouths, eyes bugging out. The silence, once again, is wonderful; hopefully today will provide a lot more of it.

"Why are you two in your underwear, anyway? Afraid of him crawling into your pants?"

"Ew! I didn't even think of that!" Servando shrieks.

"We were…"

"You were about to fuck, weren't you?" I ask, knocking a garbage can away from the wall with my lacrosse stick.

No rat.

"And what if we were?" Rowan asks righteously.

"Nothing," I say, opening cabinets in the studio's connected kitchen area. "Not like it's weird that two ex-boyfriends still live, sleep, and fuck together. You do know exes are supposed to hate each other, right? Avoid each other like the plague, at all costs?"

"Don't judge us!" Rowan says, pointing.

"Especially at a time of crisis!" Servando adds.

But of course I'm judging them. I have since we all became friends. Rowan and Servando are one of the world's greatest unsolved mysteries. They broke up over a year ago, and yet they still do everything together—including live and fuck. The true mystery is that they seem to be the only two people in Manhattan who don't realize that they ARE boyfriends. But don't tell them that, unless you want Servando to monologue the fuck out of you and waste half your day in the process.

On the other hand, while their thinking makes zero sense, it's a far better situation than Brayden's. He can't hold down a relationship for longer than a week and a half and has a must-kill list as long as a gay directory of Manhattan. Servando and Rowan's rationales may be bizarre, but at least there will be no casualties as a result.

Except one rat, maybe.

I shush the boys again and go back to slowly tiptoeing around the apartment, cocking my head, as if that'll make the little fucker easier to hear. I wonder if there even IS a rat. Maybe they just thought they saw it? This place is a mess—underwear and clothing all over the place. It's like me and Gully's room back in the frat house. But while we both grew up and learned to put our shit in drawers and cabinets, apparently Servando and Rowan have yet to reach that point of maturity.

I should have brought Señor along. He'd find the creature, if indeed there was one. Probably kill him with his Beefaroni farts too.

"Todd?"

"Shut the fuck up!" I whisper at whoever tried talking. Because I think I hear something. No—I DO hear something. It's a light crinkling noise, like some asshole in a Broadway theater opening a candy wrapper despite the prerecorded announcement instructing him to cut that crap out before the show started.

The sound is coming from the bathroom. Switching on the bathroom light would probably scare the thing away, so I grab my iPhone and, creeping into the john, shine it in the direction of the noise.

He (or she) appears in the small beam of glow from my phone. He's in the corner by the toilet, up on his hind legs and scratching excitedly at a discarded toilet paper wrapper. He's barely larger than a muffin, sorta cute in that anthropomorphic children's-movie-mouse type of way. Still, I wouldn't want him running around in my apartment, either. He needs to be disposed of.

I hold a hand up behind me to keep Servando and Rowan quiet, then slowly, carefully step closer. It'll have to be a quick attack, perfectly aimed, or my stick will crash off the toilet or wall. One wrong move and the fucker will fly out of the room and wreak havoc for the rest of the day. And while it might be fun to chase after him, I have too much else to take care of. All those other Root Beer Tapper customers, crossing their arms and turning red with little anger squiggles coming out of their heads. *Order up!*

Teeth clenched, I raise the lacrosse stick halfway off the floor and take a swipe.

Perfect shot! He's caught right in the netting.

"Sorry, Fievel, that's the end of your rodent rampage," I say, smiling.

"You got it?" Rowan or Servando asks from the other room. "Did you kill him?"

"Ew, no, bitch. Just imprisoned him. We'll put him outside so he can go back to the sewer with all of his gross friends."

I get down on one knee and drag the lacrosse stick closer. I'll need to slip something underneath the opening so he can be transported back to the streets he came from. His cousins and parents must be worried sick.

The furry thing looks at me as I get closer, its tiny eyes fixated on me like it's not sure what's going on.

"Time to go home, little buddy! How's that sound?"

Its tiny mouth opens far wider than I could ever imagine. I blink. A warped screech the likes of which you'd hear coming from a monster in a Japanese horror flick comes out. It is...SCREAM-ING!

I scream. Then Rowan and Servando scream. We are all screaming, and I'm running away from the bathroom, leaving the trapped, shrieking beast stuck in my lacrosse stick's netting.

And my phone, not wanting to be left out, rings. Another emergency.

"Aren't you going to get it out of here?" Servando cries as I sprint out of the apartment.

"Fuck that shit! You figure it out yourselves!" I yell back up the hall. "And bring back my lacrosse stick when you're done!"

***

Too drunk. Way too fucking drunk.

Because of Gulliver.

It's the weekend of my huge party on Fire Island, and I had to send my best friend home by himself, the morning of the event. Why? Because he was stupid. He got his ass kicked by Brayden the night before. Like, REALLY handed to him. Blood everywhere. Puke everywhere. I didn't find out 'til the next morning why Brayden laid into him: for fucking around with Brayden's ex, Marty, behind his back. Not once. Not twice. For A MONTH.

No—make that behind ALL of our backs. Of COURSE Brayden kicked his ass. I'd have done the same goddamned thing! I wanted to, and Marty wasn't even my boyfriend.

Gulliver lied to us. Lied to ME.

What the hell was he thinking? It isn't like him. He's smarter than that. At least, I thought he was. Has so much changed in the few years since I left UCLA? What has he become? When did he turn into some typical sneaky cunt?

I don't want to believe this is the case, that my best buddy turned into just another fresh-faced, fresher-acting, new-to-New York gay boy, but what else can I think? For every pang of loss for the friend I thought I had, I take another shot. The worst drinking game of all time.

It's a beautiful June evening. Well, at this point, June morning. We're on a raised platform built on the beach in the Fire Island Pines. Surrounded by crashing waves and blasting tunes. Nothing but disembodied lights in the background. There's a chilly breeze that cools the remaining party people who haven't already stumbled home to sleep or fuck or both. My event blew the fuckin' houses down on Fire Island, sent the sand scrambling back into the damn ocean. Over four thousand guys came out. Those numbers are typical for Gay Days and Southern Decadence, not a weekend on Fire Island.

We clogged the dance floor like a bear's shower drain gets stopped up with curlies, almost ran out of well vodka. The ticket sales probably beat the opening night of Harry Potter. *Even after paying out to everyone else, I'm going back to Manhattan with a huge chunk of cash. Even more exciting is that this is one of the events my boss Xavier let me basically run myself. I catch him toward the end of the night, drinking with a gorgeous boy under each arm. "Look at the famous Todd DiTempto," he says through a drunken smile. "Keep an eye on him, he's going to take this city over before you know it."*

But the joy of success crashes into my anger at Gulliver like two opposing waves. Trapped. Before I can smile, I wince, then walk away from my boss, cursing Gully for what he did.

The guy was like my fucking brother. We had BOTH been through bullshit with cheating ex-boyfriends and come out on the other side as even better friends. Then he goes and fucks one of my best friend's exes? And lies about it? Over and over again? Fuck no. FUCK NO. It's like he cheated on ME. He fucked that kid while living with me. While eating food I bought, watching my cable, using my Internet. Taking my drink tickets and comp entries to parties.

I'm not just angry, I feel like a fucking tool.

What should have been a celebratory weekend has been completely fucking destroyed by my bestie, who decided to think with the head between his legs instead of the one on his fucking neck. Seriously, Gullzo? I thought you were better than this.

Now I don't know what to do. And when I don't know what to do, I drink. When the party is yours, they don't make you pay for drinks.

And when you're not paying for your drinks, you lose track of how many you're swallowing. I drink because it's the easiest thing to do when I'm pissed. Easier than thinking, easier than feeling. The world's sharp edges go fuzzy, and that's just fine by me.

Thanks to the alcohol or Gulliver or whatever, on this night-of-nights, I have broken a rule I've always lived by. Rule Number One: never get fucked up at your own parties. Done and done.

Speaking of, it's time to refresh the ol' cocktail. I walk through the sizable mass of remaining party people, who kindly part so I can get through. I collide with the bar, sending a jolt of pain through my pelvis. It seemed so much farther away in my eyes. Ow.

"Enough to drink there, hot stuff?" my ex-boyfriend Kenton asks, approaching me.

"Almost," I say, smiling. "Citron and soda. In a big-boy cup, please."

Usually reserved for nonalcoholic drinks, the big-boy cups are my container of choice this evening. Fewer trips to the bar, more alcohol for me. Yum.

I sip, finding the potency agreeable, and leave a five-dollar tip.

"Great job tonight, Toddy," Kenton says, pouring himself a shot. Kenton is a guy I dated for a few months over a year ago, my first (and to date, only) boyfriend since college. Buffer than me, which must take a lot of work and commitment. Cute face with a button nose. Blond hair he combs to one side like a kid from a

black-and-white sitcom. He's thirty-something, but no one ever guesses older than twenty-six. He still has an adorable speck of a Southern drawl to his accent, even though he moved to the city for college over a decade ago and never left. He's in a tiny bathing suit, his huge thing trying to break free of the fabric. We made out last night, right before Gully got his ass kicked and had to be taken to bed.

I wonder what might have happened otherwise.

Well. No, I don't.

"You're pretty wasted." He laughs, shaking my shoulder. I almost face-plant, but catch myself on the bar. YouTube material avoided by the skin of my teeth.

"I'll tell YOU when I've had enough!" I say, slamming my fist on the bar, doing my best angry drunk impression—which must be pretty awesome, considering I'm already working with a baseline of being both angry and drunk.

"You heading back to your place soon?"

Ugh. Home. I do NOT want to go back there. Not with the guys waiting to hear what I'm going to do about Benedict Gully. What the fuck can I tell them? That I'm going to let him stay in my apartment and they should all get over the fact that he's done such a ridiculously shitty thing? Or that I'm going to kick Gulliver out, when I'm the only reason he left his old life behind and moved across the continent in the first place? He's MY fucking responsibility.

Goddammit. Is this somehow my fault? Did I do this to him? It was his decision to betray us, but he wouldn't have made it if he weren't in New York to begin with.

FUCK Gulliver. Fuck you for coming between me and my friends. Fuck you for not acting like the you I knew.

"No," I say, swallowing the drink quickly. "I think I might stay with Xavier, if he hasn't already filled his place with twinks."

"He just left with four of them, actually," Kenton says, pointing behind me. I don't even bother turning around. That sounds exactly like my boss. The lucky fucker.

"Fuck," I say. "Can I have another?"

"Last one, then I'm taking you home."

"Bitch, I just said I CAN'T go home!" I say, reaching for the big-boy cup as he refills it.

Kenton yanks the cup away, my eyes following it, and says, "I didn't say WHOSE home."

"Wha?"

"You're coming home with me. I'm not letting you sleep on the beach like a day-tripper who missed the last ferry."

That's not a good idea. It's a TERRIBLE idea. We just snogged last night, and I'm even drunker now than I was then. I'm sure Kenton's digs only have one bed, since they stick all the Fire Island staff in single rooms at the Hotel Ciel. My feelings about Gulliver are complicated enough without adding a rekindling with an ex to the mix.

Then again, if I'm looking for a distraction…

"Nah, I'll find somewhere," *I say, finally wrestling the cup out of his hands.*

"Okay," *Kenton says, raising his eyebrows like he's saying,* You missed your chance, bud. *"Invite's still open, in case you change your mind."*

An hour later, I do. Everything is spinning at this point, like I'm riding in one of those UFO-shaped things at the carnival in Central Park. I'll probably fall off the fucking dock if I try to stumble home. Kenton's place, meanwhile, is just forty or fifty feet away. And my friends aren't there, waiting for me, like they are at my house.

Thirty minutes after the party has ended and everyone else has gone home, Kenton and I are headed to his place. But not before we kiss on the empty dance platform, the waves now the only sound around us.

"Pretty beautiful, don't you think?" *he asks, looking at the ocean, rubbing my dick through my bathing suit.*

"Yeah, def," *I say, thinking only of Gulliver.*

As I assumed, Kenton is staying in one of the hotel rooms that the staff get for free for working on Fire Island all summer. It's a tiny, un-air-conditioned room with a full-size bed and a chair and a minifridge. Just a hole in the wall where he can lay his head and take home his tricks. Tonight, that's me.

His door closes and our mouths open. All over each other.

I stop thinking. Turn off my memory-maker. Dive into the blackness of the room like I'm being wrapped in a tarp. It's suffocating. His hand goes here. My hands end up there. Our mouths flutter. Tongues come out. Cocks come out. My head spins and my stomach lurches. The sheets of his bed—warm, maybe even warmer than the room. I want to open a fucking door, run out of here. Dive into the water and swim back to Long Island. But that's stupid. Every bit of that idea is retarded.

I think we fuck. No, I'm sure we do. Who's top and who's bottom? Good question. Do we use a condom? Maybe. All I can think of is Gulliver and wanting to scream. And then I can think of nothing more.

That's all I remember the next morning when I wake up to find Kenton gone: Gulliver. Rage. Darkness.

***

Shane still hasn't gotten in touch with Brayden, but there's something more pressing—Mikey Drama has had seven consecutive meltdowns on my voice mail since I popped into Servando and Rowan's apartment. I delete them all, allowing him a single screamed syllable in each one before I send it to the trash.

I grab a bagel from a street vendor and chow down as I walk home. I'm nauseous, but my stomach is growling. Another not-fun thing that's been happening a lot recently. This tasteless carby thing will hopefully shut it up.

The first bit of drama I'll handle is editing the screen projections that will be all over the club tonight. The thought of giant projections calling my event partner "Mikey Dromo" is pretty funny, but it's clear he doesn't find the situation as humorous as I do. The change shouldn't take long. Fifty minutes of Michael screaming will equal one minute of image editing. I'm not a graphic design genius, but I know my way around Photoshop. You have to when you work in nightlife, because if you don't, you end up like Michael: pulling your hair out in clumps and praying that SOMEONE took the time to learn. Half the excitement of an event is how it looks on a promo ad. And when you produce as many flyers as I do for GuyTime, you quickly realize you can save a lot of time by making your own tiny revisions instead of sending it back to the designer.

The creator of GuyTime is Xavier. He's short, handsome, soft-spoken, in his mid-thirties, with a head of closely cropped black hair. He's done this shit for over a decade. I owe all of my night-life superstardom to him, though he'll hear nothing of it. Xavier wants nothing to do with celebrity. The first thing he found attractive about me is that I'm willing to step into the spotlight, go on TV and radio and speak on behalf of the company without running away with the fame he granted me and starting my own separate outfit. This is the first event I've done completely on my own, without any of Xav's guidance and advising, because he's on vacation in Europe for three weeks with a few of our regular party boys. I would kill to be able to ask him what to do with Drama, who's STILL blowing up my phone. But Xavier deserves this time off, and I want to prove I can handle a personality like Drama and a party as massive as eWrecksion on my own. Xavier has taught me everything, guiding me through the bumps and curves of nightlife for over two years, and it's time to show him I was a worthy pupil. I owe him that much.

I wave to my doorman, who's drinking a Diet Coke and reading the *New Yorker*. I take the elevator to my apartment. The living room smells like faded dog fart, and I gag at the scent. I run to the bathroom, grab the Febreze can from beside the toilet, and spray it all around the apartment like I'm tagging the side of a subway tunnel with my name. Now the room smells like dog gas and freshly laundered sheets, a significant improvement. Señor, the guilty gassy party, hops around and nips at me like he's proud of his noxious contribution.

I park myself at the long wooden desk at the far end of the living room where I keep my computers—one a PC, for the boring day job, and a Mac, which I use for anything nightlife related. The clock on the screen tells me it's already 1 in the afternoon. Time flies when you're chasing rats.

Mikey Drama has clogged my inbox with forty messages. My head throbs seeing his name stacked on top of itself like that, pushing any other communication off the first page of e-mails.

Including Drama's, there are 100 total unread messages awaiting me. Make that 105. Make that 110. This will not stop. I need to hire a secretary.

I ignore the incoming messages and sort through the pile to find the e-mail with the projection art files attached. They download quickly and pop open on my screen. The graphic is dominated by the boys of New York Screwniversity, a gay porn site that Michael tapped to perform tonight. I've never heard of these guys, but Michael swears they're the next big thing, as far as jacking off to guys who aren't you having sex with other guys who aren't you is concerned.

He's ballsy, I'll give him that. I would never throw an event of this scale with a live sex show. That has "Health Board shutdown" written all over it. But Michael doesn't care about being shut down. That's why all of his parties are one-time only and change locations regularly. He's developed a reputation for throwing big blowout events that are too hot for Bloomberg's squeaky clean Manhattan. Each party gets dirtier than the last. To his credit, each outsells the last as well. He's also very generous with "donating" to the local police precincts, which I'm sure helps his events along.

It only takes a second to fix "Dromo" and save the new version. It's annoying that Michael didn't even try—just delegated and began flipping out. Whatever. I send it back to him and sit back in my chair.

The boys on the projection graphic are cute. Not really my type, though—way too glossed and shiny. Hairless and boyish. I know that makes them just like everyone I bring to GuyTime events, but that doesn't mean I want to sleep with them. I like my boys a little rougher, a little more human and a little less Bel Ami cyborg. But hey, clearly I'm representing the minority, since Michael has sold twice as many tickets to this event than even I did to my big Fire Island blowout two months ago.

Fire Island—was that really two months ago? Jesus.

A clanging sound across the apartment breaks my thought process. It's today's mail, conveniently deposited through a slot in the door. The luxury is kick-ass, but the bills and shit stacked up on the floor won't be as enjoyable.

I sigh again as I lift my heavy, tired body off the chair and trudge across the room. Señor, apparently exhausted from his gastric distress, is passed out on the floor by my TV, his tongue hanging out of his smiling face. Lucky bastard. The way I'm feeling right now, I could totally nap on a hardwood floor too.

I gather up the envelopes, menus, and magazines and take them into the kitchen. I drop them on the island and scrounge through the fridge again. I'm so fucking hungry and that bagel was a carb cock-tease.

I eat nothing but crap. Cap'n Crunch and rice milk it is! Pulling a stool up to the counter, I commence eating and opening.

So many bills. I gotta stop buying shit. Some new gay magazine is out, and they've taken the liberty of sending me their first issue. It's the same shit: photos of cute boys at parties, interviews with club acts I've never heard of, ads in the back for massages with happy endings, personal ads for the idiots who think anyone still answers a printed personal ad anymore. More bills. New credit card offers (perfect credit and heavy spending = everyone wants a piece of you).

And something else.

In the center of the stack is an oversized novelty postcard. The kind you find on rusty spinning racks in all of the tourist trap gift shops on Eighth Avenue and around Times Square. It's an old stock photo of the Statue of Liberty, the words *I LOVE NEW YORK* on the front in huge pink-and-white letters. I've gotten this postcard before, about two months ago. I flip this one over and read:

Todd,

Miss you a lot. Hope you're having fun in Hell's Kitchen. Maybe someday we'll be neighbors? I'm doing fine. Well, sorta.

Either way, I love you. And thanks for covering for me while I stumble around this city and try to make it work for me.

—Gully

Unlike the first postcard, this one has an address in the corner. And while I don't know the address, I do recognize the name of the company he's written above it. College Buddies.

I spin around on the chair so hard that I knock my cereal bowl to the floor, smashing it, sending milk to pool over where the coffee spilled before.

Shit.

I sprint back to the computer, waking Señor in the process. He barks and whines and tries to jump on my lap, but I ignore him, pushing him off. I'm clicking into my Gmail. Opening my eWreck-sion folder. Scrolling back a few days to the stack of invoices that Drama sent me and asked me to keep a record of.

The most important invoice (marked by many more exclama-tions than all the others) was the one we received from New York Screwniversity for their performance tonight. Except, their legal corporation name isn't New York Screwniversity. It's College Buddies, LLC. The address I sent the check to matches the one on Gully's postcard.

I click back to the projection file I was just editing, to the cast of New York Screwniversity and Michael's now correctly spelled name.

Gulliver?

I've been dying to see you again.

But not like this.

Fuck no. No way in hell! The guy I'm staring at looks nothing like my former roommate—he has bright-blue hair, a chinstrap, an eyebrow ring. I just looked at him ten minutes ago, zoomed in to make the name correction, and didn't even think...

It's not him. It can't be.

Gulliver would never do this.

But Gulliver would also never fuck a guy behind my back and lie about it, jeopardizing my other friendships—until he did, that is.

I move closer to the screen, staring the blue-haired twink in the face. His squinting eyes. His dimpled smile. I look at the postcard again, like the words on it could have changed somehow. Then back at the invoice, like THAT could have changed.

Nothing has changed. Except my mood, for the worse.

I type the Screwniversity's address into a browser and am greeted by the same photo of the boys that is on the projection. There's a button under the blue-haired boy's picture that says, *Get to know Marty Brayden—click right here!*

Marty Brayden, huh? Fuck.

It's a video testimonial—just "Marty" in a booth introducing himself. It starts playing as soon as the page loads. I hear his voice. See his smile. He stands, showing off a tiny pair of underwear and a growing bulge. He lifts his eyebrow and laughs.

I know that laugh.

Motherfucker.

I can't watch anymore.

***

Sometimes it's good to NOT be in charge of the party. Like this weekend. I'm back on Fire Island. It's been a month since we were last here, for my event, and four weeks before eWrecksion, my next event. This is my last chance to just chill, get smashed, do stupid shit, all with my boys, before I jump into the whirlwind of planning Mikey Drama's historic party. Servando, Rowan, Shane, and Brayden are along for the ride, everyone but you-know-who. We're even crashing in the same house.

Not a word is spoken of Gulliver, wherever the fuck he is. No one cares to open that can of worms. For the purposes of my crew, it's like he never came to New York at all. And I can ALMOST pretend along with them that he's still safe and happy on the West Coast.

Almost.

I leave my boys in the roped-off VIP corner by the long wooden bar, instructing the bartender to take special care of them and warning them to not take advantage. (Shane has a thirst for the fanciest-looking bottles on the top shelf.)

"Todd!" a voice shouts from across the club. "Todd!"

It's Kenton, pushing his way through the crowd like he's in a race to get out, his face a mask of concern. As a bartender, surely he's had his share of shit to deal with on a night packed like this. But I'm off. Tonight, I party. I'll redirect Kenton to Drama, who gets to be the bad cop to unruly drunk patrons; I'm the good cop, the one who bends rules and pulls strings and might let you borrow his hand-cuffs for sexy recreational purposes. A few screams from Drama will settle any dispute, and I can go back to getting fucked up.

"What's up, lover?" I ask. Kenton seems put off by my smile, shocked by it. "What's going on? Tell me there's drama. Let me text Mikey now. I haven't seen him in an hour. If he ducked out early, I'll kill him. This is HIS event, not mine."

"You didn't get my voice mail? My texts?"

"Tonight? No," I say, checking through the hundreds of texts that remain unread on my phone. When they stack up as high as mine do, you just sorta give up, figuring that the truly important matters will keep bubbling to the top.

"No, WEEKS ago. Did you get them?"

"Maybe?" I ask, scrolling through the texts. "They may have been lost in the pile..."

"I left you voice mails too, Todd."

"I check those less than I check my texts, babe. What's up?"

I usually tell people not to bother with voice mail. I may be able to work out two hours a day; I'm on my feet from 9 in the morning 'til 4 the next morning juggling a full-time day job and another, more-than-full-time nighttime career. But for some strange reason, I just can't muster the energy to dial my voice mail, put in the pass code, and sit there while someone speaks from the past about something they probably already tried texting me about too. Especially when there are forty damn voices with all sorts of shit to tell me. Just text, I advise. Then the chances of me getting back to you increase exponentially—though, clearly, not even that works sometimes.

Did Kenton call me a few weeks ago? Yeah, I remember now. Did I avoid getting back to him? Yes. I was busy. There were other priorities, like Gulliver disappearing and ramping up for eWrecksion and day job shit and who knows what else. The last thing I needed was ex drama added to the heap. What happens on Fire Island is meant to stay on Fire Island, not follow you home so you have to deal with it back in Manhattan.

ESPECIALLY when "what happens" involves hooking up with your ex. I suppose I meant to give Kenton a jingle once I got everything else out of the way—but who am I kidding? Everything else is NEVER out of the way.

"Fuck," Kenton says, rolling his eyes. "Can't you tell when a text might be important?"

I put my hands up, trying to get Kenton to tone down his voice, which is carrying despite the blasting music. "What's up, K?"

Kenton's face screws into a grimace. "Can we go talk somewhere, please?"

My stomach is in my shoes. I have so much shit to do, even if this isn't my fucking event. My guests are bitching about the door guy, who apparently isn't comping them when they drop my name, even though Drama promised it would be okay. One of the bartenders is having issues with a drunken partygoer who is refusing to leave him alone, and apparently he's one of my guests who DID get in. The last thing I have time to do is take a stroll with my ex.

"Can it wait?" I ask, flashing him a smile. "You know how crazed I get at these things."

"Todd, for once, please give me two minutes of your fucking time!"

It takes me a minute to realize he's crying. I nod and tell him to lead the way.

We escape from the party, down the stairs, and out to the edge of the adjacent docks. We're at the end of Fire Island, with Long Island just a dot on the horizon. Around us, houseboats and fishing boats bob up and down in the water, the boardwalk creaking as if ghosts are dancing around the planks. It's still loud out here, even though we're over two hundred feet from the club. The sounds of DJ Christian Robert blare out of the second-floor windows and waft down to us. Christian was my recommendation to Drama, and Brayden seems to think he's SUPER cute—which I'm sure will prove to be a negative in no time.

"Dude, what the fuck is going on?" I ask finally, after what feels like an hour of silence.

Kenton, who I never saw cry even once when we were together (or apart), has regained his composure. He stares out at the bobbing boats, his head shaking slowly. "Fuck, Todd..."

"What, babe? What's going on? You know if this were any other night, I wouldn't rush you. But they need me up there. Drama will be blowing up my phone any second."

"And you'll respond to that. Right? Because THAT'S what's impor-
tant. Parties."

"Not parties. WORK. For me, it's WORK. How many times do I
have to tell you that?"

"Yeah. Rough life." Kenton catches himself and turns to face me.
His face looks drawn out, skinny, deep circles around his eyes. "I'm
sorry. I didn't mean that. And I'm sorry about, uh…"

"Sorry about WHAT?" I ask, losing my patience. "What the FUCK
is going on with you?"

And then he tells me.

At approximately the same moment, the world ends.

I make him tell me again.

"Are you sure?" I ask. Now I'm the one staring at the boats and the
black water. I can feel Kenton's eyes on me.

"Yes," he says.

I nod. I get up. I walk away. Kenton calls after me only once, know-
ing full well I won't be turning around and coming back.

I return to the party and switch to drinking water. Two hours later,
when the event ends and hundreds of sweat-soaked boys trek back to
their weekend shares, I head home with my crew. They want to pull an
all-nighter. I tell them to have a blast, but I'm going right to bed. They

stay up drinking and dancing; I can hear them through the windows of my room. At some point, they trade indoors for outdoors, head out to the pool. I hear guests arrive. I hear sex—loud, drunken—all around me. I hear silence when everyone finally passes out.

I don't sleep.

The next morning, I leave the island, telling the boys they can stay for the rest of the weekend, but I have business back in the city. No one questions that. No one protests. Todd DiTempto does what he has to, and what he says is rarely challenged.

On the ferry and then the train, I don't turn on my phone, don't check e-mails or voice mails or texts. What might have been urgent yesterday is now a frivolous waste of time and energy and life. It's not important. Nothing is anymore.

Back in the city, I walk to my apartment alone, close the door behind me, and go to bed.

I sleep for sixteen hours. And even that isn't enough.

***

I tear up the postcard and throw it in the trash. Then I walk around the apartment in circles for what becomes an hour, Señor yipping and following me, perplexed and wondering if this will count as his evening walk.

I sit back at the computer and go back to the New York Screwniversity website, where I find hundreds of photos and videos of blue-haired Gulliver. I don't enlarge a single photo, don't play a single preview video. I don't want to see my traitorous best buddy having fun for the past two months, given what I've been going through.

I don't know what the fuck to do.

The boys are texting me. Shane first. Then Servando and Rowan. I don't respond. If they recognize Gully, see him up on that stage getting fucked by a dozen of his dorm mates, then that would be it. That would be the end of any respect they ever had for him. However much might be left after what he did to Brayden.

Fuck, how much respect do *I* even have for him? The little shit got into this situation by thinking with his dick and lying about it. And his way out of it is to fuck even *more* people and continue hiding it from those of us who still care about him?

It's not like he didn't have options. Friends here. Friends in LA. One of the most loving, functional families you could ever meet. Christ, think of how ashamed they'd be if they found this out.

Gulliver moved here for a fresh start. Now that's shot to shit, if anyone ever finds out who Marty Brayden really is. And putting on a live sex show in front of a crowd filled with boys you once knew? Well, that's a really great way to blow your cover, amongst other things.

I call Drama to tell him I won't be coming out tonight.

"What?" Drama screams on the other end of the phone. "Of course you're coming! You HAVE to."

"I feel like shit, Michael. I can't. But don't worry, bro, I got your projections taken care of. The place is going to be packed. You don't need me there."

"Excuse me? Who the fuck is this, and why are you calling me from Todd DiTempto's cell phone?"

Michael's right. At the moment, I'm not Todd DiTempto. Todd DiTempto is a man who has all the answers, who always knows what to do. He deals with shit. Confronts it head-on. Or at least, he used to.

Todd DiTempto was invincible—but he's not anymore. If only they knew.

I can't be at eWrecksion tonight. If I see Marty Brayden, I don't know what I'll do. Hit him? Hug him? Throw up? Most likely all three, right before I pick him up and physically drag him kicking and screaming out of the club and out of that life. I'll lock him in a trunk and ship it express back to California, preferably back in time too, if it's possible. Why would he do something so fucking dangerous? Put his health and future at risk? Even if he was disease-free, those fucking tapes come back to haunt you when you least fucking expect it. The idiot. The fucking moron. Does he think he's hit rock bottom? He has NO idea how much worse shit could get.

"DiTempto, come on, man! What the fuck is going on with you? Since when are you one of those bullshit promoters who don't go to their own events? Forget the fact that I need you there. It's going to be the fucking party of the century! Where are you going? What's better than this? Did Lady Gaga personally invite you to her VIP party on the moon?"

"Actually, I was thinking I would just stay in," I say, looking out the window. It's 6 and the sky is way too dark. It's going to rain. The Weather Channel says it's going to be a fucking storm and a half too. "The weather is turning to shit. Plus, I'm exhausted."

"Todd, don't pull this shit with me." Michael's voice has changed from a scream to a whisper. It's much scarier. I'm half expecting him to jump out of a closet brandishing a knife. "You WILL come to the party tonight. And you WILL be there by nine."

"Michael, please?" I beg, at my wit's end. "I really can't be there, okay?"

Michael says nothing. I can hear him breathing on the other end of the line. Thinking? Maybe he's getting it. I've never pulled anything like this, never had a reason to. But if I see Gully in that sex show, I'll never be able to look him in his fucking pierced face ever again.

Please, Drama. Please understand.

"Okay. Here's what you're going to do. You're going to make yourself a cocktail, right fucking now. You're going to drink it. And then get showered, get dressed. And all the while, I want you to think about whether or not you REALLY want tonight to be the last party you throw in this city. EVER again."

Oh, God, here it comes.

"Because if you aren't at eWrecksion tonight, gorgeous and sociable and all the other fucking words we use to describe Todd fucking DiTempto, I will call Xavier and tell him that we're done. And I'm pretty sure you and he will be done too if I have to make that fucking call. You'll never work in this town again."

Ah, there it is.

"What the fuck, Michael? Can you not see I have a good fucking reason not to be there tonight?"

"You said tired. You said weather. Those are NOT good fucking reasons. Those are lame-ass, shitty reasons! If you have a good fucking reason for committing to throw the party of the century and then backing out at the last minute, you can tell me. Come on, spit it out, I'm sure it's quite a fucking story."

Outside, people are running for cover. The sky has opened up like God just spilled the universe's largest bottle of Dasani. From nothing to pouring in half a second. Umbrellas are out. Others are scrambling to duck under awnings and apartment entryways. Cabs fill and speed away as people dive in to avoid the soaking assault.

"Well?" Michael asks.

"I'll see you at nine," I say, then hang up. "Asshole."

I sit in the living room in silence, hearing myself blink. I have to get outside before I start screaming at the walls. I stick a leash on Señor and take him down in the elevator. Outside. Señor stops every few feet to shake himself out before skipping ahead and pulling me along with the leash. I'm wet and don't care.

My phone is beeping, pinging, chiming. Exploding. I pull it out and watch the notifications fly in: new Grindr chats, new Facebook invites, new text messages, e-mails from both day job, night job, and personal life. Foursquare updates. LinkedIn e-mails. I want to fling the phone into the street and buy a drink for the first cab driver who will agree to drive over it. Shut up, just SHUT UP. Give me five fucking seconds by myself.

Instead, the phone rings. And it's the last number I want to see at this moment.

Incoming call: Mama Leverenz.

I can't not answer. Never once have I pushed Ignore on my surrogate mama. I just can't.

"Mama Leverenz!" I say, sucking it up and trying my best to sound as chipper as I usually do when I talk to Gully's mom.

"Todd, are you okay?"

Fuck me.

"Yeah! I'm fine! Just walking Señor. What's going on? Everything okay out west?"

"I just wanted to check in on my boys and see how your weekend upstate is going. Gully hasn't picked up his phone all day, and I was worried sick about him."

Oh yeah. That. I covered for Gully as recently as a day ago, spun some fairytale about us tripping upstate. Where'd I pull that from? My ass, of course. "Oh, he's pretty busy, Mrs. Leverenz. We've been getting a little crazy up here, you know."

"And you brought Señor with you all the way upstate?"

"Um, yeah! Figured he'd enjoy getting out of the noisy city," I say as an ambulance speeds by, its sirens blaring.

"It sounds pretty loud out there."

My mouth is moving, but there's no sound coming out. Is she on to me? I should be so much better at this. I'm just so fucking shaken that I'm off my game. Dammit. And I'm not a liar. Never was, until Gulliver went away. One last favor he required without even having the fucking courtesy to ASK. *Hey, Todd? Do me a fave? Can you spend the next few months bullshitting my mom about where I am and what we're doing in case she ever asks? I'm gonna go be a gay porn star. Peace out!*

"Todd, you wouldn't lie to me, would you?"

I'm so close to telling her. Because I have to tell SOMEBODY, and that somebody can't be anyone in New York. Brayden and the gang might use the information to get back at Gulliver for lying to us. They'd smear his name so fast that, by the end of tomorrow, every busboy and cab driver and street meat vendor in the city would know Gulliver Leverenz was now taking it up the ass on camera.

But, in the meantime, the secret is burning on the inside like a bad shot of Jäger. Like heartburn and food poisoning. I need to get off the phone before I blow it and cause even more damage.

Too much silence. I finally speak up: "No, of course not, Mama Leverenz. I'll be sure to tell Gullzo to give you a ring soon, okay? He's in the shower, I think."

"You're not being a bad influence on him, are you? With those parties you throw, I bet you both drink like fish!"

Phew. "Only a little bit, Mrs. L. Kid's gotta unwind somehow, right?"

"I suppose. Just watch out for my baby, okay? You're my eyes and ears out there!"

"Of course. You know I've got your back."

This lie hurts more than all the others. This shit IS my fault. It has to be. The thought of the Gulliver I knew in California changing his name and appearance to do porn would have been laughable. And after just a few short months in the city I convinced him to move to, he's undergone an Extreme Makeover: Slut Edition. I suck. As a human being. As a watchdog. As a best friend. Fuck me.

Now what can I do? How can I help?

If Gulliver's going to live this life, I'm not sure friendship's in the cards anymore. I can't sit back and watch him destroy himself, can't wait around for the news that he's now a meth addict, now an escort, now contracted a life-altering STD. No.

But I can at least try to clean up the mess I made of him. Gully would be devastated if his family found out he was working for the Screwniversity. Devastated enough to quit? Probably. I could tell her and nip this in the bud, right here and now. Stop Gulliver from doing any more harm to himself. Hell, probably stop him from even going to eWrecksion tonight. He'd go cold turkey in a heartbeat with one horrendously awkward and painful phone call from his mother.

But in the process, I'd break Sharon's heart. And his dad's. And his brother's. They'd look at Gulliver in a completely new light. They'd still love him, but they'd never forgive him after learning that the Gulliver they thought they knew is hiding a host of unsavory things from them. And that sucks. It's probably even worse when the kid is your own flesh and blood.

So even if maybe, in the long run, telling Sharon the truth might do Gully good, it's not something I can do. It's not my place. This is one responsibility I refuse to take.

"You're sure, Todd? You sound strange today. The last few times I've called, actually."

I take a deep breath. "Yeah. I'm fine. I promise. I'm just tired and hungover."

A brief silence on the other end of the line. I can imagine Sharon pursing her lips, carefully choosing her next words, as I've seen her do anytime she suspects something is up and is trying to draw it out of someone. "You know, Todd. You've mentioned you don't talk to your own parents as often as Gully talks to us. We're lucky to have such a close relationship. But you can always talk to me too."

"I *am* talking to you, Mrs. L."

"You know what I mean. Life's tough out there, I can only imagine. I may be a little old lady from California, but I'm always here and there's nothing you can't open up to me about. Nothing. Should the mood ever strike."

I wince a smile and wonder, *When was the last time anybody saw past my can-do exterior?* I say, "Okay. I promise. One of these days, I'll ring you up and talk your freakin' ear off. And then you'll be sorry."

She giggles. "That's what I like to hear! Thanks, Todd. I love you. Now, you take care of yourself. BEFORE you take care of everybody else, you hear?"

"You got it. I'll tell Gulliver to call you."

That Sharon Leverenz is a smart lady. And she's right: One of these days, I am going to have to talk to someone. Tell someone. Make it real.

Just not tonight. Tonight, it's got to be the last thing on my mind.

We hang up and I drag Señor back to the apartment, unleashing him and letting him return to his doggy bed for yet another nap. I can only hope Gully calls his mom tonight or tomorrow. I can't keep making up his life for him. It's fucking exhausting and depressing as hell, because every lie I tell is conjured up out of some alternate reality where Gulliver and Todd are still best friends and having the time of their lives. It's the life we SHOULD be living. The life we WERE living, not so long ago. How did things go to hell so rapidly? Is there any chance of getting it back?

People say I'm lucky. I stumbled into nightlife, grabbed it like a bucking bronco, and rode it to first prize. I somehow found a job in finance and have (to date) held on to it against all economic odds. I'm attractive and financially secure and popular and successful in all things. That's what they tell me, anyway. What these fuckers don't get is that this has nothing to do with luck and everything to do with hard work. I studied my ass off in college, work my ass off at the hedge, walk my ass off at the clubs and bars to get my name into the universal New York gay vernacular. It may just be the busiest ass in the city—besides Gulliver's, lately.

And okay, some people work themselves to the bone and never get as far as I do. Some might see that as good fortune. But when it comes to actual luck, I don't have a fucking drop of it. And I'm worried about how much luck Gulliver still has to spare.

All it takes is one person. One guy who recognizes his smile or laugh like I did. What happens when he leaves the Screwniversity and future potential bosses find his videos? What happens when an old friend in LA realizes whose photos he's jerking off to and sends the link to everyone Gully ever met there? His whole fucking world will come down. What then, Gully? Who will you turn to then, if not me?

And when people realize I knew and didn't say anything, I'll look like a giant tool. Because of Gulliver. AGAIN. What would Sharon say if she found out I knew Gully was doing porn and didn't stop him?

She'd hate me. The only reason she can sleep at night with Gulliver in this city is because she thinks I'm taking care of him. That I would never let anything bad happen. Like I'm some kind of superhero who has the power to save people from themselves. Instead, I pulled Gully around with me through the VIP nightlife scene, introduced him around, got him plastered. Then when he got in over his head, I sent him packing. Instead of pulling him out of the hole he dug himself into, I left him there. What did I expect to happen? It's like I gave him the knife to stab himself with! Now I'm going to have to look at that face tonight, since Michael will surely find a way to introduce me to the evening's entertainment.

And then what happens? Do I let him know that I can see through the blue? Do I pretend he's just some fucking porn boy I don't really give a shit about?

I have no idea.

***

I arrive, early, at 8, determined to get lost in the busywork of the event's finishing touches. When I am interviewed by gay magazines and websites, they usually ask how I was able to rise to the top so quickly. After (honestly) telling them I'm nowhere near the top, I openly let them in on my secret: this is a business as much as anything else is. Whether you're running a restaurant or a hair salon or a plumbing company or a gay party, it's business. This one may be a lot of fun, as far as businesses are concerned, but still. With that mentality, I've been able to keep my head in the game and my emotions out of it, which has kept the drama at bay. Until now.

Tonight marks the first night I'm having a hard time making that split. *This is business*, I tell myself as I walk down the corridor past men running around with cardboard boxes full of decorations. This is business, which makes Gulliver a performer, which makes us colleagues for the night.

But fuck, that isn't working. My fucking best friend is gearing up to spread his legs and get fucked in front of at least six thousand guys. For a second, I consider telling Michael to cancel the Screwniversity performance, but I'm not that stupid. The money has been paid (I should know, I have the copy of the check in my e-mail), and my reasoning is of no consequence to my partner. And if I did somehow convince Michael? So what? Gulliver's been doing this shit for a while already. The damage is done.

The house lights are still on, exposing the club for what it actually is: an abandoned warehouse. Sound checks are in progress, with technicians laying and taping down wires. A speaker next to my head explodes in deafening static and whining. "Sorry!" someone calls out from across the room. The diva nobody, whatever her name is, is practicing her choreography. She'll probably end up lip-synching, like most club acts do. The lighting guys are setting up premade patterns of shifting colors. I move between the three levels, oversee the construction of the VIP area on the top floor, and tell the bartenders about the porn-inspired drink specials (of course there's one for Marty Brayden).

Tonight was going to be so amazing, and once again, Gulliver has found a way to ruin it. First my party on Fire Island, now this. Thanks so much, bro. Really great way to show your fucking appreciation for everything I did for you.

Michael finds his way to me around 9:30 and is all hugs and smiles, like he didn't just threaten my nightlife career hours earlier. He's probably completely forgotten. Although he overreacts to even the smallest potential problem, once it's solved, it's like it never happened.

"DiTempto! Get us some shots!"

What I'd like to do is take a shot at his fucking face. He's smiling a shit-eating grin, clapping me on the shoulder. He gestures out to the empty space and yells, "Tonight, we make fucking HISTORY!"

At least Xavier will see that I helped make this happen. That's the one good thing. Even with my personal life as chaotic as it currently is, I'm here, throwing one hell of a party. And just because I can't have a good time doesn't mean the rest of gay New York should suffer. Tonight, they party.

"So," I say, smiling at Drama. "You said something about shots?"

"Abso-fucking-lutely! What's your fancy?"

"Cuervo and Patrón would be perfect."

***

Blur. Everywhere. Lights and banging sounds. Drinks and more drinks. This party is awesome? Think so. Hear Drama laughing his ass off.

DJ needs the AC turned up, diva that he is. Bartenders are out of Stoli. Barback missing. Barback found. Bathroom attendant leering at customers at the urinals. Bathroom attendant fired. Extra barback promoted to bathroom attendant. Music blasting. Ke$ha. Beyonce. Britney. Gaga. Ke$ha again. 'NSync? Think so. LOVE it.

Go-go Chase is cute. Go-go Chase is flirting with me. I am letting him flirt. I am flirting back. I'm kissing him. He's huge. He's not my type? He works for me? His breath tastes good. I burp quietly and blow it over my shoulder so he doesn't smell it. I'm smooth like that. He tries to suck my dick. I stop him. No. Not here. I know not to do that here.

Or at all anymore. Right?

Go to VIP. Chase loves it. So posh, yeah? Yeah. No Gulliver yet. Er, Marty. Whoever. Slut. More drinks. Hiccup. Burp. Stomach gurgle. Sounds like someone is drowning in my belly. Talk about something with go-go Chase. Flirting? Sure. Yeah, I'll take him home.

I want to be home.

Shit. Gulliver. Marty.

Drama laughing. Drama screaming. Drama pulling me across the room. Gulliver. Fuck Gulliver. Shaking his hand. SHAKING HIS HAND. Fists sweaty. Hands trembling. Still smiling. Blinking. Not sure what to say. Something. Nothing. Moment passes. Maybe said something? Maybe said nothing. Meet other porn stars. Cuter in person. Fuck. Get me out of here.

Blur.

Chair.

Blur.

Phone.

Blur.

Back downstairs, now on the main stage. So many blurry faces. Thousands of them. Christ. Introducing the porn boys. Smack Gulliver's ass as he passes. Leave before he looks back. Through the crowd. SO many boys. So much money. So fucking drunk.

Graham? Nah. Can't be. Now I'm imagining people I haven't seen in years. Don't want to see anybody else. Whether they're really here or not. Must. Go.

Find go-go Chase. Kiss him. Pull him out the door. eWrecksion fades away. Cab door opens. Take us home, driver. Get me the fuck out of here.

***

Chase is naked and whimpering. I've got my arms around him. All part of the plan.

Except, he's crying. Not part of the plan.

Rubbing that weird pocket watch tattoo, which I've only just learned is inspired by his dead grandfather's actual pocket watch. A heartbreaking backstory. I pull his naked body close to mine and kiss him on his trembling lips. His stray tear reaches my tongue.

We're not going to fuck tonight.

It was my idea—we each share something personal. It seemed intimate, kind of sexy. A good way to get to know each other—actually, an excuse.

This is the way it played out in my mind:

I shake Marty Brayden's hand. He looks at me. "Help me," he says. "Todd. Get me out of here."

I do.

Señor yips with delight as Gulliver rushes into the apartment. They roll around on the floor, Gulliver giggling, Señor panting, both tongues wagging, and I just watch, marveling at how right it all feels.

"I don't know what I was thinking, Todd," Gulliver says later, scarfing pizza, drinking hot cocoa. For some reason, his hair is wet. He's got a blanket wrapped around his shoulders, like I just rescued him from drowning. Well. Maybe I did.

"You weren't thinking, I guess. But porn, seriously?"

"I was so lost. I didn't know how to tell you. And this guy who runs the website…Well, he said it was just one video, and no one would ever see…"

"Shh," I say. "It doesn't matter."

Gulliver looks at me. "There's something different about you, Todd."

"Nah, bro," I say. "Just happy you're home."

"No…" He looks me right in the eyes. "You look…different. Todd. Are you okay?"

I say, "It's nothing you need to worry about, Gullzo. It's my shit."

"But I do," he says, taking my hand. "I do need to worry. Todd, you've done so much for me. You saved me tonight. From having to go back to that place. From doing something that's going to haunt me for the rest of my life, on stage in front of thousands of guys. Someone would have seen me. Recognized me. My life here would be over. I can't count all the things you've done for me over the years. So please. Let me, for once, return the favor. Let me be here for you."

"Okay," I say. I'm choking up. I'm crying. I realize I've been aching to tell someone—well, not just someone. Him. My best friend. I can't go through this alone.

I wrestle with it for a minute. Maybe more.

Then I tell him.

And at approximately the same time, my world starts spinning again.

But.

This is what actually happens:

Instead of Gulliver, it's Chase.

He wants to fuck. More than wants to—he's begging for it. Willing to do it bare, even, if that's what it takes.

There's no cocoa.

I am drunk enough, and horny enough, that I really don't care at this point who knows what about Todd DiTempto. Tell a go-go boy. Let him tell the other go-go boys about it. Let it spread through the nightlife world like they're playing a game of gay-sex telephone. If I'm lucky, maybe I'll only have to have this conversation once; let gay gossip take care of the rest and that's the end of my career as the up-and-coming golden boy of the New York gay party scene.

But didn't we already establish that I'm not lucky?

Gulliver looked right through me like he was a complete stranger tonight. I guess that's what he is. Whoever this Marty Brayden guy is, I don't know him.

Chase, on the other hand, is a sweet kid.

I want him. I want to feel like my old self.

Unfortunately, that means telling him. My mistake: suggesting he tell me something personal first.

I was planning to be the emotional drunk tonight, but Chase has that covered. He's talking about his mom in prison, his grandfather's death. Heavy shit. "I'm sorry, I don't usually get so worked up about this stuff," he sniffs. "I guess it's just been a while since I actually talked about it out loud." I pull him in tight and let him weep and shake in my arms.

"It's okay, bro," I tell him. "Let it out."

And he really does.

At the same time, I am giving myself the opposite advice. *Keep holding back, DiTempto...*

I stroke the back of his head, shush him. When he's done crying, he says, "Wow. Thanks for listening. It's been a long time since anyone did that for me."

"No big," I respond.

"Now it's your turn to tell me something."

I nod. I reach for his underwear, crumpled on the floor. I hand them to him.

We were supposed to fuck tonight, but I can't do that now. He's too exposed. Too vulnerable. Too naked—emotionally, that is. He's just a kid, really, and there's nothing sexy about this interaction. Despite my recent muscle loss, I'm still a good deal larger than this boy, making it all too clear who is the comforter and who is the comfortee. I console him, because that's what he needs. He's just the latest Root Beer Tapper customer to walk into the bar after all the others left. I've done my job, but he can't return the favor. That's not how this works.

I'll never be able to fuck him. Once I take on this role with somebody, our relationship changes. Mikey Drama. Irwin. Servando and Rowan. I'm the guy they come to when something's gotta get done. And done it gets.

It's not so bad, being needed—not usually, that is.

There was a time when Gulliver and I might have had sex, a long, long time ago. And then that first time I saw him flipping out over some text his boyfriend sent him. Tears and drinks. The door was closed on fucking, leaving us to explore a more fruitful path: best friendship.

A lot of these relationships are essentially one-way streets. Anything but give and take. But not Gulliver. He's seen me at my weakest. He's been there when I needed him. He's taken care of me as much as I've taken care of him—well, almost. Maybe it's selfish, but right at this second, I don't care about Gully's self-destructive porno bender. I don't care how Brayden and the other guys feel about being betrayed. I care about having my best friend back in spite of it all, because I need him.

Yeah. This time it's ME with the need.

"What're you giving me these for?" Chase asks, taking the dangling skivvies. "I thought we were gonna fuck."

"Are you really in the mood to fuck after those waterworks?"

Chase shrugs. "I guess I'm just tired. Like I said, I didn't sleep last night." He yawns, then shakes it off, like he's trying to muster some energy. "But I still want to! Come on. What did you want to say?"

"How about we save talking and fucking for the morning, and go do what the night was made for?"

"I thought that WAS fucking," Chase says sleepily as I help him step into his briefs. "Okay, but in the morning, it is ON."

I nod in agreement, knowing full well that nothing will happen.

I get Chase a glass of water and walk him to my bedroom. I turn the AC on low, filling the room with a soothing hum. He slips into the sheets, and I tuck him in tight, kiss him on the forehead.

"Are you coming to bed?" he asks, weakly.

I will be sleeping on the couch tonight, but he doesn't need to know that. "In a few, bro. Just gotta feed Señor."

"Thank you, Todd," Chase says, eyes already closed. He is lightly snoring before I've even closed the door.

What a fucking night. No—what a fucking summer. My head is spinning, and not just from all the caffeinated booze Drama poured down my throat. I don't know how I manage to take care of people in this state; I can barely take care of myself. But somehow, I do. More than manage, actually—I succeed with flying colors. At least, that's what they think.

I'm good with people. When they're around, I function. I thrive. It's being alone I have to watch out for. When there's no one but me to take care of, that's when I don't know what the fuck to do.

I switch on a lamp, filling the living room with warm yellow light. Señor hops up from his doggy bed and skips to me, his tail shaking excitedly. I pick him up in my hands and take a whiff of him. He'll need a bath soon, but in the grand scheme of things, this slutty pooch has the easiest problems to solve. A pill here. A bath there. Man's best friend, indeed—one I will never discover has secretly been doing porn under a false name or fucking my good buddy's ex and lying about it. Thanks to Señor, I never come home to an empty apartment. And of all those who require my constant attention, he doesn't leave me feeling taken advantage of. I don't think I'd take care of myself half as well if I didn't know Señor was depending on me.

I carry him to the kitchen in one arm and grab a doggie treat shaped like a miniature bacon-wrapped filet mignon with my free hand. The slobbering starts immediately, his legs swimming in the air as if that'll get him closer to it. I have to smile. Have to laugh. Both feel so good.

"Chill out there, poop," I say, putting him down on the tiled floor.

Señor raises his eyebrows, cocks his head to the side.

"You want this?" I ask, moving the treat around above him. "You hungry?"

Señor's eyes follow the treat, his head rotating and shaking along with my movements. I lay the treat down on the floor. Señor approaches it.

"Wait!" I say, loud enough to get his attention, but not loud enough to wake Chase. Señor obeys, stopping in his tracks, even though his eyes don't leave the ministeak. A light rumble of a growl slips out from between his bared teeth.

"Sit!"

Without a moment of hesitation, Señor sits.

"Lie down."

He obliges, plopping his face on the floor, his eyes still fixed on the treat. No wonder every gay boy in the neighborhood is obsessed with Señor. He really is the cutest fucking pup this side of the Hudson.

I grab the treat and stand up straight. Señor's eyes follow, but he remains on his belly.

"Roll over."

He does.

And then, all of a sudden, I'm crying. Not big, loud crying. But there are tears and I have to sniff to stop snot from falling down my face. I don't know why.

Yes, I do.

If only everyone would listen like this. Be as loyal as this. Trust me, as he does. Because most of the time, I really do know what's best. People come to me for help when they've made a mess of themselves; what they DON'T do is listen beforehand and avoid the trouble altogether. It's an endless cycle. Tomorrow, I'll wake up to another ringing phone, the same people with roughly the same problems they had the day before, still no wiser about how to solve them.

"Beg."

Señor hops up on his hind legs, his paws scraping at the air like he's using one of those hand-bicycle machines at the gym. He's also panting from all the effort. I love this dog so fucking much. I scoop him back up, mashing my nose against his significantly smaller and wetter nose.

"You're a good dog, Señor. I love you, bub."

Señor responds by assaulting my face with his tongue. Drenching my cheeks and forehead. I laugh again, holding him back as he still somehow finds a way to get his tongue to my cheek. "Enough, you slut! Cut that out!"

I hold the treat up in my free hand, and Señor goes still again.

"Hey, buddy, can you keep a secret?"

Señor's eyes meet mine, his tongue still hanging out.

"It's a pretty big deal, and I haven't told anyone. Yet. But for some reason, tonight feels like the night."

Señor blinks, his gaze unbreaking.

"Daddy's positive, pupster."

The words come out easy, but once they leave, they pull every-thing else along for the ride. Now I'm really crying. Like all of a sudden, it's official. Not when Kenton told me. Not when the nurse confirmed it at the clinic. Not when I stopped having sex. Not when I started taking the meds. Now. This moment. In my fucking kitchen.

"I made a stupid mistake," I say, gasping. "A really fucking stupid mistake. Oh, and Gulliver is doing porn. Can you believe it? 'Cause I don't!"

Señor takes this all in stride. I have to say, he's handling it pretty well.

Now Gulliver and I both have our secrets. Cue more tears. More heaving.

It should be him I'm telling this to. A human being. Not a fucking animal. Haven't I earned that? What more can I do?

Señor makes a sudden movement in my arm, stretching himself across the expanse of my chest to snatch the treat. I look down at him, chewing contentedly. That fucker spent the past two minutes scheming. That sneaky slut.

"You fucking thief," I laugh. "That was a pretty sweet move."

Señor licks my face. I reach into the cabinet to grab him another treat. He deserves the reward for those mad skills. His mouth hangs open, waiting for his prize.

"I love you, bud," I say, nuzzling his cheek. "Thank you for being here."

Señor barks quietly, shaking his head.

"Down the hatch, boy!"

I pop the treat into his mouth and watch him chew until it's gone.

ACKNOWLEDGMENTS

For Mom. Always, for Mom. For my father, who finally is resting in peace. For my brother, Jared, already on Broadway and making me sicker with pride every day. For my partner, Joe—my muse, my man, my music, and my miracle. A kick-ass mash-up DJ too. For Ray, my family's Beatles-loving, computer-security-installing, guitar-playing knight in shining armor. And for Alan Picus, my truest friend, smartest teacher, and most kick-ass business partner.

To editor/collaborator Chris Alexander for his continued polishing, fluffing, soul finding, and shining. To the team of sick geniuses at AmazonEncore, led by the valiant Terry Goodman, who found me in the first place. To David Downing, who made my first novel so spectacular that I demanded he be my editor for the sequel.

Also, to all of my wonderful fans and supporters who spread the Gully Gospel, cheer me on, fill my events, write me awesome reviews, and serve as first eyes on any of the crap I initially produce.

And to you, reader, for buying these books and spreading the good word to YOUR friends. Without you, I'd be nobody, and these stories would be buried under the stuff in my sock drawer.

Photo © Richard Burrowes

Justin Luke Zirilli is the co-director and head promoter of BoiParty.com, a New York–based gay nightlife events company. He and his business partner, Alan Picus, throw weekly dance parties around New York City and larger events across the United States. He also works at XL Nightclub, New York City's largest and newest gay dance club. In addition to event planning, Justin feeds his addiction to social media as the creator of Gorgeous, Gay and Twenty-Something, a private international Facebook group; as the New York correspondent of the national gay talk show, *The Swish Edition*; and by moonlighting as a social media and new business consultant. When he isn't glued to his computer screen, or traversing NYC's gay party scene, he spends his time in Hell's Kitchen, playing PlayStation and watching *Game of Thrones* with his boyfriend, Joe.

Made in the USA
Charleston, SC
28 November 2012